PURSUIT OF JUSTICE

MIMI LATT

SIMON & SCHUSTER

SIMON & SCHUSTER
Rockefeller Center
1230 Avenue of the Americas
New York, NY 10020

10   9   8   7   6   5   4   3   2   1

Library of Congress Cataloging-in-Publication Data
Latt, Mimi Lavenda.
    Pursuit of justice / Mimi Latt.
       p.   cm.
     I. Title.
PS3562.A7598P87   1998
813'.54—dc21   97-29855   CIP
ISBN 0-684-81184-7

ACKNOWLEDGMENTS

My heartfelt thanks to my husband, Arron, for his loving support and encouragement. Living with a writer is not easy, and he has truly been there for me through the difficult times. To my daughter and fellow writer Carrie, we have shared so much as we both make our way through the complex publishing world. Your love and empathy help me more than you could ever know. To my daughter Andi and son-in-law, Stuart, thanks for the way you are always cheering me on with such great enthusiasm. Bless you also for my wonderful grandchild, Spencer, who is the joy of my life. I love you all.

To my agent, Anne Sibbald, my undying gratitude for believing in me and my abilities. Your generous heart and nurturing spirit are a great comfort to me, and I am fortunate to have you in my life. Thanks also to my foreign agent, Dorothy Vincent, and everyone else at Janklow & Nesbit for all your help in attending to the details of my career.

To my incredible editors, Michael Korda and Chuck Adams, thank you for your support, encouragement, and skillful editorial guidance. You have both made my career possible and continue to do everything in your power to help me. I love you, guys. Also a big thank you to Julie Rubenstein at Pocket Books and to all the other wonderful people at Simon & Schuster who give of their time and expertise to make my books the best they can be.

This book would not have been possible without the expert guidance of my dear friend of many years, The Honorable Loretta Murphy

Begen, Municipal Court Judge. Thank you, Lori, for giving so unselfishly of your limited time.

A big thank you also to my other experts: professional engineer Marvin Sachse, for the maritime details; Sandy Gibbons and Harvey Giss at the Los Angeles District Attorney's Office; Eugene Carpenter, M.D., at the L.A. County Coroner's Office; pharmacist Harvey Schiller; insurance agent William Payne; probate lawyer Vicki Fisher Magasinn; those at the Marina del Rey Sheriff's Station and the U.S. Coast Guard; Enid Zaslow, Ph.D., my dearest friend and resident shrink for her help with the psychological profiles of my characters and for keeping me reasonably sane during the writing process. I appreciate the way all these professionals shared their knowledge. Any mistakes in this book are solely mine.

Writing can often be lonely and isolating. To function well as a writer one not only needs the company and support of other writers, but also constructive feedback. In this regard, no one could be more fortunate than I. All my love and thanks to my dearest friends and fellow writers, Lisa Siegel, Ellen Jones, Lisa Rojany, and Mary Firman. I honestly don't know how I would manage without you.

In Loving Memory

OF

Suzanne, Sarah, & Betty

Three Courageous Women
Who Danced to Their Own Music

CHAPTER ONE

A six-piece band played as Rebecca Brownstein Morland and her husband, Ryan, danced on the top deck of the huge private motor yacht. The boat, called the *Majorca,* was covered with tiny twinkling lights that reflected back off the inky water, lending the scene a magical aura. Night had fallen a short time ago, and over Ryan's shoulder, Rebecca watched the lights of Santa Monica receding as the yacht motored farther into the San Pedro Channel, away from the breakwater of Marina del Rey and the California coastline.

In spite of the music, the raucous laughter emanating from the various decks, and the hum of the large diesels, Rebecca found it peaceful to be out on the water. With Ryan's arms wrapped around her, she tried to make believe that the last three weeks had never happened and that their life was still perfect.

She glanced around. Tonight's party was a political fund-raiser, and the yacht was packed with the most powerful men and women in the state. The men, looking handsome in dark dinner jackets, and the women, elegantly clad in fancy cocktail dresses and magnificent jewelry, all added to the glamour of the event.

Brandon Taylor, the stately managing partner of Taylor, Dennison & Evans, the law firm at which Ryan recently had been named a partner, was making his way around the deck, shaking hands and stroking egos. As a high-profile lawyer as well as the son and grandson of two former United States senators, Brandon was intent on becoming his party's candidate for the next Senate race. So far, no one of any importance had chosen to oppose him for the nomination, and Brandon was busy ensuring that no one would, especially Paul Worthington, the multimillionaire owner of this magnificent yacht.

Rebecca tossed back her head of red hair, which cascaded over her shoulders in a mass of curls, and nudged closer to Ryan.

"I love you," he whispered in her ear, his breath warm against her cheek.

"I love you too," she murmured.

When the music stopped, Ryan pulled away and immediately began to glance around. Watching him, Rebecca could see that the haunted look was back on his face. He was a handsome man, and she particularly loved the boyish way his light blond hair fell forward over his brow. But tonight, Ryan's face was lined with exhaustion. Gone too was the devilish sparkle in his blue eyes.

His gaze still focused on the crowd of people around them, he leaned against the rail, and his tall, muscular body slumped forward as if the air had been let out of his chest. Ryan usually looked younger than his thirty-five years, but not tonight.

"You look so tired," Rebecca said, gently admonishing him.

Ryan's mouth twisted into the crooked grin that when she first met him had melted her heart. In spite of his weight loss and his pale, gaunt face, that smile reminded her of the man with whom she had fallen in love.

How could things have changed so drastically and so fast?

A mere three weeks ago everything in their lives had been wonderful. They were in love and trying to have a baby. They were both excelling in their legal careers. At twenty-nine, Rebecca had a responsible and fulfilling job as a staff lawyer in a legal clinic for lower-income people. Ryan's lifelong passion had been politics, and he'd been thrilled when, recently, Brandon Taylor had asked him to join his campaign staff. Rebecca and Ryan were often amused by the fact that their only arguments were not about the differences in their religions, which didn't seem to pose a problem, but about politics—she was a Democrat while he was a Republican. Then something had happened. Without warning, she had begun to live in a nightmare.

Memories of the last several weeks came crashing into her head. The nights Ryan hadn't been able to sleep—his almost hostile silences, his moodiness, the abrupt flashes of temper. It was clear to Rebecca that he was deeply troubled. Yet he'd told her virtually nothing, insisting that what was bothering him was work related and therefore confidential. She'd sensed that wasn't completely true. During their two-year marriage—without divulging any specifics that would violate their ethical obligations—they'd always discussed everything, including their legal cases. Besides, his eyes gave him away—he was hiding something from her. Well, if she was going to help him, she had to find out what it was.

Ryan started searching his pockets, looking for a cigarette. "It was your idea to stop smoking when we started trying to have a baby," she reminded him wryly, the corners of her mouth turning upwards.

"Please, babe." He took the pack out and removed one. "I'm at least trying to keep it down to two a day."

Rebecca decided not to press him. He still had a lot of mingling to do tonight, locking up as much support as possible for Taylor's candidacy. She'd wait until they were in the car on their way home to try and find out what was disturbing him so much.

A crewman dressed in a crisp white uniform with epaulets approached Rebecca and Ryan. He nodded to them and smiled. "Your host has asked that any smoking be confined to the stern of the boat, in the fishing cockpit. May I show you the way?"

Ryan glanced at her, a question in his eyes.

"Go ahead," Rebecca said softly. "I've got to fix my contact lens. I'll meet you back up here in a little while."

"Okay." He looked at her lovingly, then brushed his lips against her forehead. "See you soon."

Rebecca watched him follow the crewman to the circular stairway that led to the lower levels of the boat. Just before Ryan's head disappeared from view, their eyes met, and he gave her a smile. It sent a rush of warmth and hope through her. Somehow they would work things out.

Rebecca checked her contacts, covered the few freckles on her nose with powder, and put a touch of mascara on the lashes of her green eyes. Then, satisfied with her repair job, she closed her purse. Gazing at her image in the mirror, she thought her simple black sheath complemented her tall, lithe figure. Yet compared to the other guests, she felt slightly underdressed.

Shopping had never been Rebecca's favorite activity. She'd bought this dress off the rack at Loehmann's, a discount clothing store not far from the legal clinic, without even trying it on. If she worked at a firm like Taylor, Dennison & Evans, where appearance counted as much as performance, she'd be forced to have, as Ryan did, a closet full of finely tailored suits. "Oh well, *c'est la vie!*" she murmured as she left the powder room.

Heading back to meet Ryan, Rebecca was struck by the opulence of her surroundings. Everything shrieked of money, from the crystal chandeliers and the ornate mirrors to the plush carpeting and the furniture upholstered in shades of white and beige, shot through with threads of silver and gold. The Worthington yacht was a world apart from the sailboats and small powerboats she was used to.

On the upper deck, Rebecca quickly surveyed the crowd but couldn't spot Ryan. Checking her watch, she realized that fixing her contact lens had taken longer than she'd anticipated. She decided to explore the lower decks. As she made her way through the crowd of people she became aware that someone was watching her. It was Maxwell Holmes, a political insider, whose behind-the-scene support was said to be vital to winning any and all elections in the state of California. Rebecca thought Holmes slightly attractive in a rough, unpolished sort of way, but she was repelled by the man. His unwelcome attention to her earlier in the evening had clearly upset Ryan, who ordinarily would have laughed something like that off.

She heard someone calling her name and glanced around. It was Jeremy Rogers, an old law school chum of hers, beckoning her to join him at the rail where he was standing with two other people. While she was anxious to find Ryan, she didn't want to seem unfriendly.

"Hello, Jeremy," she said.

"Rebecca, it's good to see you." He introduced her to his companions, both lawyers, a woman with a lively face and a stiff-looking young man. He then explained to his friends that Rebecca and he had attended law school together.

As Rebecca shook hands with Jeremy's friends, her eyes continued to roam the crowd, searching for her husband.

"Do you go by Brownstein or Morland now?" inquired Jeremy.

"Both," she nodded, smiling.

"Brownstein," said the other man, turning to Jeremy with a smug grin on his face. "Isn't she the one who beat you out for editor-in-chief of *Law Review?*"

Jeremy's neck grew red with embarrassment. "Yeah."

Wanting to ease his discomfort, Rebecca quickly interjected, "If the truth be known, I think it was decided by the toss of a coin."

Her old classmate flashed her a grateful smile.

"And where do you practice?" The other man's arrogant tone of voice told Rebecca that he was probably a lawyer at a stuffy firm in downtown L.A., the kind of place where they checked your pedigree before offering you a job.

"I'm a senior staff attorney at the Fairfax Neighborhood Legal Clinic."

"A legal clinic?" The man raised one eyebrow, clearly surprised. "I would have thought with your class standing and other qualifications you could have had your pick of any firm in the country?"

"I did," Rebecca replied with a smile. "And I chose exactly

where I wanted to be." She was about to excuse herself, when the woman, who was standing next to her, spoke.

"I just figured out where I've seen you. Aren't you the lawyer who was profiled a few weeks ago in the *Daily Journal?* Something about tackling a bunch of developers on behalf of an elderly woman?"

"Yes," Rebecca responded.

"Going up against all those powerful law firms took a lot of guts," the woman said, looking at Rebecca admiringly.

"I'm just glad it worked out," Rebecca replied, as she scanned the people who were passing in front of them.

"Looking for someone?" Jeremy asked.

"Yes. My husband. I was supposed to rendezvous with him on the upper deck, but we seem to have missed each other. I really need to find him. It was nice meeting you both." She nodded. "Take care, Jeremy."

Crossing the main deck, Rebecca saw that a lavish buffet dinner was being served. She gazed at the huge silver trays of fresh clams, oysters, and mussels. Other silver trays were filled with shrimp and crab, poached salmon surrounded by boiled new potatoes and mounds of steamed fresh vegetables. There were all sorts of sauces too, along with lots of fresh fruit, hot bread and rolls. Inhaling the delicious aroma, she realized she was hungry. As she hurried off to find Ryan, she wondered if he might still be smoking in the cockpit.

Pacing back and forth in the salon behind the bridge, Rebecca kept glancing at her watch. Almost an hour had passed since she'd last seen her husband. Having become extremely concerned, she'd finally asked the crew for help and was now waiting for them to locate Ryan. The owner of the yacht, Paul Worthington, had also been by to reassure her that his crew would be thorough and that she shouldn't worry.

"Ryan Morland, please report to the pilothouse."

She heard the loudspeaker paging him again. Why was he taking so long to respond? Was it possible he had not heard the announcement?

Glancing through the windshield, she saw that the party

was still in full swing. It didn't appear that anyone was even paying attention to the loudspeaker. Trying to squelch the uneasy feeling in her stomach, she assured herself the crew would find Ryan before long.

Abruptly, the boat slowed, then began to turn. She heard voices approaching. A man with weathered skin, dressed in a white uniform and wearing a cap with insignia, strode into the salon. "Mrs. Morland?"

"Yes."

"I'm Captain Henry." He straightened his shoulders, his feet planted firmly apart as he spoke to her. "My crew has searched the entire yacht and we are unable to locate your husband."

Every nerve ending in her body sprang to alert. "How can that be?" She waved her arm in a wide arc. "A boat this big must have a million nooks and crannies you haven't yet checked."

"It's large," he admitted with a nod of his head. "But I guarantee you, ma'am, we've covered it all."

Rebecca fought the feeling of dread welling up inside her. "Please ask the crew to give it another try," she said, forcing herself to remain composed. "It might also be wise to see if anyone else is missing."

"That was our next step, ma'am," he acknowledged. "In the meantime, we've turned the yacht around, noted our position, and we'll be retracing our course." Captain Henry paused before adding, "We've also notified the Coast Guard and the sheriff's department. They should be arriving shortly."

"The Coast Guard?" A chill ran up Rebecca's spine, causing her to shiver involuntarily. "Why the Coast Guard?"

"When someone is missing at sea, we always notify the Coast Guard as well as the sheriff's department."

His words startled her. "You don't mean you think he's *in* the water?"

"It would appear to be a good possibility," he replied, his mouth compressed into a thin line. "You see, the transom gate to the swim step is open."

"The what?"

"The swim step is aft of the fishing cockpit," he explained. "It's a platform that goes across the stern of the boat a little bit above the waterline. It's used to transfer to a dinghy or a shore boat—also to go into the water for a swim."

She shook her head. None of this was making any sense. "Can you show me what you're talking about?"

"Of course." He guided her to the rear of the yacht, down a set of stairs, along a carpeted passageway, and finally through the door to the outside cockpit.

Rebecca realized she'd been in this area before while looking for Ryan, but at the time she'd merely glanced around. An overwhelming stench instantly caused her to feel ill. "What's that terrible odor?" she asked, holding a hand to her nose.

"We're right over the aft end," the captain explained. "The smell is the exhaust from the diesel engines that power the boat." He gestured toward the guardrail. "The swim step is below there. But be careful."

It was quite chilly now. The cold night air hit Rebecca like an icy wall. She saw that a hinged half door hung open. Holding onto the rail for support, she inched close to the stern and peered down. A platform ran along the back of the boat. Water churned up and over it, at times obliterating it from view.

She turned to the captain. "Ryan wouldn't have gone out there," she insisted, loud enough to be heard over the din of the engines. "It's way too dangerous—wet and slippery too."

His eyes softened. "Yes. But let's say, ma'am, that he did go out there." It was obvious he was trying to be patient with her. "It's quite easy to accidentally slip and then fall into the water."

"No," she protested, holding up her hand to ward off his words. There had to be another explanation, she thought as she struggled to stay calm. "Captain, you mentioned this swim step is used to transfer to small boats?"

"That's right."

She peered around. "Are there small boats on this yacht?"

"Oh, yes. We carry three smaller vessels, a speedboat, a Boston Whaler, and a personal watercraft."

"That's our answer," said Rebecca, a half smile breaking through her terror. "I'm not sure why, but it's obvious my husband must have left the yacht in one of them."

"No, ma'am," the captain countered, his brow furrowing. "I'm afraid they're all still here."

"Then maybe another boat picked him up? Can't you get on your radio or whatever you use to communicate between vessels and see who was near us?" She struggled to keep the panic out of her voice.

"We've put out a 'Mayday' to all the vessels in the area," he assured her. "When the Coast Guard gets here, they'll coordinate the rescue operations."

"How long before they get here?" she asked.

"The helicopters should be here immediately. We should also see the sheriff's department search-and-rescue operations soon and the Coast Guard cutter within the hour."

"If you seriously think my husband could be in the water, we can't wait." Rebecca's voice was strong, a perfect cover-up for the horror she felt inside. "Don't you think it would be best if your men took down the small boats and we started looking ourselves?"

"The Coast Guard and other agencies are much better qualified than we are to conduct a search of this kind, especially at night."

She pulled herself up to her full height and fixed her gaze on him, ready to bend this man to her will by force if need be. "Captain, if my husband *has* gone overboard, we must try and find him ourselves."

He stared at her for several seconds. Then, as if realizing Rebecca wouldn't be dissuaded, Captain Henry nodded. "Very well." Turning to one of his crew, he barked out some orders. His eyes on Rebecca again, he asked, "Is there someone who can wait with you while I attend to things?"

"I'd rather go with you. If you could get me some pants and a top, I'd like to go out in one of the rescue boats."

"Oh no, ma'am," he said firmly. "I strongly recommend against that. Way too dangerous out there. Besides, there will be people arriving and they'll want to talk to you. You'd be of more help if you stayed here."

Part of her wanted to take immediate action, convinced that

this whole thing was a crazy mix-up and the sooner they found Ryan, the better. At the same time, she realized the captain could be right.

"Okay. I'll stay. But I want to speak to the Coast Guard myself on the radio. They've got to dispatch boats and planes and helicopters. I also want this whole yacht to be searched again thoroughly."

"Fine. If you will come with me, ma'am"—Captain Henry motioned with his arm—"we'll get started."

Rebecca followed him, her mind racing. There had to be a sensible explanation for all this—there just *had* to be. She shook her head. Obviously, she wasn't thinking very clearly at the moment or she would have figured it out by now. After all, she told herself, no one just disappears off a yacht into thin air.

CHAPTER
TWO

Detective Nancy Solowski, of the L.A. County Sheriff's Department, watched as the boat she was riding in approached the *Majorca*. It was so huge she decided it must be one of those charter-type party boats.

Her partner, Glen Walters, was already aboard, having been brought out to the yacht earlier. Solowski, who was a widow with two children to support, had had trouble finding a baby-sitter at such short notice. Neither she nor her partner were supposed to be on tonight, and she wondered again why they'd been summoned instead of the detectives who were on duty.

Seeing the stout, middle-aged figure of Walters, she waved. "Sorry I'm late."

"As long as you're here now," Walters said, nodding at her.

Solowski tucked some loose strands of dirty-blond hair into the ponytail at the nape of her neck. "What have we got?" she asked, glancing around to assess the situation for herself.

"Seems they were cruising about two miles outside the breakwater, here in the San Pedro Channel, when a Mrs. Morland noticed her husband, Ryan, had disappeared. He's thirty-five and a lawyer."

She gave him a sharp look. "He go overboard, or what?"

"I'm not sure yet—I've kind of had my hands full." He rolled his eyes as if to make sure she appreciated the difficulty he'd been experiencing before her arrival. "Anyway, the Coast Guard's coordinating the search operation and leaving the investigation to us. Our job's to speak to the guests—all two hundred of them." He snorted.

Solowski whistled. "So—what are they doing to find him?"

"I'll take you to the wife and fill you in on the way." Walters started climbing the stairs to the upper deck, talking as he went.

Scrambling to follow him, Solowski noted that the boat looked more like a big hotel than a vessel. It was unreal—like something out of *Lifestyles of the Rich and Famous.* Tomorrow she'd tell her kids all about it.

"Is this a charter boat?"

"No. Privately owned. Guy's name is Paul Worthington— a rich real estate developer. His wife, Diana, is a well-known socialite."

She whistled again, hustling to keep up with him.

"There's a photographer on board taking pictures," Walters continued. "Mrs. Worthington's upset with me because I want the rolls of film. I told her it will help us put names and faces together, but she says she needs them for the society pages of the newspaper." He paused. "So I said you'd make her an extra set of negatives."

"Sure," said Solowski, annoyed because she always got to do the scut work.

Walters stopped near the bridge and gestured toward a group of people who were standing a short distance away. "That's Worthington with the silver-blond hair. Next to the mayor."

"Mayor?" Now Solowski was impressed. She caught sight of some movement out of the corner of her eye and tilted her head toward the people standing along the rail. "Who is doing what?"

"They're supposed to throw those life rings they're holding

if they spot him. We've also got those," he said pointing toward the sky, where the noise of whirring blades could be heard. "The helicopters are from both the sheriff's department and the U.S. Coast Guard."

Solowski took a quick peek. Beyond a certain area illuminated by the searchlights on the boat and the circling helicopters, the water was pitch black.

She shivered. "It's chilly out there."

"Yeah, and getting colder. Not a good night to be in the drink," Walters observed.

She rubbed her hands together. "What do you think the guy's chances are?"

"The more time that passes, the less chance there is that he'll survive. Hypothermia kills even the best swimmers." He nodded his head in the direction of a young woman who sat huddled on a bench just inside the bridge. Someone had put a blanket around her, and she had what appeared to be a glass of brandy in her hand. "That's Mrs. Morland. She's a lawyer too. I'd like you to talk to her. I haven't had time to ask her all the usual questions."

Solowski stood politely while Walters made the introductions. Mrs. Morland appeared young, maybe in her middle twenties, she guessed. She was a good looking woman with a smooth, ivory complexion Solowski would kill for and rich red hair.

Other than a simple gold wedding band with some diamond chips, she wasn't wearing any jewelry. Compared to the way the other guests were all gussied up, Rebecca Morland was rather plainly dressed.

Mascara was smudged under her eyes as if she'd been crying, and Solowski hoped that this poor woman wasn't about to go through what she herself had faced a few years ago—losing a husband.

Walters was speaking to Mrs. Morland. "I think it would be a good idea for you and Detective Solowski to chat while I question some of the other guests." Turning to Solowski, he added, "See ya in a few."

• • •

Rebecca's face was pale as she looked at the detective standing in front of her. "I don't see what good more questions will do," she said, shaking her head. "Can't we just concentrate on finding my husband?"

"There are plenty of people looking for him," Solowski responded, taking out her pad. "In the meantime, something you say might help. Now why don't you tell me exactly what happened, as you remember it."

"Very well," Rebecca said with a sigh, realizing it wouldn't do much good to continue arguing. She related how Ryan had gone to smoke in the fishing cockpit while she went to the powder room, and then she described how she'd searched for him every place before notifying the crew that her husband was missing.

"You and Mr. Morland been married long?" Solowski asked.

"Two years," responded Rebecca, twisting her wedding ring. "But we've been together for three."

"I see." Solowski jotted something down. "Do you know, ma'am, if your husband had any alcoholic beverages to drink tonight?"

The question made Rebecca uneasy. Had Ryan drunk more tonight than he should have? she wondered. "I believe he did," she answered.

"Know what he was drinking?"

"I'm not sure," Rebecca admitted. Then realizing how that must sound, she rushed to explain. "You see my husband normally drinks wine. For some reason he switched to hard liquor tonight."

"Any idea how many drinks he had?"

Exhaling loudly, Rebecca said, "I don't know."

"You think it was one or two or maybe three?" The detective's gaze was probing.

Shrugging her shoulders, Rebecca felt herself becoming defensive. "Whatever he had, he wasn't drunk."

"How do you know that?"

"He wasn't falling down or anything," Rebecca stated emphatically. As far as she was concerned, Ryan had not been in the least bit inebriated.

The cop's eyes were focused on Rebecca. "But you think he could have had as many as three?"

"It's possible. But as I said, he looked okay to me."

"What about food? He eat anything on this boat?"

"I'm not sure but I doubt it. They were just putting out the buffet when I started searching for him." Rebecca remembered how delicious everything had looked. That seemed so long ago.

"Did your husband have any medical problems, like fainting spells, dizziness, a heart condition? Something that would make him fall or maybe lose his balance?"

The detective's questions were unnerving Rebecca. She'd never thought about anything like that. Yet, if something had been wrong, surely Ryan would have told her. "Not really," she finally answered. "Although he did complain recently of headaches. I'm sure that was only stress, though."

Solowski wrote something on her pad before asking her next question. "Was Mr. Morland taking any medication?"

"He might have had some aspirin for a headache. That's all." Rebecca looked about. People were whispering and pointing at her, and it was making her uncomfortable.

As if she'd read Rebecca's thoughts, the detective glanced over at the crowd. "Don't let it get to you. People are just naturally curious." Her smile was kind. "Any idea when Mr. Morland's last checkup was?"

"About a year or so ago," said Rebecca. "No more than that."

"Did your husband get seasick?"

Rebecca was pensive. She remembered sailing several times with Ryan. They'd eaten everything in sight, kissing and hugging —laughing until they were doubled over. He'd never gotten the least bit sick. "Not usually. Though I suppose it's a possibility since he was drinking hard liquor." She glanced at the detective. "But if he'd felt sick earlier in the evening I'm sure he would have told me."

The detective nodded. "Does Mr. Morland swim?"

Rebecca shuddered at the thought of Ryan in the cold, dark water. "Yes, he's a good swimmer."

"Has Mr. Morland been depressed or maybe unhappy lately?"

Rebecca felt the detective appraising her, and her stomach muscles tightened. Ryan's recent behavior had nothing to do with this situation, she was sure of that. Nothing at all. "He may have been a little moody the last few weeks, the way everyone gets sometimes, if that's the kind of thing you mean."

"Was he seeing a shrink?"

What was this woman implying, Rebecca wondered, repressing a desire to scream. "Certainly not."

"How about sleep? He okay there?"

"Well—recently he was up a lot during the night."

Nodding sympathetically, Solowski confided, "I don't sleep too well myself."

"Normally he slept very well," Rebecca added quickly.

Solowski went on. "What kind of law does Mr. Morland practice?"

"Up until recently, he did a lot of contract and labor negotiations. But since Brandon Taylor, the managing partner for his firm, decided to run for the U.S. Senate, my husband's been spending most of his time working on Taylor's campaign."

"Mrs. Morland, you keep saying 'recently.' Do you think your husband was having some kind of business problem, something out of the ordinary?"

"Every lawyer has problems," Rebecca said, irritation flaring. She shook her head and pointed her finger. "Look, Detective, I know where you're headed, and you're wrong. My husband would never intentionally have jumped off this boat, if that's what you're driving at. Never!"

Solowski dropped her eyes. "Sorry, ma'am, but I have to ask these kinds of things." Taking a deep breath, she added, "Do you think Mr. Morland was in any kind of trouble? Gambling. Drugs. Money problems. Ex-wife. Drunk driving. Anything like that?"

"No." Rebecca straightened into an upright position. "I'm telling you, you're on the wrong track."

"I know it's hard to accept, but sometimes . . . sometimes when life gets really stressful, people do crazy things they wouldn't ordinarily do."

"If Ryan wound up in the water, it was an accident!" Rebecca stubbornly insisted. "He wouldn't, he couldn't have done anything like that deliberately." She felt close to losing control. "What difference does it make *how* he got in the water?" she demanded, her voice rising. "Shouldn't everyone just concentrate on finding him?"

"We're doing everything we can, Mrs. Morland."

"But you're not! It's taking too long! You've got to get him out of the water before . . ." Choking up, Rebecca found herself unable to finish—the thought was entirely too frightening to put into words.

A short time later, Rebecca became alarmed when she realized that something had changed in the pulsating rhythm of the boat's diesels. When she saw Detectives Walters and Solowski headed her way her fear and panic escalated. "What's going on?" she managed to say.

"The water's getting rough," Walters explained. "They're reassessing the situation."

Rebecca practically leaped off the bench. "They've got to keep looking for him!"

"They're trying," he said. "But we've got us some lousy weather coming in. They don't know how much longer they can continue. It's getting very risky."

Rushing out the door and to the rail, Rebecca came up against a curtain of impenetrable mist. She couldn't see a thing. The blood drained from her face as an icy fear gripped her heart. "What's happened?"

Solowski had followed her outside. "A wall of fog rolled in about five minutes ago," she explained, leaning over the rail and peering in both directions as if trying to ascertain something.

Filled with abject dread, Rebecca asked, "What does it mean?"

"If it doesn't clear soon," Solowski replied, her brow furrowed, "the helicopters will be turning back."

A roaring sound filled Rebecca's head. She put her hands up to cover her ears. "They can't do that!" she shouted.

Solowski gently brought Rebecca's hands down. "It's dangerous, ma'am," she said patiently. "In this kind of fog you can smash into each other."

The Captain, his face lined with exhaustion, joined them. "Mrs. Morland, I'm afraid the Coast Guard has advised me that the helicopters have to head back to shore. They can't see anything in this soup."

"No!" Rebecca cried, her body trembling now. "They can't just leave him out here! Please!" She pulled at the captain's jacket, her panic rising as she tried to make him understand. "They can't stop now. He'll die!"

"I'm sorry, ma'am. But they can't risk the lives of the pilots."

Rebecca searched his face for some kind of hope to hold on to. "This boat can still keep looking, can't it?"

His eyes were weary, and he couldn't meet her gaze. "I'm afraid not. Staying out here would be endangering the other passengers. But the Coast Guard cutter can stay longer. And I'm sure they'll be able to send helicopters out again at daybreak."

Frantic, Rebecca turned to Solowski. Her teeth were chattering, and as she spoke her voice started to crack. "You've got to get these people to understand that they all have to keep on going! They can't stop!"

With a grim nod, Solowski turned to the captain. "Think we can stay out here a little longer?"

He shook his head again. "I'm sorry. We really can't."

"No!" cried Rebecca. "You can't stop, I won't let you!" She began striking the man's chest with her fists, tears rolling down her cheeks.

Solowski grabbed Rebecca's arms, trying to get her back inside. Others were crowding around, offering words of encouragement. All the noise and confusion only made Rebecca feel cornered, trapped. Everyone was talking at once, but she could barely hear what they were saying.

She saw Brandon Taylor standing with the firm's other partners, Catherine Dennison and John Evans, and ran over to him. Brandon had not only been Ryan's mentor, he'd been like a father to him too. "Brandon, the helicopters are leaving. Can't you make them understand they've got to continue?"

A tall, distinguished-looking man with a full head of dark hair that was beginning to turn gray, Brandon listened to Rebecca. She saw the worry lines in his face and the concern in his eyes. When she finished, Brandon nodded and spoke quickly to various people who only repeated their reasons for stopping.

Tired of listening to the same excuses, Rebecca grabbed Brandon's arm. "Let's hire our own plane and helicopters," she begged him.

"We've already asked," he told her sadly. "Unfortunately, no one will fly in this fog." His arms around her, he murmured, "At least the Coast Guard cutter is staying. Try to stay strong, Rebecca. I promise you—we're not giving up. Somehow we'll find him."

When Detectives Walters and Solowski had a few minutes alone, they both leaned tiredly against the rail.

"I talked to all three of Morland's law partners," Walters said, taking his notepad and flicking back some pages. "Brandon Taylor, the managing partner, says Morland had been difficult to talk to lately, real moody and erratic."

"Who are the others?" Solowski asked.

"There's a lady lawyer. Name of Catherine Dennison. She said Morland had been drinking a lot tonight. Unsteady on his feet. Eyes bloodshot. That kind of thing."

Thinking back over the answers the wife had given her, Solowski wondered if Rebecca Morland had merely not noticed these symptoms or if she was just in denial.

Walters flipped a few more pages. "The last partner is a John Evans. He also says Morland was drinking too much. Real depressed lately. In his opinion, the guy could have jumped."

"According to the wife," Solowski pointed out, "Morland would never take his own life."

"Despite what the wife says, there's a good chance he decided to call it quits. In my experience, when there's a suicide the family don't accept it too well."

"You think the guy's partners knew him better than his wife?"

He shrugged evasively and scratched the stubble on his chin.

"So—did you learn anything else?" she asked.

"Just that lots of people visited the cockpit at some point during the evening."

"But no one knows who saw our guy last, right?"

"Correct," he rubbed his nose. "I'm pretty sure we got us either a guy who jumped or some kind of crazy accident. He might have been drunk. I don't see any signs of foul play or any need to have the crime unit out."

"I'm not so sure about the crime unit," she countered. "This was a guy from a big law firm. Seems to me we should go the extra yard, do a totally thorough job, you know, to cover our asses."

"Naw. With so many people in on the rescue efforts, the cockpit's a mess. We won't find anything worthwhile anyway."

"I still think—"

He cut her off. "Listen, Solowski, I'm the one in charge here, and I've decided that we definitely do not need the crime unit."

CHAPTER THREE

Throughout the rest of the seemingly endless night, Rebecca, at home, had held fast to her unshakable belief that Ryan would be found. So at eight o'clock the following morning, when there was a loud knock at the door of their house in Sherman Oaks, she flung it open. Finally, some news about Ryan, she thought, her heart hammering wildly in her chest.

"Was your husband depressed lately, Mrs. Morland?" called out one of the reporters.

She was horrified. Seeing the news cameras aimed at her, she was bitterly disappointed. "I've got nothing to say. Please leave me alone," she muttered, slamming the door. It seemed to her as if everyone from the *Los Angeles Times* to *Hard Copy* was outside.

Rebecca turned to her friend who was keeping her company. "I can't believe they expect me to talk to them. Can't they understand what this feels like?" Her eyes filled with tears.

Lucy Valdez nodded sympathetically, her pretty face uncharacteristically drawn. A part-time law student, Lucy earned school credits by working in the legal clinic as Rebecca's intern. Her brown eyes reflected sympathy, while her hands played nervously at her long dark hair, which was twisted into a knot and then neatly clasped with a red barrette at the back of her head.

"I've no intention of speaking to anyone until Ryan is found," Rebecca said. "And then I'll let *him* explain to everyone how this crazy mix-up occurred."

"Good idea," agreed Lucy.

Brushing her hair back from her face, Rebecca sighed. Other than changing into sweats when she got home, she'd done nothing but wait by the phone for news. "That must have been the umpteenth reporter. What if one of their loved ones was missing? Don't they have any compassion for what I'm going through?" Her voice was ragged.

"People are ghouls," Lucy said, shaking her head. Peering closely at Rebecca, she added, "You don't look so good. Let me make you something to eat."

"No thanks," Rebecca mumbled.

Lucy shot her a disapproving glance. "I'm going outside to see if I can get some of those reporters to go away."

"That would be great," Rebecca responded gratefully. Without Lucy, she'd never be able to manage her large caseload at the clinic. And this morning, Lucy had again proven to be indispensable. Afraid that her and Ryan's families might hear something on the news, Rebecca had had Lucy contact her parents in Pittsburgh and Ryan's mother in Florida, to tell them what had happened. When everyone had insisted on coming to California, Lucy had made all the necessary travel arrangements, charging the flights to Rebecca's credit card.

Standing in the family room of her country-style home, Rebecca gazed out the French doors at the beautiful backyard. From the moment she'd seen this house with its white siding, weathered brick trim, and terra-cotta pots waiting to be planted with flowers, Rebecca had fallen in love with it. She and Ryan had bought it two years ago, and they had been remodeling it ever since. Now the work was almost finished. Only their future "baby's room" had to be completed.

She felt the panic rush up inside her again.

"Catherine Dennison's here to see you," Lucy said, standing in the doorway of the family room. "Isn't she one of Ryan's partners?"

Rebecca's heart sank as she nodded. She didn't want to talk to anyone, especially not that woman. Catherine was not an easy person to be around even when things were going well. She recalled that when Ryan and she had first met, he'd told her how the other lawyers in the firm found Catherine difficult, if not impossible, to work with. Sure that the old double standard was in play, Rebecca had protested how men with the same aggressive qualities as Catherine were usually admired and encouraged. That had been Rebecca's opinion *before* she'd actually met Catherine. Afterwards, she had better understood Ryan's assessment.

"I'm afraid she insists on seeing you." Lucy raised her eyebrows for emphasis.

"Tell her—" Before Rebecca could get the words out, the woman they were talking about came striding into the room.

While Catherine wasn't beautiful, she had done everything possible to make herself attractive. Her carefully applied makeup and her streaked blond hair, falling loosely around her face, artfully succeeded in hiding the sharp, squarish lines of her jaw. Moreover, she dressed in elegant, understated clothes that hinted at her excellent figure.

"Is there any news yet?" Catherine asked without preamble.

"Not yet," Rebecca told her, glancing quickly at the phone beside her on the white oak table.

Catherine's eyes had followed her gaze. "Well, I'm sure there will be soon. In the meantime, you must be positive, Rebecca. Ryan would expect it of you, and it won't do any of us any good if you fall apart."

Tensing, Rebecca didn't bother to hide her irritation. "I have no intention of falling apart," she said firmly. Although Rebecca was willing to concede that the woman's take-charge attitude might be fabulous in a courtroom—Catherine was a tenacious trial attorney to whom winning was everything—she didn't appreciate it in her own home, especially under these distressing circumstances.

Rebecca had always felt uncomfortable in Catherine's presence. She supposed it had to do with the fact that she knew Ryan and Catherine had had an affair. He had told her. It had been over long before Rebecca had met Ryan, but it bothered her nonetheless.

"I still don't understand how something like this could have happened." Catherine shook her head. "The only information on the news is that they've resumed the search." Her large hazel eyes were fixed on Rebecca. "Is there anything I can do for you?" she asked absently, straightening a gold pin on the lapel of her jacket.

"No," Rebecca replied, surprised by the woman's offer. "But thank you for asking."

"No problem. Has Brandon been here yet?"

"Yes. He insisted on coming back with me last night—he didn't want me to be alone. After Lucy got here, he went home. That was about an hour ago."

"Oh." Catherine seemed momentarily preoccupied. "Well then, I'd best be heading to the office." She drummed her fingers on the back of the couch. "If you would give me Ryan's briefcase, I'll get out of your hair."

"His briefcase?" Rebecca was taken aback. They still didn't know what had happened to her husband and this woman had business on her mind. "You must be joking," she blurted out.

"No. Why would I joke about that?" Catherine appeared puzzled.

Lucy put her arm protectively around Rebecca. "I'm sure you'll agree that Rebecca has more than enough to contend with right now without worrying about your office."

"Of course," Catherine agreed. She cleared her throat. "That's why if you could just . . ."—she paused to gaze at Lucy —"I'm sorry . . . I didn't get your name."

"Lucy. Lucy Valdez. I'm Rebecca's legal intern."

"Well, Lucy, if you'd get the briefcase for me, I'll be on my way."

"What exactly is in it that's so important?" Rebecca asked, stepping forward.

A forced smile played around Catherine's mouth. "Just some business documents."

Rebecca shut her eyes tightly. The thought of handing over Ryan's briefcase made her feel as if she were giving up all hope, which she absolutely refused to do. "I'm sorry," she finally said, shaking her head. "I'm not comfortable with that."

A flicker of impatience crossed the other woman's face. "I can understand how you feel at the moment, Rebecca." Her husky voice was filled with compassion. "I wouldn't even ask except there's an important meeting today that can't be rescheduled, and we'll need those documents."

The sympathetic words were so out of character for Catherine that they instantly put Rebecca on alert. She shook her head.

"Really, Rebecca," Catherine said, this time not bothering to mask her vexation. "I need those documents. As sad as it is, the world unfortunately hasn't stopped because your husband is missing."

"I know that," Rebecca replied. "Nonetheless, I expect Ryan to walk in that door before long with a very good explanation as to where he's been. And then he'll be able to take care of whatever is in his briefcase himself."

"I'm surprised that you're acting so childishly. We'll just have to see about this." With an icy glance at Rebecca, Catherine turned and briskly left the house.

Detective Nancy Solowski gazed at the picture of Ryan Morland on the front page of the *Los Angeles Times* and the headline next to it. POLITICAL FUND-RAISER ON MEGAYACHT TURNS INTO DISASTER AS LAWYER MYSTERIOUSLY DISAPPEARS. I hope they find him, she thought, rubbing her stiff neck.

Picking up the phone, she dialed her home. "Carla, hi it's me. The kids up yet?"

"Sure are," responded the cheerful voice. "Polly is getting dressed and Timothy is finishing his homework."

After spending five minutes on the phone assuring herself that her kids were okay, Solowski turned back to the newspaper article on Ryan Morland.

"Nancy?"

Solowski looked up as Walters handed her a cup of coffee. "Thanks." She moved the papers on her desk to one side to make room for the cup.

"What're you reading?"

"An article on Morland. It says here that if Brandon Taylor won the election he was expected to take Ryan Morland to Washington with him."

"Guess he'll have to go without him now."

She ignored the sick joke. "With all the rescue people out there last night, we should have found him."

"Maybe, but it was dark. He was wearing a black jacket. Too bad it wasn't white—woulda been easier to spot."

"I'm still hoping he made it to shore," she said, thinking of Morland's wife.

"I dunno. Without a wet suit it's doubtful he coulda swum more than a mile. He had a lot to drink. He coulda hit his head. He was probably disoriented. Anyway, I still believe we got us a suicide."

"You think Morland just hauled himself up and over the rail?"

"That's one possibility," he admitted. "He also coulda gone out on the swim step and jumped from there. To me, that seems a more likely prospect, since the transom gate was open."

"But say it was an accident? How do you figure it? A guy doesn't accidentally hurl himself over a rail."

"No. He woulda had to be out on the swim step for some reason, then slipped and fallen."

Solowski was thoughtful as she tried to make all the facts fit into some scenario. "Other than on purpose," she finally said, "I can't figure why Morland would go out there."

The phone rang and Walters reached for it. "Yes. Of course. Thanks for calling, we're on our way." After hanging up, he turned to Solowski. "We got a lead. Let's go."

John Evans nervously paced the floor of his office. Thirty-eight, John possessed a five-foot-eight wiry body that seemed to be constantly in motion. An upsweep of sandy hair framed a not wholly unattractive face, but because his bright blue eyes were a fraction of an inch too close together, people often thought John had a perpetually cunning look.

What was keeping his uncle? he wondered. Brandon Taylor was usually the first one at the office, often arriving as early as six. It was almost nine now, and there was no sign of him.

John glanced at the newspaper lying on his desk. Ryan Morland's photograph was staring up at him. His disappearance was certainly getting a lot of media coverage. The firm was, too —all of it favorable. John thought about last night. It had seemed to take days instead of hours for the yacht to return to the marina. Could his uncle still be sleeping? In spite of all that had happened, that didn't sound like Brandon.

With an appraising eye he took in his surroundings. It still annoyed him that he'd been given the least prestigious of the partners' offices. He remembered how thrilled he'd been five years ago when his Uncle Brandon had finally done the right thing by bringing him into his law firm. His elation had lasted exactly two days. Then he'd found out that besides Catherine— whom he'd already known about—there was another lawyer being specially groomed by Brandon. When his uncle didn't immediately make him his protégé, instead of Ryan, John had felt humiliated in front of the entire firm. For a moment, the familiar bitterness washed over him.

He'd hated having to listen to Uncle Brandon brag about Ryan and what a financial and legal whiz he was, with his dual degrees in accounting and law. Big fucking deal. His uncle was overly impressed by academic credentials. In John's opinion, it was crap to want only lawyers who went to a top-ten school and were in the upper five percent of their class as well as on *Law Review.* In John's experience, these things had nothing to do with performance in the workplace.

The truth was that if a person wanted to practice law in the state of California, he had to pass the California Bar Exam. It was very clear cut. Pass our test, practice in our state. Don't pass, don't practice. It didn't matter that John had gone to a second-rate law school and had barely passed. He possessed his California State Bar number and he knew he was as good a lawyer, if not better than, any of the Ryans in the state. Now that Brandon's fair-haired boy was gone, maybe his uncle would finally realize what an outstanding lawyer his own nephew was.

His intercom rang. It was the garage attendant informing him that Brandon was on his way up. John straightened his tie and slipped on his suit jacket. Then he walked briskly down the hall and went into his uncle's huge corner office.

A sense of awe always came over John when he entered this impressive room with its floor-to-ceiling bookcases and posh leather furniture. Brandon was the founder of the firm and as its managing partner he ruled it as if it were his private kingdom. However, he'd have to relinquish his throne if he got elected senator, something that John longed to see happen.

As soon as his uncle came in through the private entrance, John started to speak. "Where have you been? I was concerned. I've been calling your house for hours."

"With Rebecca Morland," Brandon replied tiredly, smoothing down his thick hair.

John cursed himself for not thinking of that. "How's she doing?"

"Actually, I'm impressed. She's quite a strong young woman."

"What's the latest news?" John asked.

"The search started again at dawn."

"That's good. But shouldn't you get some rest? You look tired."

"I am," the older man admitted. "Rebecca refused to even try to close her eyes, so I stayed up with her."

"Why don't you go home, Uncle Brandon?" John's manner was solicitous. Although he knew his uncle would prefer to be called Brandon, John liked to remind him at every opportunity of their family connection. "I can take care of things here."

"I'm fine," Brandon replied, shaking his head. He clasped his hands together. "Now what's on your mind?"

John handed over a piece of paper. "This." He watched

carefully as his uncle's face turned pale. John already knew what was written on the paper. Still, over his uncle's shoulder, he read it again.

I've been thinking about this for a long time. There is nothing anyone can say or do to make me change my mind.

"Where did you find this?" Brandon's jaw was rigid.

"On Ryan's desk."

"I see." Brandon seemed to be reading it a second time.

"Anyway, the police will need to see it," John said.

"No," Brandon countered quickly. He stopped to take a deep breath as if he needed time to regain his composure. "I mean let's not be too hasty."

Unused to hearing any kind of equivocation in his uncle's voice, John was startled. "What do you mean?"

"We have to think of the damage this could do, to this firm, to my campaign—to all of us." Brandon waved his hand dismissively.

"If Ryan was crazy enough to kill himself, how can that harm any of us?"

"Use your head, John." There was a testy edge to Brandon's words. "You know how the press is. They could blow this whole thing way out of proportion. And for that matter, anyone opposed to my candidacy could twist the facts to their own advantage. A valued member of my campaign team's taking his own life could be totally misconstrued." Brandon abruptly sat down in the massive chair behind his desk and leaned back, closing his eyes. "It could be ghastly."

John started to pace back and forth in front of his uncle's desk. "Are you saying we should destroy this note?"

"No. And stop pacing—it's very distracting. I'm merely pointing out we might not need to bring it to anyone's attention."

"After Ryan's body is found there's sure to be some kind of investigation," John reasoned. "You realize that what you're suggesting could be viewed as obstructing justice."

The older man's face suddenly turned red. "Don't be impertinent, John. I'm suggesting no such thing and you know it!" His voice rose in anger. "I can assure you the authorities will conclude on their own that Ryan either committed suicide or had an unfortunate accident. All I'm saying is that an accident would be easier to accept for everyone concerned. Why make this any harder for Rebecca than it is already?"

John found Brandon's gaze so piercing that he had to look away. "Don't you think she'd rather know the truth?"

"She'll have enough difficulty just dealing with Ryan's death. Assuming of course he's dead," Brandon added quickly.

John took a deep breath. "I'm afraid we have no choice." He steeled himself for his uncle's inevitable explosion.

"And why is that?" Brandon asked warily.

"Because I've already called the police and told them what I found. They should be arriving any minute now."

CHAPTER FOUR

Rebecca had remained in a daze while the well-wishers and sympathizers came and went. But as the hours passed and there was no news of Ryan, the numbness wore off and she became desperate. When she saw the car pull up outside her home and Detective Solowski get out, she ran to open the door. "Have they found him?" she cried, her heart racing expectantly.

The detective shook her head as she came in. "Not yet."

Rebecca's shoulders slumped. "What's taking so long?" Her voice rose in frustration.

"We're doing our best, but it's a big ocean," Solowski explained gently. "We've got boats, helicopters, and airplanes out there looking for him."

"What if Ryan swam ashore and was found?" Rebecca prodded impatiently. "Or maybe he's lying unconscious on a beach somewhere?"

"We've notified the hospitals. The California Highway Patrol is monitoring the beaches, the coastline, the areas where there are big rocks and crevices." Solowski gave Rebecca an encouraging smile. "Everybody's on the lookout."

"Couldn't he have hit his head when he fell? And maybe he has . . . amnesia or something?"

"We got 'em watching for that too," Solowski assured her.

"Perhaps someone on a boat saw something." Rebecca was determined to find a logical explanation for Ryan's disappearance. "There must have been other boats out there in the ocean. Maybe one of them picked my husband up?"

"They've contacted all the marinas just in case."

"Well, they're obviously not doing enough or they'd have found him by now!" Rebecca didn't care if she sounded totally ungrateful—she wanted her husband back.

The detective stiffened. "I understand your feelings," she replied, as if choosing her words carefully.

Rebecca tried to hide the tremor in her voice. "They've got to find him."

Nodding, Solowski walked over to the window and looked out. "Mrs. Morland, I was over to see your husband's law partners this morning and . . ." She paused for a second as if unsure of how to proceed. "And they found what appears to be a suicide note."

"No." Rebecca tensed, feeling a sharp pain in the pit of her stomach. She shook her head stubbornly. "I know my husband, and he didn't—he wouldn't commit suicide."

"The note says—"

"I don't care what it says—he wouldn't do that!" She forced down the panic threatening to engulf her. "Let me see this note."

"It's being booked into evidence," Solowski explained matter-of-factly. "But I've got a copy." She reached into her jacket and took out a piece of paper, which she handed to Rebecca.

Rebecca glanced down at it. "It's not even signed," she scoffed, slapping the paper. "How do I know my husband wrote this?"

The detective straightened her shoulders. "Two of his partners, John Evans and Brandon Taylor, said it looked like Mr. Morland's handwriting."

"Just because it looks like something doesn't make it so. I'm Ryan's wife—I know him better than they do—and I'm not at all sure it's his handwriting!" The words rushed from her lips in a torrent of denial. "Besides, it's ridiculous to think he'd leave a note at the office instead of home!" She quickly reread the contents. "I demand this note be checked by an expert as well as tested for fingerprints!"

"Look, Mrs. Morland—" Solowski started to say.

"No. You look, Detective Solowski." Rebecca could feel the color rush to her cheeks. "You don't know anything about me and you don't know anything about my husband. We've been together three years and are very much in love. We are trying to have a baby and . . . everything."

There was an almost imperceptible softening in the detective's face. "I'm sorry."

"In fact," Rebecca went on, her eyes brightening with a fierce intensity, determined to get through to this detective, to make her understand that Ryan had to still be alive and would never have taken his own life, "Ryan asked me on the boat if I thought I was pregnant. I told him it was too early to tell. Would a man whose wife might be carrying their child jump off a boat?"

"I admit that doesn't fit, but still—"

Rebecca cut back in. "Let me show you the room we've been decorating for the baby." She reached for the detective's hand and pulled her down the hall, intent on convincing the woman that she knew her husband far better than anyone else.

As she opened the door to the yellow-and-white room, Rebecca's head was spinning. She tried to forget how troubled Ryan had been recently—his strange silences, the miserable look in his eyes. Was it remotely possible he had wanted to die? Could she have been that blind? No! her mind screamed. Ryan would never do that. Any second now, he'd walk through the door and the nightmare would end.

"It's very nice." Solowski seemed to be ill at ease as she glanced around the unfinished room.

"My husband thought suicide was a cowardly act," Rebecca pointed out. "You see, his father died when he was only ten. Shortly after that, he came home from school one day to find his mother unconscious. Unable to cope, she'd taken some pills.

They pumped her stomach out and she recovered, but it left a deep mark on him. He wouldn't do that to his own child."

Solowski didn't respond. She just walked back to the front door. "Well, I better be going. I'll call you the moment we have any news."

After saying good-bye, Rebecca felt drained. Why couldn't anyone understand? Ryan wouldn't take his own life. Nothing could ever make her think otherwise. More and more she was beginning to wonder if something more sinister had happened to her husband. Maybe he'd been abducted for ransom and she'd be hearing from the kidnappers any moment now. There were other possibilities, but her mind rejected anything that went against her firm belief that her husband was still alive.

Later, as Rebecca was changing her clothes, she noticed Ryan's briefcase on the floor next to the closet. He'd obviously left it there when he came home to dress for the party. What if it contained another note—one addressed to her? Go ahead and open it, she dared herself. Prove to yourself once and for all that you're right—Ryan would never kill himself.

Rebecca was tense as she squatted on the floor, propped the case on its side, and flicked the latch. Nothing. It was locked. What was the combination? Almost everyone she knew used their birth date as their combination because it was easy to remember. She aligned the numbers to form the correct date and tried again. Nothing. Next, she tried their anniversary. Wrong again. What else, she thought, racking her brain.

Maybe he'd used her birthday? She spun the tumblers until those numbers were displayed. Click. It opened. It was a reassuring feeling to know that he'd picked something of hers. Inside, the leather smell of the case mingled with the scent of Ryan's cologne. She felt light-headed as longing for her husband swept over her.

Forcing the dizziness away, she rifled through the briefcase's contents. There were several manila folders. After a quick perusal, she ascertained they were client and campaign files.

She spotted another file. Peering at the tab, she read, *Ryan*

Morland, Personal. Her pulse began to race. Inside, she found a copy of a letter addressed to an insurance agent, requesting information on a policy, along with some insurance brochures. Ryan had talked about getting life insurance a few months ago, when they'd started trying to have a baby, but she doubted he would have purchased it without telling her.

For a brief moment, she felt nauseated as her mind struggled to grasp the implications of the insurance letter. No. Even with all these unexplained things, she refused to consider that Ryan might have planned for any of this to happen. He wouldn't have done that to her—not when he thought she might be pregnant. Knowing how Detectives Solowski and Walters would view this information, and in the event she decided to give the briefcase to the partners, Rebecca stuck the personal file into a drawer.

She heaved a sigh of relief. At least there was no note. Just to be absolutely sure, she ran her fingers along the crevices of the case. At first, she found only some matches and a penny. Then she saw that, in the left corner, there was a tear in the lining of the case. Her fingers felt something that had been wedged behind the lining, as if Ryan had wanted to hide it.

She took a deep breath. It was a small bankbook, and she examined it carefully. The register showed two years of large deposits, equally large withdrawals, and a current balance of zero. Flipping the pages to the front, she saw that the name *Earl Anders* was on the account. Rebecca had never heard of him. She wondered who he was and why his bankbook was hidden in Ryan's briefcase. She quickly stuck the bankbook into the drawer where she'd put the file.

At daybreak on the second day after Ryan Morland's disappearance a sheriff's department helicopter pilot spotted an object in the water off Malibu. The pilot squinted, trying to determine whether it was a human body or that of a seal. The rocks and crevices in this area were dark and the water murky. Sea conditions were also quite choppy for so early in the day. He looked back up. The light in the east was still dim, but he knew that in another minute or two visibility would improve. Concentrating his gaze again on the small area below him, he finally grabbed his radio. "I think I've spotted something—could be a floater."

A voice crackled back. "Can you give us an exact location?"

The pilot relayed his bearings.

"Stay over it if you can. I'll get someone out there ASAP."

"Roger."

Solowski kept her gaze focused skyward for the signs of a hovering helicopter, as Walters drove down the Pacific Coast Highway toward Malibu. Turning in her seat toward Walters, she finally asked, "Think it's him?"

"Yep. It's been two days. More than enough time for the gases to cause the body to float."

She grimaced at the thought of decomposing, rotting flesh, then sighed. "If it is Morland, I hope we can tell his wife before she hears it on the news."

"Me too. But the press doesn't always give us the chance."

Solowski pictured Rebecca Morland's face. How well she knew what that poor woman would be feeling. Disbelief, then unbearable pain—the kind of pain that took your breath away. She thought back to that sorrowful time in her own life when she had lost her husband.

"Did you hear what I said?" Walters asked, sounding annoyed.

She shook her head. "Sorry."

"How're the kids?"

"Both have colds for a change," she said facetiously. "Kept them home for a few days, but as soon as they went back to school they got sick again." She could barely concentrate on what she was saying. Images of the night her husband had been shot while on duty kept interfering.

"I'm a three-time loser," Walters said with a sad smile, "but never had kids."

"I don't know what I'd do without my kids," Solowski admitted softly, gazing out the window to the ocean. She'd feel better if she knew that Rebecca Morland would at least have a child to comfort her.

Fifteen minutes later, Solowski peered at the corpse, or what was left of it. It was floating facedown and appeared to be a male Caucasian with light hair. When the medical team lifted him out of the water, she gasped. The bloated body was disfigured and mangled.

"Looks like some sharks had themselves a feast," observed the medical examiner, shaking his head at the gory sight.

"Yeah," agreed one of the deputies standing near Walters.

Solowski saw that Walters was turning green.

"Try to discourage the family from viewing the body," the medical examiner suggested.

"For sure," Walters responded grimly.

At 6:30 A.M., Rebecca was already up, pacing her bedroom, half listening to the television news. Two days and nothing. It didn't make sense. If she didn't hear something soon she'd lose her mind.

At the moment, she hated everyone. The police for not doing more, the Coast Guard for calling off their search in the fog, the captain of the yacht for turning back—they were all more worried about protecting their stupid boats and helicopters than finding her husband.

The rage boiling inside her threatened to explode as she heard the newscaster finish the weather report, then say, "This just in. A body has been found floating facedown in the waters off Malibu. There's no official word yet, but sources say it could be missing lawyer Ryan Morland."

A scream pierced the air. Rebecca clutched at her chest, then slid to the floor. It was several seconds before she realized that the horrible keening sound was coming from herself.

"What happened?" her mother cried as she rushed into the room.

Mutely, Rebecca pointed to the television. Sobs racked her body. "It's Ryan, he's . . . he . . ." She couldn't get the words out.

As if realizing what Rebecca was trying to say, her mother

murmured, "Oh, you poor, poor child." Quickly, she wrapped her arms around her sobbing daughter.

The buzzer sounded on Paul Worthington's desk. When his assistant told him who was calling, he quickly punched in the line. "What's going on?" he asked.

The man on the other end cleared his throat. "They've just found Ryan Morland."

Worthington immediately became guarded. "Where?"

"Off Malibu."

"And?"

"My guy says the body is messed up pretty bad. They'll have a hard time figuring out whether Morland fell or jumped off your boat the other night."

A large sigh escaped from Worthington's throat. "Good."

"I'd say with the suicide note they found, it's going to be easy to prove the guy killed himself."

"Perfect. Let me know if anything else develops."

"Will do."

After Worthington disconnected the caller, he leaned back in his chair and gazed around his office, which was on the top floor of the most prestigious building in Newport Beach. Done in an Art Deco motif, incorporating the original paneling and mirrors from an old theater he'd taken over and renovated, his office had been featured in magazines across the country. From here he could gaze in every direction, proudly surveying many of the buildings he owned. His growing real estate empire already stretched from San Diego to San Francisco and soon he would be expanding into Oregon and Washington.

Abruptly, he leaned forward and buzzed for his assistant. "Have my El Dorado brought around," he ordered, referring to the car he used when he didn't want to be chauffeured.

"Right away, sir."

Paul drove to the Newport Four Seasons Hotel. After leaving his car with the valet, he rode the elevator directly up to a suite on one of the top floors. Until a couple of days ago, he'd been sure it would be impossible to beat Brandon Taylor in the primary. He'd given up on the idea of challenging him and instead had tried to gain influence over the man by hosting the fundraiser for him on his yacht. But, suddenly, everything had changed.

He walked into the suite's pastel-colored living room. "Let's have a drink, Clay."

Clay Zalian, who had a reputation as a shrewd political campaign manager, smiled at him. "What's going on?"

"Morland's body has been found." He filled the man in on what he knew. "Lucky for us, it looks like a suicide."

Clay filled two glasses with bourbon and handed one to Worthington.

"It will be great if the press picks it up as a suicide too," Worthington told Zalian.

"I'll get right on it."

Smiling, Worthington sipped his drink. "With Brandon Taylor's esteemed family name and their history of public service added to his own years behind the scenes in politics, he was owed a lot of favors," he mused. "That's the only reason he got so many of the political honchos behind his candidacy."

"That and his national reputation as a dynamite lawyer," Clay pointed out.

"Reputations can be deceptive," Worthington replied curtly, giving the other man a displeased look. Whenever he thought about Taylor, his blood pressure rose. Years ago, on one of Worthington's very first land deals, he'd been about to steal a fabulous piece of property when Brandon Taylor, the seller's lawyer, had squelched it. In the process, Taylor had treated him like dirt, and for that he'd never forgiven the man.

Clay took a few gulps of his drink. "You know," he said, "you never told me what happened when you met with Morland?"

Worthington shrugged. "He was totally unreasonable. Anyway, what do you think?"

"The first thing we've got to do is start planting rumors about Morland as well as Taylor. When the voters start to doubt Taylor, his polls will drop and his supporters will desert him. If you jump into the fray quickly and come out punching, I think you could gain the upper hand. Especially if we get some of the party's big guns on your side."

Worthington thought about the ultraconservative members of his party who saw Taylor as too moderate. Cowards. They were afraid of having the party split by a bloody primary battle, which they felt would only benefit the other side. Yet these same men had let Worthington know that they were willing to support him if he somehow managed to destroy Taylor's credibility.

"If we play our cards right I'm sure they'll have no choice but to agree I've come through for them," he pointed out.

"The death of Taylor's troubleshooter along with the right media spin should change things dramatically," Clay assured him with a grin. "Besides, you've got the ultimate weapon."

Worthington smiled as he held his bourbon glass forward to toast Clay's words. With thirty million dollars of his own money that he was willing to spend on the primary and then the election campaign, he was well on his way to becoming first a senator—and then, someday, President.

CHAPTER
FIVE

Having waved good-bye to her parents and Ryan's mother, Rebecca drove home from the airport on automatic pilot, struggling the whole time not to cry. The last ten days seemed a blur, including the funeral. She was numb, unable to believe that Ryan was really gone and that she'd never see him again. It just didn't seem possible. She kept expecting the phone to ring—or for him to walk in the door, a smile on his face. Whenever she remembered how it felt to have his arms around her, she experienced such intense pain she thought her heart would break.

The media, the police, his partners—everyone—had accepted the note that had been found on Ryan's desk as proof of his suicide. Only Rebecca had remained steadfast in her belief that his death was not. Nor did she think it had been an accident. The only other possibility, then, was murder, and the more she thought about those recent nights when Ryan hadn't been able to sleep, when she remembered his moodiness, his strained silences, the more convinced she became that something sinister had happened to him.

While the family was around, Rebecca had hidden her suspicions. They'd only be frightened and worried for her. Besides, there was nothing they could do, and it would surely upset them. She herself was dangerously close to breaking down. Only Lucy knew of the turmoil she was experiencing.

Pulling into the driveway of the home she'd shared with Ryan, she felt herself gripped by apprehension. This would be the first night she'd spend alone in the house since her husband had disappeared. She was suddenly overwhelmed by a sense of loneliness that engulfed her. God, she missed Ryan so much. Would she feel like this for the rest of her life? She shut her eyes tightly against the onslaught of tears, but it was no use.

With every ounce of determination she could muster, Rebecca fought the feeling of dread that was welling up inside her and forced herself to open the car door. At the front of the house, she fumbled with her key before fitting it into the lock. As she stepped inside, she turned on the light.

"Oh my God!" she cried out. All around her was chaos. Everything had been ransacked and strewn about. Suddenly, her every nerve was on alert as she realized that the intruder could still be here. Move, she ordered her frozen body, as the adrenaline pumped through her veins.

Struggling not to scream, Rebecca ran over to her next-door neighbor's house. It was late, after ten, but she rang the doorbell and kept ringing it anyway. Finally, she heard someone coming.

"Who's there?" Mr. Olson asked, looking through the peephole.

"It's me. Your next-door neighbor, Rebecca Morland," she cried in a breathless voice. "Please, open the door."

"Mrs. Morland?" There was a shocked expression on his face as he threw the door open. "What's wrong?"

"Someone's broken into my house," she cried, gripping his arm. "Call the police—tell them to come quickly. The burglars may still be inside."

Two hours later, when the police had finished their report and were getting ready to leave, Rebecca glanced up and saw that

Detectives Solowski and Walters had finally arrived. Her nerves were still on edge, but she'd calmed down enough to be able to think more rationally. "Thanks for coming," she said, bringing them into the kitchen, where she introduced them to the investigating officers from the Van Nuys police station.

Walters glanced around. "Quite a mess. What's going on?"

"There's been a burglary," explained Rebecca, "and it's obviously connected in some way to my husband's death. That's why I felt both of you needed to see it. These officers can verify what I found."

"What have you got?" asked Walters, speaking to the older of the two officers, a burly, red-haired man.

"There's been a burglary—no question," the man confirmed, one hand on his baton. "There are signs of forced entry at the back of the house. We've had the place dusted for prints, but they came up with very little. We'll run what we've got, but I'll bet they're going to belong to the people who had a legitimate reason to be here. Almost everything appears to have been wiped clean."

He peered at his fellow officer, a tall Latino, who nodded his agreement.

"That means," said Rebecca, cutting in, her gaze going from Walters to Solowski, "that this had to be a professional job. Whoever broke in was searching for something, and to cover up what they were doing they tried to make it look like an ordinary burglary."

Jingling his keys, Walters started to pace. "What seems to be missing?"

"Far as Mrs. Morland can tell, two cameras, a VCR, a small television, and a few pieces of jewelry," replied the Latino officer.

"Those are all things that are easy to sell," Walters pointed out, with a shrug of his shoulders. "Sounds like a regular kind of job to me."

"That's not necessarily all they took," protested Rebecca, putting the broken pieces of a vase into the trash. "I have no idea what else is gone until I do a total inventory."

"What makes you think they were looking for something in

particular?" Solowski asked, stepping forward, her eyes scrutinizing Rebecca.

"Every drawer was opened and turned upside down," Rebecca replied, waving her arm in a wide arc. "All our personal papers and things were in disarray. But even more than that, it seemed like they had messed up the papers once they were on the floor."

"Got any idea what they might have been after?" Solowski asked.

"I wish I knew," Rebecca answered. "Look, I was going to call you both in the morning anyway. With the funeral, and our families being here, I couldn't really talk to you before." She paused, feeling slightly uncomfortable because everyone was staring at her.

Inhaling deeply, she plunged in. "I've been doing a lot of thinking and I've come to the only conclusion that makes sense. What happened that night on the boat was not a suicide nor was it an accident." She paused again. "I'm convinced someone wanted my husband dead."

Walters broke the brief silence that followed Rebecca's pronouncement. "We know you're upset, Mrs. Morland, and that's understandable, but we didn't see anything at the scene to suggest foul play." His smile was polite, but patronizing.

Rebecca walked over to the window and glanced out. The police cars had attracted spectators, and some of her neighbors were milling around outside. It seemed as if her life had turned into a soap opera for the world to watch.

She turned back. "There wouldn't necessarily be any evidence if he was either lured to his death, or disabled in some way and then thrown or rolled into the water," Rebecca argued.

"That could be true," Solowski said slowly. "But even when there's no direct evidence of foul play, there's usually circumstantial evidence."

"You know," Walters interjected quickly, "something that shows a motive." His dark eyes challenged her. "Know of one?"

"Not yet," she admitted, coming back to stand with the others. "It's just a feeling I have, because—"

"Ma'am, the sheriff's department can't expend manpower and resources on an investigation that's based on no evidence." Walters rolled his eyes at Solowski.

"But also—" Rebecca began.

He interrupted her again. "Mrs. Morland, you're a lawyer," he chided. "You ever seen a jury convict a defendant of murder based on a *feeling?*" Walters winked at the uniformed officers.

Rebecca saw the police officers and the detectives exchanging amused glances, including the woman detective, Solowski, who had seemed more sympathetic to her than the others. Walters was doing a good job of making her appear foolish. "Of course not. All I'm saying is that if we look hard enough we'll find the motive."

Solowski turned to the other officers. "She may have a point about the burglary. You don't usually see personal papers and things rifled unless the perps are searching for something specific."

Rebecca watched for Walters's reaction. He was scowling, but he said nothing. Only the muscle moving in his jaw revealed his displeasure. He didn't seem to like his partner's suggesting that he might be wrong.

"There's another important point," Rebecca said. "Since my husband disappeared that night, I've had family staying here with me. Even when we were at the funeral, there were people in the house. The intruders must have been watching and waiting for the right opportunity."

She paused to take a breath. "Tonight I took our parents to the airport. So you see, it's the first time the house has been empty since Ryan disappeared." Her gaze traveled from one face to the next. "That's an indication of something, don't you think?"

Walters shrugged. "I don't know. Burglars as a rule like to enter empty houses, and your place happened to be dark."

"For God's sake, why can't you understand the significance of this?" Rebecca's mouth twisted in frustration. "My husband was killed because of something he knew. Whoever broke in here tonight obviously had to make sure that any evidence was destroyed."

All the blood suddenly rushed from her face as the truth hit her. "Of course. Why didn't I think of it sooner? His computer." Her heart pounding, she raced to the den, the others following her.

Switching on Ryan's computer, Rebecca fought the fear rising in her throat. As soon as the machine booted up, she entered the main directory.

"Oh my God," she kept saying as she tried different things, punching key after key. "They're gone! All of his files are gone!" Panicked, she started plowing through the stuff that had been dumped on the floor. "His backup files are gone too," she cried.

Standing up, she crossed her arms over her chest. "My husband worked at this computer every night for the last three weeks of his life. He seemed obsessed. He wouldn't even let me see what he was doing; he said it was confidential." Her voice kept rising. "Someone found out what he was working on and that's why they killed him. Tonight they came for the files they were afraid could incriminate them." Her eyes felt like two burning embers. "Now do you believe me?"

As the two detectives drove away from the Morland house, Solowski voiced her opinion. "The woman may be right. A burglary is one thing. But wiping someone's computer clean and stealing their backup files sure smells like something else to me."

"Gimme a break," Walters scoffed. "Mrs. Morland is nothing more than a hysterical lady who can't accept that her husband jumped off the back of a boat. The family never admits the victim was depressed. They all give you the same crap. 'So-and-so wasn't that unhappy. Got to be some other reason.' " His voice mimicked a high-pitched wail.

"But how do you explain the computer wipeout?" Solowski asked.

"We don't even know if that happened tonight," he replied, putting his directional on to make a right turn. "If they did break into the computer, why didn't they leave it running? Everything else was a mess. Doesn't it seem a little fishy that they took time to turn *off* the computer?"

"No," she countered. "Makes sense to me they'd turn it off if that's why they broke in—and they didn't want their motive to be obvious."

"I don't buy it," he said belligerently.

"Then what happened? Are you saying Rebecca Morland faked this burglary and wiped out her husband's computer files so she could claim he was murdered?" She paused, then answered her own question. "That's ridiculous."

Walters stiffened. "You telling me I don't know my job?"

She didn't like him putting words in her mouth. "I didn't say that."

"Good," he snapped. "Your old man was a friend of mine—that's why I try to cut you some slack. But don't go taking advantage of it. I'm your superior—I don't have to take lip from you."

Solowski flinched at his mention of her husband. Why was Walters bringing that up and pulling rank on her again? He was overreacting, and she knew for sure that arguing with him wouldn't help. "Look," she said, calmly, "you're entitled to your opinion and I'm entitled to mine." She glanced at her watch. "Anyway, I gotta get home. Want to drive me back to my car?"

In reply, he floored the accelerator and, tires squealing, took off down the street.

Rebecca felt jittery the next morning as she watched the computer expert, who was sitting at Ryan's IBM, make one last attempt at learning its secrets. Glancing at her watch, she realized he'd been there for several hours.

After a tense few minutes, he stood and faced her. "Sorry, ma'am. I can't retrieve any of that missing information."

"That can't be," she said, her heart sinking. "There's just got to be a way."

"I've tried everything I know," he said.

She refused to accept that. "Should I call someone else?"

He shook his head and shrugged. "You can if you want. But

if I can't retrieve it, no one can. These guys sure knew what they were doing," he remarked, stuffing his tools and things into a large navy blue backpack.

Dispirited, Rebecca handed him his check and watched as he drove away. What on earth was she going to do now?

Those long nights Ryan had spent at his computer—how careful he'd been not to let her see what he was working on. The first time he'd shut off the screen when she'd come into the room her feelings had been hurt and she'd told him so. That's when he'd explained that it was a confidential matter. But she could tell from the look in his eyes at the time that it had been much more than just that.

Only once during those weeks had Ryan forgotten and left the computer on while he was in another part of the house. She'd come in to borrow his three-hole punch. Now she racked her brain trying to remember what had been on the screen. Something that had to do with foreign banks, she recalled thinking at the time.

The expert had checked Rebecca's computer too, which was kept in the kitchen, and agreed with her that it didn't look as if it had been tampered with. That fact reinforced her belief that the person who had broken in had only been interested in Ryan's files. She thought about the bankbook she'd found hidden in his briefcase and wondered if the burglars had been searching for that too? Could it be connected in some way to the missing computer files?

It was ironic that she'd put the bankbook in her handbag yesterday morning because she'd intended to make some inquiries at the bank. However, she hadn't gotten around to it.

What also worried Rebecca was not knowing whether the burglars had found what they were looking for. If they hadn't, did that mean they would be back?

CHAPTER
SIX

Early the next morning, Rebecca received a call from Gloria Powell, the office administrator at her husband's law firm, who told her that the partners would appreciate her coming in for a meeting.

A few minutes before 2:00 P.M., dressed in a tailored black suit and a white silk blouse, Rebecca headed down Rodeo Drive in Beverly Hills in her red Jeep Cherokee. Midway between Santa Monica and Wilshire Boulevards, she turned into the driveway of a beautiful two-story weathered-brick office building with a gold plaque on the front that read: TAYLOR, DENNISON & EVANS LAW OFFICES. She felt her chest constrict. Tears welled in her eyes. It was painful remembering all the happy times she'd met Ryan here after work to go out for dinner or to the movies. It seemed impossible that he was gone.

Grabbing the ticket from the parking attendant in the underground garage, Rebecca entered the elevator and exited at the first floor. Drawing a sharp breath, she felt the urge to turn around and run. Be strong, she ordered herself.

When the receptionist saw her, she seemed flustered. "Oh

Mrs. Morland, we're . . . we're all so sorry. Such a terrible thing. Are you okay?"

"Yes, thank you." Once again, Rebecca fought back tears, trying to maintain her composure.

"They're waiting for you in Mr. Evans's office." The young woman smiled shyly as she stood up to escort Rebecca. "That's okay," Rebecca said quickly. "I know the way."

She strode across the foyer, the heels of her black leather pumps clicking on the rose marble floor before she entered a wide hallway with beautifully detailed mahogany paneling and plush rose-beige carpeting. She steeled herself as she passed Ryan's office. Thank God the door was closed. The thought of going in there . . . The image of the last time she'd seen him in his office flashed through her mind. His jacket off, his shirt-sleeves rolled up, the hundreds of documents on his desk—all in neat piles in order of priority—his blue eyes lighting up when he saw her.

At the threshold to John Evans's rather garishly decorated office, Rebecca stopped. Her pulse quickened.

John jumped up and rushed toward her in his usual frenetic manner. "Rebecca, I'm glad you could come. Here, sit down and make yourself comfortable," he said, guiding her to a chair. "Is there anything I can get you? Some coffee, tea?" Because John's eyes were so close together, when he focused on her it seemed that one of them was slightly off.

"No, thank you," she shook her head. She wished the queasy feeling in the pit of her stomach would go away.

They made small talk for a few minutes—mostly about the weather, which had turned cooler. There was an edge of tension in the air as Rebecca waited anxiously to find out why they had wanted to see her.

Finally, Catherine Dennison, clad in a stunning chocolate brown suit and matching suede pumps, briskly entered the office. Knowing Catherine was a workaholic, Rebecca could never figure out how the woman always managed to appear as if she'd just had her nails and hair done.

"How are you bearing up?" Catherine's voice was unusually cordial, but Rebecca sensed that the other woman was straining to sound sympathetic. Then Catherine reached over to pat Rebecca's shoulder, and just as quickly, withdrew her hand.

Rebecca was unnerved. It was as if Catherine knew how someone was supposed to behave in this type of situation and was doing her best to play the part. "I'm doing as you might expect," she finally replied. Instinct told her not to show these people the extent of her misery.

"We need to discuss a few things with you," John paused, his blue eyes solemn as he appraised Rebecca's face. "We hope it's not too soon. Think you're up to it?"

"I'll be fine," she said firmly. She shifted her position so that she was able to see both partners better. "Isn't Brandon joining us?"

John flashed a worried glance at Catherine, who was perched on the edge of his sofa.

"One of his clients is in the middle of a major crisis," Catherine explained. "He said he'll call you later."

"Oh." Rebecca was disappointed. Since she didn't know John or Catherine very well, she would have felt more comfortable if Brandon were there.

"As you know," John began, "Ryan became a partner this year. According to our partnership agreement and its provisions, partners acquire equity in the firm based on a formula having to do with their years here. I won't go into all the details. If you can't find Ryan's copy of the agreement, I'll be happy to provide you with one."

He stood up and began to pace. "Unfortunately, having been a partner for such a short time, Ryan's equity won't amount to much money." John paused. "Even so, before we can discuss that we need to talk about another matter."

Curious to learn what he meant, Rebecca nodded.

"You see," he said, clearing his throat, "since Ryan's death, we've . . . we've had the unfortunate experience of discovering some irregularities." John stopped to face her. "Believe me, I wish there were another way of saying this, Rebecca, but there isn't." He clapped his hands together and went on. "It seems that Ryan was . . . helping himself to money that belonged to the firm."

Unsure if she'd heard him correctly, Rebecca frowned. "Helping himself to money? I'm not sure I understand."

"Maybe Catherine can explain it better," he said quickly, nodding nervously at his partner.

In a fluid motion, Catherine brushed her streaked blond hair away from her eyes. "This is very hard to say, Rebecca." She paused. "It appears Ryan was stealing from us."

"I don't believe that!" Rebecca felt her face flush. "Ryan would never steal anything!"

"We can understand how you feel," replied Catherine, crossing one shapely leg over the other. "To be honest, we're quite shocked too."

"What evidence is this accusation based on?" Rebecca asked, her heart pounding.

"I'll try to clarify it for you," the other woman said. "We'd been having some cash flow problems for a while, but no one paid much attention. That happens sometimes. A firm may have large receivables, but collections are slow. Finally, our outside accounting firm noticed something was wrong."

John jumped in. "As best as we can tell, Ryan's misappropriation of funds has been going on for about two years. It looks like someone in accounting was helping him. We're investigating it now. In the meantime, the person we suspect has been put on administrative leave."

Rebecca continued to shake her head. This couldn't be true. For some hateful reason they were playing a joke on her. Even though she knew the accusation was false, she forced herself to ask the necessary questions. "How much money are we talking about?"

"I'd say hundreds of thousands of dollars." As he spoke, John looked down at the floor.

Rebecca's green eyes opened wide in dismay. "That's a lot of money," she cried. "But why would Ryan even need it—let alone take it?"

"We were hoping you could tell us," John said, with a sidelong look at Catherine.

"Someone's made a mistake," Rebecca insisted, sitting forward. "I knew my husband. He was not a thief. Why, Ryan was the most honest person I ever met."

"I certainly thought so myself," agreed John. "I mean, we weren't the best of friends, but I would have sworn he was trustworthy."

Rebecca turned to Catherine. "Surely you can't believe this about Ryan?"

Catherine focused her large hazel eyes on Rebecca without flinching. "I don't want to. However, the evidence points to Ryan. If it would help, we'd be more than happy to show you what we've discovered." She turned to John. "Isn't that right?"

"Of course," he hastily agreed.

"I'd like to see this evidence," said Rebecca.

"Let me call accounting." After John spoke to someone, he explained, "They're going to put together some paperwork we can show you. I'll call you the moment I have it."

"Fine."

"In the meantime, if you can find something, anything to show us we're wrong . . ." He glanced at Catherine once more.

"We'd be happy to take a look at it," Catherine said, taking over.

Aware of all the looks the two partners were exchanging, Rebecca wondered what they were not telling her.

"As a matter of fact," Catherine continued, "we'd like you to try and find out if any of this money is left."

"But how?" Rebecca countered, absolutely bewildered. "All of our bank and brokerage accounts are joint accounts. If my husband had hundreds of thousands of dollars lying around, I would know about it." Suddenly, she remembered the bankbook in Ryan's briefcase and felt faint. "Could you get me some water, please," she said, her voice no more than a whisper. The room was tipping precariously.

"Get her some water," Catherine ordered.

John ran out the door, calling for one of the secretaries.

Rebecca prayed she wouldn't be sick in front of them—the humiliation would be unbearable.

"Take some deep breaths, Rebecca," Catherine advised from her perch on the couch.

A secretary came in and handed Rebecca a glass, then left. While drinking the water, she fought to regain her composure.

"Look," said John, "we know this is difficult for you. We'd like to be fair."

Rebecca struggled to understand.

"Give us back what's left of the money and we'll work out a payment plan for the remainder," He took a deep breath and exhaled. "If you agree, we won't release this information to the police or the media. No one but us will know about it. Right, Catherine?"

"Yes."

Rebecca wondered how many years it would take her to pay back hundreds of thousands of dollars—probably the rest of her life if she continued to work at the clinic. "Suppose I can't find this money?" she asked, swallowing hard. The memory of the other night flashed into her mind. She sat forward. "I'm not sure how this figures in, but there was a break-in at our house the other night."

John and Catherine exchanged alarmed glances before Catherine asked, "What kind of a break-in?"

Rebecca explained about coming home to find her house ransacked and burglarized.

"Are you aware of everything they took?" John asked.

"Other than the items I've mentioned, not really, except that they wiped out all the files on Ryan's computer."

John started pacing again. "This is terrible. Terrible." He stared off into space. As if realizing they were waiting for him, he quickly said, "Perhaps Ryan had the money hidden at home?"

"But who would have known about it?" Rebecca asked, then, in the same breath, she answered her own question. "Unless it was the person in the accounting department you say may have helped him." She stared at John. "Maybe that person broke in to destroy any incriminating evidence Ryan had against him."

Looking worried, John seemed to digest that information. "Rebecca, do you have any idea what kind of data Ryan had on his home computer?"

"No, not really," she responded.

He spoke to Catherine next, his brow furrowed. "Do we have any backup disks for Ryan here at the office?"

"I'll check it out, but I doubt we'd have copies of his personal files from home." She tapped her red fingernails along the back of the couch as if trying to make a decision. "Tell you what, Rebecca. We'll give you some time. Go through Ryan's papers and see what you can find."

Catherine stood and straightened her skirt. "I've got a meeting to attend. Take care, Rebecca. I'm sorry you have to contend with this." Turning to John, she added, "I'll talk to you later."

Once Catherine was gone, John took over again. "It's important to get on this right away, because obviously we can't reach any kind of a settlement until we know how much money can be recovered."

"May I at least have Ryan's last draw? I've got a lot of bills to pay."

John shook his head. "I don't see how. As things stand, Ryan's estate owes this firm a minimum of several hundred thousand dollars. We'll do a full audit, of course. There could be even more money missing."

Rebecca felt as if she were sinking into quicksand. With every passing second the situation seemed to be getting worse. "I see."

"I know that this is a lot for you to take in at one time, and I'm sorry about that," John said. "However, there is another matter of vital importance which *must* be brought to your attention."

Rebecca braced herself, dreading what might be coming next.

He came over to stand directly in front of her as he pulled himself up to his full five-feet-eight inches. "We'd like the police to close the investigation into Ryan's death as soon as possible. The longer it stays open, the more the media speculation hurts this firm and Brandon's chances in the primary." He stopped to exhale. "As you know, Brandon's future political career was important to Ryan. We think it's vital for you to keep that in mind."

"*You* don't have to remind me of what was important to my husband," Rebecca countered, unable to hide the bitterness in her voice. "And it's far too soon to close the investigation. The past two weeks have been an ordeal, and I'm still in a fog. But one thing is very clear to me, Ryan did not commit suicide nor did he embezzle money."

"As hard as this is for you, Rebecca," John said, "you must look at the facts. Ryan was depressed those last weeks before his death. He was acting very strangely. We all noticed it." He shifted from foot to foot. "The missing funds are the key. Ryan must have realized he wouldn't be able to hide what he'd done much longer and . . ." He hedged, "Well, I guess things got too much for him and he did the only thing he felt he could."

"No," Rebecca insisted furiously. "He wasn't a thief. Besides, he didn't believe in suicide." She paused. "He also thought I might be pregnant."

John looked surprised. "Are you?"

"I don't know for sure. I'm awaiting the results of a blood test." She felt a catch in her throat. "But in any case, I'm convinced Ryan was murdered."

"Murdered!" John was incredulous. "You're distraught, Rebecca. It's obvious the strain is getting to you. Would you like me to have someone drive you home?"

"No," she said firmly. "I can manage." She picked up her purse to leave.

"By the way." He put his hand on Rebecca's shoulder. "Did you remove files, papers, or anything else, even something you thought wasn't important, from Ryan's briefcase before you gave it to us?"

Rebecca's heart lurched. She shook her head, praying her face wouldn't give her away—her fair complexion and red hair made blushing a curse she had to bear. His eyes held hers for a long moment before she blinked. Did he know about the bankbook? she wondered.

Unable to absorb all they had said, she only knew she had to get out of this office before she collapsed. With a hurried good-bye to John, Rebecca rushed away. It couldn't be true—someone had made a terrible mistake. Unless—she hadn't really known Ryan as well as she'd thought.

CHAPTER
SEVEN

Alerted by Brandon's secretary that he was back, Catherine strode into Brandon's office as he was removing his jacket.

"How's the crisis at A&M?" she asked, sitting down on his posh leather couch and crossing her legs.

"Under control for now." After hanging his pin-striped jacket in the closet, he walked over to the old English armoire he used as a bar and opened the doors. "Want something?"

Catherine was surprised to see him drinking so early in the day. "No." She observed him closely, noticing how tense he appeared. Brandon had just turned sixty. Was he getting too old for all these last-minute emergencies? she wondered.

He poured himself a drink and raised his glass. "How did it go with Rebecca?"

"As expected," Catherine told him matter-of-factly. "She totally refused to believe it."

Brandon nodded his head. "I'll have to have a talk with her."

"That might help," she agreed. "However, in spite of what we told Rebecca, I personally think we should notify the media that Ryan had been diverting the firm's funds."

"No," he said curtly, a frown on his still-handsome face. "I don't want to do that."

"Why not?" she asked, puzzled. "He took the money. I've been getting a slew of calls from clients wanting to know what happened to him. It would make it much easier for people to understand why Ryan committed suicide."

"I think things are difficult enough without that."

She was perturbed. His reluctance gave her an uneasy feeling. It was as if he knew something he hadn't chosen to share with her.

Catherine had been the first lawyer Brandon had ever considered good enough to become his partner. She was proud of that distinction and what she'd accomplished by hard work and sheer guts. Not too many women in the legal profession had achieved her status as a name partner in a prestigious firm.

It wasn't until Ryan Morland had come along that Catherine's place in the firm's hierarchy had been challenged. It had rankled her to watch Brandon lavish attention on his protégé. She'd been here first. Now that Ryan was dead, she had expected things to change. Yet for some reason, Brandon seemed to be protecting Ryan's reputation.

"Is there something about this misappropriation of funds that I don't know?" she inquired suspiciously. For a brief moment she was positive she saw fear in his eyes before he quickly covered it up.

"Don't be ridiculous," he said with a scowl. "It's just that I'm not so sure how it would play in the media. And we don't want to make our clients nervous about the way we run the firm."

She glanced at him askance. "You know, Brandon, the authorities investigating Ryan's death are entitled to any facts that might shed light on his actions. Besides, you keep complaining that all the speculation is hurting your campaign. The missing funds give the police the motive they've been looking for in order to close the investigation."

"Not yet!" he retorted angrily.

Catherine was startled; unable to understand why Brandon was being so irrational on this subject.

He took a deep breath and said before she could respond, "And speaking of the election, I received a rather disturbing piece of news a little while ago."

The tone of his voice made her apprehensive. "What's that?"

"Paul Worthington may be getting ready to declare he's opposing me in the primary."

"You've got to be kidding," she blurted out, shocked. Catherine was counting on Brandon's becoming the next U.S. senator from California.

"I wish I were." His eyes narrowed with displeasure. "Didn't you assure me that the Worthingtons were solidly behind my candidacy?"

"That's what they told me." Catherine was deeply distressed. Diana Worthington had been her first friend when she'd arrived in California fresh out of Harvard Law School. Although they lived very different lives—Catherine totally wrapped up in her career and Diana immersed in being Mrs. Paul Worthington —they had remained close over the years.

"I can't believe Diana would do this to me—to us. She and Paul let us use their yacht for your fund-raiser." Catherine shook her head, pressing her fingers to her temples. She could feel one of her debilitating headaches coming on. "If you recall, there was a similar rumor a few months ago, which I checked out as you requested. Paul and Diana both adamantly denied that he was going to run."

"Yes. That's what you said. I was still worried, however, so I asked Ryan to do a background check on Worthington. You know, look around without making it too obvious."

Catherine's curiosity was piqued. "What did he find?"

"I don't know," he grumbled, taking another sip of his drink. "Shortly before he died, Ryan said he was working on a vital lead, but that he didn't want to discuss it unless it panned out. Now he's dead and I have no idea what it was."

"I'd be happy to look through Ryan's papers for you and try to recreate what he was researching."

"I've already done that. There's nothing there." He shook his head gloomily.

Her headache was getting worse. "Have you got any aspirin in your bathroom?" she asked, rubbing her forehead.

"In the medicine cabinet."

Done in black marble and black onyx with gold fixtures, Brandon's private bathroom had a steam shower, a commode, and double sinks. Grabbing the aspirin, she quickly washed three of them down with water before going back into the other room.

"I was thinking," Brandon said. "Ryan might have kept the information on Worthington at home. We need to check there."

"It may be too late. Rebecca told us her house was burglarized a few nights ago, and all of Ryan's computer files were wiped clean." She tapped the couch with her fingernail. "I wonder if Worthington got wind of the fact that Ryan was digging around?"

"Good God!" A cloud darkened Brandon's face. "Why didn't Rebecca turn the files over to us before that could happen?" He stood up and shoved his hands in the pockets of his trousers. "Aside from any information on Worthington, who knows what else Ryan had on those files."

He turned to her, his eyes narrowed. "At this very moment Worthington could have the plans for my entire campaign laid out in front of him! This could be a disaster!"

"I just can't understand it," Catherine reiterated. "Why would Worthington do this now?"

"I'll tell you why," he replied. "That supposed friend of yours thinks he can use Ryan's death to his own advantage and undermine me in the process."

"Are you implying this is my fault?"

"I did expect you to know the Worthingtons' intentions," he countered.

"They gave me no indication whatsoever that they were changing their minds," she said sharply. Straightening her posture, Catherine tried to think of what to do. Her future was also at stake. She wanted Brandon to go to Washington so she could stay here and run the firm. She wasn't about to let Worthington ruin her plans—not now. She had to stop his campaign before it could get off the ground. "Would you like me to talk to Diana and see if she can't dissuade Paul?"

Brandon stared out the window as if studying her suggestion. "Yes," he finally said. "I think that's a good idea. Tell her—"

She cut in, "I know what to say."

Having wasted no time in arranging a meeting, Catherine sat waiting for Diana Worthington in the restaurant of the Regent Beverly Wilshire Hotel. Outside, she watched several women cross Wilshire Boulevard and then Rodeo Drive, talking and laughing with each other as they visited stores like Valentino, Chanel, and Hermès.

Catherine didn't have the time to shop that way. Besides, it would bore her silly. Buying clothes and accessories was merely a necessity. Two or three times a year, a saleswoman from Barney's brought a suitable selection of designer garments to Catherine's office. The woman knew Catherine's measurements and taste, and most of the time she was right on target.

Glancing up, Catherine saw Diana heading in her direction. With sleek dark hair pulled back into an elegant chignon, an olive complexion, green eyes, and high cheekbones, Diana was an exotic-looking woman. Tall and extremely thin, she wore her expensive clothes with style and grace. And thanks to cosmetic surgery, Diana looked younger than her forty-two years. Catherine noticed that more than one man turned to stare at her friend as she made her way across the room.

Arriving at her table, Diana bent over to kiss the air near Catherine's cheek. Catherine responded by giving her friend's hand a light squeeze. A waiter pulled out Diana's chair, and when she was seated, she gestured toward Catherine's glass. "I'll have the same."

As soon as the waiter was gone, Diana leaned across the table. "I'm glad you called. Lately, it seems we barely see each other."

"We're both too busy," Catherine said with a smile. "I really must tell you, Diana, how terribly disappointed I am in you."

There was a puzzled look in Diana's eyes. "What's wrong?"

"Why didn't you inform me that Paul had decided to run?"

Diana looked embarrassed. "I've been meaning to discuss it with you. But Paul hasn't declared his candidacy formally. We're still weighing the pros and cons."

"We had a deal," Catherine pointed out. "You both promised me Brandon would have your full support."

"I know," Diana said, sighing. "But you've got to realize that Ryan Morland's death has changed things." She paused before going on. "The speculation in the media has opened up a window of opportunity for Paul. It's a fabulous chance, and we're thinking quite seriously of taking it."

Catherine shook her head. "It seems to me he's rushing things."

"What do you mean?"

"He needs some political experience. It takes more than *money.*"

Diana gave her a cool look. "My husband is a natural leader. Look at the empire he's built from nothing. A self-made man always appeals to voters."

Catherine laughed shortly. "A self-made man—with a quarter-of-a-million-dollar trust fund?"

"In today's world that's peanuts," Diana contended. "Paul has single-handedly turned those funds into a fortune worth hundreds of millions of dollars. In addition, he's even made the Forbes's list of the four hundred wealthiest Americans the last two years. So there." She straightened her bony shoulders.

Realizing she was getting nowhere, Catherine softened her tone and changed her tactics. She leaned toward Diana and took her hand. "You and Paul are very important to me. I just don't want to see this decision backfire on him."

"What do you mean, backfire?" There was a questioning look on Diana's face.

"Well, he's angered some very influential politicians," said Catherine. "But then you know that, don't you?"

"No," said Diana, "I didn't."

"There are some key people in both California and Washington who must be won over by any elected official who hopes to have influence and power." Realizing she was sounding like a political science textbook, Catherine exhaled and then said, "Do you want Paul to get to Washington and have no support behind him?"

Suddenly Diana looked worried as her dark brows came together in a frown. "Do you think that's really possible?"

"Absolutely."

"But like who are you talking about?"

"People who have dominated California's Republican Party for the last decade." Catherine mentioned some prominent names. "People who have known and worked with Brandon for years," she added pointedly.

Diana was silent. "I see what you mean. Paul tried talking to a few of them, but they were noncommittal."

"Paul needs someone like Maxwell Holmes."

The other woman glanced up, startled. "Maxwell Holmes? Why?"

"Because they allow a man like him to work for them behind the scenes. He's one of the most politically connected men in California. And he's been actively garnering supporters for Brandon."

"I didn't know that." Picking up her glass, Diana took several quick sips.

"Not only that," Catherine continued, pressing her advantage, "what Paul's planning to do will weaken the party by splitting it into factions."

"Why?"

"It will force the Republican Party to spend millions on a primary—millions it needs if we're going to win against the Democrats in the general election. It won't matter which one of them becomes the candidate, Paul or Brandon, if the Republicans lose the election, they'll blame it on Paul." Catherine pointed her finger at Diana. "You can count on that."

Diana looked glum.

Catherine sat back. "Paul is young yet, only in his late forties, while Brandon is already sixty. Many party members are supporting Brandon because he's been there for them over the years. That's why it's important to play by the rules. It makes much more sense for Paul to cut a deal with Brandon."

Catherine then patiently outlined the plan she had concocted on her way to the restaurant. "Think about it. When it's Paul's turn to run, he won't have to worry about any challenges, except from people who don't really matter." She lowered her voice to a confidential tone. "Diana, do you trust me?"

"Of course I do. You're my best friend."

"I'm telling you that Paul could be *very* sorry if he goes forward." Catherine pretended to be carefully considering her next words. "Did you know that before he died, Ryan Morland had been doing a full background check on your husband?"

Diana paled. "No. Did he find anything?"

Catherine immediately detected the anxiety in her friend's voice and arched her brows. "Is there something *to* find?"

"Of course not," Diana responded, her eyes unable to meet Catherine's.

"If there *is* something in Paul's past," Catherine said, enunciating each word clearly while watching Diana out of the corner of her eye, "you'd better be prepared to see it in print."

The other woman had composed herself. "There is nothing, Catherine, I assure you."

Very few people possessed the ability to play poker with a completely impassive face. It was a skill Catherine had honed to perfection and one that served her well as a litigator. She could see that Diana was definitely worried. Why? There must be something a background check might turn up—and she had to find out what that was.

"Think about what I've said," Catherine urged. "Convince Paul to discuss the situation with Brandon. If it's done quickly, I'm sure a deal can be worked out. But if he waits too long . . ." She let her voice trail off.

Diana reached for her glass. "You may be right," she conceded. "I'll try."

They sipped their drinks quietly for a short time. "You've changed a lot," Diana finally remarked, watching Catherine from beneath lowered lashes.

"What do you mean?"

"You used to talk about other things besides business—now it seems to consume you."

Shrugging, Catherine took another sip of her iced tea.

Clearing her throat, Diana went on. "I've been wondering how you're coping with Ryan's death. After all, the two of you had quite a thing together."

"That was three years ago," Catherine said, annoyed when she felt she had to go on the defensive. "There have been several other men in my life since then."

"You've never been short of suitors—that's for sure," Diana agreed. She sat back in her chair, a half smile forming around her lips. "It was interesting at the party to finally meet the woman who took Ryan away from you. Rebecca's quite lovely." She paused before adding, "And young."

Catherine stiffened. She didn't appreciate being reminded of the only time in her life that she'd been dumped for another woman. It still galled her. Especially since Catherine had been positive her relationship with Ryan was a good one. He'd been a few years younger than she, but that was okay. Actually, she found younger men more eager to please and less set in their ways. Their sex life had been outstanding too, which was always a major requirement for her. She'd never put up with a passionless marriage like the one Diana found herself in.

"Ryan didn't leave me for Rebecca," she lied, smiling. "You see, I dropped him first because I met someone else who was better in bed." Swiftly changing the subject, she inquired, "So how are things between you and Paul?"

Diana played with one of the charms on her bracelet. "We have a beautiful life. There's nothing I don't have, materially." Exhaling deeply, she added, "He's just one of those men who doesn't have much need for intimacy or physical contact."

"You're forty-two now, Diana. Have you totally given up on having children?"

Her friend shook her head sadly. "Paul's adamant on the subject—he doesn't want any."

Catherine's curiosity was piqued. "Did you ever ask him if there's some medical reason why he doesn't want children?"

"Yes. But he refuses to talk about it."

"Well, I hope you're taking my advice. There's no reason why you have to do without sex as long as you're circumspect."

"I've had my flings. I'd be a dried-up old prune if I hadn't," admitted Diana. "Still, it's not easy because I have to be so careful." She drew in a sharp breath. "I get frightened, Catherine. I know Paul would leave me if he ever found out. And I would die if that happened."

"Then make sure he doesn't find out," Catherine cautioned. She wondered if what Ryan had discovered about Paul had anything to do with the fact that the man refused to have sex with his wife. If it did, Diana would be miserable if such information got out. It would be far better for all of them if Diana could talk Paul out of running in the next election.

"And while you're at it," Catherine added, in a confidential tone, "remind Paul that when a person enters politics, all their little secrets have a way of becoming public knowledge. Especially any sexual secrets he may have buried along the way."

CHAPTER
EIGHT

Diana Worthington was pensive as she waited for the valet to bring her car around. Some of the things Catherine had said were bothering her more than she cared to admit. It worried her especially that Brandon Taylor's camp was investigating her husband, since it most likely meant they'd be checking her out as well. That thought made her shudder. She couldn't decide whether to tell Paul about this background check. Just thinking about discussing it with him made her jittery. If she did and he picked up on her nervousness, that could be dangerous.

She sighed deeply and hoped with all of her heart that Ryan Morland hadn't found out anything before he died. But then, if he had, she was sure Brandon Taylor would have used it by now. For the time being, she decided to wait and see what developed.

As she straightened her skirt, Diana realized it was actually loose on her. Since that horrible night on the yacht, she had been unable to eat. While ordinarily, she might welcome the loss of appetite—her weight was an obsession with her—she was now getting too thin, and it worried her. The whole thing was a torment to her. She wished the police would close the case.

Diana felt an aching need to be held by her husband, to be reassured that everything would be all right. Just last night she'd put on a sexy new lace cover-up and tried to entice him, but Paul had disengaged himself, reminding her that they were getting older. His rejection had pained her deeply. She felt tears pushing behind her eyelids. Don't do that, she cautioned herself —crying will only ruin your makeup.

Out of the corner of her eye, she saw the valet had brought her white Jaguar up from the underground parking garage. Tipping him, she slid into the leather seat and turned right on Rodeo Drive. She had just crossed Wilshire Boulevard when her car phone rang.

"Hello."

"Hi, Diana."

Hearing his voice, her pulse started to beat rapidly. "Why are you calling me in the car?" she whispered. They tried never to talk on the open airwaves. It was too risky.

"I need to speak to you. Stop somewhere. Call me. I'll be waiting." He hung up.

"Oh dear," she mumbled. She had a dressmaker's appointment, and if she stopped, she'd be late. Nevertheless, she pulled into the first parking spot she found, dropped some coins in the meter, and rushed into a restaurant.

"Do you have a public telephone?"

The man behind the cash register tilted his head toward the rear. "Back there."

Diana found the phone, put two dimes in it, and dialed the number. Something must be wrong, she thought. Maxwell Holmes never called her in the car. She waited nervously for him to pick up.

When he answered, she said, "Hi. It's me."

"I've heard something very disturbing," he said. "Rebecca Morland supposedly told one of her husband's law partners that Ryan was murdered."

"Murdered?" Her stomach dropped. "Do you know which partner said that?"

"Why do you ask?"

"Well, I just had a drink with Catherine Dennison, and she didn't say a word about that. If she knew she would have told me, I'm sure of it."

"That's interesting," he responded. "Well then, it must have been one of the others. In the meantime, I wanted to make sure you keep your cool and stick to what we discussed."

"Of course."

"I don't like this," Holmes said. "The Morland woman has to be stopped. How, I haven't decided yet." He laughed cynically. "At any rate, I think we should get together tomorrow. Be here at one."

"Okay," she replied, glancing at her watch. "I'm sorry to rush you, but I'm late for an appointment."

"Then I'll see you tomorrow."

Maxwell Holmes, political insider and influential power broker, was still frowning as he hung up the phone. He would have liked to have Diana come over this evening—but now was not the time to put her in such a compromising position. He wished the timing were right to let Diana's husband discover what was going on between them. Just thinking about that delighted Holmes and instantly made him feel better. God, he couldn't wait to see Paul Worthington's face when he found out that Holmes was screwing his wife. It would kill the bastard.

Holmes repositioned himself under his sunlamp. His tan, healthy appearance was a point of pride with him. Whenever his picture showed up in newspapers or magazines, or on television, which happened quite often, it didn't matter with whom he was standing, from the governor of California to Warren Beatty, Holmes always looked better than the other guy.

He'd certainly come a long way since the days when he'd hung around the El Rey Country Club, running errands, going after golf balls, doing odd little jobs—anything anyone asked of him, including servicing some of the men's wives. In the early days a lot of entertainment people had belonged to the club, and Holmes had quickly become friends with some of their sons and daughters. As he got older, his boyish good looks developed into a rugged handsomeness—some even said he resembled a heavier Tom Selleck—and by purposefully dating starlets, many of whom became stars, he had managed to live on the edge of celebrity. It also helped that his prowess with women was legendary; they sought *him* out.

Interestingly, it had been his extensive Hollywood connections that had helped him to carve out a special niche for himself in the world of California politics. Politicians always had been enamored with the entertainment world, while Hollywood movers and shakers liked to think they had something besides money to contribute to their government. By bringing these two groups together, Holmes had turned himself into one of the most influential nonelected officials in the state. He was continually being appointed to powerful state commissions. At the moment he was chairman of the state's Beach Commission—a position that afforded him virtual control over all of the state's coastline.

Holmes focused again on what to do about Rebecca Morland. She'd certainly looked lovely that night on the boat. A lot of the women there had been stunning, but Rebecca had a freshness to her that was extremely appealing. He chuckled remembering how her husband had caught him ogling her. If looks could kill, then he'd be the one who was dead. While a lonely widow might be a tempting dish, he didn't think that would be a good choice right now. The damn woman's accusations of murder could ruin his plans. He certainly didn't need her stirring things up.

Feeling troubled, Rebecca rang the bell and waited. There were several lights on in the house, but that didn't necessarily mean that he was here. Many people used timers on lights and radios to make it seem as if someone were home after dark. She waited sixty seconds, then she tried one more time.

Disappointed that no one had come to the door, she went down the slate stairs to the circular driveway, where she'd left her car. Suddenly, headlights blinded her as a vehicle turned in and headed for the three-car garage. Her pulse started to race— it had to be him.

A few seconds later, a large figure stepped out of the garage. "Rebecca, is that you?" he called out in a booming voice, as he caught sight of her.

"Yes."

"Are you all right?" Brandon Taylor sounded worried as he came toward her.

"I doubt I'll ever be all right again," Rebecca muttered.

Brandon hugged her tightly against his strong chest. "I know."

She squeezed him back. It felt good to have someone holding her. How she wished she could dump all her problems in his lap and have him take care of everything.

"Come on inside where it's warm."

Rebecca followed him through the garage and into the house. It was a beautiful old colonial-style home that Brandon's grandfather had built and he and his father had expanded and modernized.

Brandon used to say that since he didn't have any children of his own, he expected Ryan and Rebecca to live here someday, with all their kids. Remembering that thought brought a lump to her throat.

"Let's go in the den," Brandon suggested, turning on more lights as he led the way.

It was an attractive and comfortable room, with bookshelves, a media center, and soft couches and chairs. The walls were filled with political mementos and pictures. Having spent many wonderful times here with Ryan, Rebecca felt safe for the first time since her husband had died.

"Want something to drink?" Brandon asked as he took off his jacket and loosened his tie.

He was a handsome man—Rebecca could easily imagine what he must have been like twenty or thirty years ago—and smart, charming, and worldly. No wonder he'd been so successful with women. It was well known that Brandon had dated some of the most beautiful women in the world. Yet he'd never married. Ryan had speculated it was because Brandon was too set in his ways.

"Some mineral water would be fine, thanks."

"Make yourself at home. I'll be right back."

Rebecca sank into the deep leather couch, feeling some of the tension leave her body. She should have come to see him sooner, but it hadn't been feasible while her folks were in town. She prayed Brandon would have some of the answers she needed in order to figure out what had happened to her husband, and why.

"Here." Brandon handed her a Waterford crystal goblet.

He had poured himself some brandy and, holding his glass in one hand, he settled his tall frame into the chair facing her. He gave a tired sigh and fixed his eyes on her. "Now, tell me what brings you to my doorstep at twelve o'clock at night?"

"I'm sorry," she said. "I knew you'd be late getting home. Your secretary told me you were speaking at the country club this evening. How did it go?"

"Very well," he replied, smiling and nodding his head. "Thankfully, most of the members are generous with both their support and their dollars."

"That's good." She cleared her throat. "I was sorry you couldn't make the meeting this afternoon."

"I was planning to be there," he said, sounding apologetic. "Then one of my clients had a court order served on him and all hell broke loose. I hope you will forgive me?"

She nodded. "It's been such a horrible two weeks. Then to have John and Catherine accuse Ryan of taking money from the firm . . ."—her voice caught in her throat—"it was almost more than I could handle."

"Yes. I can imagine it was quite a shock."

"I want you to know, Brandon," she said solemnly, her green eyes fixed on him, "that I don't believe it."

Brandon took a sip of his brandy before answering. "I didn't either when I first learned about it. It made no sense to me." He paused before adding, "If Ryan had needed anything, all he had to do was ask."

Rebecca's stomach twisted into a knot as she sat forward. "I can't believe I'm hearing this! Ryan was like a son to you. You were like a father to him. Do you honestly believe he would have stolen money from you?"

Brandon winced. "I would have sworn on a stack of Bibles that the answer was no—I prayed it wasn't true," he said sadly. "Still, I don't know how to contradict the evidence. Apparently, on his orders, checks were deposited to another account rather than to the firm's regular account."

" 'Apparently?' " She frowned, her heart beating rapidly. "Does that mean you don't have any personal knowledge of it?"

He smiled at her, his eyes crinkling at the corners. "I forgot I'm dealing with another lawyer. With the upcoming primary and my cases, as well as all the things Ryan usually handled for me, I've been up to my ears. It was John who brought the matter to my attention. However, I also had Catherine check it out."

Brandon stopped to take another sip. "According to her, the evidence showed that over a two-year period Ryan had taken at least two hundred fifty thousand dollars and perhaps much more."

"But there was no motive and nothing to show for it. Ryan didn't have any new clothes or jewelry. There were no new cars. I can't imagine that he'd buy a boat or a plane without one of us finding out about it, can you?" Her gaze challenged him.

"No," he acknowledged.

She felt a rush of frustration. "Then if he took the money, what did he spend it on?"

"It doesn't add up," he admitted readily, running a finger over his mouth. "But maybe he was in some kind of trouble and he didn't tell us. In light of what happened later, I think it's clear he must have taken the money, even if we don't know why."

Rebecca raised her chin, not taking her eyes off of him. "What do you mean?"

Dodging her stare, he dropped his own gaze to his hands. "He did leave a suicide note," he pointed out. "And . . . well you . . . you know the rest."

"Ryan did not kill himself," she said firmly, then paused to catch her breath. "The night Ryan disappeared, you said over and over again, if only you'd realized how upset he was, maybe you could have done something more. What did you mean?"

He picked up the antique box sitting on the table next to his brandy snifter. Opening and shutting it, he appeared to be going over something in his mind before responding. "It was clear that Ryan wasn't acting like himself," he finally said. "I asked him several times what was wrong. He kept saying it was nothing. I figured maybe the pressure of working on the campaign was more than he'd bargained for." He shrugged. "And I wanted to give him a little space, you know, time to adjust."

Brandon stopped and cleared his throat. It sounded like he was choking up. "If I had realized Ryan was suicidal, I would have gotten him some help." There were sudden tears in his eyes, which he wiped away. "I'm sorry. I feel like I failed him somehow. But I had absolutely no idea." Without warning, he stood up and quickly left the room.

Seeing Brandon cry affected Rebecca deeply. It made her realize that she wasn't the only one suffering in the aftermath of her husband's death. Brandon obviously didn't understand the missing money situation any better than she did. Maybe she'd been too harsh on him.

When he returned, he looked more in control. Picking up his brandy, he sat down again.

She softened her stance. "What convinced you Ryan wasn't himself?"

He rubbed his forehead thoughtfully. "One of the things everyone loved about Ryan was his sense of humor. It was easy to be around him. But all of a sudden he had stopped smiling. Some of the support staff complained that he'd yelled at them, which was very uncharacteristic." Brandon shook his head. "In the seven years we'd worked together I'd never heard Ryan raise his voice to a member of our staff. He might dress down an attorney—always in a reasonable manner, of course—but never a secretary or a clerk."

"Was that all?"

"No. I'd catch him staring off into space, or I'd ask him a question two or three times before he'd answer. It was strange —as if he were lost in another world."

Rebecca felt a chill run down her spine. Brandon was mentioning disturbing aspects of Ryan's behavior that she had noticed as well. "What else?" she asked.

Brandon stared at her for a long moment before he spoke. "Why are you doing this to yourself, Rebecca? To me? I know how much you loved him. We both did. Don't make it any worse than it is."

"You of all people should want the truth to come out," she said, her voice rising.

The muscles in his jaw tightened. "I know you're angry and probably lashing out at me for lack of a better target," he said, "but it would help to remember we're both on the same side."

She held her glass up to the light, watching the bubbles. She knew her nerves were on edge, yet she couldn't seem to bring herself to apologize. "Did you talk to Ryan on the boat that night?" she finally asked.

"A number of times," he said, watching her warily now. "As for what we discussed, I doubt I could repeat it. It was innocuous party conversation."

"I thought Ryan was there to rally support for you. I wouldn't think of that as innocuous."

"It wouldn't be if Ryan had been doing his job." He swirled the liquid in his brandy snifter. "Sadly, your husband was drinking that night, heavily. I'd never seen him do that before, and I tried to get him to stop. He shook off my concern. I didn't feel it would do much good to confront Ryan in that condition, although I did intend to discuss it with him the next morning."

Brandon peered down at his hands, and Rebecca couldn't tell if he was crying again or not. When he spoke, his voice was so hoarse she could barely hear it. "As we both know, that chance never came."

She went to the mantel and picked up a photo of Ryan and Brandon that had been taken the year before. They were both smiling happily. How could things have changed so drastically in such a short time?

"Catherine told me about the burglary," he said.

Rebecca turned around. "It was awful. They destroyed all of Ryan's files, his entire computer was wiped out. It was a professional job. That's one of the things that started me thinking someone wanted Ryan dead."

She saw the flash of caution in his eyes. Other than that, he didn't seem overly startled by her accusation. One by one, she took him through all her reasons for believing her husband had been murdered, starting with the hours at the computer, the break-in, and the missing files; their trying to have a baby, how Ryan felt about suicide because of his mother, and lastly the things her husband had said to her that night. She mentioned everything but the letter and bankbook she had found in Ryan's briefcase.

Brandon was again looking into his brandy glass, which made it impossible for her to read the expression in his eyes. When she was through, he was silent for a moment. "Rebecca, this is very important, so think carefully." There was an ominous tone to his voice. "Do you know what was in those files?"

"No."

"Were there any backup files?"

She shook her head. "They were all gone too."

"I see. Is there anywhere else you can think of that Ryan might have kept some important papers?"

His eyes were now riveted on her. She wondered if he was looking for the bankbook. She debated telling him that she had found it in the briefcase, but something in his body language stopped her and she changed her mind. "There is no other place I know of," she answered.

Did he look relieved, Rebecca asked herself, or was it her imagination? It was her turn to ask a question. "Is there anything Ryan might have known that could have gotten him killed?"

"Nothing I can think of."

Rebecca thought she saw his eyelid twitch. She sat down and tucked one foot underneath her. "What exactly was Ryan doing for you?"

"Troubleshooting. Getting me some beneficial spin in the news. Ryan was brilliant at handling things like that. He saved me a number of times." He gave her an indecipherable look. "Didn't he tell you about it?"

"No. Ryan was very circumspect and whatever he was

doing for you he kept to himself." Again, she could have sworn he seemed relieved.

"I suppose that's good. Although his sharing things with you was fine with me."

"Thanks for the vote of confidence."

Brandon cleared his throat and took a swallow of his brandy. "Ryan was also supposed to be doing a background check on Paul Worthington. Did you know anything about that?"

Her heart began to beat rapidly as she sat forward. "Maybe that's it! What if Ryan dug up something bad on Worthington and the man found out about it? He could have figured Ryan put the information in his computer, so he killed him or had him killed and then had the files destroyed."

"I admit that thought entered my mind too," Brandon intoned, nodding his head. "But I just can't see Worthington killing Ryan because of what he found. If Worthington had something that damaging to hide, I doubt that he would even have considered running for office."

"Nothing is ever that simple," she muttered.

"Speaking of Worthington," Brandon added, "I suppose he could have wanted those files for another reason. I mean, so he'd have inside information on me and my campaign."

"I never thought of that," she conceded, mulling the idea over.

"Who else have you mentioned your suspicions to?"

"I told John I thought Ryan was murdered. That was after Catherine left. I also told the detectives, but they don't believe me." She exhaled slowly. "Would you talk to Solowski and Walters? Maybe they'll listen to you."

He didn't respond immediately. "I'll see what I can do," he finally said.

Setting his brandy on the table, he came over and put his hands on her shoulders. "I think you need to go home. You look like you could use several weeks of sleep."

When she started to protest, he put his finger over her lips and lowered his voice to a confidential murmur. "I'm worried about you and I want to see you get some rest. In the meantime, it's getting late and I'm a man running for office. I can't have a beautiful young woman leaving my house alone after one in the morning."

In spite of herself, Rebecca managed a half smile.

Brandon waited until Rebecca's car was out of sight before he closed the door. He felt sorry for her and for what she was going through. It wasn't easy to lose someone you loved. He rubbed his temples. Ryan had been like the son he'd always wanted and never had. How he'd cared for that boy. But Ryan had become a different person those last weeks—and so very difficult it pained Brandon to even think about it.

Ryan had been young, with his whole life ahead of him. Why hadn't he listened when Brandon had warned him he was playing out of his league?

CHAPTER NINE

The next morning, Rebecca was stepping into a pair of jeans when she heard the doorbell. Grabbing a sweatshirt, she went to the front door. She was relieved when she saw that it was a friend and not another reporter. "Come on in," she told Lucy in a dull voice.

"I hate to say this, Rebecca, but it sure looks like you've had another sleepless night." There was a worried frown on Lucy's face.

"Last night *was* rough," Rebecca confessed. "In fact, I just got out of bed a few seconds before you rang."

"Let me fix us some coffee, and you can tell me about it." Lucy headed for the kitchen.

Ordinarily, Rebecca wasn't the type to tell others her problems. Without Ryan, however, she needed someone to confide in, and talking to Lucy would help to clear her head. Besides that, she trusted Lucy with her life.

Lucy came back with steaming cups of coffee and handed one to Rebecca. "Okay," she said, "let's hear it."

Haltingly at first, then more animatedly, Rebecca filled Lucy in on her meeting with Ryan's partners. She told her also about the late-night stop at Brandon's house.

Lucy rolled her eyes as if to say what she was hearing was unbelievable. "No wonder you're so down. Accusing Ryan of taking funds from the firm! Jesus, it must have been devastating!" She reached over and squeezed Rebecca's hand.

"But what if it's true?" The moment the words left her mouth, Rebecca felt like a traitor.

"Oh, come on now," said Lucy, shaking her head emphatically. "I don't believe it for a second and neither should you."

"That was my first, second, and third reaction yesterday," Rebecca admitted. "But all night long the doubts kept creeping up. Maybe I didn't know Ryan as well as I thought I did. One person, or even two, might make a mistake. But they can't *all* be wrong, can they?"

"Stop being logical," Lucy said. "You know in your heart Ryan wouldn't steal."

"I want to believe that, but they say they have proof Ryan took the money. That's why they are all so sure he killed himself." In spite of her resolve, the tears spilled down Rebecca's cheeks.

"Have you seen this proof?"

"Not yet. I've asked for it. They say they're putting the paperwork together for me."

"I'll bet." Lucy reached out and took her hand. "Look at me. Give me all the reasons you believe Ryan wouldn't have killed himself?"

"Well, there was the way he felt about suicide because of his mother and the fact that I might be pregnant. I just can't believe he'd want his child to live with that burden or that he'd leave me to raise our child alone." Rebecca wiped her eyes with a tissue.

"Speaking of a child, when are you going to get the results of that blood test?"

"They said to call this morning, but I'm almost afraid to."

"You really want to be pregnant, don't you?"

"Very much," Rebecca admitted both to herself and to Lucy. "It's all I have left of Ryan."

"Go ahead and call," Lucy urged her.

A few minutes later, when Rebecca came back from her conversation with her doctor's office, her heart had lifted. "It's positive," she said, smiling, still unable to believe it was really true. She was going to have a baby. Now she knew why her stomach had been so queasy.

"That's great!" Lucy exclaimed, jumping up and giving Rebecca a hug.

When Lucy took her seat again her face had become serious. "Now you have even more of a reason to look for the answers. Think about this: They claim Ryan stole that money, then couldn't live with it so he killed himself. If that was the case, then it sounds like he expected you to face the music for him. Was your husband that kind of a person?"

"Oh, no," cried Rebecca. "I can't imagine Ryan intentionally leaving me in such a mess." She sipped at her coffee. "I'm going to have a terrible time holding on to this house as it is, even if I can prove he didn't take that money. And then, we also support Ryan's mother, or at least we supplement what little she gets from social security. Ryan's father died when he was only ten."

"That sure doesn't sound like a man who would steal from his partners," reasoned Lucy. "Besides, the two of you weren't exactly into a lavish lifestyle."

"That's what makes it all so crazy," Rebecca agreed, nodding. "Ryan had no motive to take that money."

Lucy got up from the table and helped herself to more coffee. Turning around, she said, "My gut tells me that you need to trust yourself, Rebecca. Trust your belief in your husband."

"I'm not sure if I can do that."

"Of course you can. The biggest problem right now is that you're not thinking like a lawyer. Make believe this whole mess involves a client. Then figure out what you'd do to help her. I've seen people come in all upset, and you immediately start writing letters and making phone calls on their behalf." Lucy raised her eyebrows for emphasis. "I've seen you in action. You're formidable."

"Thanks for the nice words."

"They're sincere. The other thing," Lucy said, coming back to the table, "is that you're too personally involved. Detach yourself." She waved her arms. "You said Ryan was troubled those last weeks. Go over every detail, every fact in your mind the way a detective would. Question everyone he dealt with—question everything that happened."

Lucy's words struck a chord in Rebecca. She recalled all the strange things that had happened on the boat that night. How ill at ease Ryan had been around Brandon. He'd also been terse with Catherine, as well as with Paul Worthington. She concentrated harder and remembered the apparent argument she'd witnessed between Ryan and John. And that weird incident with Maxwell Holmes, where Ryan had taken offense because the man was ogling her. Did any of these things have something to do with his death?

It was time to make some decisions. Not only for herself but for their baby. She hugged herself and inhaled deeply. "You're right, Lucy. I've got to handle this whole situation differently, starting now. I knew my husband better than anyone else, and I don't care *what* proof anyone has that he stole money or that he committed suicide. I just don't buy it."

"That sounds like the Rebecca I know," Lucy said, smiling.

Suddenly Rebecca started to feel a lot better. "If it takes my final breath or my last dollar, I'm going to prove Ryan did not steal that money." She patted her stomach. "I owe it to our child. I'm also going to find out who killed him and why." Tilting her head, she added, "And then I'm going to see that, whoever they are, those bastards pay for what they've done."

A few nights later, Rebecca was parked on Rodeo Drive, across the street from the Taylor, Dennison & Evans law firm. She'd decided she had to examine Ryan's office for clues and she had to do it without interference from anyone. It was after eight, and from this vantage point she could watch everyone departing the building. John had driven out at six, Brandon around seven. Most of the other lawyers and staff had left too. The only one she hadn't seen go was Catherine. But then Catherine might have left before Rebecca had taken up her vigil.

There was a light on in Catherine's front office, although that didn't necessarily indicate she was there. Even if Catherine or someone else was inside, once Rebecca reached Ryan's office and closed the door, the lights couldn't be detected except from the street, and she'd make sure the blinds were closed.

At the locked double glass doors fronting the street, an older man who was wearing the uniform of a private security guard smiled at Rebecca and let her through.

"How ya doing, Mrs. Morland?" he asked as she signed in.

Her hands were clammy. "Not bad, Gus."

He walked her over to the elevator and with his key called for the car.

"I'm just getting a few of my husband's things," she explained, feeling self-conscious.

"Sure." He nodded. "See ya on your way down."

She breathed a sigh of relief as the elevator started its climb. Somehow, she had been expecting him to stop her.

Rebecca experienced an eerie sensation as she stepped out of the elevator into the deserted office. She tiptoed across the marble foyer until she reached the hallway. There, luckily, the carpeting was a deep pile, so there were no loud footsteps to announce her arrival. She tried to recall what time the cleaning crew came—if her memory was correct, it wasn't until much later.

Heart pounding, she came to Catherine's office and stopped, holding her breath. The door was closed. She didn't hear anything. For a moment, Rebecca was tempted to turn and leave, but then she forced herself to listen again. It was quiet. Deciding she'd take the chance, Rebecca turned the corner and continued on to Ryan's office.

Once there, she quietly slipped inside and closed the door. Her pulse was racing furiously now.

She was relieved to see that all the blinds were drawn.

She flicked on the light, and the full impact of being in her husband's office hit her; it felt exactly like a hard punch in the stomach. Most of his personal effects had already been boxed up and brought to the house, so the office looked as forlorn as she felt.

While not a corner office like the ones occupied by Brandon and Catherine, it was nonetheless extremely large and had a number of windows. Ryan had loved light woods with beautiful grains, and his furniture had been custom made.

Going to his desk, she ran her hand over the smooth surface, wondering who would get this furniture now. It was heartbreaking to think that Ryan would never again sit behind his beautiful desk. She sighed deeply.

Pushing her memories aside, Rebecca sat down in Ryan's chair and quietly began going through the drawers in his desk. Somewhere, there had to be a clue, a lead she could follow.

It quickly became apparent, however, that the drawers had already been cleaned out; only a few things remained in each of them. Still, Rebecca patiently examined each and every item that was left, starting with a box of staples. She even checked several matchbooks for writing on the inside of the covers. Maybe there was something she'd recognize as being important, even if no one else had.

She lifted out one drawer at a time and put it on the carpet while she searched all around the inside of the desk with her hand, trying to see if Ryan had secreted a message, a key, or anything else.

The last drawer was out on the carpet when the door suddenly opened.

Rebecca froze, her heart hammering in her chest.

"What do you think you're doing?" Catherine's eyes were glaring at Rebecca as if she were a criminal.

Her stomach dropped. "I . . . I just wanted to sit in Ryan's chair." Rebecca couldn't seem to string two words together in a coherent manner. "You know, to be close to him," she finally managed to say.

Catherine had come around to the other side of the desk and was gazing at her with a skeptical expression on her face. "And it makes you feel closer to him with one of his drawers on the floor?"

"Oh, that," Rebecca shrugged, trying to make light of it. "I was looking for some tissues and pulled the drawer out too far."

"Really, Rebecca," Catherine said, arching her eyebrows. "If you wanted to sit in here, why didn't you just ask for permission instead of sneaking around like a thief?"

The color rushed to Rebecca's cheeks as she bit back a sharp retort. She straightened her shoulders. "I'm hardly a thief. My husband was a partner here, after all."

Catherine stiffened. Then, as if she'd realized she'd been coming on too strong, she backed off. "I'm sorry. It's just that you startled me."

Rebecca nodded. As they both continued to stare at one another, she decided to put Catherine's unexpected presence to good use. "Since we're both here, I'd like to ask you something." She leaned forward. "Did you notice any changes in Ryan during the last few weeks of his life?"

"Of course," Catherine nodded. "Everyone did. He was sullen and argumentative. A total reversal from his usual personality."

So far, these were things Rebecca had seen also. "Was there anything else?"

"Now that you mention it," Catherine said, watching Rebecca as if to gauge the effect of her words, "he was also gone all the time."

A shiver of apprehension ran up Rebecca's spine. "By gone, do you mean he didn't come to work?"

"Oh no. He'd actually be here in the morning. But the next thing we knew he'd have canceled several appointments and left. This happened at least four or five times that I know of."

Rebecca struggled to hide her feeling of shock. "And he didn't tell anyone where he was going?"

"No." Catherine shrugged her shoulders. "Who knows, maybe he was . . ."—she paused—"involved with someone or something."

Rebecca tried her best to ignore the obvious meaning behind Catherine's remark, vowing not to let the woman get to her. "These changes that you noticed in Ryan—did you ever ask him if something was wrong?"

"I did, but he brushed me off." Catherine's response sounded defensive.

"Tell me about the night on the boat," Rebecca said. "Did you talk to Ryan?"

"I'm sure we spoke."

"Can you remember what about?"

"It was a party, Rebecca," Catherine reminded her with a touch of annoyance. "Who can recall what one says at those affairs."

It was difficult not to lose her patience with Catherine's offhand attitude. "Please try."

Catherine sighed loudly. "Very well. It was probably about the yacht. It was impressive and everyone was talking about it."

Rebecca's gut told her Catherine was lying. "Did you ever visit the cockpit?"

"Yes," Catherine admitted. "Much earlier in the evening than when Ryan was supposed to have been there. I told the detectives about that," she added.

Making a mental note to check out that statement, Rebecca continued, "Where was the last place you saw Ryan that night?"

"On the upper deck." Catherine brushed a piece of lint from her cream-colored skirt. "He was drunk."

Her stomach clenching, Rebecca tried to remain calm. "How can you be so sure?"

"Really, Rebecca, when someone is gulping down scotch, his eyes are bloodshot, and he's slurring his words and is unsteady on his feet, I'd say that person was drunk."

Rebecca hadn't seen Ryan look or act that way. Why was she the only one who hadn't noticed these things? Or was everybody else lying? Standing up, she came around to the front of the desk. "Were you aware that Brandon had asked Ryan to investigate Paul Worthington's background?"

There was a sharp intake of breath. "Yes, I was," Catherine acknowledged. "However, I would advise you to forget about it. If Worthington ever got wind of that fact, there might be some unpleasantness over it."

Disregarding Catherine's warning, Rebecca pushed on. "Do

you think that Ryan may have discovered something about Worthington that upset the man or worried him?"

"I suppose anything is possible." Catherine's eyes narrowed. "Why? Did Ryan mention anything to you relating to Worthington or his investigation?"

Feeling the intensity of the other woman's gaze, Rebecca waited a moment to answer.

"If Ryan said anything at all about Worthington, I want to know," insisted Catherine sharply.

Rebecca wondered why Catherine was so anxious for that information. "I'm not sure. So much has happened. I'm trying to go over things in my mind. We talked all the time and shared practically everything." Rebecca gave a half smile. Let's see if that rattles her, she thought.

There was a long silence while Catherine appraised her. It was Rebecca who finally spoke. "Do you truly believe that Ryan killed himself?"

Catherine looked pensive, as if she were mulling over her answer. "Since he left a suicide note, I'm afraid that's the only possible conclusion."

It bothered Rebecca the way everyone was placing so much importance on a note that wasn't dated or signed. She considered sharing her news about the baby, then decided instead to keep asking questions. "Do you know who found the so-called suicide note?"

With a nod, Catherine said, "It was John."

Rebecca hadn't known that. "How did it happen to be him?"

The other woman arched her eyebrows again as if to say, How stupid can you be. "I would suppose because he was the first one here."

This news surprised Rebecca, since Ryan had complained about how late John came in every morning and how much that habit had infuriated Brandon.

Looking at her watch, Catherine stood up. "I'd really love to continue our chat, but I must get back to work." She swept her hair back from her face. "Why don't I escort you to the elevator?"

"No need," said Rebecca, leaning over to get her purse.

"Good night," Catherine called out.

As Rebecca walked down the hallway, she felt the other woman's gaze on her back. Good. Let her wonder what she knew.

Stepping out of the elevator and into the lobby, Rebecca had an idea. "Gus?"

"Yes, Mrs. Morland."

"I'm trying to piece something together about the night my husband died. Can I take a peek at your book?"

"Sure." He guided her to his desk and set the book down in front of her.

A small lamp threw light on the pages as Rebecca quickly flipped through them. With a sharp intake of breath, she found what she was looking for. "Were you on duty this night?" she asked, pointing to an entry on the date Ryan had disappeared.

He glanced down. "Yep. Those are my initials. Looks like I had the late shift."

"Do you remember Mr. Evans signing in?"

"Says here he signed in at one forty-three in the morning." He was quiet for a second. "Yep. It was real late. Don't usually get anyone coming in at that hour."

Rebecca's mind raced. "Do you remember anything else, like what he was wearing or how he was acting?"

The guard rubbed his chin. "Let me see," he mused. "I recall he was dressed up. A tux, I think. Not real friendly, but then he's one of the few here that never is. Not at all like your husband or Mr. Taylor." The old man smiled. "Now Mr. Taylor—he's a real gentleman. Always says hello and asks after my wife."

She smiled and tried to sound nonchalant. "Did Mr. Evans give any reason for showing up here so late?"

"Nope." He scratched his head. "You know, usually if it's real late, they say they forgot a file or they couldn't sleep because they were worried about a case. But him. Naw. He never said a word."

"What time did he sign out?" Rebecca asked, running her

finger down the pages in the book to locate the entry. "I don't see it."

He peered down at the page. "That's funny."

She glanced up at him. "Is that unusual? I mean for a person to sign in and then not sign out?"

"Yep. When I'm on, I always make sure they do both." He seemed lost in thought. "Wait a minute. I think the reason was he came down after seven. I was on from eleven at night to seven in the morning. I was just going off. We don't bother with signing in or out at that time because lots of lawyers start arriving as early as six. There was one fella used to work here, showed up at four-thirty every morning like clockwork."

Rebecca smiled at him. "Did you notice if Mr. Evans was carrying anything?"

"I think a couple of files, maybe. I'm not real sure."

"I see. Well, thanks for your help." She tore off a scrap of blank paper from a pad lying on his desk and quickly scribbled her home number on it. "If you remember anything else, please call me at home."

The old man put the note in his pocket. "Will do."

"And Gus?" She paused, her heartbeat accelerating. "I'd appreciate it if you wouldn't tell anyone about our conversation. Not until I can get the police to make a copy of your book."

"Whatever you say, Mrs. Morland."

Rebecca left feeling certain that she'd just learned something of vital importance. It was clear that John had come to the office directly from the yacht and stayed there the rest of the night. What she didn't know was why.

About a minute after Rebecca left, Catherine stepped out of the shadows.

"I didn't hear you come down in the elevator, Ms. Dennison," Gus said.

"I took the stairs. I needed some exercise." She gestured in the direction of the retreating figure crossing the street. "What did Mrs. Morland want?"

"Oh, nothing," he said. "Just to chat."

"I see."

"She's a real nice lady." Gus smiled and shook his head. "Too bad about her husband."

"Yes, isn't it," Catherine agreed. "Listen, Gus, I don't want Mrs. Morland in the building after hours unless I'm here to approve it. Understood?"

He gave her a funny look. "Whatever you say, Ms. Dennison. You're the boss."

CHAPTER
TEN

Early the following week, after learning from John's secretary that he was at the dentist's office a few blocks away from the firm's Beverly Hills location, Rebecca decided to meet him there. It would give her a chance to speak to him privately.

Although John was clearly surprised to see her when she showed up, nonetheless, he invited Rebecca to join him on his walk back to the office.

"I'm still waiting for the documents you promised me regarding the missing money," Rebecca said, trying to keep up with John, who compensated for being short by walking so fast he seemed almost to be running.

"They're working on it. It shouldn't be much longer."

"I hope not," she replied.

"Is that the only reason you wanted to see me?"

"No." She cleared her throat. "John, had you noticed anything different about my husband those last weeks before his death?"

"Yes," he nodded perfunctorily. "He was moody and depressed, as if worried about something."

"Did you ask Ryan what was upsetting him?"

"No," he replied, shaking his head.

"Why not?"

"Ryan and I . . . just were . . . never that close, you know." He seemed to be searching for the right words. "I figured that if he had wanted to talk about it, he'd tell me." He turned toward her, a strange intensity in his eyes. "You were married to him. What did he tell you?"

"Nothing of importance to you."

He stiffened slightly and started speed walking again. "Well, it's clear now what was going on. Ryan had been stealing money and probably realized he couldn't get away with it for much longer."

Rebecca recoiled, but steered clear of that subject for the moment. They came to a corner and had to wait for the light to change. "Weren't you angry when Ryan was asked to join Brandon's campaign staff instead of you?"

"Actually, I rather liked it." John's eyes seemed to draw even closer together. "I couldn't wait for them both to go off to Washington."

She was caught off guard by his apparent honesty. "Why was that?"

"So that I could finally run the firm as I thought proper."

That was interesting news. Rebecca had always gotten the impression that Catherine would be taking over as managing partner after Brandon left. The light turned green and they crossed the street. "I understand you're the one who found what the police are calling the suicide note?"

"Yes."

"How did that happen?"

John looked annoyed. "I'm not sure I understand the question."

Not wanting him to guess that she was suspicious of his actions, Rebecca lightened up. "What I mean is, did you go into Ryan's office looking for a note?"

He seemed to relax. "When I got to the law firm that morning, Ryan's disappearance was very much on my mind. To be quite frank, a number of people who'd been on the boat were convinced that he'd taken his own life. So I thought it prudent to check his office. I went in and found the note on his desk."

"Was this note in an envelope addressed to someone in particular?"

"No," he acknowledged, shaking his head again. "It was just lying there on the blotter."

She felt a chill. Ryan would never have left a note on his desk that way. It was too cold, too impersonal. "Was anyone else around at that time?"

He hesitated slightly. "No. I was the first one at the office that morning."

"And what time was that?"

John rubbed his chin as if trying to remember. "I think it was about six."

His answer stunned her. According to the security guard's book, John had signed in at 1:43 A.M. Why was he lying to her about that? Quickly, she glanced over at him, fearful she might have given herself away. He didn't seem to be aware of her reaction. She smiled, and trying to keep her voice as even as possible, said, "I didn't think you usually got in that early."

"No, I don't," he said, smiling back. "But I couldn't sleep."

"What did you do after you found the note?"

"If you must know," he said, stiffly, "I waited until shortly before eight and then called the sheriff's station."

Rebecca paused for a moment as if thinking, even though she already knew her next question. "If you got in at six," she finally said, "why did you wait almost two hours to call them?"

"How do I know?" he snapped. Then he must have realized his response had been inappropriate, because he hurried to explain. "I guess I figured I'd wait until more or less regular business hours." John frowned at her and added, "Why are you asking me all of these questions, Rebecca?"

"I'm just trying to understand things." She smiled again, hoping to put him at ease while cautioning herself to be more subtle. John was obviously hiding something, and she needed to find out what it was. "You're being very helpful, and I really appreciate it."

"That's okay," he said curtly. "But enough is enough."

Rebecca took a deep breath. "You and Ryan had some sort of argument on the boat that night—what was it about?"

His glance was wary. "What makes you think we argued?"

"I'd gone to get a glass of soda, and when I returned, neither of you saw me, but I overheard your raised voices."

"You're mistaken. We didn't argue," John insisted. "That never happened."

Another lie, Rebecca realized with a jolt. She frowned at him. "I don't know why you're not leveling with me, John. But I promise you, I will find out." Without another word, she turned on her heel and strode quickly away from him.

Later that day, still shaken from her encounter with John, Rebecca drove to the sheriff's station in Marina del Rey. There a friendly deputy took Rebecca to Detective Solowski's desk.

"Mrs. Morland." The detective stood up so quickly she knocked over a cup, which luckily turned out to be empty.

"I was in the neighborhood," Rebecca explained, not wanting to admit that she'd come there on purpose.

Solowski gestured to her chair while she herself perched on the edge of her desk. "Have a seat."

Detective Walters, whose desk was next to his partner's, nodded at Rebecca perfunctorily. "What can we do for you?"

Rebecca sat down in the woman detective's chair. "I wanted to know how the investigation is coming."

Slouching back, Walters put one knee against his desk. "Well, for one thing, we've just gotten the autopsy report on your husband."

She leaned forward. "What does it say?"

"There was enough alcohol in his system that if he'd been at the wheel of a car he'd have been arrested for driving under the influence."

Her heart sank. So all the people who said they had seen Ryan drinking were right. Nonetheless, it didn't necessarily mean that Ryan was inebriated. It only took two glasses of wine to register the legal limit of 0.8 percent. In the three years they'd been together, she'd never once seen her husband drunk. "Was there anything else? Wounds on his body or other marks?"

"Ma'am, your husband was in the water a couple of days. His body was attacked by sharks and other fish and it washed up and over some rather sharp rocks. There were a lot of marks on his body."

She cringed. Thinking of Ryan being attacked by a shark made Rebecca feel physically ill, and she prayed he'd been unconscious or already dead when it had happened.

"Says here," Walters read, "that nothing the medical examiner found was inconsistent with the conditions of his death."

"What about stab wounds or gunshot wounds?" she asked, fighting back a wave of nausea.

"No, ma'am," he said, a flicker of impatience in his eyes. "There was nothing to indicate your husband died under suspicious circumstances."

A large sigh escaped Rebecca's lips.

"Listen, I know we haven't exactly seen eye to eye, but I really think it's time for you to let it go." Walters dropped his voice to a confidential tone as if he were now her best friend. "Your husband's dead and nothing is going to bring him back. Over the years I've seen a lot of people cause themselves all sorts of unnecessary grief. It's much better just to accept things."

"I can't," she replied.

Walters flexed his shoulders. "Well," his voice took on an edge, "with the note, the autopsy findings, and the reports from his partners and other guests that he'd been depressed, et cetera, we feel the evidence surrounding Mr. Morland's death points to it being a suicide."

"I knew Ryan better than his partners or any of the guests on board the yacht that night," she shot back. "My husband would never have taken his own life. He thought I might be pregnant, and it turns out—I am. Doesn't my word count for something?" She glanced from Walters to Solowski.

"Sure it does," Solowski replied with an understanding smile. "And good luck on the baby."

"Thank you."

"In spite of your news," Walters said, cutting in, "it's been our experience that relatives of suicides all say the same thing."

Feeling her anger rising, she asked, "And what's that?"

"That their husband, mother, brother, kid, whatever, would never take his or her own life. Everyone has a hard time accepting it."

"As I told you before," Rebecca said, fighting to control her emotions, "I've been reliving those final weeks. The last night of his life, Ryan said something, and it didn't dawn on me until now what he really meant."

"And what would that be, ma'am?" Walters's voice was now condescending.

"He told me that politics was a lot dirtier than even he had thought. Also, that it was *terrifying* to realize how far someone would go to get what he wanted."

There was a skeptical look on the detective's face. "Do you know, ma'am, who it was your husband was talking about?"

"I'm not exactly sure," she acknowledged. "But it had to be someone on the boat. That's one of the reasons I'm here." She peered intently at both of them. "I need your help."

"So we're supposed to ask every person who was there that night—all two hundred of them—how far they're willing to go to get what they want?" Walters seemed to be mocking her.

"I know it sounds . . ." Rebecca started.

With a worried glance at her partner, Solowski turned to Rebecca. "Mrs. Morland, do you have any ideas, any leads we could follow up on?"

Rebecca saw Walters glare at Solowski. At least the woman detective seemed to understand the significance of what Rebecca was saying. "I'm not sure," she replied. "I've just learned that as a member of Brandon Taylor's campaign staff, my husband had been asked to do a background check on Paul Worthington—a potential opponent to Taylor in the Republican primary." She brushed her hair back from her face. "It occurs to me that Ryan may have discovered something about Worthington and that's why he was killed."

With that, Walters abruptly stood up, his chair scraping so

loudly on the floor that others in the room turned to stare at him. "You want us to talk to a substantial citizen like Paul Worthington, a man who provides jobs for thousands of workers and who pays his taxes, and ask him what? Did you kill Ryan Morland so you could run for the U.S. Senate? Gimme a break."

"Come on, let's go in there," Solowski whispered hurriedly, pointing to a side office. "The captain won't be back today."

Once they had some privacy, Rebecca responded forcefully to Walters's angry question. "As I understand it, ambition is right up there with greed and lust as one of the prime motivations for murder—not to mention the fact that Worthington might have something to hide."

"Ma'am, there's no need to lecture us about crime statistics," Walters retorted with an air of superiority. "We're very well aware of them all."

Rebecca wondered what it would take to break through to this obstinate man. "Don't forget that my house was broken into and Ryan's files were destroyed. On top of that, some of the people who were aboard the yacht that night have lied to me."

"Why don't you tell us about that," suggested Solowski with an encouraging smile.

Walters continued to glare at Solowski as Rebecca explained how John had lied to her, first about the time he'd arrived at the office the morning after Ryan had disappeared, and then again when he'd denied having argued with Ryan at the party. She also mentioned her suspicions regarding Catherine.

"Look, ma'am," Walters said, "sometimes when there's a traumatic event, people forget things like what time they went somewhere or what they did. Maybe Mr. Evans and your husband argued and now Mr. Evans feels guilty about it so he's blocked it from his mind. That doesn't make him a murderer. The fact that you believe Ms. Dennison was less than truthful doesn't make her a murderer either."

He gave her a patronizing smile. "Trust us, we're the professionals here. We don't see a single shred of evidence to suggest foul play."

"But I've given you all the reasons why Ryan didn't kill

himself." When she began listing them again it was clear from the expression on his face that she was hitting a brick wall. Shaking her head, her voice rising, becoming shrill, she said, "I don't see how you can arbitrarily refuse to investigate the possibility that someone wanted my husband dead."

"Glen," Detective Solowski interrupted again, yanking on her partner's arm. "Can I speak to you alone for a moment."

Walters glowered at her. "Can't it wait?"

"No, it can't. Please."

Peering from Solowski to Rebecca and then back again, he finally said, "We'll be right back, Mrs. Morland."

Rebecca sat there, trembling with rage. It was bad enough that her husband's partners were being less than forthcoming with her. But having Detective Walters dismiss her suspicions out of hand was something else entirely, and she didn't intend to let him get away with it.

"You're not being fair, Glen," Solowski told her partner after she'd led him out of the captain's office to a quiet corner of the main room. "This woman lost her husband less than three weeks ago and she's also pregnant. She's made some good points. I think we should check a few of these things out."

"There's nothing to check out," he insisted stubbornly.

Frustrated, she put her hands on her hips. "Fine. Then I'll investigate them on my own."

"Oh, now that's a really brilliant idea. Aren't you the lady who's always complaining she has no time for anything—her kids or herself. The same one who's always coming in late and usually half asleep?"

For a moment, Solowski didn't know what to say she was so astounded by her partner's nasty response.

"If you've got any extra time," he went on, "there's a load of cases on both our desks that haven't been touched in weeks, maybe even months."

"I'll get to them," she assured him.

Walters gestured toward the private office where Rebecca was waiting for them. "You can finish with her. I've got more important things to do." He started to walk away, then turned back. "And if I were you I'd ask that woman about life insurance. I'll bet you a thousand to one, her husband had a policy and it's got a suicide clause."

Solowski frowned. "You mean a clause that says she can't collect if his death is found to be a suicide?"

"Right. If it's murder, they have to pay her. I guarantee you, something like that is behind her insistence that his death was murder."

"Even if there is a suicide clause in her husband's life insurance policy, it doesn't necessarily prove anything."

"Just ask her," he said.

Back in the captain's office, Solowski found Rebecca Morland sitting ramrod straight, as if she'd steeled herself for more of Walters's insensitivity.

In the short time since Solowski had met her there had been a big change in Rebecca's appearance. On the boat that night, although she'd been crying, her beauty had been unmistakable. Now she looked thin and wan. Her gorgeous red hair seemed dull; her green eyes lacked their earlier luster. A pregnant woman was usually brimming with health, but in this case it was as if someone had turned off Rebecca's inner glow.

Solowski thought back to how she'd felt right after her husband died. It had taken her months before she accepted that he wasn't coming back. She hadn't looked so hot then either.

"Look, I apologize for my partner," Solowski said gently. "But he has a lot more experience as a detective than I do, and he really feels there isn't much to go on."

"I see," Rebecca replied stiffly.

"But call us with anything else you come up with. Maybe something will click."

Rebecca focused her gaze on Solowski. "Are you at least running the prints from the burglary at my house?"

"Yep. I'll call you as soon as I learn anything."

"And how about the authentication of the note?"

Solowski hesitated. Walters had said it wasn't necessary, but she felt Mrs. Morland deserved to have every avenue explored. "I'm going to send that off to the lab," she said, hoping her partner wouldn't find out.

"Can you also check into John Evans's story?"

"I'll try," Solowski hedged, "but . . . we'll just have to see about that one."

As if realizing she couldn't push her, Rebecca drew in a deep breath, then stood and held out her hand. "Thank you, Detective Solowski, I appreciate your help."

"No problem." Watching Rebecca pick up her purse to leave, Solowski realized she hadn't asked about the insurance. "Mrs. Morland?"

Rebecca turned around. "Yes?"

"I forgot to ask. Did your husband have any life insurance?"

The other woman looked as if she'd been slapped across the face. "I'm not sure," she said, shaking her head. "Why?"

"It's a standard question," Solowski explained as she led her visitor back to the front entrance. "Why don't you go home and check through your papers and get back to us on it."

When Solowski returned to her desk, Walters leaned forward and pointed his pencil at her. "I don't want you wasting any of our precious time on that woman's foolish ideas. Understood?"

"No problem." Solowski forced herself to smile as she opened one of the files that were piled high on her desk. But she was upset at the way he was handling this case and wondered why he was trying to close it so quickly.

When Rebecca returned home from doing research at the UCLA Law Library for one of her clients at the clinic, the first thing she did was check around. Ever since the burglary, it had made her nervous to enter the house. She kept wondering if something horrible had happened while she was gone or if someone was inside waiting for her.

The ordeal with the detectives had been brutal. On top of that, she missed Ryan every second of the day. Her body ached to have him with her, touching her. Sometimes the pain was so bad that she felt like crawling into bed and never getting up.

Stop that, she chided herself. Ryan wouldn't want you to give up. He'd expect you to fight for him. Besides, there was the baby to think about too. No matter how much Rebecca hurt inside, she had to be strong to pursue justice for her husband.

The next thing on her agenda was speaking to Brandon. She curled up on the living room couch with the phone and punched in his number.

A full three minutes passed before he came on the line. "Sorry, Rebecca, things are crazy here." He sounded genuinely contrite.

"That's okay. I hate to bother you, but I don't know where else to turn. Do you have a few minutes?"

He exhaled loudly. "For you, always."

"Thanks," she responded. "The day after Ryan disappeared, he was supposed to bring home his draw for the month, but John says the firm can't give me any money until we settle up on the missing funds. I haven't gone back to work yet and in the meantime I've got lots of bills."

"I'm sure you can understand that we need to know what's left from the money Ryan took?"

"*If,*" she said, emphasizing the word, "Ryan misappropriated that money from the firm. But, I've found nothing to indicate he had another account or safety deposit box." As she said the words, she felt guilty. There *was* another account, albeit with a zero balance. But Rebecca still didn't know who it belonged to. There hadn't been time to check into it. The account could even belong to a client. *If you really believe that,* a nagging little voice said, *then why don't you turn it over to the law firm and find out.* "I've no idea where else to look at the moment," she added.

"I see." She heard him breathing and waited to see if he would add anything. Finally he spoke. "Listen, my dear, if you need money to cover bills, I can certainly lend you some."

"That's very kind of you, Brandon. But I have to know where I stand on the partnership. And speaking of that, I can't find a copy of the agreement."

"No problem. I'll messenger it to you."

"Thanks. As for the missing funds, John keeps promising to

send me the backup paperwork, but I haven't seen it yet. And anyway, if you're planning to offset the monies due Ryan against the funds you say are missing, I think it would be best to do a full accounting."

"Aren't you getting a little technical, Rebecca?" There was a hint of annoyance in his voice. "I thought we were all friends here."

Brandon was trying to put her on the defensive, and she didn't like it. "We are. I'm just in a difficult position. I respect you, Brandon. You know that. But I'm not great at numbers. I'd like someone else to check this out for me."

He was quiet for several seconds. "Rebecca, I can imagine what you must be going through. At the same time, I've also lost someone who meant a lot to me, and on top of that, I've got to find someone to take Ryan's place. He was handling a million things for my campaign. He was also in the middle of turning over his cases to some of the younger lawyers in the firm who have no idea what's going on, so that burden too falls on my shoulders."

For a moment Rebecca wanted to shout out at the top of her lungs that she didn't give a damn about his problems. "I know you've got a ton of stuff to contend with," she finally said.

There was the sound of his chair revolving. "Listen, give me a couple of weeks to get things squared away. In the meantime, I'll put John in charge of providing you with the information you want. And to ease things for you at home, I'll send you a personal check to cover Ryan's draw."

"I don't want your personal check," she protested, annoyed by his attempt to manipulate her. "What I need is to get the ball rolling, and John's been stonewalling me. I've got financial decisions to make." She was about to tell him she was pregnant, then held her tongue, not wanting him to help her because he felt sorry for her. "I just don't understand why the firm can't advance Ryan's draw to me."

"Can I speak in confidence?" Brandon's rich baritone voice dropped low.

"You know you can."

"Good." He stopped to clear his throat. "I'd consider it a personal favor, Rebecca, if you'd let me send you my own check. Since I announced my candidacy, John and Catherine have been at loggerheads over which one of them is going to head the firm when I'm gone. I don't want to stir up who is owed what right now."

She sighed. It might be best to acquiesce for the time being. "I suppose that's okay. I just don't want charity."

"I wouldn't do anything to take away your dignity," he protested. "Ryan was like a son to me. And I've come to love you, too, Rebecca. Helping you will be my pleasure."

Rebecca bit her tongue. If Ryan had been like a son to him, why the hell wasn't he giving him the benefit of the doubt?

"I promise you that at the first opportunity, I'll start looking into things myself. In the meantime, I'll tell John that he's to cooperate fully with you. I'll also see that he calls you tomorrow morning."

Now she knew why Brandon was considered such a good negotiator. He could just talk and talk until the other person gave up. "Fine. By the way, have you spoken to the sheriff's department about widening their investigation?"

"No. As I've said, I've been snowed under. However, I've given the matter a great deal of thought. Unless you have some concrete evidence of foul play, I believe it would be in everyone's best interests not to mention the subject of murder."

Stunned by his advice, she could barely speak. "Don't you want the truth to come out?"

"Of course I do. But right now, all you have are suspicions —and they are providing Paul Worthington with a windfall. He's manipulating this tragedy to his own personal advantage, and I know you don't want that."

Rebecca sensed his subtle warning not to do anything to ruin his campaign. It made her want to scream. Ryan was dead, and this man's sole worry was his damn political future! "There are more important issues at stake here than an election," she said.

"I don't think you really mean that, Rebecca." His voice was as cold as ice. Then, as if realizing it, he turned the charm back on. "Think about Ryan and what he wanted. This was more than an election to him. To your husband—it was everything." Brandon paused. "Ryan and I had worked closely on all the issues, the things we hoped to accomplish in Washington. Do you want all of his magnificent dreams to die with him?"

"Of course not," she retorted, jumping out of her chair and moving angrily around the room. "If the sheriff's department would give me some help, I might find the answers. What if Paul Worthington had Ryan killed—wouldn't you want him punished?"

"Certainly, my dear. However, accusations and proof are two different things. Shouting accusations of murder from the rooftops can have severe repercussions."

Rebecca had no intention of stopping. She'd keep shouting until someone took notice—Ryan deserved that from all of them. "I'll think over what you've said, but I'm not happy about it."

"That's all I ask. Just give it some thought, my dear. I know you, Rebecca. You're a bright, lovely, sensible woman."

No I'm not, she thought, angrily hanging up. Once again she realized she was facing this nightmare by herself.

CHAPTER
ELEVEN

J ust as Brandon had promised, John called Rebecca the following morning. But she soon hung up from talking to him, both angry and frustrated. While he agreed to send her a copy of the firm's partnership agreement, he claimed that he still hadn't received the papers from the accounting department dealing with the missing funds. What incensed her even more was his refusal to divulge the name of the employee who had supposedly helped Ryan embezzle the money. He blamed it on the firm's insurance company and labor lawyers who were requiring strict confidentiality on the matter until they worked out a deal with the departing employee.

So much for cooperating, thought Rebecca. As far as she was concerned, it was just more of John's usual bullshit. Facing the fact that her husband's partners were proving to be more of a hindrance than a help to her, Rebecca went down her list of things to do, which she'd compiled with Lucy's help.

Her finger landed on an item labeled *Insurance.* She'd been postponing calling about the letter to an insurance agent she'd found in Ryan's briefcase. Part of the reason was that Detective

Walters had acted as if he thought she were guilty of something, and although the woman detective had been more sympathetic, she'd been the one to actually ask about Ryan's insurance.

You're supposed to pretend you're handling this matter for a client, Rebecca chided herself, remembering Lucy's words. Having run out of excuses, she reluctantly placed the call.

Ryan's letter had been addressed to a man named Fred Jackson. Rebecca quickly ascertained that he was the agent who handled all of the law firm's insurance. After Jackson conveyed his sympathy over the loss of her husband, Rebecca described the letter she'd found.

"Oh yes," Jackson remarked. "I got that letter a day or two before he died."

"I'm afraid I'm at a disadvantage," Rebecca admitted. "My husband and I had discussed insurance, but I wasn't aware he'd actually done anything about it. What else can you tell me?"

"Mr. Morland first contacted me several months ago. He said the two of you were planning a family and were interested in life insurance, so I mailed him some information."

Rebecca remembered the night they'd decided to start trying. It had been unusually mild weather, and she and Ryan had driven to the beach for dinner. Afterwards, they'd removed their shoes and run on the sand like a couple of kids—and then, behind a sand dune, they'd made love without using any contraception.

"Mrs. Morland?"

With a start, Rebecca realized she'd been daydreaming. "I'm sorry. Did you hear from my husband again?"

"Yes. He called a few weeks later. Said he wanted a policy for one hundred thousand dollars. Because of his age, all that was needed was a cursory physical. In fact, the insurance doctor went to Mr. Morland's office. Everything checked out and the policy was issued."

Rebecca's stomach dropped. She couldn't believe Ryan had actually purchased insurance without discussing it with her. "How long ago was that?"

"Hold on, let me get the file."

Waiting for him to return, she tried to calm her racing heart. Soon he was back on the line. "Let's see." She heard papers rustling as he searched for something. "Here it is. Looks like it was exactly one week before he died."

She felt chilled. Why hadn't Ryan told her?

"Mr. Morland also paid the first year's premium," he volunteered as an afterthought.

It was hard for Rebecca to digest this information. Still she managed to ask, "What exactly do I do next?"

"You have to fill out claim forms. Of course—" he stopped and cleared his throat—"the payment won't be automatic. On a policy of this short a duration there will have to be an investigation."

Her pulse accelerated. "What kind of an investigation?"

"Into the nature of his death." He hesitated, then continued, sounding cautious. "The policy had a standard suicide clause, which states that if an insured commits suicide within two years of purchasing the policy, the company isn't obligated to pay out on it."

"It wasn't a suicide, though," Rebecca insisted. "I believe my husband was murdered." She heard a sharp intake of breath on the other end of the line.

"Well, we usually do our own investigation," he said, then cleared his throat again. "So I'll send you the necessary claim forms. As soon as we get them back, we'll get started. That's about all I can say for now."

She hung up in a daze, her mind spinning. What did this say about Ryan's frame of mind at the time of his death? To her, the purchase of this insurance before he died strengthened her assertion that Ryan wouldn't have taken his own life. After all, he was a lawyer. He would have read the policy and been familiar with the suicide clause. It made no sense that he would plan his own death and then purchase a policy he knew she couldn't collect on.

Of course, the police might argue that he purchased it and then decided to take his own life. And that because of the suicide clause, Rebecca was trying to make her husband's death look like a murder so that she could collect. In light of this, Rebecca decided not to mention the policy to the detectives until they asked her about it again.

Then another possibility entered her mind and she shivered. Didn't the fact that Ryan bought this policy without telling her prove that he was afraid for his life? Couldn't this have been his way of providing for her and any unborn child in the event something happened to him?

Remembering that before his death, Ryan had spent a lot of time at the campaign headquarters set up by Brandon Taylor in West Los Angeles, Rebecca decided it was important to check the place out. It had only been in existence a month or so before his death, and she had never even visited the office.

It turned out to be a storefront location on Santa Monica Boulevard, a drab, almost seedy space, with its only decoration a display of Brandon Taylor campaign posters. Inside, however, there was a lot of activity as people folded, sorted, and stamped mailings, and answered the ringing phones.

After finally locating the person in charge, Scott Reed, a casually dressed young man who wore his sandy blond hair in a tight ponytail, she managed to convince him to give her a few minutes of his precious time.

In between frequent interruptions, most of them phone calls from "important" people, Rebecca breathlessly listened to him as he related to her one of the first real clues she had had so far in her husband's death.

"So, you're saying that a few days before his death, Ryan received a phone call here from Paul Worthington?"

He nodded.

Finally, thought Rebecca excitedly, she might be on to something important. "And after an apparently heated conversation, my husband stormed out of the headquarters?"

"Right, he told me he had to go meet the guy." He shrugged his shoulders. "Who else could he have meant?"

Her adrenaline was pumping as she digested this significant information. Whether or not Ryan had actually met with Worthington was something Rebecca most definitely would have to follow up on. When she had told the detectives that Worthington could have wanted her husband dead, she'd had nothing to support that possibility. Now she did.

"If I could just look through the things in my husband's desk, I'll let you get back to work."

"Sorry," he said, shaking his head, "but the morning following Ryan's disappearance, Brandon Taylor had me pack up everything in and on Ryan's desk and deliver it to him."

Rebecca was incredulous. That was at least a full day before her husband's body was found. Why would Brandon have felt the need to clean out Ryan's papers before he even knew Ryan was dead? Contemplating the possibilities gave Rebecca a sick feeling in the pit of her stomach.

Two days later, Rebecca was in her Jeep heading for the San Diego Freeway, which she then planned to take to the exclusive community of Newport Beach. After trying unsuccessfully to reach Paul Worthington by phone at his office, she had decided a more aggressive approach was in order—she'd visit him at home. That way she could also ask his wife, Diana, a few questions.

After getting the Worthingtons' address off the envelope containing the condolence card they had sent her, she had left a message at Worthington's office that she'd be in Newport on Sunday in the early afternoon and would appreciate some time.

As she drove, Rebecca tried to make sense out of what she'd learned from Scott Reed, the chief coordinator at Brandon Taylor's campaign headquarters. It was strange that Ryan had never mentioned to her that he'd even talked to Worthington—that's why she felt it might be the key to finding out what really had happened on the boat that night.

As she approached the entrance ramp to the freeway, she noticed in her rearview mirror that a gray Ford appeared to be weaving in and out of traffic as if trying to stay behind her. The hairs on the back of her neck stood up. Why would anyone want to follow her?

She made a quick right turn and then another turn at the first block. Her pulse was racing. Was the car still there? She no longer saw it, but just to make sure she repeated her evasive actions several more times, until she was positive she'd lost the car. Had she imagined it? Or was someone really following her? Feeling a bit shaken, Rebecca tightened her trembling fingers on the steering wheel and found her way back to the freeway.

A half-hour later, she exited and turned toward the Pacific Coast Highway and the ocean. The Worthingtons lived on Harbor Island, a finger of high-priced land that jutted out into Newport Harbor. She'd read somewhere that their home had cost eighteen million dollars. What kind of a place would that much money buy? she wondered.

As she arrived at the narrow bridge that crossed over the channel to the island, Rebecca was surprised to find that the entrance to this exclusive area didn't have security gates or guards. In fact, the bridge itself was only wide enough to allow one car at a time to pass over it.

She came off the bridge onto a private cobblestone street no wider than a charming alley. Since the homes here were all built to face the water, almost nothing about them could be ascertained from the street.

Finding the right address, she pulled her car to the side of the road. From this vantage point the Worthington home appeared modest—the property no more than forty feet wide. The windows, shuttered. But the massive front doors, along with a beautiful teak sculpture that stood off to the side surrounded by lush green ferns, gave the home a stately presence.

Rebecca lifted one of the huge brass knockers and rapped it against the door, taking a deep breath as the hollow sound reverberated in her ears.

The door was opened by a man dressed in a white jacket and dark pants. "Yes?" His tone was crisp.

"Hello. I'm Rebecca Morland. I'd like to see Mr. Worthington, please."

He looked puzzled. "Was he expecting you?"

"Yes. I telephoned to say I was coming."

"I'm sorry, ma'am. He's not here at the moment."

Her heart sank. "Oh dear. I drove all the way from L.A. Do you know when he'll be back?"

"I'm not sure. Mrs. Worthington is here. Shall I see if she's available?"

"Yes, please," she said eagerly.

He stepped back to allow her in. Her eyes were immediately drawn to the open expanse in front of her, a panoramic view of Newport Harbor, from the waterways and yachts to the beautiful homes and fancy restaurants lining its shores. The green lawns of the Worthington property ran down to the edge of the water. It was breathtaking.

The living room was huge, but broken up into small seating areas, the decor all soft whites, beiges, and earth tones. On most of the surfaces stood interesting sculptures or other beautiful objects. Works of art that looked as if they had cost millions of dollars hung on the walls.

The man led her to a small area in one corner of the vast room, directly in front of the floor-to-ceiling windows. "Please wait here. I'll be right back."

Too restless to sit down, Rebecca gazed out the windows at a stone-and-brick patio filled with flowering plants, a large pool, and then the rolling green lawn that extended to the water. The frontage on the property had to be over two hundred feet across.

Suddenly, she caught her breath. Off to one side was the dock, and tied to it was the *Majorca*. Rebecca hadn't seen the yacht since that awful night. In the distance she glimpsed someone wiping down the teak railing on the starboard side.

The sound of high heels clicking on marble made her turn around. Wearing cream-colored wool slacks, a vivid green silk blouse, and simple but elegant gold jewelry, Diana Worthington came into the room, looking like she'd just posed for a photo in *Town & Country* magazine.

"Rebecca?" Diana Worthington's face registered a mixture of surprise and worry. "What brings you all the way to Newport Beach?"

"I was hoping to find your husband at home. I called on Friday. When I couldn't reach him I left a message at his office that I was coming."

"Oh, I see." Diana nervously fingered the charms on her bracelet. "If you'd like to wait, that's fine. I expect Paul to be back before long."

"That's very kind of you," Rebecca said, wondering if it was her presence that was making the woman anxious, and if so, why. "You have a beautiful home, Mrs. Worthington."

"Thank you." Motioning for Rebecca to sit, she took the chair across from her. "And please call me Diana."

"I hope I'm not disturbing you," Rebecca remarked, feeling as if all of her nerve endings were on alert.

"Not at all." Diana uncrossed her legs and leaned forward. "Actually, I'm glad to see you. I wanted to tell you again how sorry I am for your loss."

Rebecca nodded. There was no mistaking the genuine sympathy in the woman's voice, but the way she seemed unable to meet her eyes was making Rebecca uneasy.

"It was a terrible thing," Diana continued, then gazed off into space for a moment. Unexpectedly, she looked up. "I'm sorry. I'm forgetting my manners. May I offer you something to drink?"

"Some water would be fine, thank you," Rebecca said, realizing she actually was thirsty.

Diana put her foot on a small brass button in the carpet. A few seconds later, the houseman appeared. "Bring Mrs. Morland a glass of Pellegrino and a soda with lime for me." She turned back to Rebecca. "Now, what did you need to see Paul about?"

"I'm trying to understand some of the things that were going on before my husband's death." Rebecca paused to take a breath. "And I've been visiting everyone who had any dealings with him the last few weeks of his life as well as those who were on the boat that night."

A flicker of concern briefly crossed Diana's face.

"In fact, there are a few questions I'd like to ask you. That is, if you wouldn't mind?" As Rebecca spoke, she was again struck by Diana's evasive eyes. Clearly something was troubling her.

"No. Of course not." Diana waved her hand.

"I was wondering, if you talked to my husband at the party?"

"Yes. I always try to speak at least once with all of my guests."

The houseman handed Rebecca a glass of water, and she thanked him before continuing. "Do you remember what the two of you discussed?"

Diana shook her head. "I had conversations with so many people, I'm quite sure I've gotten them all mixed up." She laughed uneasily.

"Had you ever conversed with Ryan before?"

"Other than just to say hello, I don't believe so."

"So you don't have any context in which to judge his behavior that night, correct?"

"Right, except that . . ." Diana's voice dropped off as she continued to finger one of her charms.

"Go on," Rebecca urged.

Diana clasped her hands together. "Rebecca, what I have to say may upset you, but I feel that since you've come all this way, you at least deserve to be told the truth."

"Go on," said Rebecca, feeling a twinge of apprehension as Diana began to speak.

"According to many people on the *Majorca* that night, including the crew, your husband unfortunately had had a lot to drink."

Rebecca started to protest, but Diana held up her hand to silence her.

"I said you might be upset, but let me finish, please." Smoothing back her hair she continued, "I've been at many parties on yachts, both mine and others. I can't tell you how many times someone has drunk too much and almost fallen in the water." She shook her head sadly. "It's hard to keep your balance on a boat, especially when it's out to sea."

"I was with him a short time before he disappeared and he seemed fine," Rebecca insisted, her heart beating rapidly.

"I've probably had a lot more experience in these matters than you," Diana advised, a slightly condescending smile on her lips. "Men, you see, can consume great quantities of alcohol and not appear to be falling-down drunk—but they are drunk just the same. And when a person is already in an unhappy frame of mind . . ." She hesitated briefly before adding, "Well then . . . sometimes the unexplainable happens."

Rebecca was unnerved by Diana's apparent sincerity along with her certainty about Ryan's condition. Still, she couldn't let it stand undefended. "Mrs. Worthington . . . I mean Diana, I don't think you understand—"

The other woman interrupted. "I do understand," she asserted firmly, then lowered her voice as if perceiving she was coming on too strong. "I really do. I realize you're distraught and that's to be expected . . ." Her voice trailed off as she turned around.

There were voices coming from the foyer. A few seconds later Paul Worthington strode into the room. "I heard we had a guest," he said to Diana, then stopped when he saw Rebecca. "Mrs. Morland?"

Tall and thin like his wife, Worthington was wearing a pair of dark brown brushed-velvet cords with a soft yellow cashmere sweater. Underneath the sweater was a plain white shirt. With his light hair turning silver, he presented a magazine-perfect façade, just like his wife.

"Rebecca said she left a message at your office that she was coming down to see you," Diana explained.

"Oh?" His light blue eyes were questioning as he faced Rebecca. "I'm sorry. I didn't get it."

Still shaken by Diana's comments, Rebecca quickly composed herself. "I called several times Friday and yesterday, but you were never in. That's why I decided to drive down here. I left a message to that effect."

He shrugged his shoulders. "It's been an unusually busy week."

She fought down her urge to confront him. It was best to appear polite if she wanted to learn anything from these people. "So I've been reading in the newspapers," she responded, forcing a half smile to her lips. "Are you planning to run for the Senate?"

Worthington appraised her openly. "I'm not sure. However, the enthusiastic response I've been receiving has convinced me that a significant portion of the party wants a more conservative candidate." He tilted his head proudly. "I should be making my decision before long."

Glancing at his wife, he added, "Diana, ring for Sven and have him bring me my usual." He pointed to Rebecca's glass. "Can we freshen whatever it is you're drinking?"

"No, thank you. I'm fine."

Sitting down, he crossed one leg over the other. His arm swept in front of him in a wide arc. "How do you like our view?"

"It's incredible," she replied honestly.

"When I saw this piece of property, I knew immediately I had to *possess* it no matter what it cost."

The way he said the word "possess" frightened Rebecca. It sounded so ruthless.

The houseman handed Worthington his drink and left. He took a rather large sip. "Well, I'm sure you didn't come here to discuss the view. Was there some particular reason why you wanted to see me?"

"Yes." Rebecca repeated the reasons for her coming that she'd related earlier to his wife.

"I'm not sure how much help I can be," he said tensely, when she had finished, "but go ahead."

She tried to appear more relaxed than she felt. With both of them watching her warily, it wasn't easy. "Prior to the party, I was wondering how well you knew my husband, other than to maybe say hello at political gatherings?"

"I knew him," he responded, his manner guarded.

"May I ask how you knew him?"

"We'd talked a few times over the years."

"Do you recall when you might have spoken to him last, that is before the party?" She took a sip of water as she waited for his reply.

Worthington shook his head. "Not really. I believe not for quite some time."

So, he wasn't going to level with her. "It was my understanding that shortly before Ryan died, you telephoned him at Brandon Taylor's campaign headquarters?"

He rubbed his forehead. "I'm sorry, it must have slipped my mind. You're right, I did call Ryan. I had to ask a quick question."

Rebecca was relieved that instead of lying, he was at least admitting he'd had the conversation. Nonetheless, his apparent willingness to skirt the truth made her cautious. "May I ask what you discussed?"

"Nothing terribly important," he said in a dismissive tone of voice. "Something to do with Brandon's availability for a speaking engagement at my club."

His response didn't ring true. "It's also my understanding that a few days before the party, my husband and you had a disagreement on the telephone. And after that, Ryan left the campaign office to meet with you."

Before all of the words were out of her mouth, Rebecca saw the surprise on Diana's face as she turned to her husband. Pretending not to have noticed, Rebecca finished her inquiry. "I'd like to hear your version of what happened."

The man seemed to be taking his time as he casually fingered the crease in his trousers. Uncrossing his legs, he leaned toward her, and she detected an air of restraint. "Rebecca, I don't know where you're getting your information, but it's not true. We had a brief phone conversation, as I just told you—and that's all."

"I have a witness who overheard Ryan's conversation with you," she countered.

His smile was chilly. "Then for some reason he or she is lying to you." He paused. "I'm not a psychiatrist, Rebecca. But from the way Ryan was acting on the boat that night, he seemed to be a very unhappy man."

He was trying to shift the focus away from himself by attacking Ryan—it made her angry. "What you don't know is that my husband would never have killed himself. You see, we thought I might be pregnant."

Diana looked stricken as she sat forward. "*Are* you going to have a baby?"

"Yes—I am."

The pallor of the other woman's face was quite noticeable. "I'm so happy for you," she mumbled, looking at her husband.

Worthington finally realized he was expected to say something too. "Yes. Congratulations."

"Thank you."

"If Ryan didn't commit suicide, then what do you think happened?" Diana asked, tensely searching Rebecca's face.

"Diana," Paul said softly but with a warning glance at his wife. "We're not interested in any other theories. The authorities think it's a suicide. It's their place to decide these things, *not* ours." While he sounded reasonable, the tightness in his jaw gave away the fact that he was upset.

"My husband was murdered," Rebecca stated, firmly. "And I intend to find his killer."

Again the Worthingtons exchanged looks. "It must be difficult to accept that someone you loved has taken his own life," Paul remarked coldly.

"It's *very hard*," Rebecca admitted, "especially when it isn't true. You see, the Ryan Morland I knew would never have voluntarily left your yacht." She took a deep breath and exhaled. "Before I go, there are a few more things I need." She faced Diana. "I'd like to have a guest list from that night as well as the name of the catering company you used."

Diana nodded. "I'll need to get that information from my secretary, and she's not here today. I'll have her send it to you tomorrow."

"I'd appreciate that. Let me give you my home phone and fax numbers." Rebecca opened her purse, scribbled the numbers on a piece of paper, which she then handed to Diana. "And now, if I may, I'd like to talk to the yacht's crew."

"Of course," Diana said.

"Today is their day off," Paul interrupted, "and there's no one aboard the vessel."

"Oh, but I saw—" Rebecca started to say.

Worthington's mouth hardened into a grim line, although he smiled to cover it up. He stood up, putting his hands in the pockets of his slacks. "My crew has already spoken to the detectives. I don't see any need for them to go through it again. If you need additional information, I suggest you speak to those same detectives."

It struck Rebecca as odd that he wouldn't let her talk to the crew or go aboard the yacht after she'd seen someone working on it less than fifteen minutes ago. What could he be so afraid of her finding out?

She stood up also. "Just one more question," she said, keeping her voice purposely low and nonthreatening.

He was watching her with hooded eyes. "What's that?"

"Were you aware that Ryan was checking into your past?"

His eyes widened, and Diana's hand came up to cover her mouth, but not before Rebecca heard a small gasp. Worthington must have heard it too, because he glared at his wife. Then he turned back to Rebecca. "I'm not surprised Taylor would stoop that low, considering the level politics has sunk to lately."

As she swiftly took her leave, Rebecca was positive that Worthington had been aware of Ryan's search. His wife's reaction was far more interesting. Did that gasp indicate Diana hadn't known about it, or did it mean that she was afraid of something unpleasant coming out?

The very fact that Worthington didn't want Rebecca on his yacht, meant she had to get aboard, even if she did it without his knowledge. This visit cemented her belief that Paul Worthington knew more about Ryan's death than he was telling.

Outside on the cobblestone street again, Rebecca walked quickly to her car, started it, and drove until she was sure she was out of the Worthingtons' view. Then she pulled over.

Making her way back toward their house, she tried to stay hidden behind bushes and other shrubbery. Was there some way she could reach the dock from the neighboring property? Not all of the estates had gates. She walked along the side of one large house until she caught a glimpse of the water. Maybe she could reach their property from here.

"Where are you going?" asked an angry voice.

Rebecca's heart jumped as she swiveled around and saw an

elderly woman in gardening clothes. "I was just trying to get a glimpse of the property a few doors away. The house is for sale and I wanted to see it from the front." She forced a wide smile to her mouth. "Unfortunately, I don't have a boat."

"Well, this is private property you're on," the woman retorted, stiffly. "You shouldn't be here, so get along now."

"Of course. I'm so sorry," Rebecca said and then rushed back to her car. Damn! She needed to find a way to get on that yacht without the Worthingtons' knowledge.

CHAPTER
TWELVE

With a big sigh, Rebecca looked at the modest one-story building that housed the Fairfax Neighborhood Legal Clinic. She was nervous about visiting the place. Most people didn't know what to say to her about Ryan's death, so she dreaded facing all of her coworkers. Yet, she needed to pick up her paycheck and talk to the director.

The first person she encountered was Lucy, who whispered in her ear. "You said it was okay to tell everyone about the baby —so I did."

Rebecca nodded. If people like the Worthingtons knew, certainly her friends and coworkers should too.

It wasn't long before several other people had gathered around her to offer their congratulations, and she soon realized that the news about her pregnancy made things less awkward.

Finally, the director escorted Rebecca back to her office and closed the door behind them.

Leaning forward in her chair, Rebecca spoke. "Trudy, I know how shorthanded you are already, and I hate to make your job any harder. But I can't come back full time for a while. Ryan's death has left me with a lot of things to take care of."

The director nodded sympathetically. "We are shorthanded, but take whatever time you need, Rebecca. We'll manage somehow." She cleared her throat. "We appreciate the way you've continued to help your clients by making phone calls and writing letters from home. I don't have to tell you that most people wouldn't have done that."

"I couldn't just let everyone down because of what had happened to me," Rebecca explained with her usual forthrightness.

"Will you be able to keep doing that?"

"I hope so," Rebecca replied, nodding her head. "But I'm afraid we're going to have to take it day by day. In the meantime, with Lucy bringing me the work, I'll do as much as I can." As hard as it was, she gazed at Trudy unblinkingly. "If you have to hire someone else, I'll understand."

"I'd rather not do that. I'm very happy with your work."

Trudy's praise pleased Rebecca. "Thanks," she said.

"You know," Trudy said, sighing, "if our grant doesn't come through soon we might be out of operating funds altogether. We're trying to get help from someplace else, but it doesn't look good. State funds for legal clinics are drying up too."

"It seems the needs are increasing while the resources are dwindling," Rebecca observed sadly.

From the director's office, Rebecca went to her own to pack up a few things she might need. Her windowless space with its battered file cabinets, sagging steel shelves, and cardboard boxes hemming in the table she used as a desk, looked more like an overcrowded file room than the office of a senior staff attorney, but she still missed it.

Lucy came in with a carton. Rebecca began filling it with personal items and books. She picked up a photograph, which had been taken on their honeymoon in Hawaii. It showed Rebecca and Ryan on the beach with their arms around each other. The sun had bronzed Ryan's body and whitened his blond hair. As for Rebecca, she resembled a bright pink lobster. For her, the sun was deadly. God, they had been so happy, she thought. Tears came to Rebecca's eyes, but she blinked them away.

"I guess that's all," Rebecca finally said with a quick glance around the room.

"Things will work out, Rebecca. You'll see."

This time the tears spilled down Rebecca's cheeks as she hugged Lucy. "I know. Thanks." Calling out a good-bye to the others, Rebecca strode quickly through the crowded waiting room. She vowed silently that after she found her husband's murderer, she'd be back.

Rebecca had decided to try to speak to someone at the Taylor, Dennison & Evans law firm other than a partner. Ryan's secretary hadn't been there very long, and Rebecca hadn't yet gotten to know her. She wondered if Gloria Powell, the office administrator, would be willing to help her. Ryan had respected Gloria, and from what he'd told Rebecca, the feeling had been mutual.

She'd also been deeply touched by the sympathy note Gloria had sent her. On the other hand, Gloria had been with the firm a long time. Her loyalty might make her feel uncomfortable about talking to Rebecca. Still, she had to try.

Later that evening, after getting Gloria's address from Ryan's phone book, Rebecca found the large apartment complex in the Baldwin Hills area of L.A. where Gloria lived.

After Rebecca rang the bell and identified herself, Gloria opened the door. Her smooth face with its rich dark brown skin and high cheekbones had a worried look on it. "Hello, Mrs. Morland."

Rebecca disliked the policy at Taylor, Dennison & Evans which required that all lawyers as well as their spouses be formally addressed. "Please call me Rebecca," she insisted.

"I'll try." Gloria's smile was friendly as she tugged her sweater down over her slacks. "Please come in."

This was the first time Rebecca had seen Gloria in anything other than office attire, that is, a skirt or dress, and heels. She looked younger. "Forgive me for showing up here unannounced, but I wanted to speak to you and it's difficult to do that at the office."

"That's okay, Mrs. Morland . . . I mean Rebecca. I understand. Would you like some coffee or a soda?" Gloria asked as she led Rebecca into the living room.

"Black coffee would be fine," replied Rebecca, still feeling awkward about barging in on this woman at home.

While Gloria went to get the coffee, Rebecca tried to quell her anxiety, hoping that coming here was the right thing to do.

Returning with two cups of coffee, Gloria joined Rebecca on the couch. Rebecca pointed to the pictures on the end table. "Are those your children?"

"Yes." Gloria nodded, smiling proudly. "Justine is my oldest, she's in law school now. And Everett's finishing his senior year at UCLA and wants to be a professor."

"Sounds wonderful," Rebecca said, returning the smile. She put her cup down on the coffee table. "Gloria, I've got some questions, but I don't want to put you in an uncomfortable position. If you feel you can't or don't want to answer them for any reason, I'll understand."

"I appreciate that." Gloria sat up straighter. "Mr. Morland was a nice man to work for, kind and considerate. I liked the way he talked about his mother." She tilted her head. "He was very proud of the fact that she'd worked as a secretary to put him through school."

Rebecca smiled. Their shared experiences had obviously formed a bond between Gloria and Ryan.

"Anyway," Gloria finished, "if I can help, I will."

Grateful, Rebecca took a deep breath. "The last few weeks before"—she paused—"before he died, my husband had been very troubled. I asked him what was wrong, but he wouldn't tell me much. Was there something unusual going on at the firm?"

"I think that gearing up for Mr. Taylor's Senate race was making everyone nervous, especially your husband. Problems cropped up on a daily basis."

"Were the other partners upset about the upcoming campaign, or the fact that Mr. Taylor would be leaving?"

The woman rubbed the side of her coffee cup. "From what I gathered," she glanced up, "and some of this I don't know for sure, but when you've worked in a place a long time, you get a feeling about things, I don't think Ms. Dennison or Mr. Evans were upset about Mr. Taylor leaving. They were more concerned about which one of them would become the head of the firm."

"Did this power struggle affect my husband?"

"I'm sure it did. It affected everyone. You see, there were a lot of arguments at the firm ever since—" Gloria stopped as if she had said more than she wanted to.

"Ever since what?" Rebecca asked softly.

"Oh, dear," Gloria began twisting her hands nervously. "I'm not sure I should talk . . . about this."

"I understand. You're worried about your job. I won't repeat anything without your express permission."

With a weary sigh, Gloria gave in. "Well, all right. Let me start back a ways. Before John Evans came, Taylor & Dennison was a good place to work." She paused. "Ms. Dennison can be demanding. But I know how to handle lawyers like her. And Mr. Taylor was the best. Your husband too."

"And after Mr. Evans came?"

Gloria frowned. "It all changed."

"How?"

"From the day he arrived, Mr. Evans was constantly competing with your husband for Mr. Taylor's attention. I hate to say this, but I felt Mr. Evans would have done anything to get Mr. Morland out of the firm."

Her words were chilling to Rebecca. Did *anything* include murder? "What kinds of things do you mean?"

Gloria shrugged. "For one, Mr. Evans was always bad-mouthing Mr. Morland."

"Was Mr. Taylor aware of this?"

"In front of his uncle, Mr. Evans was nice to Mr. Morland. But behind his back, he blamed him for all sorts of things."

Rebecca was surprised. She'd known Ryan and John hadn't gotten along particularly well, but Ryan hadn't mentioned this. "How did my husband handle it?"

"For the most part he ignored Mr. Evans. However, he voiced his concern to me a few times about how Mr. Taylor didn't seem to be aware of the way Mr. Evans was manipulating him."

"Did you think Mr. Evans was manipulating his uncle too?"

"Yes. It was very subtle. We knew there had been a rift between Mr. Taylor and his sister, John's mother, and that they were estranged, but we didn't know what caused it. It made us wonder if maybe that was the reason Mr. Evans behaved the way he did."

"How was it that Mr. Evans came to the firm in the first place?"

"Out of the blue one day, he telephoned for Mr. Taylor, saying he was his nephew." Gloria paused, then shook her head. "After that call Mr. Taylor was extremely upset—not angry, mind you, but very agitated. He even had me cancel a bunch of appointments, which is something he never does. Then he just left the office without a word about where he was going."

"Then what happened?"

"Well, when he finally came back later that afternoon, we learned that Mr. Taylor's sister had died. He and Mr. Morland were in conference for hours, not taking any calls. When he came out of the office later, your husband seemed concerned, and maybe even a little upset."

Rebecca wondered why Ryan had never told her this story. "Is that when Mr. Evans came to work at the firm?"

Gloria's eyes locked with Rebecca's. "About a week later he showed up. Mr. Taylor introduced him around and told us Mr. Evans was joining the firm as a partner."

"Just like that?" asked Rebecca, surprised.

"Yes."

"How did Ms. Dennison react?"

The other woman pursed her lips. "She wasn't pleased. I can tell you that."

"And my husband?"

"He didn't say much about it." Gloria looked down at her hands. "But I could tell he wasn't happy."

"I see." Rebecca was thoughtful. Ryan had griped about John's shortcomings, but he'd never explained these other details to her. Because John was Brandon's nephew, she'd figured his working at the firm was just a family obligation sort of thing.

"Later," Gloria said, "when I happened upon a file with Mr. Evans's vital information, I learned why everyone was so upset. Why, even I was shocked. Mr. Evans had gone to one of those fly-by-night law schools from which he graduated near the bottom of his class. And" — she paused for effect — "he'd taken the California State Bar Exam four times before he'd passed it. Why, we'd never taken on a lawyer like that before at any level, much less as a partner."

Rebecca smiled inwardly at the law firm's snobbery. "Did you learn anything else?"

"In four years, Mr. Evans had already worked at three different firms. Not a good sign either. Anyway, from the day he started, the firm changed. There was more tension. Doors were closed more often. The staff complained about the way Mr. Evans treated them." She stopped for a moment. "You can tell a person's character from things like that, you know."

"Yes." Sipping her coffee, Rebecca digested this information, wondering what light, if any, it shed on Ryan's behavior. "Gloria, do you think my husband committed suicide?"

Gloria shook her head decisively. "No, and I told the detectives that. He wasn't the kind of man to take his own life."

"I don't think so either," Rebecca said, relieved finally to hear someone echo her feelings, especially someone who had known Ryan longer than she had.

"But," added Gloria, "there was that note."

"I'm not at all convinced my husband wrote that note."

The other woman blinked several times as if surprised. "Are you saying someone forged his handwriting?"

"I'm still waiting for the police to authenticate it." Rebecca paused. "Do you remember anything about the night of the party? Did the partners all go together?"

"Mr. Taylor doesn't like bringing his things with him, so he went home to change. So did your husband." Gloria smiled. "However, Mr. Evans and Ms. Dennison both dressed at the office."

"Did they leave together?"

"No. She left a little before him."

"Was John the last person to leave the office?"

"Oh, no. I'm usually the last one. If I have time, I like to take a peek around before going home."

Rebecca's heart started beating faster. "Do you ever check any of the lawyers' offices before you go?"

"Quite often," Gloria told her. "I'm not snooping or anything. It's just that many of them forget and leave work on their desks that is intended for the night computer shift. But those people don't have access to the entire office—they can only do what's left by their work stations."

"Did you happen to look on my husband's desk that night?"

"Yes. Everyone left so early I had plenty of time."

Rebecca's pulse quickened. "Did you see a suicide note?"

"No." Gloria frowned. "Is that where they said it was found—on his desk?"

"Yes."

"That's real strange." Gloria shook her head, the puzzled expression back on her face. "I'm sure I would have seen something like that if it had been there."

Sitting forward, Rebecca felt the adrenaline pumping through her veins. "Now can you see why I question that note?"

Gloria bit on her lip. "It's funny, no one even asked me about it. Not the partners and not the detectives."

"Is it okay if I mention this to Solowski and Walters?"

"I guess so. If they had asked me I would have told them."

Grateful, Rebecca hesitated before proceeding. "Gloria, do you know about the firm's missing money?"

The other woman's posture grew stiff as if this was a subject she was not comfortable discussing. "I do."

"Are you aware the partners think Ryan is responsible?"

She nodded her head. "Yes."

"What do you think?" Rebecca held her breath as she waited for the answer.

"I know they've got some evidence. Still, I find it real hard to believe. Mr. Morland just wasn't that kind of person."

Rebecca wanted to hug the woman. "Are you also aware that someone in the accounting department supposedly helped him take the money?"

"Yes."

She wondered if Gloria knew that John Evans had refused to give her the person's name. Feeling a little underhanded, Rebecca said nonchalantly, "Who was that again?"

"Zoe Olin," Gloria replied.

"Right." Rebecca swallowed hard. "As I understand it, Zoe was put on administrative leave while they investigate?"

"Yes."

"Did you ever speak to her?"

"No. Mr. Evans and Ms. Dennison took care of that."

Taking another deep breath, Rebecca asked, "Could you get me her address or phone number? I'd really like to contact her."

At that, Gloria appeared uneasy again. "I'm not sure. I feel bad about what you're going through," she said sadly. "But I just don't know."

"That's okay," Rebecca murmured. "I understand. Would you call me if you think of anything else that might help me in trying to sort all this out?"

"Sure. I could do that." There was both a delicacy and a strength in Gloria's face, and Rebecca had a tremendous amount of respect for her. Not too many people in her situation would have been willing to help.

She opened her purse and quickly scribbled her number down. "Here. I know you have this at the office, but I want you to keep it here as well, in case anything should come to mind. Please call me if you do think of anything else."

"I will," Gloria promised with a smile.

The phone was ringing as Rebecca opened the door to her house. She ran for it. "Yes?"

"Rebecca Morland?" The voice sounded like it was coming from far away and she didn't recognize it.

"This is Mrs. Morland. Who's calling?"

"Never mind that. Just listen. You've been making some

nasty accusations and upsetting folks. This is a warning to stop saying your husband was murdered or you'll be sorry."

Her heart was pounding in her ears, and her knees felt weak. "Who are you?" she asked, sinking into the nearest chair.

"Don't matter. Just stop with the murder accusations or you may end up like your husband." Without another word, the caller slammed the phone down.

She rubbed her ear at the deafening sound. Shaking, she tried to imagine who the caller could be. It was obvious her questions were making someone very nervous. Burglaries, files wiped clean, strange automobiles following her, threatening phone calls—she dreaded what might be next.

CHAPTER
THIRTEEN

John Evans waited nervously for his uncle to get off the phone. His earlier meeting with Catherine Dennison had not gone well. Having been instructed by Brandon to work out the division of the cases Ryan Morland had been handling, they had begun bickering immediately.

Clearly Catherine still viewed John as a lightweight and was taking for herself all the plum clients, especially those who would generate the highest billings—on which their annual bonuses would be based.

After almost an hour of unabated argument, Catherine had stormed out, declaring her need to meet with a client outside the office. Now, John faced the uninviting task of telling his uncle of the impasse they had reached.

When his uncle was through, John explained what had happened, then listened quietly to Brandon's admonition that he make more of an effort to get along with Catherine. When there was a break, he jumped in, ready to plead his case. "I think the bonus system as it's structured now is unfair. It favors those who have greater skills in luring clients to the firm, like Catherine, over those like me who actually do the tedious work."

"What are you getting at, John," Brandon asked, impatience showing both in his face and his voice.

"You took Ryan under your wing, trained him, and let him handle a lot of your clients. Well, Uncle, I'd like the same chance; let me show you and the others what *I* can do."

Brandon Taylor eyed his nephew warily.

"Look, I've never really had a chance at anything," John continued. "I grew up in an impoverished household, both financially and culturally lacking. No one ever asked me my opinion, but they wouldn't have listened to me anyway." The bitterness in his voice was apparent. "If I work with you, others here would give me more respect. They'd even take the time to listen. And I do have some good ideas."

The senior partner looked thoughtful. "I hear you, John," he said finally. "Give me time to think this over. I'm sure we can work something out."

John was ready to shout with joy as he left his uncle's office. Maybe what John had longed for was finally going to happen. He couldn't believe it—and all it had taken was Ryan Morland's timely demise.

Catherine Dennison hadn't gone to a meeting as she'd told John Evans. She'd been too stressed out. In addition to working for weeks nonstop there was the emotional strain of Ryan's death. She'd needed to crash. Unfortunately, ever since that night on the yacht, Catherine had been having nightmares, so going home hadn't been too appealing. Instead, she'd ended up at her lover's place, where after taking a long hot bath, she'd fallen into a deep sleep for hours until she'd been awakened with a kiss, and they had made love.

Now she looked appreciatively at the nude body stretched out on the bed next to her. Anthony Necosia was lean and muscular, with a golden tan. She rubbed the thick, brown hair on his chest, thinking how much she enjoyed being with him.

Tony could make slow, languorous love to her, savoring every inch of her body, starting at her toes and working his way up her legs, his tongue seeking all of her most sensitive spots.

However they tried it, sex with Tony was always amazing,

whether he was on top, riding her until she was sore and screaming for him to stop, or she was the dominant one—her breasts
bouncing wildly as she sat astride him while he rubbed the place
between her legs.

He had a sense of playfulness too, which was rare in a
lawyer. It was those times, when they laughed and made love,
that meant the most to her, for Tony brought out a fun side in
Catherine that even Ryan hadn't known she had. Ryan used to
tell her she was too serious—that she needed to lighten up.
Well, maybe if he'd given her more of a chance . . . If only Rebecca hadn't entered Ryan's life, Catherine was sure that Ryan
and she would have worked out their relationship.

For a moment, she felt a deep sense of loss, but only for a
moment, as she felt a stirring beside her and Tony's mouth
sought out her nipple. "Mmm," she murmured, feeling the tin-
gling sensation shoot straight through to her groin.

Tony opened his eyes and gazed deeply into hers as he
rubbed the now erect nipple with his finger. "Feel good?"

"Wonderful."

He pressed his lips against hers. "Ready for more?"

"With you Tony, I'm always ready for more."

He took her in his arms. "You are one insatiable lady."

Her answer was a deep, hungry kiss.

"What do you want this time?" he teased.

"Plain, ordinary fucking," she moaned, opening her legs to
receive him.

Later, after she showered, Catherine scrutinized her face in
the mirror. She'd had her eyes done last year without telling
anyone. Back in Minnesota where she'd grown up and gone to
college, she never would have even considered it—but in L.A.
the competition was deadly. Her eyes roamed over her body.
The few extra pounds she had allowed herself to carry the last
several years gave her figure a soft, rounded appearance. At her
age of thirty-nine, it wasn't good to be too thin, like Diana. She
had high cheekbones, and the added weight also gave her
cheeks a slight fullness instead of the sunken look she'd favored
when she was younger.

In various places her body was beginning to show a minor loss of muscle tone, although certainly nothing Tony would notice while they were making love. Still, she rarely allowed herself the freedom of walking around nude in his presence. Somehow she'd have to find the time for a personal trainer.

She felt better than she had earlier. Making love always calmed her down—probably because it drained all of her pent-up energy and emotions. Removing a lavender satin kimono from the hook on the back of the door, she went into the other room to retrieve her clothes. As she started to slip into her silk panties and lace bra, her movements awakened Tony.

He stretched, sitting up on the bed. "Where are you going?"

"Home." She reached for the thigh-high hose lying in the open doorway to his bedroom.

"You mean three times and you're through?" His tone was light and teasing.

"I've got a mountain of work to do." Her glance swept over him. Tony was certainly a handsome boy, only twenty-nine. But in those twenty-nine years he had somehow learned to do things in bed that many men twice his age had never learned.

Yet when the sex was over, she was anxious to leave. She liked to be in her own home where she had a fully computerized study.

After she dressed, she bent over the bed and brushed Tony's cheek with her lips. "I'll call you."

"It's been weeks and we still haven't discussed Ryan's death," he said as she headed for the door.

Catherine stiffened. "There's nothing to discuss. I've already told you—he was depressed and obviously decided to end it all. If you watch television or read the newspapers you'll know everything that the rest of us know."

He stood up and came over to her. Although he was nude, he seemed not to be the least bit self-conscious.

"I know what the media are saying. But I also know that you once loved Ryan and now he's dead. Are you sad, glad, what?"

"The way he died was a shock to all of us."

He grabbed her arm to turn her toward him. "I'm trying to talk to *you*, Catherine, about *your* feelings, *your* thoughts."

"And I don't want to talk about them."

"It's unhealthy to keep things bottled up inside the way you do," he warned.

"Tony, please. We've been over this before."

He started to say something, then stopped. "Fine," he muttered before he kissed her hard on the lips to assert himself the only way he could with her. "I love you."

Without responding, Catherine broke away from him, lifted her purse off the floor, and went to the door. "Take care," she called out.

Outside, she hurried to her car, anxious to be home. Truthfully, she didn't find Tony's one-bedroom condominium in Santa Monica all that comfortable. As an associate at another law firm, Tony made about eighty thousand a year, which was good, but certainly nowhere near the million dollars she earned.

Not overly complicated, Tony had been the perfect choice to ease her pain over losing Ryan. Tony also abided by her strict conditions. He had to be monogamous and tested regularly for STDs and HIV. Even then, she insisted he use a condom. It didn't pay to be careless.

When Tony had first proclaimed that he loved her, Catherine had felt nervous. It was one thing to find passion with a younger man—it was another thing to plan a future with him. As for talking about her feelings, she couldn't do that with anyone. Yet it was obviously important to Tony, so one of these days she'd really have to try.

Stopping for a red light, Catherine thought about the meeting she'd had earlier in the day with John, to reassign Ryan's cases. Who the hell did he think he was, trying to take all of the important cases and muscle in on all she'd worked for?

She had previously seen Ryan as her only serious competition, because on top of all his charm he'd been a damn good lawyer. Catherine had never figured she'd have to compete with John too. Brandon was crazy if he thought she would stand by silently while he awarded lucrative cases and clients to his nephew. There was no way in hell she'd go along with that.

• • •

Rebecca pulled up in front of her house, surprised to find Brandon Taylor standing outside, obviously waiting for her. His face looked lined, and she could tell from the way he followed her into the house that he was exhausted.

"What's wrong?" she asked.

"I'm just tired," he confessed, sitting down in an armchair. "I understand you were at the office today, reviewing the documents on the missing funds?"

She nodded.

"Were you satisfied?"

"I don't know. As I told you before, I'm not good with numbers, so I didn't fully understand what I was looking at. And there were many lines that had big black marks through them."

He frowned. "We couldn't let you see things that were confidential."

"No. Of course not," she said. Those deletions could also mean that the documents had been altered, she thought, but she wasn't yet ready to accuse them of that.

"Anyway," he said, changing the subject, "as I promised, I went to the sheriff's station."

She caught her breath as her eyes searched his. "Did you speak to Detective Solowski and Detective Walters?"

"Only Walters was there."

"Oh." She was disappointed that he hadn't spoken to Solowski. The woman cop gave more credence to Rebecca's suspicions than Walters did. Besides, Walters hadn't been at all helpful when she'd telephoned to inform him about the threatening phone call she'd received. He'd told her there was nothing the police could do and to notify the telephone company if she got more threatening calls.

"I found out from Walters that you're pregnant." There was a hurt expression on Brandon's face. "Why didn't you tell me yourself?"

She felt a momentary pang of guilt. "It just never seemed to be the right time."

He gazed at her as if debating whether to accept her explanation. "I see," he finally said in a tense voice.

Before he could say anything more, she changed the subject. "So, what else did Walters say?"

"Not what you want to hear, I'm afraid," he admitted, shaking his head. "Walters was firm—there's no evidence of foul play. He also explained that they've got a lot more experience in these things than we have. And frankly, after listening carefully to the man, I must admit he made a lot of sense."

"What exactly do you mean by that?" she asked, alarmed.

"The way the facts add up," he said, as if not noticing her reaction. "I mean, Ryan's strange behavior. At times depressed, other times sullen—then the way, without warning, he'd become quarrelsome." He gazed up at her. "We've been over this, Rebecca. According to Walters, these are all common emotional symptoms exhibited by people who later take their own lives."

"Not you too!" She felt her anger and resentment bubbling up and spilling over.

"Come on, Rebecca, don't act like it's you against the world. We're all in this together. I don't want it to be true either. Suicide makes me feel like I failed Ryan."

"But you knew how Ryan felt about suicide," she insisted.

"I appreciate how traumatic his mother's suicide attempt must have been for him as a child," Brandon said, clearing his throat. "Nevertheless, when a person feels desperate enough to kill himself, he isn't thinking coherently. He's lost in some dark place where his pain is so bad and the future looks so bleak that he isn't rational."

She kept shaking her head. "There are too many facts that still don't add up," she said. "Like John Evans saying he came in at six the morning after Ryan disappeared, when he really signed in much earlier, at 1:43. And the way he claims he found the suicide note on Ryan's desk that morning, when Gloria Powell maintains it wasn't there the night before. Gloria's positive that on the night of the fund-raiser, she was the last one to leave the building and that she checked the offices before going home."

Brandon paled. "What are you talking about?"

Rebecca detailed her findings for him. After she was

through, he sat there in silence for a few minutes. Then he leaned forward and took her hands in his. "Think back, Rebecca. You know in your heart Ryan hadn't been himself. Could we just accept for the moment that he was depressed, okay?"

Reluctantly, she nodded. But inside, she resolved that Brandon wouldn't change her mind.

"And wasn't it also true that he had a lot to drink that night on the boat?"

"Not that much," she protested.

"Enough," he countered with a knowing glance. "According to all the psychology books, the worst thing an unhappy person can do is drink. Alcohol depresses the central nervous system and can make someone feel like they're in a long, black tunnel with no way out."

"I don't care what those books say. I was with him. We danced together, he held me in his arms and told me he loved me." Tears started streaming down her face. "He wasn't despondent. I would have been able to tell. He was troubled, I'll give you that, but not depressed and not drunk."

"If you don't want to believe it was a suicide, Rebecca," he said, "how can you rule out the possibility that it was an accident? He'd had too much to drink, on top of the depressed state he was in. They said Ryan was drinking hard liquor. You and I both know that Ryan seldom did that. Your husband loved wine. That was his drink of choice. Given those facts, it's hardly far-fetched to think he might have become sick."

"No. If he'd been sick, I would have known."

"Not if it came upon him suddenly," he shot back. "Think of it this way. Ryan goes down alone to the cockpit to smoke. Which, by the way, is something he hadn't done for months. Smoking after a long abstinence can make a person nauseated. So he's feeling sick and thinks why look for a bathroom when the ocean is right there. He probably didn't want to vomit all over the yacht, so he opens the transom gate and tries to throw up from there."

"No—that didn't happen."

As if he didn't hear her, Brandon went on. "Maybe he didn't

go out on the swim step—maybe he just opened the transom gate. And as he's hanging over, a swell comes along, or he loses his balance and . . . the next thing he knows, he's in the water. Think about it for a minute—it's not that hard to imagine."

"I don't want to think about it!" she cried, putting her hands over her ears.

Gently, he pried them away. "Once he's in the water he panics. I would, you would, anyone would." Brandon was gathering steam now as if he were making his summation to a jury. "It's dark, the water is cold, and the boat is moving swiftly away from him. He probably tried yelling, but with the noise from the diesels and the music, no one would have heard. Later, people said they barely heard the loudspeakers when you were having him paged. In the meantime, he tries swimming after the boat. Who knows what happened next. Whether he got tired and couldn't go on, or if a shark—"

"Stop it!" she cried. "That's enough. I don't want to hear any more." Rebecca ran out of the room. The picture of her husband struggling in the water, reaching out for help—was devastating. Locking the bathroom door behind her, she threw herself down by the tub and sobbed.

She had no idea how long she'd been crying when she became aware of a voice calling to her from the other side of the door.

"Please open up, Rebecca."

"I'm . . . all right," she managed to say, even though she felt empty and scared. "I just want to be alone. Please . . . go."

"I don't want to leave you like this, especially not when you're pregnant."

She heard him trying the doorknob again. "I'm really . . . okay." She grabbed some tissue and wiped her eyes. "I just need to be . . . alone."

He cleared his throat. "Are you sure you're all right?"

"I'm fine," she said, forcing her voice to sound normal. "I'll . . . call you later."

After a few minutes, she heard his footsteps as he walked away, then the sound of the front door closing. Rebecca felt as if a train had rolled over her. This time when the tears came, she didn't try to stop them.

Within twenty-four hours of Brandon's upsetting visit, Rebecca suffered her second devastating loss. Her doctor felt the stress associated with Ryan's death had probably caused her to miscarry. At first, she felt as if she didn't want to go on. How could God be so cruel? She stayed in bed, not eating, not answering her telephone, wanting to die.

Worried because she couldn't reach Rebecca by phone for two days, Lucy went to the house and rang the doorbell for close to a half hour before Rebecca finally opened the door. Together, they'd both cried, and then Lucy got tough with Rebecca again. "All pain that doesn't kill, strengthens."

Rebecca frowned at her. "Who says?"

"My mother," stated Lucy. "She claims God never sends you more than you can handle."

"Well *she* did this time," Rebecca said.

But after a few more days of depression and soul searching, she realized that Lucy was right. There were two ways to handle what life dealt you. You could either give up, or you could fight back. So, once again, Rebecca plunged herself into the search for her husband's killer.

In a busy shopping center in Marina del Rey, Rebecca sat at a back table in Jerry's Deli. She'd telephoned Detective Solowski, asking for five minutes of her time alone, away from Detective Walters. Although the woman had been hesitant, Rebecca had pleaded with her until she'd finally given in.

When Rebecca saw Solowski enter the restaurant, she waved her hand.

"Hi ya," said Solowski, pulling up a chair.

Rebecca noticed that, as usual, Detective Solowski looked messy. Her dirty-blond hair was windblown, and her mascara was smeared under her eyes. Still, there was a sweetness about the woman's face that Rebecca liked and that made her trust her. "Thank you for coming."

"That's okay."

"You said something that first night about being a widow," Rebecca reminded her, inwardly shuddering at the word "widow" because she still didn't feel that it pertained to herself. "Did I get that right?"

"Yep," admitted Solowski, her eyes meeting Rebecca's.

"May I ask what happened to your husband?" Rebecca asked gently.

"Sure." Solowski nodded. "Randy was a sheriff too. One night he stopped a car—two young men jumped out and started running. He chased them, and one of the men turned around and shot him. He died there on the street."

As Solowski told her story in direct, unflinching words, Rebecca sensed the other woman's pain. "How awful," she exclaimed. "And you have children?"

"Yeah. Two. A boy, Timothy, and a girl, Polly." She told Rebecca a little bit about each child.

Trying to ignore the pain she was feeling, Rebecca said, "You're so lucky. They sound darling."

"They're wonderful," Solowski said, beaming. "To be honest, I don't know how I could have gone on without them."

Rebecca nodded sadly. "I was hoping I'd at least have our child too, but with the stress I've been under . . ." her voice trailed off. "I guess it just wasn't meant to be."

Solowski looked startled. "You mean you lost the baby?"

Nodding, Rebecca had to glance away from the detective to keep from crying.

"That's too bad." Solowski's eyes filled with sympathy.

"Yes," said Rebecca. With a sigh, she reminded herself it was time to get on with the reason for this meeting. Lifting her cup of coffee, she took a few sips, trying to get beyond the sadness. "Have you had a chance to do any of the things we talked about last time?"

"Nope," Solowski said, shaking her head. "I'm sorry, but it's been hectic."

"Look, Detective, I hope you don't mind my asking to see you alone. I wanted to speak to you woman to woman," Rebecca confessed. "I don't know about you, but frequently I use my intuition. In my work I take a lot of depositions and question a lot of people. And from that, I've come to know when someone is lying."

The woman detective smiled as if she knew exactly what Rebecca was talking about. "I do too. That's an important part of being a cop."

"I've been questioning people who were on the yacht that night. I've found many of them are not telling the truth or, at the very least, are leaving pertinent information out."

There was a curious expression on Solowski's face. "Can you give me some examples?"

Even though she had mentioned some of these things to Solowski before, this time Rebecca went into more detail. She started with her husband's partners, describing the argument she'd heard between John Evans and Ryan on the boat and John's later denial that it had occurred; Catherine Dennison's almost threatening demand for her husband's briefcase the morning after his disappearance and before his fate was known. She debated, then decided not to say anything about Brandon Taylor, but went on to relate her conversation with the Worthingtons, from the lie Paul Worthington had told her about not having met with Ryan a few days before he died to his refusal to let her speak to the yacht's crew.

Lastly, she mentioned what Gloria had said about the suicide note not having been on Ryan's desk when she left the office the night of the fund-raiser. She also reminded the detective that John had been at the firm most of the night. Since the partners hadn't yet told the detectives about the missing funds, Rebecca decided not to mention it either.

When she was through, she sighed tiredly. "I know everyone thinks I've got my head buried in the sand, but that's not true. I know in my heart Ryan's death wasn't suicide. I'm convinced he found out something terrible and was afraid to tell me because he feared it might put me in danger too. That's the only thing that makes sense. Anything else he would have discussed with me."

Solowski stared off into space as if she were mulling over what Rebecca had just told her.

"Think about it," Rebecca continued. "Wiping out computer files would be overkill unless someone had an awful lot to lose. And don't forget the threatening phone call I received."

The woman detective raised her eyebrows. "What phone call is that?"

Rebecca was surprised. "You mean Detective Walters didn't tell you?"

Solowski shook her head.

Amazed at the man's cavalier attitude, Rebecca filled her in. Solowski appeared troubled but said nothing further, so Rebecca went on. "I don't believe my husband was talking in generalities when he said it was terrifying to realize what some people would do to get what they wanted. I feel he was trying to warn me about something."

She took a deep breath and exhaled slowly. "Please, Detective Solowski, can't you look around a little on your own? I know there's evidence out there—if only we can find it."

The detective sat silently for a moment. "I guess I can check a few things out," she finally said. "But don't call or ask me any questions in front of Walters, okay? When and if I have anything to report, I'll come by your house. No need to get my partner any more riled up than he already is."

"Absolutely," Rebecca agreed, wanting to hug the woman. "Thank you so much," she added, her eyes shining with gratitude.

"Save it until we see how I do," muttered Solowski, with a nod of her head.

CHAPTER
FOURTEEN

Rebecca waited in the shadows of the parking garage for the lawyers and support staff from Taylor, Dennison & Evans to start leaving the office for the day. John Evans was usually one of the first, and when she saw him swing through the door, she quickly maneuvered over to his car, where she planned to intercept him. While he unlocked the door of his Porsche, she put her hand on his arm.

"What the hell!" he yelled, jumping away from her.

"I'm sorry, I didn't mean to scare you," Rebecca said.

"What the hell do you think you're doing, sneaking up on someone that way?"

"I wasn't sneaking up on you, I was merely waiting for you. You must have been daydreaming," she said lightly, "and that's why you didn't see me."

"Shit! You almost gave me a fucking heart attack."

Realizing he was genuinely shaken, she apologized again.

"Okay, okay," he said, waving her off. "What do you want, anyway?"

"To ask you a couple of questions."

"Now?" He seemed incredulous.

"Yeah. It will only take a few minutes. Can I sit in your car with you?"

After looking around, he checked his watch and finally motioned. "Okay, get in. But make it quick. I've got a date."

"I will." She climbed into the front seat and turned so that she was facing him. "Since you and Ryan worked together for five years, you're in a unique position to know certain things."

John eyed her carefully. "Could be."

"Was there anyone with whom Ryan did not get along?"

"He wasn't universally loved, but I'm not really sure what you're getting at."

"Did you know of anyone at the firm who was angry with Ryan? Brandon or Catherine. Or maybe one of the support staff?"

"The staff kissed his ass. As for Brandon, Ryan was his golden-haired protégé who could do no wrong," John grumbled.

"And Catherine?" she prodded.

There was a glint in his eyes. "Ryan was not her favorite person after he dumped her."

Swallowing hard, she continued. "Do you know why their relationship ended?"

"Sure," he chuckled. "He dumped her for you." John started to laugh. "You should have seen the jealous bitch's face—she was royally pissed."

Rebecca was startled at this news, and her eyes must have shown it.

"Didn't Ryan ever tell you that you're the reason he broke up with Catherine?"

"No," she replied truthfully.

"Ah." John's smile was malicious. "Well, it seems that our dear Catherine had dreams of home and hearth with Ryan. Then again, maybe not; her dreams are different from most people's. She probably saw herself heading the law firm with Ryan as her second in command. An unequal partnership more than a marriage—one without children, I'd wager."

She felt her cheeks growing warm. She'd had no idea the relationship between her husband and his former lover had been so serious. Certainly she'd never known that they had been contemplating marriage. "You talk as if it were common knowledge that Ryan and Catherine were planning a future together."

"All I'm telling you is that I saw some of what was going on." He tapped his fingers on the steering wheel. "I'd say it was one of the only times dear Catherine didn't have the last word. Ryan and I didn't always see eye to eye, but I was proud of him for walking away from her."

"What do you mean?" she asked.

"Come on now, Rebecca," he said, raising one eyebrow. "Catherine was second in seniority to Brandon. Ryan was still an associate. Hooking up with her was one way to lock up his future at the firm."

"Ryan wasn't that kind of a man," she protested. "His relationship with Catherine must have been based on something besides what she could do for his career."

The corners of John's mouth curled up in wry amusement. "You are so naïve, Rebecca."

"Am I?" She found her patience thinning.

John didn't reply. He just smiled back at her mirthlessly.

"Well, they broke up three years ago," she pointed out. "Catherine couldn't still be mad at him."

"You don't know much about women like Catherine," John said, laughing again. "I'd venture she's capable of carrying a grudge for a very long time, secure in the knowledge that someday she'll get even."

The thought of someone remaining angry for so long made Rebecca uncomfortable. "Is there anyone else who had a grudge against my husband?"

"No one I can think of at the moment." He eyed her carefully. "You're not still pursuing that ridiculous murder theory of yours, are you?"

She shrugged without responding.

"You're an interesting woman, you know," he said, leaning back against the door and appraising her. "You're always chasing after windmills. From the people you help down at that clinic, to the way you believe things are either black or white, good or evil." John shook his head. "Life is never that simple. And Ryan wasn't a paragon of virtue either."

Rebecca stiffened. "What are you getting at now?"

"Nothing much. I'm just pointing out that your husband had his good points and his bad. He had his vanities, his ambitions. He knew what he wanted and he went after it, not caring who he ran over in the process."

"And just who did he run over?" she asked. "You?"

"He certainly tried," he responded. "However, I'm a much more worthy opponent than he ever gave me credit for."

Not feeling up to listening to more of John's self-aggrandizing b.s., Rebecca opened the car door. "Thanks for answering my questions."

"That's okay." His eyes roamed over her. "Need a ride?"

His gaze was making her uncomfortable. "No thanks. My car is outside on the street."

"Good night then, and drive safely," he said, as with tires screeching, he pulled out of his space and headed up the ramp.

After Detective Walters left that evening, Solowski pulled out the Morland file and began reading it from the beginning. She was anxious to see the reports both she and Walters had submitted that first night. She also wanted to reread the autopsy report.

Perusing the file, she was reminded of how she'd wanted a crime scene unit to go over the yacht's cockpit the night Ryan Morland had disappeared, and how Walters had vetoed her suggestion. In fact, he'd been adamant that it was not necessary. Why? she wondered, not for the first time. And the fact that it had not been their night on duty had also perturbed her. Was there a hidden reason why Walters had been summoned to the boat?

Picking up the autopsy papers, she quickly scanned for the toxicology test results. It wasn't there. All they'd screened for was alcohol, and that test had come up positive. That was odd. She and Walters had agreed to have a full toxicological work-up done on Morland.

Needing to talk to the medical examiner, she punched in

his phone number, wondering if he'd still be in this late. No answer. That meant she'd have to wait until tomorrow. Quickly she made copies of the documents she wanted, then put the file back in the drawer.

Slipping the copies into her purse, she left the station and then headed home. She'd been upset earlier when she'd learned that Walters hadn't told her that Rebecca Morland had received a threatening phone call. Her review of the file tonight hadn't improved her mood. More and more things with the Morland case weren't adding up, and she wanted to know why.

John knocked softly, then put his key into the lock and opened the door. The apartment was dark. He went directly to the bedroom, where the television screen was flickering images across the unlit room and the walls. Standing by the bed, he looked down at the woman's sleeping form. Then, leaning over, he brushed his lips against her neck.

"Mmm," she murmured, rolling over.

When the sheet fell away, he saw that she was nude, and immediately he felt aroused. Sitting down next to her, he lightly ran his finger from her neck down through the valley between her breasts, over her smooth stomach, until his entire palm came to rest on the area just above her pubis. He gently applied pressure, satisfied when her hips began to lift in response.

He took one of her nipples into his mouth and began to suckle. Instantly, it was taut, and she arched toward him.

"Hold on a second," he whispered in her ear. Quickly, he removed his clothes, throwing them on the floor, kicked off his shoes and tore off his socks and shorts.

Fifteen minutes later he rolled over, spent. He felt her move against him, her fingers trailing lightly down his chest and through his matted hair.

"Can you stay tonight?" she whispered.

"Please, Meggie O," he said, using her nickname. "Don't ask, okay? You know what's going on at my fucking firm. With Ryan dead and Brandon spending all his time campaigning, I've got hours of work to do tonight."

"I hate that firm," she said, pouting. "I spend hours and hours waiting for you. And when you do show up, you come in, make love to me, and then leave. Wham, bam, thank you ma'am. It makes me feel cheap and used."

"How can you say that? Don't I always take good care of you?" He nudged her gently, but she continued to sulk.

"Come on, don't be like this. I've promised you things would be changing soon, and they will. You've got to believe in me. Uncle Brandon is coming around. I think I've got a good chance to take over the firm when he goes to Washington."

"Sometimes I have a sneaking suspicion you're really married."

He kissed her lightly on the nose. "I'm not, and there's no other woman in my life—I swear to you."

A short time later, showered and dressed, John kissed her good-bye, pulling up the corners of her mouth to coax a smile out of her.

Back in the car, he looked at the clock on the dashboard. Only 10:30 P.M. Not too bad, he thought. He'd still have a few hours to spend with his other love.

Brandon Taylor glanced at his watch again. Ten in the morning and his nephew was still not in. After their talk last week, Brandon had been sure John was going to mend his ways. It had sounded to him like John was finally ready to accept the responsibilities that came with being a partner in a firm of this caliber. But arriving this late in the morning was not acceptable. For sure, Brandon didn't need problems like this. Not when the newspapers today were full of Rebecca Morland's accusations.

There was a knock and the door opened. Brandon saw John and waved him in. "Where have you been, it's after ten?"

"I had a client conference this morning out of the office," John said quickly, flashing a big smile.

For a moment, Brandon contemplated calling him on it. After carefully checking all the office calendars, he hadn't found any such conference scheduled, but he decided against that tactic. He had more important matters to address. Ever since his talk with Rebecca, Brandon had been anxious to question his nephew. However, his campaign schedule had kept him away from the office. "Sit down," he ordered.

"Certainly," said John, looking surprised. "Is something wrong?"

"That depends. I'm going to ask you some questions and I want honest answers—is that clear?"

"Of course. I'm always honest with you."

Brandon let that one go by as well. "Why did you lie and tell Rebecca that you got into the firm at six the morning after Ryan disappeared, when the book shows you signed in at 1:43 A.M.?"

A brief flicker of alarm crossed John's face before he swiftly covered it up. "I never said that. She must have made a mistake. I told her I came here directly from the boat."

He gave his nephew a long look. "Why did you come here at that hour?"

"I felt someone should be at the firm in case the sheriff's department needed us for some reason." John shrugged. "I don't know, it just seemed the sensible thing to do."

"And what did you do here all night?"

"I fell asleep when I got to the office, and I woke up at six." John hit his head as if he'd just remembered something. "That must be why Rebecca got mixed up," he theorized.

Either John was quicker on his feet than Brandon had previously thought, or he was telling the truth. "And the note. When did you find it?"

"Shortly before I called the police. I meant to check for a note when I first got here, but the trauma of the night had wiped me out, and the next thing I knew it was morning. I had no choice but to wash up in your bathroom and put on my suit from the day before."

"And you're sure you found the note on Ryan's desk?" Brandon's eyes narrowed as he appraised John carefully.

John began to fidget under his gaze. "Why do you ask that?"

Brandon folded his arms across his chest. "Because Gloria was the last one to leave the office the night Ryan disappeared, and she didn't see any note on Ryan's desk."

There was a sheepish expression on John's face. "You've

got me on that one, Uncle Brandon. You see, the note wasn't actually on his desk." He jumped up and began to pace. "The note was on the floor behind the wastebasket. It wasn't crumpled up or anything. But I thought if I told the police where I really found it, they might surmise Ryan had meant to throw it away." He made a hapless gesture with his hands. "I was positive Ryan had been depressed and killed himself, so I just said it was on the desk."

He came to stand by his uncle. "I'm sorry, Uncle Brandon. I should have told you the truth. I was just trying to be helpful."

Drumming his fingers on his desk, Brandon was still deciding what to do when his buzzer sounded. "Yes. Okay. I'll be right with him." He glanced over at John. "I've got a visitor. We'll discuss this later," he said angrily. As John left his office, Brandon was sure he saw a smug smile on his nephew's face.

A few minutes later, Maxwell Holmes came striding across the large office, his hand outstretched. "Brandon, glad you could see me on such short notice," he said in a booming voice. A newspaper was clutched under his other arm.

"Hello, Maxwell," Brandon replied, shaking his hand and gesturing to a chair.

Maxwell shook his head. "Naw. Let's sit on the couch."

"Very well." Brandon told his secretary to hold all his calls and reluctantly joined the other man, wondering what was on the Beach Commissioner's mind.

"I suppose you saw this?" said Holmes, unfolding the newspaper and hitting it with his hand. The face of Ryan Morland stared out at them. In big bold print the headline said: WIDOW OF ATTORNEY CLAIMS HUSBAND WAS MURDERED.

Brandon nodded glumly. "I saw it."

"This is bad, very bad," Maxwell said. "Can't have that gal creating headlines like this. It's only going to hurt your election chances. She's got to be stopped."

"I've tried," Brandon assured him. "I've already spoken to her about it, several times, but it's no use."

Holmes shook his head disapprovingly. "I've talked to some of the other guys—this kind of thing makes them real nervous."

There was an edge to Holmes's words that made Brandon uneasy. He was well aware that Holmes's support and that of the people he controlled were absolutely vital if Brandon was to remain the party's choice for the nomination. "I can understand their concern," Brandon replied. "After all, Ryan worked closely with me. However, I can't stop the media from printing Rebecca Morland's accusations."

Maxwell fixed his dark eyes on him. "There is something you can do. You can call a press conference. We'll see that all the right people show. You tell those damn reporters why you're sure Ryan jumped off the back of that boat."

"Don't you think that dignifying her statement with a response would lend legitimacy to her accusations?" Brandon countered. "I think the best thing to do is not to acknowledge this at all."

"Nope," Maxwell said firmly. "We can't have our candidate tainted by something like this. The reporter hinted that Ryan may have uncovered something that could reflect badly on you. Now I don't know what that gal told him, but it doesn't take a genius to figure out it sounds like you've done something dirty."

"That's not funny and you know it," Brandon said angrily.

Holmes stretched his legs out in front of him, a lazy smile on his face. "You've got to make a statement—if not, the party might have to look elsewhere."

"They'd do that to me after everything I've done for them over the years?"

"They might not want to," Holmes said with a smirk. "But Worthington is scurrying around like a mad rabbit, trying to make you look bad while he locks up support for himself."

"I can't believe either you or any of the other members of the party would even consider him my equal as a candidate," Brandon said, indignantly. "He's too extreme. And what's the man done for us over the years? Nothing as far as I'm concerned." He shook his finger at Holmes. "For all we know, and I certainly wouldn't put it past him, Worthington is behind this distortion in the media."

"It's true he's done nothing for the party," Maxwell agreed. "And the guys are deeply grateful to you. There's no question you've paid your dues. But the objective is to win in November against the Democrats. We can't have the slightest scandal touch our candidate—it gives the opponent too much ammunition."

Brandon exhaled loudly. He resented this man ordering him around. Brandon's father and grandfather had been prominent in state politics long before this idiot's family probably even knew what it was like to vote. Calm down, he cautioned himself. After he won the election, he'd be in a much better position to take his revenge. "Fine," he said, straightening his shoulders. "I'll take care of it."

Rebecca called directory assistance to get the address of Zoe Olin, the bookkeeper who had supposedly helped Ryan steal the money from the firm. But there was no listing in the telephone directories of Los Angeles County or the neighboring counties for the woman.

When she turned to Gloria Powell for help, all Gloria could provide was the address of Zoe Olin's mother as that was the only information the firm had on file for the bookkeeper. Gloria also mentioned that a secretary had overheard Zoe talking about moving to a new place a couple of days before she was put on leave.

Rebecca doubted the mother would speak to her if she identified herself as Ryan Morland's widow. How else could she find out the information she needed? Racking her brain for ideas, Rebecca came up with one she hoped would work.

Since her picture had been in the newspapers and she didn't want to run the risk of being recognized, Rebecca dressed as plainly as she could, bought herself a plausible but cheap wig, and put on a pair of glasses.

When she reached the address in the San Fernando Valley she identified herself as an investigator for Taylor, Dennison & Evans's insurance company, who needed to interview the woman's daughter so that the embezzlement matter could be settled without prosecuting her. The woman smiled at her gratefully and wrote down her daughter's new address. Feeling a twinge of guilt, Rebecca hurried off.

Twenty minutes later, Rebecca located the apartment building where the bookkeeper was supposed to be living. After parking her car, she walked up to the security gate and found Z. Olin's name on the directory. She pressed the intercom button next to it and a few seconds later heard a high-pitched voice answer.

Using the same phony routine she'd used with Zoe's mother, Rebecca convinced the woman to buzz her into the building. After climbing the stairs as instructed, she located the door and was just about to knock when it opened.

Zoe Olin was young, in her late twenties or early thirties, and very pretty with soft brown hair and large blue eyes. She was wearing a floral print cotton dress that showed off her curvaceous figure.

Rebecca's throat went dry. Even though she didn't believe Ryan had taken the money, coming face to face with this woman made her very nervous. All sorts of thoughts ran through her head. What if Ryan had become involved with Zoe for some reason and the whole money thing was . . .

A look of recognition came into Zoe's eyes. "You're Ryan Morland's wife, aren't you?" she asked, her head tilted sideways as if she were trying to figure out what was going on.

So much for her disguise, mused Rebecca. "I'm sorry that I had to pretend to be someone else," she explained hurriedly, feeling her cheeks grow warm. "I just want to ask you a few questions."

"No. I don't want to talk to you," Zoe said, trying to slam the door in Rebecca's face.

Rebecca put her foot in the way. "Please, it will only take a minute. I promise."

"No. Go away before I call the police."

Would this woman really want to involve the police? Rebecca wondered. "Go ahead and call them. There's no law against merely asking a few questions."

"You tricked me into letting you into the building," protested Zoe, her voice rising.

"I don't think there's a law against that either," Rebecca said, trying to stay calm. "All I want to know is if my husband took the money from the law firm as the partners say he did."

Zoe's eyes turned fearful. "I . . . I don't want to talk to you," she said again, continuing to shove the door against Rebecca's body, which was now wedged firmly against it.

"Did he do it?" Rebecca asked, searching the other woman's face for the truth.

"He did whatever they say he did," Zoe responded loudly. "Now, go before I start screaming."

Her heart pounding, Rebecca steeled herself for Zoe to make good on her threat. "Did you hate my husband that much?"

Looking stricken, Zoe shook her head. "I didn't hate him. He was a nice man. Look, my lawyer doesn't want me to talk to anyone. Please leave."

"Can I give you my phone number in case you change your mind?"

The young woman kept shaking her head. "I won't."

With an unexpected show of force, Zoe suddenly shoved so hard Rebecca lost her balance. As she fell back, the door was slammed in her face.

Leaning up against the wall of the hallway, Rebecca debated what to do next. She could camp out here hoping Zoe would have to leave the apartment, or she could wait outside the building for her. Now that she knew what the woman looked like, she could also follow her.

Rebecca was still contemplating her options when she heard the sound of footsteps coming in her direction. It was a burly man, with a red beard.

"I'm the apartment manager," he said in a booming voice. "I've got a complaint that you're bothering one of my tenants. You should leave right now, lady. The cops are on their way."

Having read about the slow response time of the police to real emergencies in this part of the San Fernando Valley, Rebecca knew they wouldn't be arriving too quickly on a mere disturbing the peace complaint. Nonetheless, she'd accomplish nothing by antagonizing the manager.

"I'm going," she said dejectedly. She picked up her purse

which had fallen in the scuffle and headed for the stairs. From the look she'd seen on Zoe's face, Rebecca knew that the partners hadn't told her the entire story about the missing funds. Somehow, she had to find a way to get Zoe Olin to talk to her.

Back at home, Rebecca turned the small bankbook over in her hands, wishing she could make sense of yet another piece of the puzzle. What she needed to do was to take it to the bank and see what she could find out. But she was afraid. What if it did belong to Ryan?

Picking up the phone, Rebecca called Gloria Powell. "I've got a quick question," she explained. "I'm just going over some notes I found on scraps of paper, trying to see if there's anything of importance scribbled on them or if I can throw them away." She took a deep breath and plunged ahead. "Does the name Earl Anders mean anything to you?"

"Earl Anders?" Gloria repeated, as if thinking. There was silence for a few moments. "No. I can't place it."

Rebecca felt that that was a good indication the man wasn't a client of the firm. If he was, Gloria would have known the name.

"Want me to run it on the computer at the office?" asked Gloria.

"Could you do that without anyone finding out about it?"

"Sure," Gloria said. "I run names all the time to make sure we don't have any conflict of interest problems. I'll do it tomorrow and call you."

"Thanks, Gloria. I appreciate your help."

"No problem." She lowered her voice. "Listen, I don't know too much about it, but Mr. Taylor's called a news conference for tomorrow morning. That's all I heard. If you say anything to anyone about my telling you, it could cost me my job."

Rebecca's heart was pounding. "I won't say a word—I promise." After she hung up, she sat and stared at the phone for a while. Why would Gloria need to whisper about a news conference? Brandon would never discuss Ryan in public without informing her first and inviting her to be present. Brandon was probably planning to formally announce his candidacy or something like that. When someone ran for office they thought everything they did was newsworthy. Still, she'd watch it just in case.

Her gaze fell again on the bankbook she was still holding. If Earl Anders wasn't a client of Taylor, Dennison & Evans, then why was his bankbook in her husband's briefcase?

CHAPTER
FIFTEEN

Slightly uneasy, Rebecca sat in her den, watching the television. Brandon Taylor, speaking from the lobby of the firm, was about to read his statement to the news media. When she heard the first words out of his mouth, she sat forward, a sinking feeling in the pit of her stomach.

"It is with great sadness that I talk about my late colleague and friend, Ryan Morland. In light of the speculation created by his wife's accusations of murder, I feel I have no choice but to speak the truth. Ryan was clinically depressed prior to his death and needed medication but refused all offers of help. I have great empathy for his wife, Rebecca. Unfortunately, she is finding it difficult to accept the reality that her husband killed himself, and that's one of the reasons why she's making such outlandish claims. It is my hope that Mrs. Morland will seek proper care to help her come to terms with the truth."

Stunned, Rebecca pressed her hand over her mouth, a suffocating sensation welling up in her throat. How could Brandon of all people do this to Ryan—to her? His betrayal was incomprehensible.

Quickly, her anguish turned to rage. How dare he say Ryan was clinically depressed and needed medication? What the hell did he know? Brandon was making it sound as if both Ryan and she were crazy.

Voices on the television captured her attention again, and she heard Brandon indicate he'd answer a few questions from the reporters, who seemed to be taking down his every word. Yes, he was still planning to run for the Senate. No, he didn't know yet who would take Ryan's place. No. He didn't want to comment on the rumors that Paul Worthington was planning to oppose him. All Brandon would say on that subject was that he believed his candidacy had the full backing of the party. He reiterated that he'd called this conference to put to rest the rumors that Ryan's death had anything to do with him or his campaign, or that any foul play had been involved in the tragic incident.

Is that what this news conference was about? Rebecca thought, her anger rising like acid in her throat. Had Brandon stabbed Ryan in the back merely to make sure nothing interfered with his political future? She was bitterly disappointed in the man. If anyone should have been able to stand up to political pressure, she would have thought it would be Brandon. How could she have been so wrong about someone?

One of the reporters called out a last question. "Is it true that the main reason Rebecca Morland is claiming her husband was murdered is so that she can collect on an insurance policy that has a suicide clause?"

Shocked by the question, Rebecca held her breath while Brandon answered.

"No comment," he said, waving his hand at the reporters and thanking them all for coming.

How had that reporter known about the policy when she herself hadn't found out that Ryan had purchased life insurance until a few days ago?

Blood pounding in her temples, she turned off the television and ran into the other room to get her notes. She found the phone number for the insurance agent, Fred Jackson. The man barely had time to say hello before she lit into him.

"Who the hell did you tell about the insurance policy Ryan bought?"

"I . . ." he seemed to be stumbling over his words. "I may have mentioned it to Brandon Taylor. I mean, I was feeling rather confused after I spoke to you, so I called his office."

Rebecca felt like she'd been hit by a double-whammy. In her gut, she was sure that Brandon or someone close to him had tipped off the reporter to ask that question.

"Why, is something wrong?" asked the agent.

"It wasn't anyone's affair," she said angrily. "My business dealings with your agency are private! I doubt your other customers would enjoy finding out what a big mouth you have. So keep it shut from now on!" She slammed the phone down.

For a moment, Rebecca felt totally overwhelmed. She was completely alone with no one to turn to, no one to ask for help.

Her gaze fell on the mantel. She went over to the fireplace where she'd put the picture from her office of Ryan and her taken on their honeymoon in Hawaii. God, they had been so happy—their whole lives together stretched out in front of them. Who could have guessed it would end like this?

"Stop feeling sorry for yourself," she muttered under her breath, fighting back tears. She had to be strong for Ryan, because now there was no one else who would pursue justice for him.

When the news conference given by Brandon Taylor came on television, Detective Solowski was already upset. Checking with the medical examiner about the tests done on Ryan Morland, she'd learned a disturbing fact. The medical examiner claimed that Detective Walters had specifically ordered him to only confirm that there had been alcohol in Ryan Morland's system— nothing more. That meant that Walters had made a deliberate choice—one contrary to her understanding with him—not to have a full toxicological screen done on Morland.

Now, Solowski experienced a queasy feeling in the pit of her stomach as she listened with Walters and the rest of the department to Brandon Taylor's statement. Walters was going to shove that damn insurance issue down her throat. She had forgotten to follow up on it. Actually, Mrs. Morland was supposed to have checked into it and gotten back to her, but she hadn't. Maybe she'd overlooked it because of everything else that was going on. Besides, life insurance wasn't the only reason why Mrs. Morland was claiming her husband had been murdered. And it didn't change the fact that Walters had ignored Solowski's request for a full toxicological screen to be done on Morland.

She felt sorry for Mrs. Morland. How embarrassing to have your husband's boss claim on television that both you and your husband were having mental problems. And that reporter's question about the insurance—even though Brandon Taylor had said no comment, the question itself had planted the idea firmly in people's minds. After this, everyone would think all the wife really cared about was collecting the money. Solowski was sure Rebecca had genuinely loved her husband. No one could fool her in that department.

Earlier that morning, when she'd asked Walters why he'd never mentioned to her that Mrs. Morland had received a threatening phone call, he'd shrugged it off, insisting that it was merely another ploy on the widow's part to convince them that her husband had been murdered.

"Let's grab something to eat," she said to Walters, indicating with a nod of her head that she wanted to get out of the station.

"Where to?" he asked, a supercilious grin on his face.

"Let's get some good coffee at the Bahamas Coffee Shop," she suggested. "We can take a look at some of the boats."

His eyes appraised her for a moment as if he were trying to figure out what she was up to. "Whatever you want."

Within a short time they had their coffee in Styrofoam containers and were heading down to the docks at one of the many boating facilities in Marina del Rey.

"So what's on your mind?" Walters asked, gazing longingly at a forty-foot sloop.

"I wanted to talk to you about the Morland investigation."

Walters gave her a sideways glance. "I'd think after this morning's statement by Brandon Taylor, you'd be ready to throw in the towel. Clearly the woman is after the insurance money."

She felt herself bristling. Don't lose it, Solowski, she told herself. Shielding her eyes from the sun with one hand, she took a sip of coffee. "Doesn't it make you wonder what the real stakes are? I mean, each of Morland's partners is only too willing to throw stones at a man who can't fight back."

"Oh, I dunno. They say business partnerships aren't exactly loving relationships. People pick business partners for different reasons."

"I've got a feeling there's something more going on in that firm than meets the eye." She started walking down the ramp.

He put a hand on her shoulder to stop her. "Why can't you leave it alone? Everyone's convinced it was a suicide. We've got enough to do without making more work for ourselves. I'm ready to close it."

Squinting up at him, she asked, "Don't good detectives owe it to the folks in this county to do the best they can?"

"Sure."

"Well, I don't think we've done that yet in this case."

A scowl crossed Walters's face. "What's that supposed to mean?"

"We didn't follow up on everything." She swallowed several times before continuing. "Like doing a full toxicological screen on Morland."

He eyed her cautiously before responding. "The autopsy showed he had enough alcohol in him to be considered under the influence. What more do you want?"

"To know what else was in his system. I read through the reports, and you didn't ask for the full screen."

"I decided we didn't need it." He shrugged. "What's the big deal?"

"We had agreed to request it."

"And I changed my mind," he said defensively. "It didn't seem to me we should waste any more of the taxpayers' money on the guy."

"Oh, is that what you were doing?" Her tone was mocking. "Saving the taxpayers' money?"

Suddenly he was in her face. "I'm your superior and I don't appreciate you telling me I'm full of shit."

"I didn't say that," she insisted. "And why do you keep pulling rank on me in this matter? Why do you refuse to look at alternatives concerning Mr. Morland's death? It's beginning to make me wonder."

He was glaring at her now. "What the hell are you getting at?"

"I think something strange is going on—that's what," she retorted.

"If you think I'm such a dumb ass, I can arrange for you to be transferred—like that." He snapped his fingers.

Solowski heard the unmistakable threat in his voice. While he was behaving badly and deserved to be taken down a notch or two, her sense of self-preservation was warning her to pull back from the brink before it was too late. Pissing him off would only hurt her, not him.

"Seems to me," he snarled, pointing his finger at her, "that you're ready to throw away your whole future for a lady who's made an ass out of you. Hell, Solowski, what's gotten into you? That fucking widow lied to you. She was supposed to tell you about the insurance and she didn't. Why aren't you pinning *her* to the wall instead of me?"

He was giving her a chance to step back. Was she ready to give up her badge for Rebecca Morland and her theories? For a brief few seconds she wavered. Then, hating herself, she gulped down her pride and forced herself to apologize. "I wasn't trying to be disrespectful. Sorry if you heard it that way." Sadly, while she might feel sorry for Mrs. Morland, Solowski couldn't afford to antagonize Walters. His evaluation of her was too important for her future.

Pulling up in front of her home, Rebecca was gathering some packages to take into the house when a man with a camera jumped out of the bushes and came running toward the car.

"What do you think you're doing?" she yelled, too surprised to do anything else.

"Mrs. Morland, did your husband kill himself because of something to do with Brandon Taylor's campaign?"

She was horrified. How could people be so insensitive? "Please leave, or I'll call the police," she shouted at him.

The man started snapping her picture, and Rebecca put her hands in front of her face. Shaking her head in response to his repeated questions, she merely kept motioning for him to go away. If she made a run for it, would he be crazy enough to try to follow her into the house? She'd have to find out. It was either that, or stay in her car all day waiting for him to leave.

Holding her purse in front of her face, she ran, feeling him in hot pursuit. "I'm going to call the police and have you arrested," she yelled, as she shoved the key in the lock and opened the door. Without turning around, she slammed it behind her. Then, for several minutes, she stood there trembling.

Diana Worthington glanced around carefully before she dashed from her white Jaguar. She tried to reassure herself that she hadn't been followed and that no one was around who might recognize her. It was the middle of the afternoon on a sunny day, and she felt completely ridiculous in her mink coat as she raced for the front door of the house.

Knocking loudly, she tried to hide behind the potted tree and prayed he'd open the door quickly. After what seemed like many minutes instead of only seconds, the door swung open.

Maxwell Holmes stood grinning at her. "Hello, Diana." He was wearing fawn-colored jodhpurs and a full, long-sleeved white shirt. His feet were ensconced in high leather boots. She'd jokingly referred to this attire as his rubber plantation owner's costume.

"You're absolutely crazy," she told him, once she was safely inside.

"Why? Because the thought of you driving over here as you did gets me so excited I could come in my pants?" He laughed and took her hand, guiding it to the large bulge in his trousers. "See what you do to me?"

She nodded.

"Let's go into the solarium," he suggested.

As she started to follow him, he swung around, an innocent

smile playing around his lips. "Would you like to hang your coat in the hall closet?"

"No thank you," she said, shaking her head.

He laughed again. "Come along then."

The room he called his solarium had been decorated to look like it was part of a prewar subtropical plantation house. Holmes had seen this, his ideal room, in an old black-and-white movie. He'd had stills made from the film and then hired a decorator to create an exact replica.

Diana had never counted the plants in the room, but she guessed there were easily hundreds if not a full thousand—all different varieties. Holmes loved both heat and humidity. He claimed it kept his skin young and supple. Diana always felt sickeningly warm in the solarium, but today, wearing a mink coat, she felt especially uncomfortable. She could already feel the rivulets of sweat gathering between her breasts.

"You're beginning to look hot, Diana." Maxwell loved to use double entendres. "I think it's time to take off your coat."

She twirled around for him as he removed it for her. Then she turned to face him as she stood there in high heels and nothing else. With the bright sunlight shining through the glass, she felt vulnerable.

"Ah," he said, stepping back and throwing her coat over one of the couches, which was covered in a rich leopard fabric. "Turn around, Diana. Hmm, yes. As usual you look exquisite." Gazing at her with a lazy expression in his eyes, he rubbed the protrusion in his pants. "My God, I haven't been this hot in ages," he said. "It reminds me of my very first time." He smiled. "Does it thrill you knowing what you do to me?"

A half smile curled up the corners of her mouth. She'd never admit it to him, but there was a definite satisfaction in reducing him to an excited adolescent—especially when this man had dozens of beautiful young women at his beck and call.

"Feel like your usual?" he asked.

"Please," she replied nervously, knowing what would come next.

Holmes went to an intercom on the wall. "Chang, bring in the refreshments."

A few seconds later, the door opened and the Chinese houseman came in, his eyes carefully averted from Diana, carrying the frosty pitcher of martinis.

The first time this had happened, Diana had almost had a heart attack even though Holmes had assured her that the man never saw anything. He'd been with Holmes for ten years and supposedly would die before he'd reveal anything that went on in this house. Still, it was most unnerving, and she shivered involuntarily, despite the intense heat.

Turning to Holmes, she watched his face. She'd noticed before how he treated his Chinese houseman as an object instead of as a human being. It seemed to be part of what turned him on.

Holmes ran his finger lightly over her nipple. It grew hard, and she felt herself shiver again. His other hand moved slowly down her nude and trembling body and over her belly, until it reached inside and was greeted with her moist warmth. Her body's immediate response embarrassed Diana, but she was helpless to do anything about it.

He then took a sip of his drink, deliberately keeping several ice cubes in his mouth before he bit her other nipple. Suddenly, that incredible melting sensation started in her chest and flowed to her loins as, unable to stop herself, she began to orgasm. Her body engulfed in sensations, she was filled with shame as she heard the houseman close the door behind him.

Later, when Diana was putting on her makeup, Holmes put his hand on her shoulder. "I've heard Rebecca Morland's been visiting everyone who was on the boat that night. Has she been to see you and Paul yet?"

"Yes. She showed up at our home in Newport Beach."

He arched an eyebrow. "Really. What did she want to know?"

"Things like what we discussed with her husband that night. She also kept insisting he wouldn't have killed himself." Diana searched her mind quickly for what else to tell him. She didn't want to mention the argument Rebecca was sure took place between Paul and Ryan, nor did she want to bring up the subject of Morland's supposed investigation into her husband's life.

"What else?"

"That's about it." She ran a brush through her hair; she felt exhausted. This man never seemed to get tired during sex—it was amazing. "Oh, she also said she was pregnant. But I've since heard that she lost it."

"That's too bad," he said.

"Hasn't she gotten to you yet?" asked Diana.

"No." His face darkened as if his thoughts were disturbing him.

Diana turned to gaze at him carefully. "What are you going to tell her when she does?"

"Don't worry about that, pretty lady," he said with a smile. "I'll think of something." His eyes now danced with amusement. "Maybe I'll say you seduced her husband that night and the poor man fell off the boat in utter bliss."

She didn't find the remark very funny and shook her head at him as she would at a child. "I've got to go."

Outside, it was dusk. Now was when the real fear began. Holmes would never let her put on any additional clothes before she left—he insisted it would spoil the whole fantasy for him.

Running to her car, again wrapped only in her mink, she glanced at her watch. It was getting late, and she was going to hit a lot of traffic. She and Paul had a black-tie affair to attend tonight. Usually, she didn't make plans to be with Holmes when she had a big event, but he'd been so insistent. She hoped she'd make it home before Paul did.

Inside the car, she yanked on a pair of loose pants and a sweatshirt. The mink coat she'd stuff in the trunk before she went into the house. That way, if Paul was home, she could say she'd been to an exercise class. He'd still be angry with her for cutting her time so short, but it was far better than having him guess the truth.

Although she'd promised Detective Solowski not to call her, Rebecca had been having a difficult time waiting for answers to her questions. So against her better judgment, she'd twice called the station but so far Solowski hadn't called her back. Unable to stop herself, she again dialed the number.

To Rebecca's dismay, Detective Walters answered. "No. Solowski isn't here," he informed her. "But I do have some results to report, if you're interested."

His jovial voice made Rebecca nervous. "What results are those?"

"Well, for starters, with regard to the burglary at your home, they found no unidentified fingerprints."

"I see."

"Also, the only fingerprints found on the suicide note are those of Mr. Morland and John Evans, the man who discovered it."

She bit her lip to keep from crying.

"Mrs. Morland? Are you still there?"

"Yes. I'm here."

"Oh. I thought maybe you got upset and hung up." He paused. "There's more."

Rebecca realized this man wanted to unnerve her and she refused to give him that satisfaction. Taking a deep breath, she quietly steeled herself for more bad news. "Go on," she told him.

"Well, it seems that the handwriting expert believes that the suicide note was written by Mr. Morland." He paused again. "Of course, I warned Solowski that having a handwriting analysis done would be nothing but a waste of time. Obviously, she didn't listen," he added in a snide tone of voice.

Rebecca was further shaken by this latest news. She'd been counting on evidence from one of the reports to help her prove who had killed Ryan. Keeping her voice even, she thanked him and hung up. Only then, with the receiver safely back on the hook, did she allow her tears of frustration to flow.

That night, Rebecca had to force herself to go to a ballet recital that Lucy's daughter, Gaby, was performing in. She didn't feel like sitting through a show, but Lucy had been so wonderful to her. And Gaby was such a darling little girl—Rebecca didn't have the heart to disappoint either of them.

Backstage, Gaby pirouetted for Rebecca, showing off her pink tulle ballet costume. Rebecca told her she looked beautiful and wished her good luck on her performance.

Nonetheless, all through the show, even though she clapped whenever everyone else did, Rebecca felt preoccupied and upset. She still hadn't recovered from the awful statement Brandon had made to the press or the assault by the reporter in her own front yard. On top of that was the disturbing fact that Detective Solowski wasn't returning her calls. Even worse was the news Walters imparted to her. It didn't seem as if anyone was on her side anymore except for Lucy. She wished she could hire a private investigator to help her find her husband's killer, but they were too expensive.

She saw Lucy gazing at her with a worried expression. Mustering up a smile, she forced herself to concentrate on the stage. Unfortunately, her mind refused to cooperate.

Between the funeral expenses, the travel expenses for Ryan's mother and her own folks, and all of the monthly bills, the money Brandon had sent her had quickly disappeared. Another huge chunk of that money had been used to pay down the balance on her Visa card.

And now she didn't know whom to approach regarding settling up Ryan's share of the partnership. After the statement Brandon had issued to the press, she wasn't sure she'd ever speak to him again. She and John Evans were hardly on the best of terms. And since John had told her how angry Catherine had been when Ryan had broken up with her, she felt less than secure about approaching Catherine. As much as she hated the idea, she was going to have to file suit against the firm. Of course, they would then countersue and claim the monies Ryan took as an offset. That meant the entire world would think of her husband as a thief. She had no idea what Ryan's partnership share was worth. It might not even be financially worthwhile to sue.

With the police ready to determine that Ryan's death was a suicide, the chances of her collecting on the insurance policy were also slim. It was really quite simple: if she didn't go back to work, there would be no more money coming in. The pay at the clinic was minimal compared to what she could earn at a law firm, but that kind of work didn't appeal to her at all. It was probably time to put the house up for sale.

Rebecca prayed for a break in the investigation. If she could only get Zoe Olin to crack. Zoe had to know more than she was telling. Rebecca just hoped it wasn't an affair with Ryan that she was hiding.

When the recital was over, Rebecca hugged Gaby. "You were great," she told the brown-eyed child, whose face glowed from the exertion of the dance as well as the pink rouge and the bright red lipstick that her ballet teacher had put on her. "And you look so grown up."

Gaby was full of giggles and childish exuberance. Lucy wanted Rebecca to join them for dessert, but she begged off. "I'm really beat," she pleaded. "Can I have a rain check?"

"Sure," Lucy nodded, her brow creased as if she were troubled over Rebecca's refusal.

Oblivious to her mother's frown, Gaby threw her arms around Rebecca's neck and gave her a kiss. For a brief second, Rebecca buried her face in the child's warmth before pulling away.

It had started raining, and she gripped the steering wheel carefully as she maneuvered away from the Beverly Hilton Hotel and into traffic.

The sound of the windshield wipers scraping back and forth dulled her anxiety for a few minutes. Soon, however, the prospect of returning to an empty house filled her with dread.

Before Rebecca met Ryan, she'd been living in an apartment in West Hollywood. It had been a security building, although that hadn't stopped thieves from breaking and entering the garage several times. Yet Rebecca didn't remember feeling afraid living there by herself. Nor had she felt afraid in her current home—not until Ryan's death. Then the burglary and the threatening phone call had heightened her fear. Lately, she'd become a nervous wreck.

She glanced in her rearview mirror. Wasn't that car behind

her following too closely? It made her apprehensive, especially considering the rain. Unused to driving in bad weather, L.A. drivers often forgot how slick, oil-coated pavement could become suddenly treacherous. Every time it rained here, television crews captured for their viewers numerous pictures of jack-knifed trucks and cars that had skidded out of control.

For a second, Rebecca considered pulling over and letting the other vehicle pass, then changed her mind. Another block and she'd be turning onto Benedict Canyon, one of the several canyon roads that wound its way between Beverly Hills, Bel Air, and the San Fernando Valley, ten miles to the north. Their home was off Mulholland Drive. Rebecca could reach it either by taking the San Diego Freeway and going east on Mulholland or this route and going west on the scenic highway. This way was faster.

To her chagrin the other car turned behind her onto Benedict. An uneasiness settled over her. This winding road had only one narrow lane in each direction, making it hard to find anywhere to pull over and let another car pass. She wished the road were better lit. The rain made the canyon, with its hills, deep ravines, and treacherous hairpin curves even more bleak and desolate than usual. It was especially dangerous in the rain because of the mud and the rocks that often came tumbling down onto the roadway.

Remembering the reporter who had jumped out of the bushes in front of her house, she wondered if it was him driving so closely behind her. She edged her car over to the right side of the lane and slowed down, hoping the other driver would cross over the yellow line to pass her. You weren't supposed to do that on this road, but everybody did—the police rarely patrolled the canyons, and there didn't appear to be any cars coming in the other direction.

She heard the engine of the car behind her rev up. Good. The driver was finally going to pass. Then she could stop worrying about being rear-ended on one of the many curves.

The black car pulled alongside her to the left. It was too dark for her to see the driver. Suddenly, with a sickening jolt, the car rammed her.

"Oh my God," Rebecca cried out, leaning on her horn as the car bumped her car again with a dull thud.

"Are you crazy?" she shouted, as fear skittered through her. The idea that it was a reporter who was following her flew out of her mind. Her heart pounded frantically. This had to be a robbery or a carjacking. Shaking, she gunned the engine. Her car shot forward, and for a few frightening seconds Rebecca felt she was plunging out of control. Don't panic, she warned herself, swallowing at the tightness in her chest, fighting not to lose command of her car.

She knew she had to get away. The most dangerous part of the canyon lay ahead, just before Mulholland Drive, which was her turnoff. Her mind raced with alternatives. She could swing a U-turn and head back, but her car couldn't make the turn in one try, and it was too dangerous to slow down.

In the middle of the first perilous curve, the shiny black car pulled alongside her again. She sensed its nearness, afraid to take her eyes off the road. Nausea crawled up the back of her throat. There was no doubt in her mind now—the other driver was trying to push her over the edge. Panic such as she'd never known before welled up in her.

Suddenly, a blinding light appeared. A car coming in the other direction seemed to have its brights on as it headed her way. Heart pounding wildly, she leaned on her horn, blinking her lights on and off, trying to convey her desperate need of help.

The menacing black car shot forward, and a few seconds later its fading taillights quickly disappeared around the curves in the road. Rebecca regretted with all of her heart that she had never installed a phone in the car.

The vehicle coming from the other direction passed her, the driver seemingly unaware of the disaster that had almost occurred and ignoring her flashing headlights and blaring horn.

Shaking like a leaf, Rebecca forced herself to think. Who had wanted to scare her? Or worse, kill her? She'd been so busy looking for the answers to why Ryan might have been murdered, that she'd forgotten the same people could also want to get rid of her. But why? She tried to figure out what she knew that could hurt anyone. Then she realized that was the whole point. Whoever these people were, they didn't know what she might have found out and were no longer willing to risk whatever it might be coming to light.

Rebecca had no idea whom she could ask or trust. How was she to determine who was telling her the truth and who was lying—or who was trying to scare or even kill her? She couldn't believe that all of these horrible things were happening to her. She wondered if this was how Ryan had felt during the last few weeks of his life. Had someone tried to kill him before that night on the boat and he'd been too afraid to tell her?

Sometimes it seemed an exercise in futility to keep hoping that she'd find the answers to her questions. As Rebecca's hands trembled on the steering wheel she fretted over what else she might have to face in the days ahead.

CHAPTER
SIXTEEN

Rebecca woke up with a start, her heart pounding. She was sitting in the large, white damask chair in the den, and sunlight was streaming in through the window. Stiff and sore all over, she glanced at her watch. It was after eight in the morning, and she realized she must have fallen asleep after the first light of dawn. Memories of what had happened to her last night came crashing into her mind.

After the car had tried to push her off the road, she'd driven directly to the Van Nuys police station, where she'd filed a police report and asked them to contact Detectives Solowski and Walters at the Marina del Rey sheriff's department, who were investigating her husband's death.

Then, still feeling petrified, Rebecca had called her private security company and asked for one of their cars to meet her in front of her house. The young guard with the shy smile had come into the residence and waited patiently while Rebecca turned on all the lights and checked to make sure everything was in order. When he'd left, she'd known she was too terrified to sleep, so she'd gotten a blanket and sat huddled in the big chair, waiting for dawn.

During the long night, Rebecca had gone over in her mind all the possibilities of who might have tried to hurt her and why. She'd also questioned again if they were really trying to kill her or only warning her to stop searching for the reason why Ryan had died. Whatever their message, her biggest fear now was not *if* they would try it again—but *when*.

Brandon Taylor was enjoying the rare tuna steak he was having for lunch in the Belvedere, a garden restaurant in the Peninsula Hotel in Beverly Hills, when he saw Maxwell Holmes enter with two of Hollywood's foremost talent agents. Brandon excused himself to his client and walked over to Holmes. He shook hands with the three men. Then, with an imperceptible nod of his head toward Holmes, Brandon made for the men's room.

A few minutes later, the men's room door opened and a confident and tan-looking Holmes strode in. "Great restaurant, isn't it?" he commented jovially.

Brandon was just finishing up and didn't bother answering. "I kept my end of the bargain," he told the other man, gazing at him forcefully, his voice low so as not to be overheard. "Now you keep yours."

Holmes glanced in the mirror, stroking down his mustache and checking to make sure his tie was straight. "No problem," he replied. "You're going to get all the support we promised. The guys all thought that was a nifty press statement you read on Morland."

"Thank you," replied Brandon, his tone chilly.

"Well, I've got to get back. See you later," Holmes said with a wink at the other man.

For a short time after Holmes had gone, Brandon allowed the hot water to continue running over his hands, wishing he could as easily erase the bitter taste from his mouth.

Solowski kept glancing at her watch and wondering where Walters was. He'd been gone for hours, and she was anxious to tell him the latest developments in the Morland case. She'd gotten a call from an officer at the Van Nuys police station and had followed it up with a call to Rebecca Morland. To her mind, the fact that a car had actually bumped and damaged Rebecca's car in an apparent effort to run her off the road, created an incident that deserved further study.

When Walters finally sauntered through the door, Solowski filled him in on her conversations with the Van Nuys police officer and Rebecca Morland.

"That Morland broad really comes up with the stories," he said, rolling his eyes.

"It isn't like that," she assured him, her stomach tightening at his response. "Mrs. Morland sounded badly frightened, and the cop saw the dents in her car last night."

"That doesn't mean her car got dented the way she said it did."

Solowski eyed her partner. Something more than pigheadedness was keeping him from objectively assessing the facts of this case; his mind was unquestionably closed.

"Look at the facts again," she persisted gently. "Things keep getting worse. After her husband dies, her house is burglarized and her husband's computer files are stolen. Then she gets a threatening phone call. Now someone tries to kill her."

In spite of her determination to make her point in a calm, professional manner, Solowski heard her voice rising in urgency and frustration. "If we don't help her, Walters, she's liable to end up dead. Do you want that on your conscience?"

"You're looking at it all backwards," he insisted, shaking his finger at her. "What's really happening is that this woman is doing more and more to convince us that something sinister is going on, when she's the one who's spinning out of control. She may very well end up dead, but it will most likely be by her own hand." He shrugged indifferently. "Who knows, maybe she should be hospitalized."

Detective Solowski gazed at her partner in stunned silence. She couldn't believe her ears.

Walters's face became very serious, and he lowered his voice. "Listen, Solowski, we're going to be closing this case. I'm telling you this for your own good. Let it be."

Solowski fought unsuccessfully to contain her rising anger. "You may be through with the case," she told him, "but I couldn't live with myself if something happened to her."

"See here," he said, jabbing his finger at her. "You don't wanna be doing anything that could hurt *you* in the long run. You hear me?" And with that final declaration, he threw her a menacing look and stormed out of the room.

Catherine Dennison slid further into the hot water. Her hair had an oil treatment on it and was wrapped in a thick white terry cloth towel. Her face had been thoroughly cleansed so that the vapors of steam from the water could enter her open pores.

"Feels wonderful, doesn't it?" Diana murmured, luxuriating next to Catherine in the whirlpool.

"Mmm," agreed Catherine. The two of them were at the Tree House Spa, a full-service facility in Brentwood. Once a month, Catherine allowed herself a few hours off. She and Diana Worthington usually arranged their schedules so that they could visit the spa together.

Hair, nails, pedicure, facial massage, whirlpool, and a full body massage were all included in the package they'd paid for today. While Diana also liked to get her body wrapped, Catherine found it too confining.

During their time here, Diana and Catherine usually kept their conversations light and gossipy. Unfortunately, Catherine had to breach their unspoken rule today.

Water reaching to her chin, Catherine stretched her body out fully until her feet touched the other end of the tub. "Has Paul made a decision on the Senate race yet?" she asked.

Diana's green eyes fluttered open. "Didn't I already tell you?"

"No," said Catherine, trying not to let her annoyance show. Diana knew damn well that she hadn't said a thing.

"He's not interested in a deal," Diana admitted, shaking her head, which was also wrapped in a terry cloth towel. "Brandon's stance on certain issues is too soft for Paul. He believes it's his duty to champion the things he feels strongly about." She repositioned her body in the water.

Suddenly, Catherine's enjoyment was ruined. She had thought she'd done a remarkable job in convincing Diana that Paul should not run, something she'd assumed Diana would get across to her husband. "Paul's making a big mistake, Diana. I really mean that. He's angering some powerful party people who will view his actions as traitorous to the cause." She paused a moment to let that sink in before adding in a cajoling tone of voice, "On the other hand, if he waits to run, it will be well worth it to him."

"Paul's got some heavy-duty backing too, you know," countered Diana, her chin stubbornly high.

Catherine chose not to acknowledge Diana's statement. If her scare tactics hadn't worked, and they obviously hadn't, she had to come up with another scenario—another way to make Worthington back down. Having Brandon go to Washington as a senator was the top priority in Catherine's life at the moment.

Finally, she spoke again. "Enough of politics. Let's relax. So, who's the new lover in your life?"

"I can't tell you his name," Diana said, splashing the water with her hand.

"Then tell me something about him," insisted Catherine.

Diana looked pensive. "Very well. He can go for hours without coming."

Catherine's eyebrows arched. "Really? Hours? He must be young, like Tony."

The other woman merely smiled, but said nothing more.

Detecting a certain tension around Diana's mouth, in spite of her smile, Catherine's curiosity was aroused. "Come on, who is it? I'm dying to know."

Her friend shook her head. "No way."

Catherine knew she could easily find out whom Diana was seeing and use that information against Paul, but that would hurt Diana too much. What she wanted to find, needed to find, was something about Paul.

Time for another tack, Catherine decided. "You know, Diana, you've always said Paul just doesn't seem to be that interested in sex. I was thinking. Maybe there's something you can do to change that."

"Believe me," Diana responded with a big sigh, "I've tried everything. I've been to those stores and bought the books, the outfits, the contraptions. I've tried the dirty movies. It only seems to infuriate him, and then he makes me feel cheap for even suggesting it in the first place."

"Mmm," Catherine murmured again, pretending to be deep in thought. After a reflective pause, she leaned toward her friend and whispered, "Have you ever thought that maybe Paul is gay?"

Diana stiffened. "Of course not! You know how Paul feels about people like that. It's strictly against his moral code."

Catherine did know how Paul felt. Although she didn't share those views, she wasn't beyond using Paul's phobia for her own agenda. "That doesn't mean those desires aren't locked deep inside him where he thinks no one can find out. Sometimes those who protest the most have the most to hide."

Shaking her head, Diana said, "No. Absolutely not."

Catherine gave her a knowing look. "Well, if I were you, I'd discuss it with my family doctor."

Diana seemed puzzled. "Why would I want to talk to him about that?"

"He might have some suggestions," said Catherine with a shrug.

"No. I don't think so."

Refusing to give up, Catherine continued. "I was also contemplating Paul's lack of desire for children. I know you said it wasn't anything medical—but maybe there's a disease in his family's history that he's afraid your children might inherit?"

"I don't think that's it," said Diana. "Did you forget? Paul's adopted. He has no idea who his natural parents are."

In the back of her mind, Catherine remembered Diana's telling her this years ago, but at the time it hadn't registered as being important. Now she speculated as to whether or not Ryan had investigated either of these things, and if so, what he'd found out.

A young attendant came into the room. "Mrs. Worthington?" she called out.

"Yes." Sitting up, Diana waved.

"There's a phone call for you."

"We're not supposed to be disturbed while we're here," Catherine reminded Diana, a scowl on her wet face.

"My staff knows that. This must be important." Diana reached for the towel the attendant held out. "I'll be right back."

Catherine was perturbed. She obviously had failed in her attempt to discourage Paul from entering the primary. But that didn't mean it was too late to keep him from beating Brandon. She just had to find something she could use to manipulate the man. And if she couldn't get any facts from Diana, there were always other ways to get the information. Yes, and who knew, she thought, it might be fun.

Standing partially out of sight in the lobby of the Peninsula Hotel, where the aroma from the huge bouquets of exotic flowers permeated the air, Rebecca watched as Maxwell Holmes exited the men's room and noticed a shapely blonde waiting by the window.

"Hi, Maxwell," the blonde called out in a breathy voice.

He waved at her. "Can't stop to chat, Dorothy, I've got people waiting."

"Catch you later." She smiled and gave him a knowing wink.

Rebecca wondered if the rumors about him were true. She'd heard that Holmes frequently took care of his political and business friends by arranging a memorable evening for them with one of Hollywood's many beautiful wanna-bes. She'd also heard that, for a price, he could accomplish just about anything.

She didn't know the man, but she was aware that Ryan had detested him. That had become clear that night on the yacht when Holmes had bumped into them on the dance floor and Ryan had so abruptly stopped dancing and escorted her to the bar.

Maxwell Holmes was definitely on her list of people to interview, and she seriously considered visiting him next.

Finally, Brandon emerged from the men's room and hurried toward the dining room. Before he could get there, Rebecca intercepted him.

"Rebecca," he said, his face turning white. "You startled me."

"Your press conference had the same effect on me," she told him icily. "I just want to know why you did it?"

"It's not that simple," he hedged. "Look," he added, putting his hand on her arm and nodding in the direction of the restaurant as he spoke in a confidential whisper. "I've got a client waiting in there. How about if we meet later to discuss this?"

"No," she replied sharply, not caring if anyone else heard her. "I want an answer right now—here." Her voice rose. "Why did you do it?"

Heads were beginning to turn. Brandon tensed, his entire posture showing how uncomfortable this scene was making him. "Give me a chance to tell my client that an emergency has come up," he pleaded softly. "Then we'll go into the lounge and talk."

She viewed him through narrowed eyes. "Make it quick." Without another word, she turned and headed for the bar.

Five minutes passed before Brandon joined her. "Let me have a Crown Royal and bring the lady a glass of red wine," he said to the bartender, obviously remembering what she liked to drink.

"Thank you, but I'll just have club soda," Rebecca stated, unsmilingly.

With his arm on her elbow, Brandon ushered her to a small table away from the few people who had been sitting at the bar.

"I regret I had to do it so publicly," he began when they were seated, "but some of my biggest supporters felt that your murder accusations were tainting me." He flashed her one of his most charming smiles. "I'm sure you can understand that you really left me no choice."

How dare he blame her! Her anger at him bubbled to the surface. "And these supporters that you're so worried about are men like Maxwell Holmes?" She didn't try to keep the disdain out of her voice.

A flush crept up his neck as he focused his eyes on her. "I'm not sure what you mean."

Rebecca stared back at him unblinkingly. "I think you do." She stopped talking while their drinks were served. As soon as the waiter was gone, she continued. "While you might think I'm mentally unbalanced and that my accusations of murder are crazy, someone else is taking me quite seriously." She paused to catch her breath before adding, "In fact, they tried to kill me last night."

He looked stricken as he reached out for her hand. "My God. What happened?"

She brushed him away, ignoring his question. "You were Ryan's idol," she lashed out harshly. "I hope you can live with yourself and what you've done. But quite frankly, if I were you, I'd be sick to my stomach every time I looked in a mirror."

Rebecca yanked open her purse, removed a ten-dollar bill and, before he could protest, threw it down on the table and then walked away.

When Rebecca reached Maxwell Holmes on the telephone the next afternoon she found him very charming. She explained that she was trying to talk to everyone who had been on the boat the night her husband had disappeared and that she would very much like to see him. "It shouldn't take more than ten or fifteen minutes of your time," she promised.

"Fine," he replied. "Come on over to my house." He gave her an address in Trousdale Estates. "How about seven this evening?"

"I'll be there. And thank you for seeing me on such short notice."

"No problem," he said.

A little later, Rebecca drove up Sunset and turned on Doheny Road. At Loma Vista she began the scenic climb through Trousdale Estates, named for the developer who had turned this valuable Beverly Hills hillside property into an enclave of exclusive homes, many with a fabulous view of the city.

Spotting the number of Maxwell Holmes's house on a concrete pillar, she pulled over to the curb. It was an imposing residence in terms of size, but it was hard to see the house itself because of the shrubbery and foliage all along the frontage of the property. She recalled hearing somewhere that Holmes had been married briefly to the ex-wife of a big Hollywood star, and that he'd never married again.

Remembering the way the man had leered at her on the yacht the night of the party, she hoped there would be someone else in the house, like a secretary or a housekeeper. Feeling anxious, she rang the bell.

Holmes answered the door himself. He was wearing a dark suit with a bright blue shirt open at the neck. There were several gold chains that stood out against the dark hair on his chest. While he certainly wasn't her type, Rebecca had to admit that with his thick dark hair and mustache and his rugged-looking bronzed skin, Maxwell Holmes was a striking man.

"I'm on the phone," he said smiling. "Make yourself at home in there." He pointed toward what looked to her like the living room.

Rebecca walked around, examining his works of art. Extremely unusual, she thought, and not particularly appealing. They were too primitive for her. There was also what she considered an overabundance of potted trees and plants that, along with the art and his extensive use of animal prints, made the place feel something like a jungle.

Holmes finally reappeared. "Sorry. Had a long-distance call. Want something?"

"No, thank you. I'll get right to the point. The police said you might have been one of the people who visited the yacht's cockpit the night my husband disappeared. Is that true?"

"Yep," he said, with a slight smile, showing even, white teeth. "They weren't letting us smoke anywhere but the cockpit." He patted his pocket, which she noticed had two cigars in it. "I went down there a few times to smoke one of these. I import them."

"Did you happen to see my husband in the cockpit on any of those occasions?"

"Once. I was down there smoking my cigar when he showed up. I had just about finished." He smiled. "We talked for maybe a minute or so before I left."

Rebecca's breath quickened. Finally, someone had admitted being in the cockpit at the same time as Ryan. "Can you remember what you and my husband discussed?"

"It wasn't a real discussion, if you know what I mean." He gave a shrug and smoothed back his mustache. "More like 'beautiful night,' 'great cigar' — that kind of thing."

"I see." She paused for a moment. "Do you recall what time it was when you saw my husband?"

Holmes shook his head. "Sorry. It was a party. I wasn't looking at my watch." He rubbed his forehead. "I think it was before I'd eaten, if that helps. Wasn't that some buffet?" His eyebrows arched.

"Mmm," she nodded, trying to remember something. They had just started serving the buffet when she first came out of the bathroom and couldn't find Ryan. Her throat went dry. That meant Holmes might have been the last one to see her husband before he disappeared.

He had taken one of the cigars out of his pocket. "Hope you don't mind?" It was more of a comment than a question.

She shook her head. "During the time you were with him, could you tell if my husband seemed upset?"

"He was quiet. But I'd noticed him at the bar a number of times. Sometimes people get real quiet when they've had a lot to drink." With a clipper, he took off the tip of his cigar.

Rebecca was getting tired of everyone telling her about her husband's drinking. Hands clasped in front of her, she cleared her throat. "Besides talking to him down in the cockpit, did you speak to Ryan at any other time during the evening?"

Holmes had reached into his jacket and taken out a gold Dunhill lighter with which he proceeded to light his cigar. He puffed in a couple times and, turning his head slightly, blew the smoke out. "Yeah. On the upper deck, earlier in the evening. I think we talked about the primary. He wanted me to be the chairperson for a dinner at the Century Plaza in support of Brandon." Fingering one of the gold chains around his neck, he added as if as an afterthought, "I told him I'd be glad to. He seemed pleased."

Behind-the-scenes support from Holmes was one thing, thought Rebecca. However, she strongly doubted that Ryan would have been eager to have Maxwell Holmes's name appear on an invitation as the chairperson to an event.

His eyes were appraising her. When she didn't say anything, he asked, "Didn't your husband inform you that he'd spoken to me?"

She decided to play along. "Yes. Now that you mention it. I do think Ryan mentioned something about it."

It was his turn to gaze at her intently. "What *exactly* did he tell you?"

The tone of his voice put her on guard. He seemed almost too interested in her reply. "Actually, I really don't remember. I'll have to think about it. I'm sure it will come to me when I've had a chance to concentrate." She gave him a dazzling smile.

He scowled and took another puff on his cigar. "What's all this *really* about?"

"As I'm sure you know, Mr. Holmes, I believe someone killed my husband and then tried to make it look like an accident or a suicide." She paused and looked down at her hands, her wedding ring. "Any help you could give me in finding out who it was would be greatly appreciated."

Fingering his mustache, he gave her a slow once-over that made her flesh crawl. "Sounds like you're having trouble accepting that he's gone."

"I am," she readily admitted. "Especially since what they're saying about him committing suicide is *not* the truth."

Putting the cigar in an ashtray, he leaned toward her and reached for her hand. "You're a pretty lady." The pressure on her fingers increased. "With looks like yours you'll have no trouble finding someone else."

She shuddered, struggling to conceal her revulsion. Suddenly, the doorbell rang.

"Damn," he said, releasing her hand and glancing at his watch. Picking up his cigar, he turned to her. "We through?"

"Yes, I think so," Rebecca said, grateful for the interruption and anxious to get out of this place.

"Good. Do me a favor, okay?"

She eyed him warily. "That depends."

He pointed to the French doors off the living room. "Those go to the patio. Turn to the left and make your way around the side of the house. You'll find a path through the shrubbery that will take you to the street."

It was a strange request, but she couldn't see any reason not to comply. As she left, however, Rebecca was careful not to close the door all the way. She held her breath and listened but was unable to hear much more than mumbling. Swallowing hard, she opened the door a fraction of an inch, peered in, and caught a glimpse of a tall, very thin man. It was no one she recognized.

Praying they wouldn't hear her, she eased the door closed. Then, her heart pounding, she made her way around the side of the house. The foliage was thick and overgrown, and she was thankful when she found herself back on the street.

Walking to her Jeep, Rebecca pondered what had just happened. Had Holmes not wanted her to see the man or had he not wanted the man to see her? And why? She slid behind the wheel of her car, opened her datebook and scribbled down the license number of the vehicle now parked behind her. It might lead nowhere, but she wanted to know who Holmes's visitor was.

As Rebecca pulled away, another car, its headlights off, careened around the corner, almost hitting her. Maniac, she thought, then froze when she recognized the driver. It was John Evans.

She stopped her car and watched in shock as John pulled up to the curb in front of Maxwell Holmes's house and then ran to the front door. What business could he have here? she wondered as she drove away.

CHAPTER
SEVENTEEN

As Rebecca ushered Solowski into her living room, she thought of all that had happened since they'd spoken last and she hoped the detective had some good news for her.

"Have you had any luck in finding out who tried to run me off the road?"

Solowski shook her head. "Without a license plate number we can't do much." She gazed around the room nervously. "I know you spoke to Walters and he told you about the fingerprints and the graphologists' conclusions on the handwriting."

"I shouldn't have called," Rebecca said, feeling bad. "I was just so anxious for the results."

"It doesn't matter. Anyway, I had your husband's note checked for something else because I noticed that the edges of the paper were uneven. The lab determined that the paper was cut with a scissors, but the guy had no way of knowing if it happened before or after your husband wrote on it." Solowski cleared her throat. "It didn't strike me that Mr. Morland was the type of person who would have grabbed a scrap of paper to write a note on."

Trying to digest this new information, Rebecca nodded. "Ryan was compulsive, he started everything on a fresh page. If you put it all together—the fact that it wasn't signed or dated and also that the paper was cut—it makes me think the note might have been tampered with or perhaps even fabricated."

"Yeah. I think so too." Solowski started walking around the room, glancing at photos. Finally, she seemed to make a decision and faced Rebecca. "Look, Mrs. Morland, let me say a few things. When my partner watched Mr. Taylor on television and the stuff on the insurance came up, it was the final nail for him, if you know what I mean? He's sure your husband took his own life."

Incredulous, Rebecca asked, "Even after someone tried to kill me?"

"He thinks you made that up along with the phone call." Solowski made a dismissive gesture. "As for the burglary, he thinks it was staged."

Rebecca experienced a sinking feeling. "About the insurance policy," she said, coloring slightly. "I'm really sorry. I didn't check into it right away as I promised you I would. I'd only found out about it myself a few days before that press conference. I should have called you."

Solowski nodded. "That's okay."

Rebecca's throat felt like it was closing up. "Do you feel the same way Walters does—that I staged everything?"

"No. I think you've raised some good points. And I don't like what happened to you on the canyon road. I really believe you could be in some kind of danger."

The tension inside Rebecca mounted as she waited for the detective to continue; clearly something else was bothering her. Solowski stopped pacing and faced Rebecca again. "Look, you ever tell anyone I said this, I'll deny it. Understood?"

The detective's discomfort was making Rebecca nervous too. "Yes. Whatever you say."

"You're a nice lady. I believe you when you say your husband wouldn't have killed himself." Solowski hooked her finger in her belt. "I'm just not sure what I can do about it."

Feeling that there was more, Rebecca remained silent.

Her expression grim, Solowski said, "Something's going on but I'm not sure what. It's strange that Walters is ignoring everything that's happened to you since your husband's death, that he's acting as if you'd made it up."

Rebecca's green eyes widened. "Are you saying that Walters may have an ulterior motive in all this?"

Solowski put up her hand as if to ward off Rebecca's words. "I'm not saying anything. I'm simply pointing out a few facts, and just between us, okay?"

"Of course," Rebecca quickly agreed.

"What I am getting at is this." Solowski paused. "If my husband was gone off the back of that boat, I'd sure pressure people to investigate his death, or I'd do it myself."

Rebecca felt her breath catch in her throat. "You think I'm right then—someone murdered Ryan?"

Solowski frowned. "I don't know. Things just don't add up. But like I said, we never talked, okay?"

Her warning made Rebecca shiver. Solowski was confirming her worst fears, her growing sense that there was a conspiracy to turn Ryan's murder into a suicide. "I promise—not a word."

"Good."

Rebecca's mind was racing as she said, "Can you give me any . . ."—she hesitated, before adding—"unofficial guidance on where you'd look if it were your husband?"

"You say lots of people have lied to you," Solowski said, making eye contact with Rebecca for the first time. "Start with your husband's partners. I spoke with that guy, John Evans. He claims he never told you he got in at six that morning. He says he went directly to the office after the yacht docked, in case the cops needed something. As for the note, he says he found it only a short while before he called us at eight."

With a sickening jolt, Rebecca realized someone had betrayed her trust. Other than Solowski, she'd told only Walters and Brandon about John's lie as to the time he'd arrived at the office. It had to have been Brandon. "I see," she finally managed to say. "Did you believe John?"

Solowski shook her head again. "Nope. If he got there at 1:43 A.M., he would have found the note earlier, and the idea of him waiting six hours to call us is bull. There's always someone on duty."

Rebecca sighed with relief. "Anything else you'd do?"

"Follow up your hunch on that Worthington guy and the others who are involved in the primary." Solowski shrugged her shoulders. "Just look at all the angles."

"I have, but I'll go over it all again." Rebecca clasped her hands together. "It means a lot to me that you believe me."

"Yeah. It's a real bitch, the spot you're in. Anyway, I got to go. Just remember, ma'am," she lowered her voice, "I've got two kids to support. You tell anyone what I've said and it could be curtains for my career."

Rebecca was double parked in the shadows when Gloria Powell came out of Taylor, Dennison & Evans on Rodeo Drive and headed for Wilshire Boulevard. Not wanting to be seen by anyone else, she waited until Gloria was halfway down the block before pulling alongside and honking her horn to attract the woman's attention.

At first, Gloria didn't notice her. Knowing Beverly Hills cops, I'll probably get a ticket, Rebecca thought wryly as she honked again. This time Gloria saw her and came over to the car.

"Mrs. Morland, is something wrong?" Her face had a worried expression on it.

"Hop in. And please call me Rebecca."

"I'm sorry." Gloria smiled sheepishly as she opened the car door and got in. "Old habits are hard to break."

Rebecca nodded, returning the smile. "I had a few more questions, so I thought I'd save you the long bus ride home."

Gloria turned around in her seat. "That's so nice of you Mrs. —I mean Rebecca. But you don't have to take me all that way. Just drop me off at the Crenshaw bus."

"I don't mind. Put your seat belt on."

"Oh, sure."

At the sound of the metal latch clicking into place, Rebecca spoke. "Gloria, is there any connection between Brandon Taylor and Maxwell Holmes besides the fact that he's supporting Mr. Taylor for the nomination? Is he a client of the firm or a friend of Mr. Taylor?"

"To my recollection, it's only a political relationship," Gloria said. "But I can check."

"I'd appreciate that." Rebecca stopped for the red light. "What about John Evans and Maxwell Holmes? Has John ever done any legal work for him?"

"I don't know. I'm not involved in Mr. Evans's day-to-day dealings." Gloria gazed at Rebecca. "Is something wrong?"

"I don't know," Rebecca admitted. "I've been trying to talk to everyone who was on the yacht the night that Ryan died. You know, to see if anyone saw or heard anything that could be important. When I called Maxwell Holmes to set up a time to talk, he invited me to his house." She then detailed how she'd seen John park his car and rush into the house.

Gloria's lips were pursed. "And you say his headlights were turned off?"

"Yes."

"That does seem strange to me."

"I thought so too," Rebecca nodded. "You know, when I spoke to John about the night Ryan disappeared, I asked him to explain an argument I had interrupted between Ryan and him." She paused. "He could have told me anything he wanted—after all, I'd only overheard their raised voices and not any particular words. Instead, he denied it had ever happened."

The office administrator's eyes opened wide with disbelief. "Sounds like he just out-and-out lied to you."

"Yes. It was very disturbing. After all, if he had nothing to hide, why lie?"

"That's true," Gloria said, a perplexed look on her face.

"It also tells me that the man is capable of lying about other things as well," Rebecca continued. "It might help me to find out more about John Evans. Do you think you could get me a copy of his résumé? I'd like to run a background check on him."

"I'll try. It should be in his personnel file." One finger over her mouth, Gloria said pensively, "You know, you might want to talk with his ex-wife. Sometimes you can learn a lot that way."

It was Rebecca's turn to be surprised. "I hadn't realized John was ever married."

"I don't recall him mentioning it to me either. But a Cindy Evans has telephoned the office several times. I know, because she's called collect and identified herself as his ex-wife."

With a quick peek in her side mirror, Rebecca changed lanes. "Did you speak to her?"

"Yes. Our receptionist can't accept collect calls without permission, and Mr. Evans was on another line, so I got on the phone. She told me who she was, and when he was done with his other call, I told him a Cindy Evans was waiting. He took the call immediately." Gloria took a deep breath. "I had barely gotten out of his office when I heard him start yelling at her."

An ex-wife might have a lot of information she'd be willing to share, Rebecca thought. "Do you know where she called from?"

Gloria looked thoughtful. "I think the operator said Costa Mesa."

"Could you get me her address or phone number?"

"Not her address," replied Gloria, shaking her head. "But the number from which collect calls are made should be recorded on our bill. I don't know if she was at home, or at a pay phone, but you can check out the number that shows up."

"That would be great." Rebecca felt her hopes rising. "I can't tell you how much I appreciate your help. And again, I promise not to say where I've gotten the information."

"I wish it could be different. But I'm not sure how the partners would feel about my helping you. And I do need my job."

"I know you do. Don't worry. It's not a problem for me," Rebecca assured her. "I've only mentioned—as you said I could —that you didn't see a note on Ryan's desk before you left the office on the night he disappeared."

Gloria nodded. "That's fine. By the way, I had a chance to check out that name you gave me. Earl Anders, I believe it was?"

"Yes?" Rebecca tried to hide her nervousness.

"I couldn't find his name in any of our files, so I don't believe he's a client." Gloria hesitated momentarily before adding, "What made you think that he was?"

"Oh, it was nothing." Chewing on her lip, Rebecca realized she was no closer to knowing who Earl Anders was than she'd been the day she'd found the bankbook with his name on it. Had Ryan had a secret life he'd kept hidden from her? No, she thought, shaking her head, it had to be something else. But what?

Rebecca had driven down to Newport Beach again, determined to find a way to get on the *Majorca* without the Worthingtons' knowledge. Of course, the captain, or whoever else was there, might not let her board the yacht without first telephoning the Worthingtons for permission. Unfortunately, that was a chance she'd have to take.

It was the middle of the week, and the Pacific Coast Highway, which had been so crowded that Sunday when she'd been here last, was now deserted. In early spring most of the beach towns were still empty during the week. She pulled her car into a large lot in front of a yacht brokerage. Inside, she inquired if anyone knew where she could rent a small boat to get out to a yacht. The salesman suggested she check out some of the marinas on the other side of the bay. For a few bucks one of the young people working on a boat might be willing to transport her in a dinghy.

Parking near one of the marinas, Rebecca noticed that the docks were all fenced in, with tall gates closing off each gangway down to the boats. She tried several of these gates but found them locked.

There were all kinds of boats there. Sailboats with their masts swaying in the wind. Powerboats with canvas covers buttoned up against the elements. A gentle breeze was blowing, and the ropes attached to the boats were making a squeaking noise as they pulled against the cleats on the docks floating in the water. The eerie sound gave the whole marina a deserted feeling. Rebecca saw several people, but she felt her chances of getting someone to help her would be best if she found a boat with only one person working on it.

Continuing along the outer edge of the fence, she spotted a young man, his blond hair whipped by the wind, washing down the deck of a powerboat that had to be at least fifty feet long. She called out to him.

He glanced up, startled. "Hi," he yelled back.

Smiling, she asked, "Could I talk to you for a minute?"

"I guess so," he said with a shrug. Putting down his brush, he approached the fence.

When he was facing her from behind the closed gate, she gave him her best smile. "Want to earn an easy fifty bucks?"

"That depends," he replied warily. "What do I have to do?"

"I want to get aboard a boat from the water and I need someone to take me to it."

The expression on his face darkened. "What do you want to do once you're aboard?"

"Just talk to some people," she said casually. "You see, one of the crew got a friend of mine pregnant. She's tried to reach him, but he won't call her back. I just have to deliver a message. I can't go through the owners of the boat because they're rich and kind of snobby, if you know what I mean."

The young man studied her face, then smiled and nodded. "I guess I could do it. Where is this boat, anyway?"

She waved her hand in the general direction of where she wanted to go. "Over there in front of a house on Harbor Island."

He squinted his light blue eyes at the sun as if he were thinking it over. "Yeah, okay. But I want the money first."

Ten minutes later, Rebecca was wishing she'd worn a warmer sweater as she hugged her cardigan around her and hunched lower on the wooden seat of the dinghy, trying to take advantage of the small windscreen. In spite of the cold, it was beautiful on the bay, and she wondered when she would be able to again enjoy all the things she used to take for granted.

They soon passed from the more commercial area over to the residential part of the bay. As for the many palatial homes facing the water, the overwhelming choice of architecture seemed to be Mediterranean, although she noted some traditional and contemporary styles too. The homes without lawns fronting on the water all had decks exquisitely landscaped with huge pots filled with trees and flowers bursting with color.

The young man, whose name was Dirk, seemed to know where he was going as he skillfully guided the boat through the bay and then under several small bridges. As they rounded a bend, he turned to her and gestured. "This is Harbor Island. Do you know the name of the boat or where exactly it's located?"

She nodded. "It's at the tip of the island, facing the bay. And it's called the *Majorca*."

His eyes opened wide. "Lady, that's not just a boat. The *Majorca* is an ocean-going yacht."

"It *is* pretty big," she admitted.

Soon he was bringing her alongside the yacht. Rebecca shivered involuntarily. For her, the boat had an evil presence, as if it were somehow responsible for her husband's death.

"Anybody here?" Dirk called out before she could stop him, his voice much louder than she would have liked.

A crewman stuck his head out of a window. "Yeah."

"I got a lady who wants to come aboard," explained Dirk. "Can you give me a hand?"

A second later, one of the crew Rebecca remembered from the night of the fund-raiser appeared on deck. She saw recognition register on his face. Her pulse racing, she waved. "May I come on board?"

He glanced around nervously as if unsure how to handle this situation. "Captain Henry isn't here at the moment."

"That's okay. I'd like to talk to you if I could." Rebecca gave him her most winning smile. "Just for a few minutes, okay?" She held her breath. Finally, the man exited through a doorway in the side of the boat and proceeded down a set of wooden stairs to the dock. When he reached for the rope Dirk was offering him, she gave a silent sigh of relief.

Rebecca stood, but before she left the dinghy, she spoke to Dirk. "You will wait for me, won't you?"

He squinted his eyes at her. "How long you gonna be?"

"Not more than thirty minutes." She quickly added, "I'll make it worth your while."

"Okay." He nodded.

She took the crewman's outstretched hand and hopped up onto the dock. In the meantime, another crew member appeared in the fishing cockpit and, from there, helped Dirk guide the dinghy around to the swim step, where they tied it off.

As Rebecca's eyes focused on the swim step, she suddenly realized that Ryan had met his end off that small wooden platform. An overwhelming sense of loneliness and pain shuddered through her, and for a moment she was afraid she might be ill.

"Are you okay?"

Rebecca started. Trembling, she forced the painful thoughts from her head and accompanied the young man up the wooden stairs and onto the deck. Out of the corner of her eye she glanced over at the large house. It was quite a distance away, too far to tell if anyone was watching. Feeling uneasy, she turned to her guide. "Can we go inside out of the sun?"

The man led her into the salon. It appeared even bigger to her than she'd remembered, probably because it wasn't filled with people and tables as it had been on the night of the party.

"I'm Rebecca Morland. I'm sorry. If I learned your name the night my husband disappeared, I don't remember it."

"It's Bob." He stood ramrod straight and ill at ease.

She'd already learned from the sheriff's reports that none of the crew members had seen anything unusual that night. One of them said he'd shown her husband the way to the cockpit. That had to be the man who'd spoken to Ryan in her presence. Another one had observed Ryan headed that way.

"Were you the crew member who saw my husband going toward the cockpit the night he disappeared?"

"No," Bob said, shaking his head. "That was Hal."

Rebecca's eyes held his. "Is Hal on board? I'd like to talk to him."

"I believe so. Let me go find him."

A few minutes later another crewman entered the salon. He smiled hesitantly. "Hi, I'm Hal."

Returning his smile, she made her voice friendly. "They say you saw my husband on his way to the fishing cockpit that night?"

"Yes," he replied, his clear brown eyes fixed on her.

"Do you remember where you saw him?"

The young man thrust his hands into the pockets of his white ducks. "He was in the lower passageway, heading toward the cockpit. I passed him going in the opposite direction."

Rebecca realized that this man must have seen Ryan shortly after he'd left her. "Go on," she urged.

"He stopped to ask if he was headed in the right direction for the cockpit. I told him to keep going and that he'd come to a door at the very end."

"Was anyone else around?"

"Not that I could see."

"Do you recall what time it was?"

"I think it was shortly before the buffet was served. We'd been out of the breakwater about thirty minutes."

"Was my husband walking unsteadily, or was there anything else you noticed that suggested he'd been drinking?"

"No," Hal replied, meeting her gaze without blinking. "He seemed perfectly okay to me."

Her eyes opened wide in surprise. His answer supported her impression of Ryan's behavior. "Did either of the detectives ask you about Mr. Morland's condition that night?"

The man squinted as if he were trying to recall. "No. I don't think so."

Aha, she thought, a feeling of excitement building. "Do you remember which of the two detectives questioned you?"

Hal nodded solemnly. "The male detective, ma'am."

Goose bumps rose on her arms. So Walters hadn't even bothered to ask the damn question. That's because he'd already decided on the answer he wanted to hear. He'd then written his report in such a way that no one had noticed his omission. "And that was the last time you saw my husband that evening?"

"Yes, ma'am."

"As you continued in the passageway, did you see anyone else proceeding in the opposite direction?"

"No."

"Is there another way to get to the cockpit?"

"Just from the water," he replied.

"I see. Was anyone on the ship that night who wasn't on the guest list? I mean besides the crew or the serving staff?"

"Not that I know of." His face scrunched up. "A security detail came aboard before any of the guests arrived; they went through the ship checking out everything."

"I didn't realize that." She found this new piece of information interesting. "Do you know who they worked for?"

"No. I don't."

"I'd like to refresh my memory. Could you just show me the path my husband took that night, to the cockpit?"

Hal stiffened as if uncomfortable with her request.

"I just want to see it—that's all," she explained. "Shouldn't take more than a minute."

With a sigh, he agreed. "I guess that will be okay, ma'am."

Down below, Rebecca was overcome by a momentary wave of nausea. What had been on Ryan's mind as he'd walked down this passage? Concentrate on the job at hand, she admonished herself.

Thinking she heard footsteps behind her, Rebecca whirled around to detect a young, dark-haired Hispanic man standing behind her with a startled expression on his face, as if he'd been caught doing something wrong. Before she could utter a word, he quickly scurried off in the opposite direction.

"Who was that?" she asked, gesturing after him.

"Only Juan—the cook's helper," Hal responded. "He was in the kitchen during the party. He wouldn't have seen any of the guests."

"Oh." She wondered why Juan had been following them.

In front of the door to the cockpit, Rebecca hesitated. She didn't want to risk being seen from the Worthingtons' house. Also, she was afraid to face any more painful memories. Her main purpose had been accomplished. She'd merely wanted to judge the distance from the middle deck to the cockpit and determine the approximate time it took to walk it.

"This is far enough," she told him. "Let's go back the way we came."

In the library of their mansion, Diana Worthington, her husband, Paul, and Clay Zalian, their newly hired campaign manager, were sharing an afternoon cocktail.

"I believe your chances are good and getting better every day," Clay said, nodding his head confidently. "My latest figures show you're gaining and Brandon Taylor is slipping. We just have to keep up our negative messages."

"Shouldn't we also be issuing some positive messages about what Paul hopes to accomplish?" asked Diana. She didn't like the tenor of the television spots they were currently running.

"We've got a bunch of those in the works." Clay leaned over, grabbed another canapé from the silver tray, and stuffed it whole into his mouth. "Delicious. Absolutely delicious. As I was saying, first we wanted to knock a few percentage points off Taylor's lead. You know, just enough to get them worried and to give us something to show the big boys, the ones Paul's going to need if he wants to lock this thing up."

"Still—" she began.

"Clay knows what he's doing, dear," Paul interrupted, coming to his manager's defense.

A smile of appreciation twisted the corners of Clay's thick lips. "Personally, we couldn't have hired a better public relations person than that Morland woman. She's stirring things up pretty damn good." He turned to Worthington. "I don't understand why you won't let me run with this murder theory of hers. I can plant some doozies that will make Taylor look like Jack the Ripper."

Worthington shook his head. "No. That kind of thing has a double edge to it. I don't want Brandon Taylor's camp throwing it back in my face, especially since Ryan's death already looks like it has been good for me."

"Hell, you can't help that." Clay beamed.

Diana tried to hide her revulsion for this man.

"I'd rather stick to the suicide angle," Worthington said. "I like the way it sounds. Young, idealistic attorney is sickened by something having to do with his mentor. Torn by guilt over what to do, he throws himself into the ocean. Let's keep playing that angle since it seems to be working."

Clay turned to Diana as if looking for support from her.

"I agree," she said nervously. "We must not give any credence to a murder theory. Although from my perspective, there's nothing wrong with it being an accident."

"It was not an accident," Paul retorted, glaring at her. "His death was a suicide—end of story."

Her hand fluttered to her neck, the jingling of her bracelet breaking the silence. "Paul and I both firmly believe that young lawyer killed himself," she told Clay.

"Fine." Clay leaned over for another canapé, which he proceeded to wash down with a swig of his bourbon. "By the way, one of the political honchos supporting Taylor isn't crazy about him. While you may be a drop too conservative for his taste, I think the man can be swayed."

"Who are you talking about?" Paul asked.

"Maxwell Holmes," Clay replied.

Diana felt her stomach drop and the blood rush to her face. She prayed Paul wouldn't notice.

Worthington frowned. "Why do we need him?"

"I've been told a lot of powerful people owe Holmes favors. He's a good man to have on your side. So far, what I know has only been reported to me by some hired guns. But I'd like your permission to approach Holmes on your behalf."

"I know he's served on several different commissions, but besides that, what else does he do?" asked Worthington.

"He says he makes his money in real estate. But I hear he has many ways of raking in the dollars." Clay chuckled.

All during their exchange, Diana felt as if she were holding her breath. She wanted to tell Paul to forget it, but she was afraid to trust her voice. It was her damn libido that had gotten her into this situation with Holmes, a situation that could destroy her marriage if Paul were ever to find out. The further removed Maxwell Holmes stayed from her husband's campaign, the better she'd feel.

After clearing her throat, she ventured, "I've heard that Maxwell Holmes is a moderate. I think we should only court the more conservative Republicans for now. After all, a lot of Paul's supporters might not want Holmes with us."

Paul glanced at her curiously. "Diana's got a good point there. Let's keep his name on the back burner. While we're getting rolling, I believe we should be identified with the conservative element. Later, when we have their support, we can expand under the guise that we're offering an olive branch to the other factions of the party."

"Okay." Clay slapped his thigh. "Sounds like a good plan."

Sipping her drink, Diana willed her breathing to return to normal.

The houseman came in to tell Paul he had another call. He picked up the phone and spoke to someone; then, as he listened, his face darkened. Hanging up, he turned to Clay. "Why don't you use the phone on the desk to make those calls we talked about? I've got something to check on. I'll be back shortly."

"Where are you going, darling?" Diana asked, going over to his side.

"Down to the boat," he responded. "I need to take care of something."

CHAPTER
EIGHTEEN

Detective Walters pulled his car over by the side of a building and got out. Glancing quickly around the deserted area, which was in an industrial section of downtown L.A., he waited until a nondescript four-door sedan came into view.

When the car pulled alongside him and stopped, he climbed into the backseat. The sheriff of L.A. County, Roland Quentin, moved his bulky frame over to make room for the other man.

"Hello Walters," Quentin said. "Beautiful day, isn't it?"

"Sure is, Sheriff," Walters replied, feeling slightly uneasy. The sheriff was a mercurial man, and Walters never knew in what mood he'd find him. For the most part though, they got along fine.

Sheriff Quentin put his hand on the driver's shoulder. "Get lost for about ten minutes."

The deputy got out of the car and walked away.

"I had a visit last night from a friend," Quentin stated. "I promised him an up-to-date report on the investigation into Morland's death."

"We're moving along," Walters assured him. "I would have had it closed by now, but Mrs. Morland keeps feeding her dumb theories to the media."

"Well, I have some news for you that should make it easier to wrap up."

"What's that?" asked Walters, thinking he could use some good news. The situation with Solowski was driving him crazy.

Sheriff Quentin cleared his throat and gave a small chuckle. "It seems our young attorney, Ryan Morland, was dipping his hand into the cookie jar at the Taylor law firm."

A loud whistle escaped through Walters's teeth. "You're kidding?" He looked at his boss for confirmation.

The sheriff shook his head. "Nope. Got it from an unimpeachable source."

"Wasn't the Morland guy a partner in that firm?" Walters asked, a puzzled frown on his face.

"Yup." The other man nodded.

"So if the guy was still alive, we probably wouldn't get involved, right?" queried Walters. "We usually leave money disputes between partners to the civil courts."

"We probably wouldn't. Except in this case we might have, because Morland wasn't a partner the whole time he was taking the money. If he had been caught stealing while he was just an employee, he could have been charged with theft. Anyway, we now have a motive for Morland's suicide."

Walters rubbed his chin. "Why didn't the partners tell us about this sooner?"

"Apparently they weren't sure until just recently. According to what I was told, there was a cash-flow problem. So they started taking a good, hard look at their books. There's hundreds of thousands of dollars that's missing."

Walters whistled again. "That's not chicken feed."

"Nope, it isn't."

"Shit!" Walters couldn't believe this turn of events. "Why would a lawyer in a fancy law firm have to steal—I thought those guys made a fortune?"

"Who cares?" Quentin responded. "All I know is that we

have a reason this guy jumped. It should be a cinch to close the investigation now. Morland stole from the firm, realized they were about to discover it, and took the easy way out."

"Yep," said Walters, rubbing his chin again. "By the way, did the wife have any idea of what he was up to?"

"My information is that she was told about it right after her husband died."

"Wow," said Walters, his pulse starting to race. "Wait till Solowski hears that."

There was a look of concern on the sheriff's round face. "Is your partner still having her doubts?"

"It seemed that way for a while," Walters said evasively.

The sheriff shook his head. "Women. Pull rank on her if you have to—but let's get this case closed."

"I don't anticipate any more problems from her. Certainly not with the information you've just given me."

"I hope not." The sheriff brooded. "I've had more than a few reservations about that woman."

"I'll handle her," Walters promised.

"Now if that Morland woman goes to the press, the picture might change," the sheriff warned him.

Eyes narrowed, Walters turned toward his boss. "How's that?"

"After Brandon Taylor made that statement on television no one would be too surprised if something happened to her." Quentin's smile showed little pointed teeth. "I mean an unstable woman who can't accept her husband's death might do all kinds of crazy things." His eyes remained fixed on Walters as he shrugged his bulky shoulders.

"Right," Walters said, nodding his head in comprehension. "And all we would need is some muckety-muck shrink to explain it to the press."

"I take it you agree that this information is good?"

"It should do what we want," Walters agreed. "With your permission, I'll arrange for my usual leaks to the media. Then in a few days, I'll announce that we've determined that Ryan Morland's death was a suicide."

"That's exactly what I want to see," Quentin told Walters with a knowing grin.

A few minutes later, as he watched his boss being driven away, Walters thought how glad he'd be when he was rid of this whole Morland mess. Solowski was sticking her neck out a mile, completely ignoring his warnings and making his life difficult. If it had been anyone else but Randy's widow, she would have been long gone. He'd done all he could to help her. But he wouldn't be able to protect her if she stepped over the line again.

Rebecca almost fell back when she came up the spiral staircase of the yacht and found herself facing Paul Worthington.

"What do you think you're doing?" he demanded, as he menacingly leaned toward her.

Heart racing, she quickly searched for a plausible answer. "I had to see your boat again," she explained, swallowing hard and regaining a measure of control. "I'm sure it's hard for you to understand, but this is where I last saw my husband." She stuck her chin out defiantly. "If you knew anything about how the mind struggles to deal with the loss of a loved one, you'd understand."

The words seemed to catch him off guard. Eyes narrowed, he turned to the young crewman Rebecca had first encountered. "Didn't you say she was asking questions?"

The other man nodded, a glint of fear in his eyes.

It was clear to Rebecca that the crew had called him. "I don't know why you're turning this into such a big deal," she said, keeping her voice even. "As I said, I merely wanted to see the boat again and ask the crew if they remembered anything unusual—that's all."

"I don't take kindly to people who ignore my wishes and trespass on my property," he replied with a stony gaze. "I could have you arrested if I wanted to."

"The last time I read the law on the subject, one can't be trespassing if they request permission and it's granted. I asked before I came aboard."

"Don't argue the fine points of the law with me," he retorted arrogantly. "I've done a lot of business over the years with Orange County officials, and if you're wondering which one of us they'll believe, I'll win hands down."

He was so sure of his own power, thought Rebecca, that he was actually bragging to her that he had law enforcement connections. There was only one reason Worthington was determined to keep her off his boat—he had something to hide.

A flash of anger welled up in her. "Call your lackeys!" she said, staring him squarely in the eye. "I can't wait to see the morning papers: WIDOW OF MAN WHO DROWNED OFF WORTHINGTON YACHT THROWN IN JAIL FOR WANTING TO SEE BOAT! I love it." She laughed. "Being cruel to a helpless widow will look especially good for a political candidate." Hands on her hips, she added, "Go ahead, call them. I dare you to!"

Worthington's eyes blazed with anger, and for one crazy second she thought he was going to strike her.

"You are as stubborn as your husband!" He stiffened immediately, almost recoiling, as if realizing his gaffe.

Triumph flooded through her. She had at last goaded him into losing control. "So—you're finally admitting that you and Ryan had an argument?"

"I've said no such thing," Worthington countered. "I was merely making a comment based upon what others have told me." He marched over to the railing and looked below. "Is that the boat she arrived on?"

"Yes sir," the young crewman responded. He was gazing at Rebecca apologetically as if trying to beg her forgiveness while at the same time fearful his boss might catch him being nice to her.

She nodded her head to convey she understood.

Worthington made a big show of pointing to his gold Rolex watch. "I'll give you exactly one minute to get off my property."

"I'll go," she told him, "but not before I tell you how I feel. I wasn't sure before this childish temper tantrum on your part. But now I'm firmly convinced that you and my husband argued about something that was important, and certainly important to you. What did he find out that had you so freaked out?"

"You're clutching at straws," he said icily, glowering at her. "I've got nothing to hide."

She flashed him a smile filled with contempt. "Just remember, if *he* found it, I'm sure *I* can too."

Still glowering at her, Worthington said nothing more as Rebecca walked down the wooden stairway to the dock and then stepped into the waiting dinghy that Dirk was holding for her.

Solowski stood by her desk at the station in total disbelief as Walters told her what he'd learned concerning Ryan Morland.

"You say the partners discovered this theft and had already spoken to Mrs. Morland about it?"

"Yep." He nodded, a smug smile on his face. "I just got off the phone. I insisted on talking to all three of them. Taylor, Dennison, and Evans all personally confirmed that Ryan Morland took the money."

She was grasping for something—anything—to make sense out of this. "Who first told you about this?"

"One of my sources," he said with a nonchalant shrug.

Solowski looked at him askance. Walters often came up with information out of nowhere. Just who were his mysterious sources? she wondered. "I can't understand why Mrs. Morland didn't say something to me about it," she muttered under her breath, stunned by this news.

"I'll tell you why she didn't mention it," he retorted. "Because she's a fucking liar, that's why. The lady pegged you for a soft touch from the night that man disappeared. She's made a patsy out of you, Solowski. If you'd get down off your grieving-widow platform, you'd see I'm right."

The phone rang, and while Walters answered it, she sat down. Feeling sick to her stomach, Solowski frantically searched her mind for answers. When Mrs. Morland had begged for her help, Solowski had been sure the woman had opened up her heart and told her everything. She'd really believed her and felt sorry for her, because she, too, had lost her husband. Had she been blindsided as Walters was claiming? Had Rebecca Morland merely been using her?

When he got off the phone, Walters turned to her. "I'm still waiting to hear what you've got to say for your Mrs. Morland now," he said in a jeering tone of voice.

She couldn't meet his gaze—not when she was feeling so betrayed. The thought that she'd been putting her entire career on the line for a woman who had been using her made Solowski sick. She felt guilty when she realized how much her kids could have suffered because of her stupidity.

It was too warm in the room, and Solowski felt like she needed to go somewhere to think this whole mess through. Grabbing her purse, she mumbled something about a doctor's appointment for one of the kids. "I'll call you later," she promised her partner as she rushed from the room.

By the time Rebecca got back to the marina, her trembling had subsided. Now she was convinced that Worthington knew more about her husband's murder than he was letting on. Briefly, she considered going straight to the sheriff's station in Marina del Rey. But what could she really prove? The fact that Worthington wouldn't allow her to question his crew was no proof that he was part of a conspiracy to kill her husband.

Just keep following up on all your leads, she cautioned herself. See if a pattern of some kind emerges connecting all the people who are not telling the truth. She recalled Gloria's saying that John's ex-wife lived in Costa Mesa. While she was out here in Orange County, she should try to talk to her too.

Calling Information, Rebecca got an address for Cindy Evans. Costa Mesa was inland from Newport Beach, and whereas Newport was a haven for the rich, Costa Mesa was more of a middle-class town.

Fifteen minutes later, Rebecca pulled up to an apartment complex on a quiet, somewhat run-down street. There was no security gate around the perimeter and she was able to traverse the pathway that ran between two identical, green-painted buildings, looking for number eight.

After Rebecca rang the bell, the door squeaked open and a skinny girl peeked out. She appeared young. Her brown hair was worn in a scraggly ponytail, and wisps fell carelessly around her face.

"Are you Cindy Evans, John's ex-wife?" Rebecca asked.

"What if I am?" Her hands were on her hips.

"My husband, Ryan Morland, was his law partner. Could I talk to you for a few minutes? It's important."

"Yeah. I suppose." Cindy unlatched the screen door.

Rebecca walked into a dismally small apartment. There was a dilapidated sofa in the corner, and a television was playing loudly. It was one of those combination living room/dining room layouts so common in California apartments.

"Sorry . . . about your husband." The young woman spoke awkwardly, as if not sure of the proper thing to say.

With a little nod, Rebecca said, "Thank you."

"Here, sit down on the couch." Cindy picked up some papers and books and dropped them on the worn floor to make room for Rebecca. "I'm going to school—studying to be a nurse. I was doing my homework," she explained.

"You're so young." Rebecca was having a hard time believing that this woman had been married to John Evans. "I was expecting someone older."

"Oh." Cindy blushed, touching her face self-consciously. "When I put makeup on, I look older." She pulled a chair away from the dining room table and sat on it.

There was an uncomfortable silence before Rebecca plunged in. "I came to see you, Cindy, because I need your help."

"You need help!" Two deep lines of worry appeared between Cindy's eyes as she sighed with exasperation. "Lady, John owes me a bundle. I was hoping maybe you could help me!"

Rebecca was stunned by the young woman's outburst. "How much does he owe you?"

"Over fifty big ones."

"Fifty thousand dollars?" Rebecca asked, her pulse quickening.

"Yeah," said Cindy.

"That *is* a lot of money. How did it get to be so much?"

"We had a small house when we were married. After we sold it, John cashed the check and took my share." Another sigh of exasperation escaped her lips. "He owes me my half plus two years of support, because I worked like a slave to put him through law school. I wouldn't be living in a dump like this if he'd just pay me what I've got coming." Cindy jumped up and nervously began straightening things on top of the table as if that would make the place look better.

"Does he send you any money at all?" Rebecca prodded, wondering what on earth John did with his earnings.

"Not in a long while," Cindy admitted, a dejected expression on her face. "He keeps telling me things at the office will be changing soon and he'll be getting some huge bonuses." Her blue eyes were guileless. "Do you know when any of this is supposed to happen?"

"I'm sorry. I don't."

A look of anger caused Cindy's eyes to narrow. "Damn. It better not be more of his usual bullshit!"

With a sense of dread, Rebecca asked, "What do you mean?"

"His gambling."

"Gambling?" She stared at Cindy blankly.

"Yeah, it's a big problem with him. That's what caused our divorce."

"Oh," said Rebecca. "I didn't realize John gambled."

"He kept promising to change, but he didn't." Cindy nodded her head as if discouraged and then slumped back down in her chair. "When I couldn't take it any longer, I left. By that time we owed so many people money it was a joke. After our divorce came through I had to file for bankruptcy."

"I'm so sorry." Rebecca wasn't sure what else to say. This was not the kind of thing she'd expected to hear. Then something occurred to her. "Did John's uncle know about his gambling?"

"Yeah," said Cindy. "He took John into the firm because John said if he had a really good job that paid decent money, he wouldn't gamble anymore and that he'd also be able to pay off his debts."

"Did he even try?"

"I think he did at first," Cindy acknowledged. "But as they say at Gamblers Anonymous, it's a hard thing to give up."

"Do you know John's uncle, Brandon Taylor?"

"No. But John sure did talk about him a lot. Just recently John called to brag that he was going to be taking over all of his uncle's cases and even his office when his uncle left for Washington and that I should have stuck it out with him."

Rebecca fleetingly wondered if Catherine knew about John's plan. "Do you have any idea how much money John owes besides the fifty thousand to you?"

"Nope. But it's easily hundreds of thousands of dollars. Maybe more." Cindy's thin shoulders drooped. "He's crazy when it comes to gambling. According to him, his next big hit is always right around the corner."

A rush of excitement surged through Rebecca. Most likely she'd just stumbled onto who had really taken that money from the firm. "What else did John say about the law firm?"

"Sometimes he liked to brag about all the famous clients and stuff. You know, to make me feel bad because I'd left him. Mostly, he just complained about the shit work they made him do." She stopped and gazed directly at Rebecca. "You think you can help me get some money? Lately, I'm barely managing."

"Unfortunately I'm having some problems of my own," Rebecca admitted ruefully. "Not only with John and Brandon Taylor, but with Catherine Dennison too."

"John talked about her a lot." Cindy gave her a knowing look. "He said Catherine was a real c-u-n-t."

Rebecca had no way to respond to that remark, so she ignored it. "Did John ever mention my husband, Ryan, to you?"

Cindy peered down at her feet as if deciding whether or not she wanted to repeat anything. "Well, he did say Mr. Morland was a stuck-up asshole."

Never having heard Ryan described that way before, Rebecca was startled. "Anything else?"

"Naw. Just stuff like that."

Rebecca forced herself to concentrate on her reasons for coming here. "Did John ever speak to you about a Paul Worthington or a Maxwell Holmes?"

Cindy looked pensive. "No. I don't think so."

It seemed that she had gotten all the information the young

woman had. Digging around in her purse for a card, Rebecca found one and wrote her home number on the back. "Thanks for your time, Cindy," she said, getting up to leave. "If you remember anything else, could you call me?"

"I guess," Cindy replied tentatively, and then added, "Can you see about getting me some of my money?" Tears had welled up in her eyes. "I'm getting desperate."

"I can try," Rebecca offered, "but I doubt that John will listen to me."

"Shoot." Cindy brushed away a tear. "I got a tuition payment coming up and everything."

Rebecca took a hesitant step forward. "One more thing. Have you ever known John to be violent? Did he lose his temper very often?"

Cindy nodded. "What guy doesn't? Sure, he got mad."

"Did he ever hit you?" Rebecca watched the other woman's face carefully.

Shrugging, Cindy gazed down at her feet again. "I don't want to talk about it."

Her mind racing, Rebecca wondered if a man who hit his wife was also capable of cold premeditated murder. The statistics certainly suggested that he was. "Did you ever hear John threaten to kill someone?"

The young woman seemed confused. "Everybody gets mad like that sometimes, I guess."

Rebecca stared directly into Cindy's eyes. "Did he ever say anything like that about my husband?"

Cindy appeared puzzled.

"I'm just trying to find out if John ever said anything that made you think he'd like to see my husband . . . out of the way."

"He told me once that he wished he could get rid of both your husband and Catherine, if that's what you mean. After all, the firm was started by his uncle, and John felt both Mr. Morland and Catherine were trying to take over and push him out. You can understand how he felt, can't you?"

She didn't reply but merely shrugged her shoulders. "Well, thanks again."

As she drove back to L.A., Rebecca wondered how Catherine would feel when she learned that she was next on John's hit list. When John had told her how angry Catherine had been at Ryan, had he merely been trying to shift any suspicions Rebecca might have away from himself and onto someone else? If so, it was possible that everything he said about Catherine and Ryan's relationship had been nothing more than a calculated lie. While that possibility certainly made her feel better about Catherine, it did nothing to abate her growing suspicion that John had somehow been involved in her husband's death.

CHAPTER
NINETEEN

Rebecca glanced down at the piece of paper in her hand and up again at the dilapidated duplex in front of her, checking to make sure she had the right address. The numbers matched. She was surprised. Somehow she'd expected John to live in a nicer place. Perhaps it was one of those buildings that was only fixed up on the inside. The area itself wasn't bad—off Olympic Boulevard near La Cienega in one of L.A.'s middle-class neighborhoods. Most of the residences were well tended, with nice yards.

She rang the bell and waited, recalling what Cindy had said and wondering if John's gambling was the reason he lived like this.

After two more rings, someone called out. "Who is it?"

Rebecca recognized John's voice but wondered why he sounded frightened. "Rebecca Morland," she responded.

The door flew open and he glared at her. "What are you doing here?"

"I'd like to talk to you," she said in a matter-of-fact tone of voice.

"Showing up unexpectedly is a really bad habit of yours," he grumbled. "Why can't you call and make an appointment like a normal person?"

"Because what happened to my husband isn't a normal thing," she said, pushing by him into the foyer.

"Hey, what do you think you're doing?" Quickly, John stuck his head out the doorway as if to peer up the street before closing the door behind them.

"Were you expecting someone?" she asked, looking at him quizzically.

"Uh, yeah," he said, then changed his mind. "No. Never mind."

She took a few more steps until she was facing a small living room. Rebecca was astonished to see that instead of drapes, sheets were tacked up over the windows, and the furniture looked like it had come from the Salvation Army.

"What is this about?" John asked warily.

"Aren't you going to invite me to sit down?"

He gestured to one of the chairs. "Now why don't you tell me why you're here?"

"I've uncovered some interesting information," Rebecca told him.

"What?" he asked, watching her carefully.

"First of all, I learned that you were once married."

John flushed. "How did you find out?"

"Oh—I have my ways."

"Well, now you can understand why I live in a dump like this," he said bitterly. "I had a lot of bills to take care of. The divorce totally cleaned me out, and I'm still paying through the nose." He started to pace.

"That's a lie. I happen to have had a nice visit with your ex-wife, Cindy." Her tone was sarcastic.

When John turned around there was an alarmed expression on his face.

"She says you still owe her over fifty thousand bucks." Rebecca's eyes were riveted on him. "She's even been forced to declare bankruptcy."

"She's full of—" he started to say.

Rebecca cut in. "She also said you're a gambler who owes big sums of money to some very disreputable people. The kind of guys who"—she arched her eyebrows—"would think nothing of breaking your kneecaps!"

John had turned crimson, and a fine line of perspiration formed on his forehead. "My ex-wife hates me. She'd say anything to make me look bad."

Standing up, Rebecca continued in an accusatory voice. "I think you're the one who stole the money from the firm. Then you pushed my husband off that boat and framed him to take the rap."

"No," he shook his head emphatically. "That's not true."

"Why did you kill him? Because he found out what you were doing and you needed to keep him from telling? Or was it because you were afraid if you merely framed him and he proclaimed his innocence they'd believe him instead of you?"

"This is total nonsense," he protested angrily.

"Did you hate Ryan that much?" she persisted, her voice rising to a shrill pitch.

"You're crazy," John declared, backing away from her. "Your husband killed himself. You just can't accept that fact."

"No," she said, her eyes blazing at him. "You were so jealous of Ryan that it was eating you up inside. According to Cindy, you planned to be taking over most of your uncle's cases and earning much bigger bonuses. You even told her you'd be moving into Brandon's office. Did you feel with Ryan around, you were being held back? Is that why you killed him?" Not giving him a chance to respond, she pushed on. "How long had you been planning to get rid of my husband?"

"Rebecca, you don't know what you're saying." John straightened up to his full height and seemed to regain some of his previous arrogance. "I think your husband's death has unhinged you mentally."

She ignored his remarks. "Do you deny you hated Ryan?"

"I've told you before, I resented him. Both he and Catherine usurped my rightful place in my uncle's firm. But that doesn't mean I'd kill anyone," he announced, shaking his head emphatically. "You're behaving in a totally irrational manner."

Rebecca took a deep breath and continued. "Are you saying you're not a gambler?"

"No." He looked down. "I admit I had a problem at one time. But it's been under control for quite a while."

"Then why are you living like this?" she shot back.

"I told you, I've had a lot of bills." His chin rose noticeably as he added, "I'm buying an incredible condominium on Wilshire Boulevard in the near future."

"With money from bonuses on cases that belonged to Ryan?"

His eyes narrowed to slits. "Someone had to take them over. Anyway, this is all speculation on your part. You have no proof of anything."

"You were lying about Ryan and Catherine and everything you told me about them, weren't you?"

A smug smile settled around his mouth. "Is that what this is all about?" He shook his head again, grinning now. "No. I was definitely telling the truth."

She had such an overwhelming urge to push him that it was frightening to her. Her mind was reeling. How did John and the money fit in with Worthington and whatever secret he was trying to hide? And what did John have to do with Holmes? She wanted to ask him about that as well, but held off. It was all so confusing.

"Would you please leave now? I've nothing more to say to you." His mouth was pursed.

"Fine," she replied through gritted teeth. "As I told you before, I intend to find out why you're lying to me and what really happened to the missing money. And when I do, you had better watch out."

Without waiting for his reply, she stalked to the front door, opened it, then slammed it behind her with all her strength.

The next morning, Rebecca felt dejected as she pulled out of the parking lot of the Century Hills Bank. Earlier, after rummaging through a box filled with pictures and mementos that Ryan and she had accumulated during their three years together, she had finally found a group picture taken at a picnic his firm had held for its staff and attorneys.

Armed with that photograph and the bankbook she'd discovered in Ryan's briefcase, she'd marched into the bank with a story that she was trying to locate the owner of an account who had come to her office seeking advice and who had left the bankbook behind.

However, just as she'd feared, the bank officers told her they couldn't give her any information about the person who'd opened the bank account unless she had a court order or a power of attorney document authorizing them to do so.

She'd tried to get one of the officers to look at the picture and see if he recognized the person who had opened that account, but he also refused to do that.

Rebecca realized that the time might have come for her to show the bankbook to the partners at the law firm—but the thought made her flesh crawl. If John had something to do with the missing money, he'd only deny having any knowledge of the bankbook. She debated whether to mention it to Brandon privately—and quickly rejected that idea. She couldn't trust him to tell her the truth. No. She had to come up with another way of finding out who had opened this bank account and why.

Lucy was sitting on the front steps of the house when Rebecca drove up. She helped Rebecca unload the grocery bags from the trunk and, as they walked to the front door, Rebecca told her what had happened at the bank.

Inside the house, Rebecca headed for the kitchen and proceeded to put her groceries away.

"I'm glad to see you finally broke down and went to the market," Lucy teased.

"I had to," Rebecca said with a shrug. "I ran out of coffee." She glanced at her watch. "You're here earlier than I expected. What happened at Zoe Olin's?" After Rebecca's unsuccessful attempt at getting the bookkeeper to talk to her, Lucy had suggested that she visit Zoe on Rebecca's behalf.

There was a hangdog expression on Lucy's face. "I wish I had some good news to report, but I don't."

Rebecca's heart sank. "What did she say?"

"Nothing. She wasn't there."

"You mean she didn't answer the bell?"

Lucy was busy washing the coffeepot. "No. I mean she's gone."

Rebecca stared at her friend in disbelief. "Gone, as in moved out?"

Lucy nodded. "According to the manager, it happened two days ago, in the middle of the night. She didn't even pay her rent —stiffed him for it."

"Did he have any information on her, like where she banked or a forwarding address?" Rebecca asked, unwilling to give up.

"Nada," said Lucy. She pointed to the can of coffee and Rebecca handed it over. "According to the manager, she paid her rent in cash and usually late, that's why he hadn't been overly concerned. He mentioned how strange it was that she never seemed to go anyplace or do anything—just stayed in the apartment all the time."

Feeling like the air had been knocked out of her, Rebecca sat down at the table. "Damn. I was counting on Zoe's talking to us."

Lucy opened the can of coffee. "I know. I wonder if the partners have any idea of where she's gone? If she's on administrative leave, she must be getting paid."

"Yeah. But if John was reluctant to share information with us before, now that I've called him a murderer . . ." Rebecca's voice trailed off.

"What a weird partnership Ryan got himself involved in," said Lucy, getting down the cups.

Rebecca agreed. "Since the night Ryan disappeared, they've put roadblock after roadblock in my way."

"Well, John and Brandon have made their positions clear, but what about Catherine? She wasn't that bad when you went to see her, was she?"

"For Catherine, she was okay," Rebecca said with a rueful smile.

"Why not try talking to her?" There was an inquiring look on Lucy's face.

"I guess I could try and speak to her at home."

"Do you know where she lives?"

"Yeah. She's got a place in Manhattan Beach. We went to a dinner there once. The problem is, she works such long, crazy hours, I have no idea what time she gets home."

Lucy finished preparing the coffee and turned the switch on. "How about catching her before work?"

"That's an idea. I think she jogs in the morning. I could get there really early." Suddenly feeling weary, Rebecca sighed.

"Don't worry. Things will work out."

Rebecca nodded and glanced at her watch. "We better take a look at the papers you've brought for me to review."

"By the way," Lucy said gently, "Trudy asked me how you were doing, and I didn't know what to tell her."

"I'm behind in the things I promised to do. But it's taking all my time looking for Ryan's killer." Rebecca bit her lip. "I may have to tell Trudy to find someone else."

"I'm sure she'll understand," Lucy said in a sad voice. "I doubt anyone at the clinic knows the whole story, but they read the newspapers and have some idea of what you're up against." She smiled. "Everyone always sends their love when they know I'm coming to see you."

"Please tell them I appreciate the support," Rebecca told her. She felt terrible that she had to disappoint Trudy as well as her clients; however, finding out the truth about Ryan's death had to take priority now. She couldn't let his killers get away with his murder. It was unthinkable, and she'd never forgive herself.

Although Detective Solowski had told Rebecca that Detective Walters had washed his hands of her and that she should try and pursue the investigation herself, Rebecca still felt she needed to tell Solowski certain things. She'd placed several calls to the woman but, so far, she hadn't heard back.

Not knowing how else to contact her, Rebecca decided to

drop in at the station again. Maybe she could get Solowski to take a walk with her so they could talk alone for a few minutes, away from the scrutiny of Walters. If Solowski couldn't manage that, she would at least realize Rebecca needed to speak to her, and maybe she'd give her a home number or something.

Rebecca drove to Marina del Rey, parked, and went inside the sheriff's station. Knowing where she was going this time, she headed for Solowski's desk.

"What do you want?" asked Walters, grim faced the moment he saw Rebecca.

Damn, she thought, he was here and wasn't even making an attempt to be pleasant today. "I was in the neighborhood and thought I'd stop in and say hello." Ignoring him, she turned to Solowski. "Want to grab a cup of coffee with me?"

Without lifting her eyes, Solowski shook her head and mumbled, "I can't." Then to Rebecca's dismay, she just kept on doing her paperwork.

"By the way, Mrs. Morland," said Walters. "We're closing the investigation into your husband's death."

"I'm afraid I don't understand," Rebecca said, glancing toward Solowski again. This time when she was unable to make eye contact with the woman detective, she became alarmed. Something had happened and she had no idea what it was.

"We've found the motive we've been looking for." There was a malicious glint in Walters's eyes.

Feeling ill, Rebecca glanced up. "Oh?"

"It appears you've been selective about what you decided to share with us," he explained. "We've just learned how your husband was caught stealing money from the law firm. As we understand it, they confronted you with this information quite a while ago. Of course, you didn't bother to mention it to us."

"Well . . ." she stammered, momentarily caught off guard. No wonder they were both treating her as if she had some kind of communicable disease. "I didn't say anything because I didn't believe it, not for one second. I'm positive someone framed Ryan for that and I'm sure I know who it is." She rushed on to tell them what she'd learned from John Evans's ex-wife.

Walters's face remained impassive. "Mrs. Morland, it may come as a surprise to you to hear we're handling many other cases at the moment besides the death of your husband. At any rate, since we now have information that has given us the missing motive for why your husband took a dive into the ocean, as I said, we're closing our investigation with a determination of suicide."

"No, you can't do that!" Rebecca felt a sense of dread enveloping her. "Please, things are just starting to fall into place. At least—"

He put up his hand to stop her. "The decision has been made. The case is closed. Now, we seriously recommend you get yourself some counseling." Without another word, he sat down and began thumbing through one of his other case files.

"Please," Rebecca implored, speaking directly to Solowski this time. "Don't do that yet. This new information I've got changes everything."

Solowski shook her head. "I'm sorry, Mrs. Morland. There's nothing I can do." The woman detective then picked up a folder and walked away.

Rebecca stood there with her mouth open. How could she get them to listen to her? They couldn't do this. Glancing around, she became aware that other people in the room were staring at her. Did everyone think she was a nut case?

As she walked out of the station, her shoulders squared, she thought about the promise from Ryan's partners not to say anything about the theft. Had the three of them decided together to go back on their word? Or had it been only one of them who had changed his or her mind and told the detectives?

CHAPTER TWENTY

A report on how Ryan Morland had committed suicide because he had been misappropriating funds from his law firm surfaced first in a newspaper column and then was picked up by radio and television news.

Rebecca felt as if she were on an emotional roller coaster. One minute she was deeply ashamed, dreading having to face people who would now view her husband as a common thief. The next minute, she was angry and even more determined to prove all his accusers wrong. Unfortunately, the vacillation between the two extremes was sapping her energy, and she'd been unable to accomplish anything productive.

Finally, she forced herself to take action, fearing that if she remained inactive any longer, she'd become paralyzed and give up on the investigation completely.

Getting up early in an effort to avoid the traffic, and hoping to catch Catherine while she was still at home, Rebecca drove to Manhattan Beach, taking the Marina del Rey Freeway and then Culver Boulevard to the beach route.

The area between Marina del Rey and Redondo Beach was the longest stretch of public beach in Los Angeles County—

more than eight continuous miles of oceanfront. Two of the nicest areas, Hermosa Beach and Manhattan Beach, in recent years had experienced a dramatic upsurge in real estate values as more and more city dwellers looked for their own slice of the Southern California good life.

Rebecca had no trouble locating Catherine's address. Soon she was ringing the doorbell of a contemporary house that faced the water on what was called The Strand. Getting no answer, and convinced that Catherine must be out running, Rebecca sat down on the low wall that edged the wide concrete path used by joggers, bikers, skaters, and those merely wanting an early morning stroll.

The morning air was still cool, and the sky overcast, yet a lot of people were out on the boardwalk even at this early hour. Every few minutes, Rebecca stood up, stamped her feet, and rubbed her hands to ward off some of the chill.

Finally, she saw two figures approaching, one of whom, from a distance, she thought might be her husband's partner. Within a few minutes, Catherine and a male companion came to a halt in front of Rebecca, who was seated on the wall.

Catherine, who was panting heavily, was dressed in designer workout clothes, her streaked blond hair tucked inside a hood, which was tied firmly under her chin.

The man with her looked like he was in his twenties. He was tall with dark brown hair and an appealingly friendly face. Quite attractive, actually, Rebecca thought, wondering if he was a boyfriend or merely a neighbor of Catherine's.

"Hi," said Rebecca, her cheery greeting belying the knot of anxiety in the pit of her stomach.

Catherine seemed stunned by Rebecca's unexpected visit and was momentarily rendered speechless. Probably for the first time in her life, mused Rebecca.

"I'm Tony Necosia," said the young man, smiling and holding his hand out to Rebecca as if trying to bridge the awkwardness that hung between the two women.

"Glad to meet you," Rebecca replied, smiling back at him and shaking his hand.

"Is something wrong?" asked Catherine, frowning.

"Yes," Rebecca acknowledged with a nod. "And I wanted to talk to you about it in private, away from the office." She fully expected Catherine upon hearing this to excuse herself from the other runner.

"Let's hear it," Catherine said simply. She had pulled a wad of tissue out of her pocket and was patting her brow and under her chin.

Rebecca glanced at Tony and then back at Catherine. "I'm not sure this is something you'd want anyone else to hear."

"I'll be the judge of that." With a wave of her hand, Catherine indicated that Rebecca should start.

Feeling she'd been left no other option, Rebecca began in a firm voice. "I've discovered some unpleasant things about your partner, John Evans, and I thought you might want to know about them. I also think they are significant, especially in light of the media coverage on the theft from your firm." She paused, giving Catherine one last chance to have the information remain private.

But Catherine merely said, "Go on."

Fine, Rebecca decided. If Catherine didn't care who heard this, neither did she. "I went to see John's ex-wife a couple of days ago."

"Ex-wife?" Catherine's large hazel eyes held a modicum of surprise at this bit of news.

"Yes," Rebecca said, gazing at her. "It would seem he didn't want anyone to know he'd been married, although I'm not sure why. At any rate, his ex-wife, whose name is Cindy Evans, complained to me how after their divorce John had taken all the money from the sale of their house and still owes her fifty thousand dollars."

"I wouldn't put too much stock in what a divorced spouse has to say, Rebecca." Catherine's voice was brusque and impatient. "Quite often they have old scores to settle."

Although she was surprised by Catherine's reaction, Rebecca continued with her story, going on to tell her about John's gambling problem and all the money he most likely owed. When she was finished, she added, "I think it's clear that John had a stronger motive to take money from the firm than Ryan ever did."

Catherine had sat down on the wall and was retying one of her running shoes. "Do you have any direct evidence of this?"

"No. But then I don't have access to the firm's accounting department."

"Well, I can't accuse my partner of stealing just like that." Catherine snapped her fingers to make her point. "I need some kind of evidence other than what an ex-wife has to say."

"That's why I've come to you. Since Ryan is dead and unable to defend himself, and I have reason to believe that Brandon may be protecting his nephew, I hoped you'd check into the matter."

"Maybe I'm missing something here," said Catherine, who had now removed her hood and was running her hands through her hair. "I've already told you I've investigated the missing funds and I was perfectly satisfied with the results. In fact, you were shown the incriminating documents."

"Correction," interrupted Rebecca. "Since neither you nor Brandon would allow an outside accountant to audit the books for me, I merely reviewed the documents you showed me. Many lines on those documents were blocked out in black ink. Surely, as a competent litigator, Catherine, you know that documents can easily be altered."

"I don't think I'm that easy to fool," Catherine retorted, sounding irritated. "Without more evidence, I just don't see how I can do anything."

Her attitude took Rebecca aback. "But don't you see that this news about John changes everything? He may have owed hundreds of thousands of dollars to people who would have killed him if he didn't pay up. As for my husband, I've found no trace of the money missing from the firm. I've uncovered no hidden bank accounts. There was nothing expensive that he bought without my knowledge. I mean, hundreds of thousands of dollars doesn't just vanish into thin air."

"I can't even begin to speculate on where that money might be," Catherine asserted, her expression inscrutable. "As for John, he has a six-figure income as a lawyer and if he has chosen to gamble some of that money away"—she shrugged her shoulders —"what business is it of mine?"

Rebecca was becoming exasperated. "My God, Catherine, I'm showing you that there's a logical connection between the firm's missing money and John's gambling addiction that could account for how and why the money disappeared. Furthermore, John may have killed Ryan to frame him."

"We need to get beyond Ryan's death and the circumstances surrounding it," Catherine insisted. "It's all speculation. The publicity is hurting the firm, and then there's the election."

"A law firm and an election are not more important than Ryan's good name and the truth about how he died—or catching his murderer!" snapped Rebecca indignantly. "You can't let him take the blame for something he didn't do." She paused to catch her breath. "Don't you feel some ethical or moral obligation to check this out?"

"It would seem to me," said Tony, speaking for the first time since he'd introduced himself, "that Rebecca has at least brought up some good points, Catherine. Can't you do some checking without John's knowledge?"

Rebecca caught the angry look Catherine gave him. It was obvious that she didn't like him interfering in her business. With Tony coming to her aid that way, Rebecca decided to take one more stab at it. "I'd really appreciate your help, Catherine."

Catherine stood for several moments as if silently going over her options. "Very well," she finally said, annoyance showing in her voice. "I'll see what I can find. Assuming there's anything *to* find."

"That's all I ask," said Rebecca.

"I've got to go in and change. I'm going to be late," Catherine declared, turning and walking toward her home.

Rebecca flashed a grateful smile at Tony and gave him a wave good-bye. He rewarded her with a reassuring wink. What a nice man, thought Rebecca, wondering what he was doing with Catherine.

• • •

At five-thirty that evening, Rebecca sat outside of the Taylor, Dennison & Evans office building, waiting for John Evans to leave for the day. Having found it strange that Catherine wasn't more interested in investigating her partner's gambling addiction, Rebecca decided to do it herself. On the seat beside her was a brown bag filled with junk food, from tortilla chips to candy bars, and a thermos of some really strong, hot coffee to keep her alert during her surveillance.

She was driving Lucy's car, which rattled and shook something awful, but at least John wouldn't recognize it and realize that she was tailing him.

Rebecca was wearing an old sweat suit of Ryan's, which was all stretched out and very comfortable, along with running shoes, even though she expected to have nothing more to do all night than sit in her car, fighting the urge to sleep.

Finally, John's black Porsche pulled out of the underground parking lot. After seeing the shabby place where he lived, Rebecca figured that whatever money John had left over after paying his debts, he spent on leasing a fancy car. Obviously, it was important for him to present at least the image of a successful attorney. She calculated also that if he dated at all, and she'd rarely seen him with anyone, he probably never took the woman to his place.

Trying not to be obvious, she stayed two or three cars behind the Porsche. Even though dusk was already falling, Rebecca had on a pair of sunglasses—the kind that adjusted to the light so that she could see as it got darker. Her red hair was tucked under a baseball cap. In this beat-up old car, she figured she would be relatively invisible to him.

She followed John down Beverly Drive, then through a series of turns, ending up on the Santa Monica Freeway. Because of the way Lucy's car shook on the freeway, Rebecca prayed John wasn't planning on going too far. She was also worried about keeping him in her sights, given the difference in power between their respective vehicles.

Traffic was heavy, and watching John move back and forth between lanes, she could see that he drove with the same nervous energy with which he did everything else. When John abruptly switched onto the San Diego Freeway, going south— she had to swerve to get over too. She hated drivers like him who didn't bother to signal their intentions.

A short time later, he exited the freeway and not long after, pulled into the glitzy Hollywood Park Casino, a card club in Inglewood, which offered limited types of gambling.

She waited ten minutes before taking off the baseball cap, putting on a knee-length raincoat, and venturing inside on her own. There were no slot machines, crap tables, or roulette wheels anywhere in sight throughout the large room, which was decorated with neon lights and fake palm trees. Just lots of tables —way over a hundred—at which people were playing cards, presumably poker.

Carefully, Rebecca circled the area until she spotted John, who was already sitting at a table, his jacket off and his sleeves rolled up. Her breathing became irregular as she watched apprehensively from a safe distance. It was easy to read the excitement on his face as he picked up his cards. It didn't appear to her as if he'd kicked his gambling addiction at all.

As she roamed around the outer perimeter of the big room, she noticed that the club had a restaurant, although it looked as if most of the patrons preferred to have their food brought over to where they were playing. Sitting down nervously at the counter, she ordered a cup of coffee and some pie. When she had finished that, she would go back to the car. While being in the club was less boring, she certainly didn't want to risk John's spotting her.

Several hours later, Rebecca finally saw John exit the building. The ebullience she'd seen on his face earlier was gone, and he now looked extremely upset. Another man followed him out, and she watched as they exchanged what appeared to be heated words. Her pulse racing, she rolled down her window and heard their loud voices but couldn't make out what they were saying. John seemed to be trying to reassure the other person about something.

Was that man one of the people John owed money to? Rebecca wondered. She made a mental note of the man's features so that she could return here and question him. For now, she decided to keep following John. When John got into his car, she counted to twenty before tailing him back onto the freeway and then in the direction of his duplex.

When she saw him turn onto his street, she contemplated returning to the club and talking to the man John had been arguing with. But she questioned whether Lucy's car would even survive another trip on the freeway and decided instead to wait and make sure John was in fact staying put for the night.

A block before his house, he turned again and Rebecca noted there was an alley running behind the residences on his block. Obviously, some of the garages could be entered that way. She drove down his street and parked about two houses away from his. She'd just wait until the lights came on in his place—then leave.

Listening to the radio, Rebecca lost track of the time. When she next checked her watch, at least ten minutes had passed and she still hadn't seen any lights go on upstairs. That was odd, she thought. Unless, of course, he was one of those people who came in and, without bothering with lights, dropped into bed. A flash of alarm skittered through her. Had he spotted her and decided to shake her by going down that alley? That didn't make much sense, though, if all he planned to do was retire for the night.

She found herself in a quandary. Should she drive around to the alley and see what she could find? The street was mostly dark and completely deserted. It was the middle of the week; the neighbors were probably already at home and asleep.

Rebecca counted the houses on the block so she'd be able to ascertain when she was directly behind John's place. It was pitch black in the alley, and she found it very scary. Goose bumps appeared on her arms. Originally intending to drive without her headlights on, Rebecca was forced to change her mind. Without them, she couldn't see where she was going.

The car crept down the narrow path as Rebecca counted

to seven. Leave it to a gambler to live in the seventh house, she thought. As she slowed, she glanced up again to see if the lights in John Evans's place had been turned on in the meantime, but the duplex was still dark.

The garage in back of John's duplex was open, and she spotted the Porsche. He hadn't left. With such an expensive car, it seemed foolish not to close the garage. Had he been too tired to close the garage door or turn on any lights? She wondered if he was already upstairs, fast asleep.

She was just about to drive off, when she heard a sound. Holding her breath, she lowered the window and listened. There it was again. A low moaning sound. A flicker of apprehension coursed through her. Get out of here, she told herself. But she didn't leave. By now her curiosity was piqued.

Opening the car door and trying not to make any noise, she quietly walked over to the garage, aware that she was trembling. The moaning became louder. At first she had thought it might be a cat, but this sounded like a human being. Her adrenaline surged.

Running the last few yards, her heart pounding, she quickly peered around, willing her eyes to adjust to the dark so she could see where the sound was coming from. It seemed to be over by the side of the Porsche. "Oh my God," she gasped as she saw the form of a man lying on the ground, his body moving as though writhing in pain. Terrified, but feeling she had no choice, Rebecca crept closer. It was John. He was covered in blood. A gurgling sound came from his throat.

Terrified, her own breath coming in shallow, quick gasps, Rebecca crouched down close to him. "It's Rebecca, John. What happened?"

The response was guttural and she could not make it out. Realizing he might be drowning in his own blood, with great effort she turned him onto his side, propping his back against one of the Porsche's back tires. Then she pulled off her sweatshirt, crumpled it into a pillow, and stuck it under his head.

Her eyes having adjusted somewhat to the darkness, she could see him clearer now. Her stomach lurched—he'd been badly beaten, and there was blood running out of his mouth. My

God, was this what they did to you if you had gambling debts? Or was it something else? She thought about all the follow-home robberies she'd read about in the newspapers. Is that what had happened?

"I'll be right back," she said, terrified and not sure if he could hear her. "I've got a phone in my car. I'm going to call for some help."

More guttural sounds emanated from him. Rushing back to the car, Rebecca grabbed her purse. Her panic rising, she found the portable phone she'd recently purchased and hurriedly punched in 911.

CHAPTER Twenty-one

Siren shrieking loudly in the night, the ambulance rushed
across intersections to the nearest hospital while Rebecca drove
behind it, trying to keep up.

Inside the hospital, the emergency personnel wheeled John
Evans away, and a young woman showed Rebecca where to wait.
It was a typical hospital waiting room with its gray-green walls
and linoleum floors, plastic chairs, Formica end tables, and scattered torn magazines.

Not long after she had arrived there, a policeman came to
talk to her, a Hispanic man in his late twenties or early thirties.

"Do you think he's going to be all right?" she asked him,
worriedly.

"They don't know," he told her honestly, his dark eyes sympathetic. "At the moment, he's unconscious." He took out his
notebook and explained that he needed to ask her a few questions.

Feeling tense, Rebecca related how she'd been planning to
visit John, that she saw him drive up, and after waiting quite a
while for the lights to come on in his apartment, she'd become

suspicious. What she neglected to mention was the fact that she'd been following him all evening.

"Do you usually visit people at midnight?" the policeman asked, a look of curiosity on his face.

Rebecca thought for a moment, then decided she'd better tell him as much of the truth as she could. "No, but these were exceptional circumstances and I needed to speak to him." Trying to remain calm, she folded her hands tightly together. "You see, John was one of my late husband's law partners, and I had some important business questions to ask him. I happened to be in the area and stopped in to see if he was home. When he wasn't, I decided to wait for a short time and the rest I've already told you."

He scribbled down a few more notes on his pad of paper and asked her a few general questions about John's age and relatives.

"Do you think this was a robbery, or what?" she asked.

"Hard to tell," he responded in a matter-of-fact tone. "His wallet was on him, but his money was gone. Credit cards, license, watch, everything else was still there. Most robbers take the cards as well. And they left the Porsche, which is even stranger. We'll have to wait and see what Mr. Evans can tell us."

Next, he took down Rebecca's name and phone number and asked if she wanted to notify John's nearest relative herself or if he should do it.

"I'll do it," she said, nodding her head. After the policeman left, she thought things over. When John regained consciousness, it might be best for her to speak to him first—then she could call Brandon. But what if he remained unconscious for a long time?

She was still trying to decide what to do when a tall, African-American doctor came out to see her.

"Are you with John Evans?" he asked, sitting in the chair next to hers.

"Yes." She nodded, glancing at him closely. "How's he doing?"

"Not very well, I'm afraid." He shook his head. "He's regained consciousness, but he's bleeding internally. We've called in a surgeon; we're going to have to operate right away."

Her heart jumped. "That sounds serious."

"It is." He nodded gravely.

Feeling slightly ill, she asked, "Can I see him for a minute?"

The doctor hesitated.

"Please," she pleaded, holding her breath for his response.

"Okay," he finally agreed. "But make it brief."

"I will," she promised.

John wasn't in an actual room, but in an area sectioned off by curtains. They had him covered with a sheet. Rebecca felt queasy when she saw how pale and waxen John's face looked. His eyes were swollen, and not all of the blood had been washed off his face. There was no question that he'd been pummeled without mercy.

Though his eyes were only slits, he recognized her when she came over to the bed. "You saved my . . . life," he whispered in a halting voice.

She hurried to explain. "I was waiting outside to talk to you when you drove up. When the lights didn't come on upstairs, I figured I better check. Was it a robbery?"

A fearful look came into his eyes. "Told cops that," he confided. "But think . . . it was . . . bookie." His voice was now very low and coming out in gasps.

Rebecca was surprised he was confiding in her. "Did you owe them a lot?" she asked gently.

He nodded.

"They want me to call your nearest relative," she told him. "I'm going to call Brandon, okay?"

"No," he groaned. "Don't tell."

"Why not?" she blurted out, shocked.

"He'll . . . get . . . mad."

"Oh, no," she insisted. "I'm sure your uncle would help you if he knew your life was in danger."

"Helped once . . . Holmes. Some kinda deal. This . . . time . . . said no." He stopped, and his chest heaved while he struggled to catch his breath.

Hearing Holmes's name, Rebecca tensed, her mind searching anxiously for the meaning behind John's words. At the same time she reached out and patted his hand. "Don't talk. Rest for a while."

As if he hadn't heard her, he said, "Went . . . alone."

"To see Holmes, you mean?" she asked tensely, remembering the night she'd seen John pull up in front of Maxwell Holmes's house with his car's headlights turned off.

John nodded. "Yeah. Has connections. First time . . . fixed things."

The word *connections* jolted her. With a shiver she speculated if that meant something like the Mafia.

"He . . . laughed . . . told me . . . get out."

A middle-aged nurse in a white uniform came over to John's bed and indicated it was time for Rebecca to leave. Someone else stuck her head in to say there was another emergency, and before Rebecca could react, the nurse rushed out of the room.

John had closed his eyes in the meantime and, not wanting to disturb him, Rebecca stood quietly off to the side. She was confused and filled with apprehension.

After a while, he mumbled, "May not . . . make it." His swollen eyes were open again.

A momentary fear chilled her. "Don't be silly," she told him, trying hard to make her voice sound as reassuring as possible. "You're going to be just fine."

"No. Feel . . . strange. Body numb."

The hair on the back of her neck rose. Could he be dying? In spite of how nasty he'd been to her, she hated to see him in such pain, and she certainly didn't want him to die. "Here, I'll get your circulation going." She took one of his hands and started rubbing it with her own.

He gave a weak smile and seemed to drift off.

Rebecca panicked. What if he died and she never found out the answers to her questions? She couldn't let that happen. When John stirred again, she asked him in a soft voice, "What kind of a deal did Brandon and Holmes make?"

His mouth began moving, although his eyes remained closed. "Didn't . . . tell."

Trembling, Rebecca leaned closer to the bed. She didn't want to agitate him, but at the same time she felt compelled to grab her chance now as it might never come again. "John, did you have anything to do with Ryan's death?" Her heart was beating wildly in her chest as she anxiously waited for his response.

"No," he mumbled. He was quiet for a few seconds. Then he said again, "No."

Swallowing hard at the tightness in her throat, she tried to absorb the meaning. Was he telling the truth? Usually in circumstances like this, where someone faces surgery, maybe even death, the courts felt you could rely on that person's statement. But could she?

Then he began talking again. "I . . . dying—don't . . . want . . . more lies." He paused. "Took . . . money. Feeling des . . . per . . . ate," he muttered. Tears started rolling down his cheeks.

Listening to him, Rebecca was frozen to the spot. Her heart pounded in her ears, and she was filled with an overwhelming sense of relief.

"That's why . . . briefcase . . . Ryan found . . . bankbook . . . guessed . . ." His voice trailed off.

For a moment she didn't know what he was referring to, then it hit her. "Are you Earl Anders?" she whispered urgently.

He nodded.

"Is that what you and Ryan argued about on the boat that night?"

Again he nodded.

So John did have a good motive for killing Ryan. Yet, Rebecca sensed that John may have only taken advantage of Ryan's death by blaming him for the theft. "But you didn't kill him?"

"No . . . Sorry . . . about money," he muttered.

Rebecca knew that if John was telling the truth it would be cruel of her not to reply. "It's okay," she told him, tears welling up in her own eyes. She patted his hand again, trying to grant him the forgiveness he was looking for, along with some added strength for the surgery.

The curtains parted, and when the nurse saw that Rebecca was still there, she became angry. "I thought I told you to leave."

"He had things he needed to say," Rebecca explained, her voice choking up. "I've been holding his hand."

"Well, out," the nurse ordered, shooing Rebecca away. "I've got to get him prepped for surgery."

"I'll be waiting outside," Rebecca told John, hoping he could hear her even though his swollen eyes were closed again.

When Rebecca saw Brandon Taylor walk into the hospital waiting room some twenty minutes after she had phoned him, she was shocked by his appearance. Having never known Brandon to look less than perfect, it was strange to see him so disheveled. Clearly he had dressed hurriedly and driven directly there without even running a comb through his hair.

"John's just been wheeled into surgery," she told him quickly. "The doctor has promised to send someone out periodically to inform us how he's doing."

Brandon's face was tense as he questioned her about John's condition.

"It was a good thing you found him," he said, his tone genuinely grateful. Then his eyes narrowed as if the implications of his statement had just sunk in. "What were you doing there, anyway?"

Rebecca repeated the story she'd given to the police, but she wasn't sure Brandon believed her.

After she was through, he sat silently for a minute, staring off into space. "Did John tell the police that he'd been robbed, or did they surmise that?"

"I believe he told them that because he didn't want them to know the truth," she said, watching his face as an understanding of what she was getting at dawned on him.

His gaze became suspicious. "What do you mean?"

She took a deep breath. "I spent a few minutes with John before they wheeled him into the operating room."

He paled noticeably, and there was a flicker of alarm in his eyes. "What did he tell you?"

She let him hang for a moment before replying. "John thought it might have been a bookie's henchmen who beat him up."

Brandon's mouth twisted into a grim line, but he didn't act at all surprised—a good indication that he had known about John's gambling all along.

"What else did he say?"

"That he'd asked for your help, but that you'd refused." From the distressed look on his face, she sensed that her statement had wounded him, made him feel guilty for something he'd done or had not done.

"I . . ." Brandon hesitated, as if searching for the right words. "I didn't realize that they would do this," he finally said, shaking his head, unable to meet her gaze.

"John also mentioned how you'd helped him once before by going to see Maxwell Holmes to fix things."

This time there was no disguising the shock that registered on his face. "He told you that?"

She nodded.

"Were there other people in the room?"

"No. We were alone," she answered honestly. The moment she saw his look of relief, she realized her mistake. Cursing herself for her stupidity, she straightened her shoulders and went on. "John explained how you and Holmes made a deal and how Holmes then arranged for the bookies to back off." She waited a few seconds, and when he didn't comment, she added, "I'd like to hear more about this deal."

He ignored her request. "What else did my nephew say?"

Rebecca's voice turned brittle. "According to John, you didn't want him to know any of the explicit details."

"That's not true," he said, shaking his head and regaining some of his composure. "I merely paid the debt along with some added interest. John knew that," he insisted.

"By 'added interest,' " she said, her mouth twisted wryly, "do you mean money or something else?"

"Money, of course," he said hastily. "Was that all John said?" His eyes were clouded with uneasiness.

"No." She took her time responding, wanting him to worry, enjoying the momentary bit of power she held over him. There was a window that faced the building next door, and she went to stand by it. Finally, she spoke again.

"Actually, John was quite frightened and made what could be called a deathbed confession. You know," she said, elaborating in a quiet voice, "the kind of statement that is considered an exception to the hearsay rule."

Brandon's shoulders stiffened; he was a proud man who wasn't used to being put on the defensive this way. Clearing his throat, he asked gruffly, "What is it you're trying to tell me?"

"Just this," she said, a note of triumph in her voice. "Your nephew confessed he was the one who misappropriated the money from the firm. The bookies were threatening him again. Desperate, and afraid you would find out, he framed Ryan." She stopped to catch her breath and to gauge his reaction to her news. "Ryan had nothing to do with it. Of course, I told you that from the second I heard about the missing funds. And the Brandon I used to know, the man Ryan believed in, should have realized that too."

He sat there staring at her, not saying a word. It was almost as if he had lost his ability to speak.

"In fact," she continued, pointing an accusing finger at him, "I've come to the conclusion that you either knew or guessed that your nephew was involved in the theft, but for reasons of your own, most likely having to do with your damn election, you chose to let the blame fall on Ryan since he wasn't here to defend himself."

Shoulders slumping, the man seemed to diminish before her eyes. "Don't blame the whole thing on me, Rebecca," he said, his voice low and hoarse. "Catherine investigated the matter too, and I accepted her results. She had absolutely no reason to lie."

"That may be, but as far as I'm concerned, neither of you really bothered to check things out carefully. John obviously doctored the evidence, and you let him get away with it." She was riding on a surge of adrenaline, and she felt vindicated for believing in Ryan when no one else had.

He nodded silently, and the light in his eyes dulled.

Relieved to have him acquiesce so easily, Rebecca clasped her hands together and said in a strong tone, "I'll expect the firm to issue a statement to the media with a full apology."

Before he could respond, a woman in a green scrub suit came in. "I'm Doctor Bailey. Are you John Evans's next of kin?"

"I'm John's uncle," Brandon advised her, standing up and going toward her.

"I'm afraid we were unable to stop the bleeding," she said, glancing from Brandon to Rebecca. "He'd already lost too much blood before he got here." The doctor paused before going on, as if giving them a moment to prepare. "I'm sorry to have to inform you that Mr. Evans died on the operating table a few minutes ago."

Brandon seemed to stagger backwards before he found the chair and collapsed into it. "He's dead? My nephew is dead?" His voice sounded strangled.

The doctor nodded sadly. "I'm afraid so. I'm terribly sorry. We did everything we could, but he was too badly injured."

Rebecca stood frozen to the spot, absolutely speechless, her last words with John echoing in her mind.

Still shaking his head as though unable to comprehend this traumatic turn of events, Brandon kept mumbling: "I don't understand. He was only beaten up—not shot. How could something like that cause such a quick death?"

Stating that internal injuries could result from a severe beating, the doctor explained in detail what probably had happened.

All during their exchange, Rebecca also was having a hard time processing this news—stunned by the suddenness of it all. John was dead.

Finally, Brandon appeared to grasp what the doctor was saying. After a few more questions and answers, he seemed to gather his strength and regain some of his former poise. He shook the woman's hand and thanked her for her help and concern.

When they were finally alone again, Brandon began pacing the room. Rebecca merely sat there quietly, giving him a chance to gather his thoughts and to deal with the finality of what had happened. For the first time, she felt in her body the exhaustion of the long day, and she was glad for a few minutes of rest and the chance to regain her strength.

Soon, Brandon came over to face her. His hands were stiff

and awkward by his sides. "Rebecca," he said, his lips compressed, "I think it would be best for all concerned if we went along with the story John told the police—that this was a robbery."

She felt a rush of anger. "Your nephew isn't dead five minutes and you're already manipulating the media spin on it?" Her voice rose to a high pitch. "Is there nothing in the world more important to you than your damned election?"

"When people are dead, Rebecca," he said, his voice low and weary, "there's nothing we can do to change that. In the meantime, I still believe I can achieve a lot of good as California's next senator and I don't see what's wrong with trying to do that." His mouth formed a stubborn line. "I think that if you mull this over calmly, you'll see that I'm right."

She was amazed at this man's sense of importance. "I disagree. As far as I am concerned, your nephew told me what happened, and I'm going to see that every newspaper in the country runs the story tomorrow." Her body was trembling with rage at the man's audacity.

He merely shook his head sadly. "No, Rebecca. You don't want to do that. First of all, you have no proof. Second, you will only end up making everyone feel sorrier for you than they already do. 'That poor woman, unable to cope . . .' You know; that sort of thing."

Rebecca could not believe what she was hearing. "What do you mean? John admitted it was him; he took the money," she practically screamed at him.

"Ah," he said, smiling at her faintly as if he'd just trumped her at a game of hearts, "you said there was no one else in the room to hear it."

"*I* was there. *I* heard it," she insisted angrily, her stomach churning, pain gripping her temples.

Brandon's voice turned hard. "Who's going to believe the wife of a man who killed himself because he couldn't face the consequences of his actions?"

"Everyone," she insisted. "Especially after you do a full audit to prove who the real culprit was."

"Did I say I was going to do such an audit?"

Rebecca felt an almost uncontrollable wave of anger wash over her. She wanted to scream at him, to shake him. "So after your nephew confessed to being the thief, you're still willing to let the world believe it was my husband?"

His gray eyes were unreadable. "I'm afraid I have no choice."

A red haze blurred Rebecca's vision. She could foresee the next few days as they played themselves out in her mind: she'd run to the authorities and the media, explaining how John had confessed; Brandon would maintain she was using an unfortunate tragedy to exonerate her husband, which only proved how unbalanced she was.

She was about to scream at him that she had a bankbook . . . when she realized that with John dead, she still had to prove his connection to the account and that he was Earl Anders. It was better not to tip her hand until she had the confirmation. "You won't get away with it," she challenged, glaring at him.

"We'll just have to see which one of us they believe, won't we?" he said, a half smile curling his lips. "But in all seriousness, if I were you, Rebecca, I'd be cautious." The look he cut her was suddenly dark and dangerous. "And it would be best for you to forget you ever heard any mention of Maxwell Holmes."

CHAPTER
TWENTY-TWO

Standing behind a large maple tree, Rebecca watched as Detective Solowski's two children hopped out of a car and helped their mother carry the bags of groceries into a small stucco house located on a pleasant street in Culver City, a small incorporated area in the middle of L.A.

Rebecca had followed Solowski here. Although she hated to intrude on the detective's time with her kids, she had no other alternative. She couldn't approach the woman at the sheriff's station—not when Walters treated her like a criminal.

Somehow, Rebecca had to convince Solowski to help her —she was her last hope. And before she could do that, she had to make the woman understand why she hadn't told her about the missing money. Praying for success, she proceeded up the walkway and rang the bell.

A little boy looked out through the curtains and yelled for his mother. Solowski came to the door. When she saw Rebecca, she frowned. "Mrs. Morland, what are you doing here?"

Rebecca tried to convey with her eyes the urgency she was feeling. "I must talk to you about something," she said forcefully.

"It's very important. May I come in? Or do you want to come outside for a few minutes?"

Solowski turned back toward her children as if deciding. "You better come in." She unlatched the door. "Let me get the kids busy in the kitchen with their homework and I'll be right back." Gesturing toward the couch, she indicated that Rebecca should sit down.

Entering the tiny living room, Rebecca glanced about. The couch had a blanket draped over it, and there were two rather dilapidated chairs, a scarred wood coffee table, and a large television. On one wall there hung a small crucifix. She noted that every surface held framed pictures and bent to examine some of them more carefully.

A burly, handsome man was in most of the photographs with Solowski and either one or both of the children. It had to be Solowski's late husband. It was obvious that the woman was trying to make her children feel as if their father was still very much a part of their lives. Rebecca would have done the same thing if only she'd been lucky enough to have Ryan's child. A deep sadness threatened to overwhelm her whenever she realized she'd never have that chance now.

"Okay, they're busy for the next few minutes," said Solowski, coming back into the room. "Now what's this about?"

"I'm sorry to bother you at home," Rebecca began, "but I couldn't talk to you at the station—not when Detective Walters is so hostile toward me."

"He's been tougher than I have," admitted Solowski in a flat voice. "But then it seems like he's a much better judge of character than I am."

Rebecca winced. "I know you're angry with me," she said softly. "And I don't blame you. Let me just explain if I can."

Nervously, she moistened her lips. "When the partners first told me about the missing money, they said they wanted back whatever was left and told me we'd work out a repayment plan for the rest. They also promised to tell no one."

Stopping for a moment, Rebecca fought for control. "You must believe me, I knew my husband wouldn't have done such a thing, but I had no idea how I was going to prove it. I also had just learned I was pregnant and I didn't want our child growing up ashamed because the world believed his or her father was a thief." Her eyes pleaded for understanding. "What would you have done if you'd been in my shoes?"

The woman detective folded her arms across her chest, not meeting Rebecca's gaze. "You should have told me—I would have understood."

"Yes. But you also would have felt it was necessary to tell Walters, and then it wouldn't have been a secret." Rebecca searched the woman's face for a sign that she was getting through to her, but Solowski was unreadable. "Anyway, remember when I came to the station and told you what I learned about John Evans from his ex-wife?"

"Yep," Solowski replied with an impersonal nod.

"Well, after that I was sure John had something to do with the missing money, so I started tailing him." Rebecca proceeded to relate the entire story to Solowski, not leaving anything out, including her confrontation with Brandon Taylor at the hospital.

"Look," said Solowski, twisting her hands in her lap. "I stuck my neck out for you before and almost lost my assignment as a detective. I'm a widow with two kids to support." She motioned in the direction of the kitchen. "I can't afford to take any more chances. Even if I believed you," she hesitated briefly, "and I'm not sure I do—there's not much I can do to help you."

"I understand that I let you down," Rebecca conceded, her tone apologetic. "But there was such a rush to judgment that my husband had committed suicide, I felt I couldn't be totally open. I'm really sorry. And I don't want you to get in any trouble. But this whole case hasn't been right from the beginning, and you know it too. So many things don't add up and so many people are hiding the truth. Please," she said, beseechingly, "just check two things out. Neither should be hard to do. Then decide."

With a wary glance, Solowski asked, "What kind of things are we talking about?"

"Even though John admitted to me he was Earl Anders, I

have no proof." Rebecca went on to explain about the bank and how they wouldn't give her any information. "If you could just take the bankbook and this picture into the bank and see if anyone there remembers who opened and/or used the account . . ." She handed the bankbook to Solowski along with the photograph that had Ryan and John in it.

There was a grimace on Solowski's face as she pointed at the bankbook. "Where did you get this?"

Rebecca's stomach dropped. "I found it in my husband's briefcase," she acknowledged. "I didn't know if it belonged to a client or what. But I was sure it was somehow mixed up in this theft of money. If the bank identifies my husband, then I won't bother you anymore. Is that fair enough?"

"I don't know," mumbled Solowski, apparently unwilling to commit. "What's the other thing?"

Explaining about how she'd located Zoe Olin only to have the woman disappear on her, Rebecca suggested that, with the computer systems and other avenues of information available to the sheriff's department, Solowski should be able to locate Zoe without too much trouble.

"I've got dinner cooking, and I want to see how the kids are doing on their homework," Solowski said. "Excuse me for just a few minutes."

Rebecca could hear the detective talking to her kids in an encouraging voice. How hard it had to be to work all day, Rebecca thought, then take care of the kids at night, supervising homework, making dinner, cleaning the house, marketing, without having a husband with whom she could share the responsibilities as well as the joys.

Soon she was back. "I don't know," Solowski said. "Walters has closed the case. I've got a dozen other things that should have been done yesterday. I'd have to do this on my own time, and I don't have much of that, if you know what I mean."

"I'll be glad to help you," Rebecca proposed eagerly, brushing the hair from her eyes. "I can do your grocery shopping, or the laundry. Pick up your children and take them wherever they've got to go. I'd be really happy to watch them while you do this."

Solowski seemed genuinely surprised by the offer. "Let's just see how it goes first."

"So will you do it?" Rebecca asked, holding her breath.

"Let me think about this some more tonight," Solowski hedged, as if she were already having second thoughts.

"Okay," Rebecca conceded reluctantly, knowing that was all she could do. As she drove away, she hoped that Solowski would find the courage in her heart to help her one more time.

Even though it was Detective Solowski's day off, the next morning, while the kids were in school, she drove to the bank in Century City. Inside the marble edifice with its deep-pile carpeting and walnut-paneled counters, Solowski showed her badge and encountered very little resistance from those she questioned. After showing the photograph of Ryan Morland and John Evans to several people who worked in new accounts, there was finally a glint of recognition in the eyes of one woman.

Taking off her glasses for a closer look, she said, "Yes. That gentleman in the picture is the man who came in here and opened the account."

"Would you please point him out for me," asked Solowski, positioning herself so she could see.

"This one."

The woman's pink-nail-polished finger pointed to John Evans. Solowski took a deep breath. So that confirmed what Rebecca had said—Evans might very well have been the thief. And if that was true, it cast a shadow of doubt on everything else John had told them about his partner, Ryan Morland, including, as she recalled it, that Ryan had been drunk and very depressed the night he'd died. John Evans had also found the suicide note and had supposedly been the one who had discovered that the funds were missing from the firm.

"Would you be willing to make a statement to that effect, under oath if need be?" asked Solowski.

The woman hesitated. "I guess so."

"It's important. This man may have committed a crime."

The woman straightened the jacket on her navy suit and smiled. "Of course."

After taking down all the information and telling the woman she'd notify her when to come in, Solowski left the bank. Before she told Rebecca anything, she wanted to check out the other lead too.

She debated about the best way to find the woman named Zoe Olin. As Rebecca had suggested, Solowski could access various computer systems, but she'd have to be careful. She didn't want anyone to see her using the computer and to mention it to Walters. Supposedly today was his day off too, so she hoped he wouldn't be around.

Several hours later, having learned Zoe Olin's new address, Solowski arrived at an apartment complex in Burbank—a burgeoning community with several television and movie studios within its borders, which lay east of the San Fernando Valley.

She rang the bell and convinced Zoe Olin to open the door and speak to her. Although the woman's eyes looked red rimmed and swollen, as if she'd been crying, Solowski could see that she was young and quite attractive.

Faced with questions from a detective, Zoe became quite forthcoming, and Solowski was able to ascertain who was really behind the theft.

"So you're saying that it was John Evans you helped, not Ryan Morland?"

"Yes," Zoe said, sniffling into her tissues. "John and I were in love, we were supposed to get married. He used to call me Meggie O. My full name is Zoe Margaret Olin, but he hated the name Zoe." The tears started flowing again. "I can't believe he's dead. He was here only two nights ago."

"I'm sorry," said Solowski, feeling bad for yet another woman who had to go through the agony of losing the man she loved.

Even though Zoe had been advised of her rights, she seemed eager to talk, wanting to clear her conscience. So Solowski set up her small tape recorder to capture the woman's statement. "Can you tell me just how you accomplished this theft of funds?"

Zoe launched into a detailed account of the elaborate scheme John had devised to divert checks made out to the law firm into the bank account he had opened for that purpose.

"Do you know why he wanted to target Ryan Morland for what he himself had done?" asked Solowski.

"According to John," said Zoe, wiping at her eyes, "Ryan Morland had cheated him out of his rightful place in the firm by somehow convincing Brandon Taylor to share his cases, clients, and fees with him instead of with John. We were not really stealing," she insisted. "We were merely remedying a wrong that had been done to John over the years."

"Are you absolutely sure that John Evans had nothing to do with Ryan Morland's death?"

"Positive," said Zoe. "He would have told me; we didn't keep secrets. And besides, John wasn't that kind of person."

Solowski let the woman's last remark pass. "Do you have any idea who might have wanted to see Ryan Morland dead?"

"No. John never even mentioned the possibility of murder. I think he honestly believed that either Ryan Morland had killed himself for some reason or that his death was an accident. He was relieved though, because it gave him the perfect opportunity to pin the missing funds on Ryan."

"Did you know that John was a gambler?" asked Solowski.

"Oh, I knew he liked to play cards once in a while," Zoe said, smiling. "But that's not really the same as being a gambler."

Solowski decided not to say anything more about Evans to this unhappy woman. It seemed she had enough to contend with for now.

When Solowski got to the station the following morning, Walters was waiting for her, a glum expression on his face. "Let's take a ride," he suggested in a gruff voice.

"What's wrong?" she asked, hoping he didn't hear the misgiving in her voice.

Walters refused to meet her gaze. "I'll tell you as soon as we're out of here." He motioned for her to hurry.

She checked in and then the two of them headed for his

car. A wave of apprehension swept through her as they got in and fastened their seat belts.

As soon as Walters pulled out of the parking lot, he started in on her. "You know, Solowski, I always figured you for a smart lady. I was positive you had the makings of a really fine detective." He spoke through clenched teeth as he added, "Now I'm not so sure."

Filled with dread, she tried to sound normal. "What do you mean?"

"A good detective learns how to follow orders, which is something you seem to have a hard time doing."

Her pulse was racing as she tried to get him to be more specific. "Why do you say that?"

"You tell me. I ordered you to stop working on the Morland case. I told you that as far as we were concerned, it was being closed as a suicide. And what happens? The next thing I know, I get a call that you're still asking questions on the case."

So he had found out. "Who told you?"

"The lady from the bank called asking for you."

Solowski began to justify her actions. "I discovered that Rebecca Morland was right about her husband and his law firm's misappropriated funds," she said, trying to keep her tone of voice calm and respectful while explaining the importance of what she'd found out. "John Evans was identified by the bank as the man who had opened an account through which hundreds of thousands of dollars had flowed. The woman who helped him in the firm's accounting department, Zoe Olin, has also confessed that it was John she helped steal the money, not Ryan Morland. I've got her statement on tape." She inhaled deeply before adding, "You can see that this throws a significant amount of doubt on everything John Evans told us."

He took his eyes off the road and glared at her. "You still don't get it, do you?"

"Get what?" she asked with a slight tremor in her voice.

"It's got nothing to do with what Ryan Morland did or did not do. It has to do with taking orders. This case means nothing to me one way or the other. These orders didn't originate with me," he told her flat out. "I was sure you were smart enough to figure that out by now."

Finally he was admitting someone else was involved. She eyed him carefully. "Who did they originate with?"

"That's not any of your business," he said coldly. "All you gotta know is that the orders came down."

"From the same person who arranged for us to be on the boat that night?"

"So what if it was? Like I said—it don't matter. You think you're some big shot who's gotta question everyone and everything? I've done all I can to try and keep you out of trouble. You can't blame me for anything that might happen to you."

"Would you please tell me what you're talking about," she demanded, dispensing with the caution she'd used up to now. "You're making it sound like I've done something terrible enough to be demoted or even fired. Is that what you're trying to say?"

"I'm afraid you've gone a lot further than that." He flicked a speck of dirt off his jacket. "All I can tell you, without endangering myself, is to be careful. Like I've said before, Randy was a friend of mine and I promised him I'd watch out for you, but I can't be expected to risk my own neck. That's where I gotta draw the line." He paused to take a breath before continuing, "And I'd sure hate to see anything happen to you . . . or those wonderful little kids of yours," he said.

A cold chill ran up her spine. It didn't make sense that someone might actually be thinking of hurting her or her children because she'd kept on investigating a case after she was told to stop. Especially when she'd been able to prove that Rebecca Morland had been on the right track. What did all this mean? It made her sick to realize she was being intimidated in the most horrible way possible, receiving threats on the lives of her children.

"Do you think you understand the seriousness of the matter now?" he asked harshly.

"Yes. I do," she finally admitted, too scared to say anything else.

"Then give me the tape," he ordered, holding out his hand.

She thought about refusing, about denying that she had it on her, but she knew it would be futile. Digging around in her bag, she found it. With a large sigh, she handed it over to Walters.

Since Solowski was one of the people who was sworn to protect the citizens of L.A. County, it frightened Rebecca to observe her behaving in such a paranoid manner. Rebecca was made to call the detective from a pay phone and wait for Solowski to telephone her back from yet another one. Finally, the woman gave her instructions for where they were to meet. It sounded rather convoluted, but Rebecca assumed Solowski knew what she was doing.

Rebecca hadn't been on a city bus in years, but after making sure she hadn't been followed to the parking lot where she left her car, she boarded one on Fairfax Avenue and took it to Sunset Boulevard, where she transferred. Besides the driver, there were only a few other people on the bus, none of whom seemed to be paying any attention to her.

Just before the bus got to Hilgard Avenue, where the UCLA campus started, a woman came on and made her way to the back where Rebecca was sitting. At first, Rebecca didn't recognize the detective; she was dressed in a pair of tight jeans and a tee shirt with DISNEYLAND emblazoned across it. She was also wearing a Mickey Mouse cap and dark glasses and had smeared her mouth with bright red lipstick. Rebecca couldn't recall ever seeing Solowski wearing makeup before, and certainly nothing this obvious. After a few minutes, Solowski began to fill Rebecca in on what she had found out.

"Didn't I tell you?" Rebecca's voice soared with elation upon hearing that the bank had identified John as the one who had opened and used the bank account. Then Solowski told her how she'd found Zoe Olin, who had admitted that she had been helping John, not Ryan.

"You were right," said Solowski, nodding her head. "But the sad thing is I'm not sure what to do about it."

"There must be someone in law enforcement we can trust," said Rebecca.

"I'm not sure who to go to," the woman detective stated. She brooded for several minutes before speaking again. "There's this deputy district attorney I've heard a lot about. His name is Daniel Black. I've never met him personally, but he's known for being honest and not afraid to tackle politically sensitive matters. However, if you ask for his help, you can't tell him who sent you, or it could be really bad for me—and I'm not just talking about my job."

Rebecca looked at the woman carefully. Was it her imagination or was there an ominous note in the detective's voice? "Have you been physically threatened in some way?"

Solowski nodded and then proceeded to tell her the details of her confrontation with Walters, along with his warnings to her.

"Oh my God," cried Rebecca, feeling a surge of panic rush through her. Things like this were not supposed to take place in this country. "I'm so sorry. I could never forgive myself if something happened to either you or your children. I'll do whatever you say and I'll never mention your name, I swear it on my life."

"I'm sure you wouldn't hurt us intentionally," Solowski ventured, "but the least little slip could prove disastrous. Until this matter gets straightened out, I'm thinking of taking the kids and leaving the state."

"Where will you go?"

"I don't know."

"I can give you some money if that will help?" Rebecca was biting her lip.

"I'm afraid I'll have to take it. I've got nothing put away." Solowski seemed to be embarrassed by this. "It's just not been possible with all of our expenses."

"That's okay," said Rebecca, trying to figure out which bills she wouldn't pay so that she could help Solowski instead. "Oh, God," she sighed, "I feel just terrible for getting you into this mess."

"Don't blame yourself. It's plain that the people involved in your husband's death have political juice. They might own the sheriff. Anyway, these people are willing to do whatever it takes to achieve their ends."

"I can see that," Rebecca agreed. She stared off into space for a short time. "I'll go see Daniel Black," she finally said. "Maybe he'll be brave enough for both of us."

Later, as she lay wide awake in her bed, unable to sleep, Rebecca fully understood the dilemma Ryan had faced those last weeks of his life when he'd been acting so strangely. He must have been terrified for himself and afraid that the people involved might harm her too. At some point, Ryan must have concluded that these people felt that whatever they were doing was more important than his life, or that of anyone else.

Now it looked like these same people were threatening to kill a detective and her children and most likely would carry it out, just to accomplish their ends. That kind of evil was hard for Rebecca to comprehend. She prayed that the deputy district attorney she was going to see would have enough guts to help her bring these people down, and she prayed too that she would still be alive to find out who they were.

CHAPTER
TWENTY-THREE

The following morning when Rebecca called the district attorney's office, asking for Daniel Black, she was given a phone number for the Special Investigations Unit, where he was assigned. She opted not to call, however, having already decided that the best way to approach the man was in person.

Downtown at the Criminal Courts Building, which also housed the district attorney's offices, she went through a metal detector and emptied out the contents of her purse before she was allowed inside.

Once upstairs, Rebecca went through more security procedures. After insisting that her business was highly confidential and that she would speak to no one but Daniel Black, she was finally shown into his office.

Daniel Black was talking on the phone, which gave her a few minutes to collect herself. He seemed friendly enough as he smiled at her and waved her to a chair.

Because he was seated, it was hard to tell how tall he was, but he appeared muscular and seemed to have a trim figure. He also had boyish good looks, deep-set hazel eyes, curly brown hair worn rather long, and a straight nose that was a trifle too large but not at all unattractive. Feeling embarrassed when she realized she'd been staring at him so unabashedly, she forced herself to gaze out the window at the downtown skyline.

Finally, he hung up the receiver. "I'm sorry," he said in an even-toned voice. "Right after I told them to bring you in, I had an emergency call." He stood up, and she could see she'd been right. He was quite well built and quite tall. Holding his hand out to her, he said, "I'm Daniel Black."

"Rebecca Morland," she told him.

"Morland? Ryan Morland's widow?"

"Yes," she nodded.

"I see." His face became a bit wary. "I was told this was a highly confidential matter."

"It is." Her heart was pounding as she tried to figure out how to begin. "I heard that you were relentlessly honest and willing to tackle politically sensitive matters." Eyes fixed on him, she asked, "Is that a fair assessment?"

He smiled at her description. "Who told you that?"

She didn't return his smile. "I'm afraid I can't divulge that. You see, this person is not only afraid for . . . their job—but their life and the lives of their family."

He ran his hand through his hair. "That's pretty heavy duty," he said, his hazel eyes appraising her carefully.

"I'm afraid the story I have to relate to you *is* heavy duty," she countered, keeping the expression on her face grave so that he'd understand how serious this was.

"Does this concern the death of your late husband?"

"Yes." She swallowed hard. "Does that make a difference to you?"

"I'm not sure," he admitted honestly. "You know the D.A.'s office has not been asked to look into the case, so I'm not positive you even belong here."

She tried not to let his words discourage her. "Please hear me out first, and then decide that when I'm through."

The deputy D.A. rubbed his chin, and she thought she saw a look of respect in his eyes as he nodded. "Okay."

Rebecca told him everything that had happened, starting

with Ryan's strange behavior during the last weeks of his life. She spared no detail, even admitting her own mistakes. The only thing she was careful to avoid was relating anything having to do with Solowski. Instead she just referred to a "law enforcement person."

Several times during her account he interrupted her to ask a question. At times she saw the amazement on his face, at others, he remained impassive. When she was through, she saw the lines of concentration deepen between his brows and around his eyes.

"And you say someone in law enforcement has told you they think there's a cover-up going on at the highest levels, but they're too afraid to come forward?" he asked.

"Yes," she said, nodding.

Daniel Black leaned back in his chair, playing with a pencil. He appeared to be deep in thought. After what seemed like a very long time, he put the pencil down, stood up, and walked to the window.

Her stomach tightening, Rebecca expected the worst and prayed she was wrong.

His back to her, he began to speak. "The story you've told me is quite unbelievable. More than that, it's frightening. The people involved are all extremely powerful, influential men and women." He started ticking them off on his fingers. "To begin with, we've got Paul Worthington, one of the state's richest developers, who wants to be the next U.S. senator. Then there's Brandon Taylor, one of the most respected lawyers not only in this state but in the nation. This man comes from a family of dedicated public servants and he, too, wants to be the next senator from California."

Rebecca remained quiet while he went through his list, which was an effort, because her nerves were very much on edge.

"Next, we've got Maxwell Holmes, who's been on several prestigious commissions and at the moment is chairman of the Beach Commission. He's a very good friend of the mayor and the governor and probably every other politician of note in this state. And according to what John Evans told you before he died, Holmes also has 'connections,' which you took to mean connections to organized crime." He turned around and glanced over at her. "Am I right so far?"

"Yes," she replied, hoping he couldn't hear the pounding of her heart.

Leaning back against the windowsill and crossing his legs, he continued. "Then we have the other partners of this high-profile firm of top lawyers, Catherine Dennison and John Evans. Mr. Evans died from a beating. But first he confessed certain things to you that his uncle now denies."

Making his way back to his desk, he sat down again. "Tell me again why you're positive your husband wouldn't have killed himself." His eyes studied her.

Swallowing hard, she went through her reasons.

He glanced out the window and then back. "And you're also ruling out the possibility it was an accident?"

"Yes."

"Why?"

"He wouldn't have gone out on the swim step. Not while the boat was under way," she explained as earnestly as she could. "Anyone could see how dangerous it was."

"You've handed me something that could either be a career-making or career-breaking kind of case," Daniel said.

"Yes. I'm aware of that."

"It could also be dangerous."

She nodded. "I'd venture to guess that these people are willing to kill a district attorney too. Does that frighten you?" Her eyes challenged him.

"Hell, yes!" he retorted. "And anyone who would tell you it didn't is a damn liar."

She smiled at his frankness. "So," she hesitated, "will you help me?"

He sighed before responding. "To be quite honest, I don't know if I can."

Her heart sank. "What do you mean?"

"As I said, the case hasn't been turned over to the D.A.'s office. And from what you've told me, it's unlikely it ever will be."

Rebecca frowned. "I'm not sure I follow you."

"You say the sheriff's department has closed it. If they've made a determination there was no foul play involved—we won't see the case at all."

A shadow of frustration crossed her face. "But surely district attorneys get involved in cases where they think the cops might have screwed up, don't they?"

"Yes." He paused before adding, "But sometimes we just can't."

Her voice caught in her throat. "Then what happens?"

"I might suggest that you take this to the FBI. But I hate to send you there cold turkey. Those guys can be rather arrogant at times."

Silently she willed him to help her. Her intuition told her that he was the right person for the job. Still, she couldn't think of anything else to say to win him over to her side.

"Tell me something about yourself," he said suddenly, catching her totally off guard.

Wondering what he wanted to know, she told him about the clinic and how much she loved working there, but that investigating her husband's death had become her first priority. He asked a few questions, which she did her best to answer. He seemed to be trying to assess the type of person he'd be sticking his neck out for, and she couldn't blame him.

"I'm not sure whom I can trust either," he said, quietly. "I'll have to be very careful in making any inquiries." He paused for a moment. "Look, Mrs. Morland—"

"Please call me Rebecca," she interjected.

"Fair enough. And you can call me Daniel. I'm not sure what I can do for you. And I certainly don't want to make things any worse. But let me see what I can find out. I have an investigator I'd trust with my own life. Let me get him to take a look around. Is there somewhere I can reach you?"

She gave him her home phone number.

He stood up and came around the desk, making it clear her time was up. She rose also.

"Please don't tell anyone that you came to see me," he said solemnly. "These charges are very serious, and the less certain people know about what we're doing, the better off we'll be."

"I understand," she told him.

The door opened suddenly, and a man walked into the room. "Oh, excuse me, Daniel," he said, seemingly surprised. "I didn't realize you had someone in your office."

He was an attractive man, Rebecca noted, handsome in a craggy sort of way, with prematurely gray, almost white hair and a deep tan.

"No problem," Daniel said. "We were just finishing."

"Thanks again," she said quickly, sensing he wanted her to leave before he was forced to introduce her. Without looking back, she exited the office and headed for the elevators.

After Rebecca Morland left, Daniel Black stood waiting for Chief Deputy D.A. Lance Renway to explain why he was there.

"Was that Rebecca Morland?" Renway asked, with a questioning glance.

Unhappy that she'd been identified, Daniel nodded. "Yes, it was."

"I thought I recognized her from the newspapers. Those photographs don't do her justice. She's quite beautiful."

"I agree," said Daniel.

The other man cleared his throat. "I hope Mrs. Morland was not here to see you in an official capacity," he said, frowning.

"No," Daniel replied quickly. "She came to see me as a friend."

The other man's eyes narrowed. "A friend?"

Feeling he needed to protect Rebecca Morland, Daniel embellished, "I meant that we have a mutual friend."

"I see," Renway said. "So what did she want?"

Daniel tried to sound nonchalant. He didn't need anyone guessing the true nature of Rebecca's visit. "The clinic where Mrs. Morland's been a senior staff attorney is losing its funding and may be closing."

His response seemed to surprise Renway. His eyes opened wide. "Are you saying she wants to work with us here at the D.A.'s office?"

"No," Daniel said, shaking his head. "She'd heard I have some friends doing public-interest law and asked me to put out some feelers for her."

The chief deputy D.A. had a skeptical expression on his face as he continued to appraise Daniel for a minute. "I see," he finally said, but he looked troubled.

"What did you want to see me about?" Daniel asked, changing the subject.

As Renway started to explain a case to him, Daniel had trouble concentrating on what the man was saying. He was too busy trying to figure out why Renway had acted so uncomfortable about Rebecca Morland's visit.

Later, after Renway had finally left, Daniel Black sat at his desk thinking about Rebecca Morland and the story she had told him. He had been following the investigation of her husband's death in the newspapers and had to admit that the media's depiction of her was quite different from the woman he'd just met. She didn't strike him as someone who refused to accept the circumstances of her husband's death just because it might reflect badly on her or their marriage, or because she wanted to collect on a life insurance policy.

Rather, Mrs. Morland came across as a very serious young woman, passionate about her work at the legal clinic and passionate about finding out why and how her husband had died.

Still, he asked himself if he really needed to take on something like this. Why not pass the buck to the FBI or the U.S. Attorney's office? They'd love to get their hands on a cover-up involving local law enforcement. There was usually a great deal of rivalry between state and federal agencies and a long history of mistrust between them.

But it was more than merely not wanting to see the gleeful Feds pounce all over the state. Mrs. Morland's story intrigued him. He certainly saw the advantages of cracking a case like this. Daniel would be able to write his own ticket—run for D.A. next year, maybe even attorney general or governor. It was quite easy to get caught up in the dreams of glory something like this could engender.

The other side of the coin was that he could anger a lot of powerful people and end up with no career at all. He'd ask Zack McKenzie, one of his best investigators, to take a look, but he'd have to warn him to be very discreet. If what this woman had told him turned out to be true, it would be one of the biggest scandals ever to hit L.A.

Catherine looked intently at the light-haired, middle-aged man standing before her, eager to hear his news. "What have you been able to find out?"

He lowered himself into the chair in front of her desk even though she hadn't invited him to sit down. "Well, ma'am, nothing so far, I'm sorry to report."

"It's been two weeks and you have nothing?" She slammed the palm of her hand on the desk.

"I've dug around quite a bit," he hurried to reassure her, "and I've got a pretty good idea where Paul Worthington's original birth certificate is, but I've run into some bureaucratic red tape."

"I thought that's what I'm paying you for—to cut through the red tape?" Her tone was derisive. This private investigator had come recommended to her as one of the best, but so far she was less than impressed.

"Well now, Ms. Dennison," he said, "these things take some time and . . ." he paused, "some other things, if you know what I mean?"

She stiffened. "No, I don't know what you mean," she retorted, thinking how stupid he was. "I'll pay you whatever you ask to get the job *done.* I don't want to hear about any 'other things,' is that clear?"

He cocked an eyebrow at her. "Yes, ma'am. I'm reading you loud and clear."

"Besides the original birth certificate, are you checking out all medical information on Worthington, going back to when he was a child?"

"Yes, ma'am."

Catherine impatiently tapped her red nails on the surface of her desk. "And all his associations both public and private before and after his marriage?"

"We're covering all the bases you suggested."

"Good. Now I don't care what it costs, I want you to spend all your time on this." She leaned forward to make her point. "I've got to have that information as soon as possible."

"I'm giving it my all, ma'am," he promised. "I hope to have something for you soon."

"I'll be waiting," she said in an exacting tone of voice.

After he left, she gazed out her window onto Rodeo Drive. The firm was located in a premier area, referred to as the Golden Triangle of Beverly Hills. It had the prestige and reputation she'd longed for her entire life. Getting here had not been easy, but the struggle was about to pay off. She was on the verge of getting everything she wanted.

Her mind flashed to the other top firm where she'd worked when she arrived in L.A. right out of Harvard Law School, to all those horrible years spent in the law library, those eighty-hour weeks with no social life. Being a woman had made it that much harder. Still, if not for those experiences, Brandon never would have asked her to join his firm as a full partner.

She thought of Brandon. He hadn't had to pay his dues the way she had. There was no doubt he was a brilliant lawyer with a first-rate legal mind, but it often took more than that to achieve such an august position in the legal community. He'd been allowed in because his father and grandfather had been influential United States senators. When clients came to the firm they were counting on all the influence and the government connections that promised.

Now it was her turn to reap the advantages of having a former partner who was a U.S. senator serving his country in Washington. That kind of connection would generate millions of dollars of new business for this firm. She wasn't about to let Paul Worthington step in and ruin her and Brandon's carefully laid plans.

She was confident that the information to stop Worthington was out there. She'd get it. And then she'd use it.

CHAPTER
TWENTY-FOUR

Daniel Black was busy working on a case that was coming to trial the following week when Chief Deputy D.A. Lance Renway strode into his office.

"We need to talk," Renway said, closing the door behind him.

There was a funny feeling in the pit of Daniel's stomach, and he had a premonition of what was coming.

Renway did not mince words. "I asked you last week if you were doing anything for Rebecca Morland in an official capacity, and you assured me you were not."

It was best to see what Renway wanted before answering, Daniel decided, as he remained silent.

"So what do you have to say for yourself?"

Trying to sound calmer than he actually felt, Daniel replied, "That depends on what the question is?"

The man scowled at him. "Do you deny you've been snooping around at the sheriff's department, looking into the Morland case?"

"Come on now, Lance," Daniel said in a cynical voice, "since when can't a deputy D.A. ask a few questions of a law enforcement agency the D.A.'s office works with on a regular basis?"

"This is an election year. Relations between Sheriff Quentin and the D.A. are already strained."

"And my inquiry has made things worse?"

"Let's just say our boss can't afford to have problems with the sheriff and his minions. He wants you to stop."

Daniel was amazed that they were even having this conversation. Finally he said, "Tell him message delivered."

Renway's neck grew red. "You've got a brilliant future here, Black. The D.A. himself has talked about grooming you for a key staff position. I'd hate to see you lose your chance to become district attorney of L.A. County someday because you were misguided by a beautiful woman."

He stopped for a moment as if waiting for the import of his words to sink in. "We have a severely limited budget and we must stick to our priorities. Am I making myself understood?"

"Absolutely," said Daniel, his eyes narrowing in displeasure.

"Good. As for Mrs. Morland, for the time being she's politically hot. It's best you stay away from the lady."

Daniel's pulse started to race. "Are you telling me I shouldn't see her socially either?"

"We're not novices here, Daniel," said Renway, glowering at him. "This is the real world, and there are some political alliances that must be maintained. Therefore, if your being friends with her gives certain people the wrong impression, then for the future of your career, I'd be careful."

"I can't believe you're—"

The chief deputy held up his hand to silence him. "Enough said. You know the game rules. The ball's in your court. Play by the rules—you stay in the game." His tone dropped as he finished. "If not, you end up in the bleachers."

As Renway walked out of his office, Daniel choked back the urge to vent his anger. How dare the man tell him whom he could associate with. Suddenly everything Rebecca Morland had told him took on a new meaning. She was right—someone with government connections wanted her stopped. He wondered which one of the suspects she had named had that kind of political clout.

He grabbed his jacket and headed out into the smoggy day.

Lance Renway went back into his office and made a telephone call. When the other person came on the line, he said, "I think he got the message loud and clear, although he wasn't too thrilled."

He listened for a minute to the voice on the other end. "No," he responded. "I think he was just feeling sorry for a pretty lady. I don't anticipate a problem.

"Yes. I see. Well, if you think tapping her phone would be valuable, I'll leave that to your discretion. Of course, I can't have anything to do with something like that. In fact, I'd prefer not to know about it.

"Yes. No. Okay. I understand. Maybe you're right. That's the best way to see who she's talking to and what about. No. Of course. You have to do what's necessary. Okay. Keep me posted."

Daniel was feeding the pigeons in MacArthur Park when his top investigator sat down next to him. As usual, Zack McKenzie had a cup of coffee in his hand. "Where did you get that?" Daniel asked.

Zack, who was built like a linebacker and going bald, pointed toward the vendor behind the small cart.

"Aren't you afraid you'll end up poisoned?"

"I've got a cast-iron stomach." Zack grinned. "So what's up? I take it something's wrong or you wouldn't have wanted to meet me away from the office where we can't be overheard."

"Right," said Daniel, not bothering to hide the fact that he was unhappy. "Looks like we've got to be even more careful than I had thought."

"What do you mean?" Zack's gaze was probing.

Daniel explained his run-in with Lance Renway. "So as you can see," he concluded, "the chief deputy as much as told me to cool it."

The investigator's eyebrows shot up. "Why does he care?"

Daniel tapped his foot impatiently. "He says it's an election year and the D.A.'s worried. But I think if you weren't stepping on some toes in the sheriff's department with your inquiries into the Morland matter, they wouldn't be trying to stop us."

"Good point," agreed Zack. "Maybe you should go to the FBI or the U.S. Attorney and let them investigate it."

"I don't know," said Daniel.

The other man fingered his tie. "I've got a few friends at the Bureau. Want me to talk to someone?"

Daniel shook his head. "I'm worried about how they might handle it. Now that I've met Rebecca Morland and heard her story, I feel sort of responsible for her, if you know what I mean."

"Yeah," said Zack. "But maybe they'd work with you on it."

"Oh, sure," Daniel scoffed. "Even if they let me do some work, it will be a one-way street. Me telling them what I know, while they give me nothing. Their egos will never allow them to share information with me."

"You may be right."

"And what if in their desire to snare the big guys and all the glory they use Rebecca as a decoy?"

"That could be bad," Zack acknowledged, making a face. "She could get hurt."

"The other problem," Daniel reminded his investigator, "is that if the chief deputy or whomever else is trying to shut us down were to find out we've made overtures to the Feds, we could both find ourselves out of a job, and then what good could we do?"

Zack snorted uncomfortably. "Yeah."

It was one thing, Daniel thought, for him to be willing to stick his own neck out, but since the game had gotten trickier, more dangerous, he had to give Zack a chance to bow out. "If you want to pass on this whole thing," Daniel said, looking Zack directly in the eye, "I'll understand."

"I'm in," said Zack without a moment's hesitation.

Daniel breathed a sigh of relief. "Okay, for the time being, let's keep doing our own snooping," he proposed. "And carefully. We've got to act like we've put the entire Morland matter completely behind us."

"Agreed. So what do you have in mind?"

"Stay clear of the sheriff's department for now. Dig up everything you can about the relationship between Paul Worthington and the other players. Holmes too. We know that both of those men have friends in high places. Let's see what reptiles we can find hiding under the rocks."

If Daniel Black did elect to help her, Rebecca wanted to have all of her witnesses ready to meet with him. She decided to stop in and see Scott Reed again at Brandon Taylor's campaign headquarters. She hadn't talked to Reed since the time he'd told her about the heated phone call he'd overheard between Ryan and Paul Worthington.

The primary was getting closer, and instead of having the nomination locked up as it had been when Ryan was alive, Brandon was now facing an uphill battle against Worthington.

She prayed Brandon himself wasn't at the storefront. They had not spoken since that night at the hospital when John Evans had died, and she hoped never to speak to Brandon again. As far as she was concerned, Brandon had betrayed both Ryan and her.

Inside, she could see that more desks and chairs had been stuffed into the room than before so that it was now quite crowded. And instead of two people sorting things, there were at least ten. The phones were ringing incessantly and it looked like controlled chaos.

A young woman in her late teens with long black hair came over to Rebecca. "May I help you?"

"Yes. I wanted to speak to Scott Reed. Is he here?"

The worker nodded. "He's in his office. Who can I say wants him?"

"Rebecca Morland."

"Sure." The young woman went off. Tired of the stares, the questions, the inane remarks, Rebecca was relieved that the young woman hadn't recognized her name. She longed for the privacy she'd once known.

Scott Reed himself came out to greet her, and she noted that his sandy-blond ponytail was gone. His hair was short now, neat and nondescript. Brandon had probably decided that Reed hadn't looked right for the part he was supposed to be playing.

"Mrs. Morland," he said, his eyes darting around nervously. "This is unexpected."

A shiver of apprehension ran up her spine. This man was uncomfortable with her being here. She wondered why. "I'd like to speak to you for a few minutes," she said, trying to make her voice friendly.

"I'm really busy," he said tersely. He glanced down at his watch. "Tell you what. There's a little restaurant about two blocks from here." He mentioned the name but she didn't recognize it. "Why don't you go over there and wait. I'll meet you in about fifteen minutes, okay?"

"Sure, if that's what you'd rather do. But it's not necessary. What I have to say won't take very long."

"No . . . well, I mean, I think that's best."

She was now positive Scott Reed wanted her to leave. It dawned on her that he might be afraid Brandon would show up. Brandon must have warned Reed that Rebecca was the enemy. "See you there," she called out.

Rebecca found the restaurant Scott Reed had suggested, a seedy, hole-in-the-wall place. An older woman stood behind the counter, smoking and watching a television set. There were only a few tables and chairs. The entire restaurant was no bigger than Rebecca's kitchen, and she was curious as to why Reed had wanted to meet her in a dump like this.

"What're you having?" the woman asked Rebecca, not taking her eyes off the television.

Rebecca ordered a bottle of Pellegrino and sat at a table to wait for Reed.

When he came in a few minutes later, she watched to see how he said hello to the woman. That would tell her if he frequented this place or if he had picked it because they didn't know him here.

He walked over to the counter. "How much for a cup of coffee?"

Rebecca had been right. He didn't want to be seen with her.

"So, what have you been doing?" he asked, stirring some sugar into his cup.

"The same. Trying to find out who murdered my husband."

"Oh?" His eyes were focused on his coffee. "I read about that theory of yours in the newspaper, but I thought it was settled. I mean when the news came out about Ryan stealing those funds from the firm—I just figured everyone finally knew that's why he killed himself."

"My husband did not steal that money and he did not kill himself. He was murdered." She paused, then added, "Anyway, I wanted to tell you that I'll be needing to take your statement soon."

Reed looked puzzled. "Why would you want to do that? I don't know anything."

"I mean about what you told me the last time we talked. You know, that you overheard Ryan having a heated discussion with Paul Worthington on the phone and then Ryan ran out to meet him."

He shook his head. "I don't remember saying that."

She was astounded. "You're going to stab my husband in the back too, like all the other bastards?"

The man's neck reddened. "I don't remember having that conversation with you."

Rebecca felt as if she were in the Twilight Zone again. "Who got to you? Was it Brandon Taylor who told you to keep your mouth shut? Or are you really a spy for Paul Worthington? Did he make it worth your while to conveniently lose your memory?"

"You have no right to talk to me like this," Reed declared indignantly. He stood up and slammed a quarter down on the table. "I've got to get back." Without another word he turned and walked out of the restaurant.

Rebecca felt tears pushing at the back of her eyes, but she refused to cry. From the way Scott Reed had reacted, she knew she had touched a nerve. What she didn't know was which one of her theories was right. After all, Ryan was dead and therefore he couldn't do anything more for Reed. But either Worthington or Brandon would be able to give him what he probably wanted —a job as part of their staff in Washington. Which horse had he decided to back?

Pulling into the Ralph's parking lot on Ventura Boulevard in Encino, Rebecca remembered how much she used to love going to the market after work, planning the dinner she would make for Ryan. Now grocery shopping was pure drudgery, just a matter of getting the few things she needed so she could keep on functioning, like coffee, orange juice, and toilet paper. Since Ryan's death she'd been eating mostly junk food. One of these days she would get herself back on her customary healthful diet, or so she promised.

Inside, she got a cart and started down one of the aisles. Suddenly, she felt someone's hand on her shoulder. She whirled around to find Daniel Black standing there.

He looked concerned. "I'm sorry if I scared you."

"That's . . . okay," she replied, getting her breath back. "Is something wrong?"

"I need to talk to you for a few minutes. How long will it take you to finish your marketing?"

"Ten minutes."

"Fine. Meet me over at the bookstore when you're done. We have to make sure we're not being followed. So this is what I want you to do." When he was through he said, "Got it?"

"Yes," she whispered back.

"See you in a few."

Back at her car, Rebecca loaded her groceries into the trunk. Suddenly paranoid, she anxiously watched another woman piling her bags into a van parked next to her. Was she possibly someone other than a woman doing the family's grocery shopping? Rebecca wondered. Or how about that man finishing his cigarette before he got into that red sports car? No, she thought, if you were following someone you wouldn't drive such a conspicuous automobile.

Her nerves were already shot from everything that had happened. Now she had something else to contend with. How much more was she going to have to go through before this nightmare came to an end?

The bookstore was really close, so Rebecca decided not to move her car. Checking her watch, she put on a light sweater before she locked the Jeep. It was almost six but not dark yet as the days were getting longer. Soon the clocks would be set forward to take advantage of the light.

She walked around to the coffee bar and bought a cappuccino along with a couple of biscotti and then entered the bookstore. It was nice the way they let you bring your refreshments in. And the comfortable couches and chairs scattered around the huge store encouraged people to stay and read for as long as they wanted.

Relieved, she saw that the couch at the back was empty. Sinking into its overstuffed cushions, she was attuned to every sound around her. Her eyes quickly roamed the stacks, taking in the people browsing there. Did any one of them look suspicious? She wished she had a better idea of what kind of person might be following her.

Glancing up, she observed Daniel approaching. So as not to appear to be waiting for him, she opened one of the books on her lap and began reading. She felt him settle into the seat next to her. They remained quiet for a few minutes as he sipped the coffee he had gotten himself.

"Did you see anyone?" he whispered.

She shook her head. "What's wrong?"

He quickly filled her in on what had happened. While he talked, Rebecca's stomach tensed with nerves. It seemed as if everyone she involved in her problems immediately found themselves in a difficult situation or, worse, threatened in some way.

"I don't have much to tell you yet. But I wanted to let you know that apparently your fears are well founded."

Rebecca already knew that, but hearing the words coming from this fearless deputy D.A. somehow gave it a reality it hadn't had before.

"I'm stunned by how quickly they got to me," he said, sipping his coffee and flipping through a book at the same time. "That's why it's absolutely mandatory that you don't tell a soul I'm doing this."

"I understand. Can I just tell Lucy?" She proceeded to explain to him about her legal intern.

"It sounds like she's really been your support system, and I'm sure she's fine," Daniel said. "However, the fewer people who know about this, the better. Not only for our own protection, but for that of the other people as well."

Rebecca nodded. She didn't need to have Lucy as terrified as Solowski was. And there was little Gaby to think about too. "I won't say anything," she promised him.

He closed his book. "I'll be in touch as soon as I have anything to report. Okay?"

"Yes."

"I doubt that they would go so far as to tap our phone lines, especially mine. But the less said on the phone the better, so I may also be contacting you in other ways."

"Like at the market?"

"Yes." For the first time he smiled at her. It was a nice smile, one probably meant to convey hope and reassurance. "Don't worry," he said. "We're going to get to the bottom of what's going on."

"I hope so," she replied. "I'd hate to think they could get away with this."

"They won't." He flashed her another quick smile, then got up and left.

Rebecca continued to sit there for a few minutes. She wanted Daniel to mean what he'd said about getting to the bottom of things. Unfortunately, she'd been trying to unravel this mystery alone for too long. She had become accustomed to trusting no one—even this really nice man. Nor could she merely sit back and wait for him to solve this mess for her. She needed help desperately, and she prayed he could give it to her, but in the meantime, she intended to keep on looking for the answers on her own.

CHAPTER
TWENTY-FIVE

In a limousine reserved exclusively for his use, Brandon was being driven to a dinner in his honor. Since they rarely had time to talk anymore, and since neither of them had an escort for the evening, Catherine had joined him for the ride.

"What do the latest polls show?" she asked.

"I'm gaining back some of my lost ground," Brandon responded, straightening his bow tie and pulling down his cuffs. "This isn't going to be a slam-dunk thing like Worthington was hoping." He grinned at her. "Now if we could only come up with a scandal to set him back."

"I've been racking my brain for ideas," she acknowledged. "It was terrible the way Worthington took advantage of Ryan's death. Of course, after the news about Ryan's theft came out, people began to see his suicide had nothing to do with you. At least the media saw John's demise for what it was," she added.

"Yes," he agreed, musing about the slew of articles and commentaries on his nephew's death. The general consensus seemed to be that John had been killed by a follow-home robber. The tragedy had actually been good for Brandon. Whereas Ryan's death had cast doubt on him, most likely helped along by Worthington's machinations, the random death of his nephew had had the opposite effect—creating a backlash of sympathy for Brandon, who was taking full advantage of it.

"I also believe most people see your continued campaigning as an act of bravery," Catherine pointed out. "After all, you've lost your closest relative and yet it hasn't stopped you from doing what's needed to help the people of this state."

"I appreciate your comments." He flexed his shoulders.

Catherine, who was wearing a flattering cream-colored satin gown, had opened her compact and was checking her lipstick.

"You look positively beautiful tonight, Catherine."

She flashed him a wide smile. "Why, thank you, Brandon. And you look very much like the next U.S. senator from California."

Brandon Taylor graciously nodded his head.

Putting the compact away in her evening bag, Catherine fixed her gaze on his. "Have you heard from Rebecca?"

"Not since I saw her at the hospital." Brandon had not told Catherine all the details of his confrontation with Rebecca, and certainly nothing having to do with John's confession. He'd decided to wait and see what Rebecca did, then he could counter it. The last thing he needed was for Catherine to figure out the truth about his nephew.

"I still don't understand how she happened to be there."

"According to Rebecca, she was parked outside John's place, waiting to speak to him, when he pulled into the alley. After the lights didn't come on, she went to check on him."

"Yes, I heard that part," Catherine said in that impatient tone of voice she was famous for. "What I'd like to know is what she wanted to talk to him about."

"I'm not sure, but Rebecca might have mentioned it had something to do with the theft."

"Hmm. On that subject she's a fanatic. I told you what happened when she accosted me on the beach that morning, didn't I?"

"I'm not sure," he said, stiffening.

"Well, with everything that's been happening, I may have forgotten. Rebecca gave me some ridiculous story about John's being a gambler who owed money to bookies. I explained I'd seen the evidence of Ryan's guilt with my own eyes, but she remained unconvinced. I don't think she can deal with the truth."

"I'm afraid you're right there," he agreed, relieved to hear that Catherine had discounted Rebecca's story.

"Rebecca also told me that John had been married. Did she make that up too?"

"No. That part was true," he conceded.

She eyed him curiously. "Why didn't he ever tell us?"

Brandon hurried to rationalize his nephew's behavior. "Probably because she wasn't the right kind of girl for him, if you know what I mean. I think he just wanted to forget it happened. As for the young lady, as lawyers we both know how a scorned spouse can make up all sorts of stories regarding the other person in order to feel better about herself. I'm sure that's what happened, and Rebecca, because she's looking for conspiracies under every rock, fell for it."

Catherine crossed her legs. "You're probably right."

Shortly, they pulled into the underground garage of the Century Plaza Hotel, where the car would drop them off directly in front of the ballroom where Brandon would be speaking. Tonight's event was an illustrious gathering of movie industry Republicans and California bigwigs. People had paid one thousand dollars a ticket for the dinner, with many of the guests purchasing several tables. They were expecting a huge turnout.

Brandon shook hands with numerous people who were waiting in the lobby of the ballroom to escort him in. The guests were already seated, and Catherine was taken to her table so she could watch Brandon's entrance.

Just as the doors were about to be opened, Rebecca suddenly appeared by Brandon's side.

"We need to talk," she told him.

His heart started beating furiously in his chest. What a mess if she chose to make a scene here, he thought frantically. Of course everyone would think that the poor girl was still distraught over the death of her husband, but if possible, he'd rather avoid any kind of unpleasantness.

The bodyguard he'd hired for these types of events had Rebecca by the arm and was ready to take care of the situation when Brandon interceded. "It will just be a minute," he told everyone around him with a reassuring nod.

He drew her over to a corner of the lobby. "Now isn't a good time, Rebecca," he whispered in a tight voice. "There are eight hundred people waiting for me inside."

"I'll leave in two seconds—just as soon as you explain what kind of deal you made with Holmes." Her green eyes had a feverish intensity. "I have a right to know."

"I've already told you." He sighed with exasperation. "You just refuse to believe me. He merely arranged for me to pay the bookie off, with something extra for his trouble. That's it."

"If you keep balking at telling me the truth, I'm going to ask Holmes myself," she asserted.

Gazing directly into her eyes, he whispered, "Rebecca, for heaven's sake listen to me, because I'll never repeat it again. Understood?"

"Yes."

"Maxwell Holmes is a very dangerous man. Do not go to him, do not talk to him—stay as far away from him as you can. You're playing with fire. I warned Ryan too, but he wouldn't listen."

Her face turned white. "What do you mean?"

"I don't know of anyone who can protect you from that man." He paused. "Now, that's all I intend to say," he added firmly and then signaled to the bodyguard that he was done.

The man came over. "May I escort you out, ma'am?" he said politely.

Brandon saw the fear in Rebecca's eyes and hoped she'd listen to his warning. "I've got to go in now," he told her. Then he turned and walked away.

The next moment, the ballroom doors were opened and Brandon was led down the red carpet as eight hundred people gave him a standing ovation, their cheers continuing as he proudly made his way to the podium.

Standing on the moving escalator, accompanied by the bodyguard, Rebecca heard the applause explode in the ballroom. She was consumed by anger and self-pity: anger that Brandon was getting away with his lies, his deceit, his betrayal of Ryan—and that he was basking in the adulation of the roaring crowd—and self-pity, because Ryan was gone and so far she'd been singularly unsuccessful in avenging his death.

What had Brandon meant when he said he'd warned Ryan to stay away from Holmes? Was he admitting that he had known the man would kill her husband? She wondered if Ryan could see what was going on from where he was, and if so, what he thought of his idol now.

The next afternoon, shortly after two, Rebecca drove into the Trousdale Estates and headed for Maxwell Holmes's house. She had thought long and hard about Brandon Taylor's warning, and in spite of what he might think, she had not taken it lightly. She had no doubt that Holmes was a very dangerous man. Still, there had to be some safe way she could get to him.

What she had in mind was keeping an eye on his comings and goings for a day or two. Maybe from someone who visited Holmes, or from someplace he went, she'd get an idea about a new avenue to explore.

Her thoughts shifted to Daniel Black, and she wondered how he was doing in his investigation. Hopefully, she'd hear from him soon.

In reaching Holmes's house, she searched for a spot to park where she wouldn't be noticed. A few doors away there was a car with a trailer attached, holding a speedboat. Rebecca pulled in behind it and shut off her motor. Once again she'd brought bags of junk food, lots of coffee, and some work. Her portable phone, which had been with her at all times since that night on the canyon road, kept her in touch with her answering machine and any messages that came in.

There were several other cars parked on the street—two expensive Mercedeses, one Jaguar, and one Rolls-Royce. She wondered if any of their owners were inside visiting with Holmes. Just in case, she wrote down the license-plate numbers.

As she sat there, her mind played over the things she'd learned about Holmes. John Evans had said the man had "connections." Even knowing that bribes and payoffs happened every day in politics, she still had a hard time believing that there could be an association between politics and organized crime, but she'd surmised from her conversation with Daniel Black that he hadn't found such a supposition to be farfetched. What she couldn't quite figure out was why Brandon would want to get mixed up in something like that. But then after what John had told her, who was she to judge what someone should do when trying to save his only nephew's life.

Rebecca had been sitting in her car for almost three hours when she detected some activity at Holmes's front door. It was hard to see from the street because of the shrubbery, so she used her binoculars. There were two people, a man and a woman, and they were kissing. When the woman turned to leave, the man pulled her back for another kiss. The woman was tall and thin and wearing a mink coat. That was strange, Rebecca thought. Not that it was too warm, but one rarely saw fur coats in California anymore, especially during the day.

Because she had on dark glasses and there was a scarf over her hair, it was hard to make out the woman's features. The man stepped farther outside, and Rebecca was able to identify him— it was Maxwell Holmes. She watched as he ran his hand under the woman's coat. The woman glanced around quickly as if she were worried someone might see them. Then she blew him a kiss and ran to the white Jaguar. There was something very familiar about the woman, and Rebecca tried to place where she'd seen her before. She'd have to ask Daniel Black to run the license number.

Suddenly an image flashed into her mind. No, it couldn't be. Rebecca held the binoculars up again. My God, it was— Diana Worthington. What on earth was she doing visiting Maxwell Holmes? Rebecca was dumbfounded. Holmes was supposed to be backing Brandon. Was he secretly plotting against him with Worthington? Could this be what Ryan had meant when he'd said politics was so dirty? Was it possible Worthington and Holmes had killed Brandon's top aide in a manner that would suggest suicide to discredit Brandon the way Vince Foster's suicide had hurt President Clinton? But that made no sense. Why not just kill Brandon and eliminate the candidate?

Don't be silly, she told herself. Mrs. Worthington was doing more than visiting Maxwell Holmes. There was no mistaking the intimate kisses Rebecca had just witnessed. But so what if Paul Worthington's wife was having an affair with Holmes? That didn't mean anything more than that the two of them were lovers. Worthington wouldn't know about it and Brandon certainly wouldn't either. Was this the secret Ryan had discovered? And if so, whom had he told?

Rebecca strained but couldn't see what was going on in the car. Diana seemed to be shucking off her mink coat and slipping into something else. Not wanting to take the chance of being spotted, Rebecca sank down in her seat. Maybe when the woman drove by, she could tell more. Then Mrs. Worthington, who was now wearing sweats and a visor as if she'd been out jogging, got out of her vehicle and dumped the mink coat in the trunk. A few seconds later, she turned the automobile around and drove off.

Rebecca contemplated following her but changed her mind. Diana was probably headed for Newport Beach. When Rebecca spoke to Daniel Black, she'd tell him what she'd seen. In the meantime, she'd watch Holmes a little longer.

Tires screeching, Diana pulled into the garage of her home. It was large and could hold nine cars, not to mention a small workshop for repairs. Her heart sank. Leaning against one of the vehicles was her husband, Paul, wearing a scowl on his face.

Usually, because of their hectic schedules, she and Holmes never got together more than once a week. Lately he'd been calling her more often. A shiver of apprehension coursed through her as she quickly composed her face into a smile and got out.

"Hello, darling," she said with a wave, reaching into the back of the car to get her gym bag. Hopefully, he wouldn't notice the fact that her heart was pounding faster than normal.

He didn't even bother to say hello as he strode over to where she was standing. "Where have you been?" Worthington asked, his eyes narrowed, his mouth set in a grim line.

Diana swallowed down her fear. Gesturing toward herself and the sweats she was wearing, she teased him. "My goodness, can't you tell? I've been working out. Why? Is something wrong?"

Ignoring her questions, he demanded, "Where?"

"The gym at the country club," she responded.

"That's funny," he snapped, gripping her arm and digging his fingers into the soft flesh. "I called there a short while ago and was told that they hadn't seen you all day."

Feeling her knees grow weak with terror, she tried to make light of it. "Whoever you talked to must be new."

He shook his head. "I had the person on the desk check with every trainer and employee in both the gym and the spa."

"Well, I was there darling, so I don't know how that can be." Diana gave a nervous laugh before adding, "You're hurting me, Paul." She tried to pry his fingers away with her free hand.

His face had darkened into a hard, angry mask. "Diana, if you are doing something to make a fool of me, you'll be sorry. I can promise you that."

"Make a fool of you?" She gave him a dazzling smile, showing the white teeth she had had bleached last year. "Why, I don't know what you mean, darling."

"Is there another man?" The question forced its way out between his clenched teeth.

"No." She knew she should leave it at that, but something inside her wouldn't allow it. "But if there were, who could blame me? It's been years since I've had any *real* sex with my husband."

The muscle in Worthington's jaw was moving back and forth. "We've been married for almost fifteen years, Diana. We share many other good things. Contrary to what you think, physical intercourse is not a necessary component of a good marriage."

"Maybe not for you," she countered, feeling her anger rise, "but to me it is. I need to be touched, held, made love to." Her voice broke. "Your thoughts on this subject are unnatural. I've even asked our doctor about it, and he agreed."

"You told our doctor?" His eyes were wide with horror.

"Yes," she nodded, pushing some loose hairs back into her chignon. "I needed to confide in someone."

Paul's mouth was hanging open as if he couldn't believe what she had just told him. "How could you do such a thing?"

"You won't ever discuss the subject with me," she said in an accusatory voice. "As far as I'm concerned, you left me no choice." She stopped long enough to take a deep breath. "Do you want to know what he asked me?"

His eyes were pools of anger, glowering at her. "What?"

"Was there any possibility you were gay."

Like a bolt from the blue, his hand came up and slapped her hard across the face. "How can you even consider such a thing?"

Holding her fingers to her smarting cheek, she became defiant. "So what if I was with a lover. What are you going to do about it? Divorce me?" Her rage was white hot, and she could no longer hold her emotions in check as the pent-up anger and frustration spilled out of her. "What would happen to your political career then? The men who support you don't believe in divorce. You leave me and your dreams of becoming President will die. I'll not only get one-half of everything we have, but I'll tell the world I'm divorcing you because you've refused to touch me for years."

Worthington stood in front of her, shaking his head.

Tears were now streaming out of her eyes. "I wanted children. You said no. Tell me—I deserve to know—why won't you make love to me?"

"Diana, stop this nonsense right now," he demanded, his voice harsh. "I thought you wanted what I did, and I thought you wanted it just as much."

As her rage subsided, her old insecurities returned. No, she didn't want to lose either him or the life they had. For fifteen years she'd put up with it all because she wanted to be Mrs. Paul Worthington more than anything else in the world. After such sacrifice, she'd earned the right to be a U.S. senator's wife and then, hopefully, the First Lady. "I do," she replied meekly.

He looked at her for what seemed an eternity, and she felt fearful. She could see what an effort he was making to swallow his pride.

"Then go take a bath," he finally said harshly. "I can smell him on you." The disgust in his voice was palpable. "We'll discuss this later when we've both calmed down."

Diana nodded and headed inside. She felt weak with relief. The crucial moment had passed. If he'd meant to kick her out of the house, he would have done it then. Thank God, he hadn't asked her who she was with. It was almost as if he didn't want to know. But she was aware he'd be watching her more carefully than ever. Somehow, this thing with Holmes had to end.

When Rebecca got home that night, she noticed a car on the other side of the street blinking its lights off and on several times. She didn't recognize the make, and it was too dark to see who was driving. Carefully, she pulled alongside, ready to put her foot on the gas if it turned out to be someone menacing.

With a sigh of relief, she realized it was Daniel Black. He beckoned for her to follow him. A few blocks from her house, he pulled over and stopped. She followed suit.

Daniel got out of his car and slid into the front seat beside her. The air immediately filled with the scent from the aftershave he was wearing. It made Rebecca realize how much she missed being around a man.

She told him quickly what she'd witnessed and gave him the license number to verify.

"Are you saying you think Maxwell Holmes and Diana Worthington killed your husband to keep him from divulging their affair?"

"I'm not sure," she admitted. Then as if realizing he had to have come to see her for some other reason, she asked, "What's going on?"

He took a deep breath and exhaled. "I've got some papers to go over with you."

Rebecca glanced at him curiously. "What are they?"

"Let me explain what I intend to do, then you take a few minutes to absorb it. I don't want to do anything without your knowing about it."

His words sent small shivers up her arms, and she felt goose bumps on her skin. "Go on," she urged, anxious to find out what he meant.

"Zack and I have talked this thing over and we've decided that we need to get a full toxicological screen done on your husband's body. If he was, in fact, thrown off that boat, it's quite possible he was given something that made him drowsy. But to be honest, we're afraid to trust the facilities where they did the autopsy. That's why I've drafted a motion"—he paused, then went on—"to exhume your husband's body and have it taken to another facility."

The moment he said *exhume*, Rebecca's stomach turned over. From all that had happened the last few days, she was already feeling fragile and vulnerable. The thought of having Ryan brought up out of the ground made her so ill she had to put her head on the steering wheel while she tried to catch her breath.

"I'm sorry. I know how hard this is." She felt his hand on her shoulder. It had been so long since she had let her guard down that she started to cry.

He reached into his pocket and removed a handkerchief, which he handed to her. "Go ahead and cry as long as you need to," he told her in a soothing voice. "Like I said, this must be really hard."

It took Rebecca a few minutes before she could get her composure back. She took a deep breath. "I . . . I don't know what to say. If you feel that's really necessary, then I guess it has to be done. It . . . just sounds . . . so horrible."

"I know. Honestly, Rebecca, I have no idea how I'd handle it if I were in your shoes." He started telling her a little bit about his family back in New York. His dad was a rabbi and his family were Orthodox Jews. He explained how his people were usually buried without embalming because they believed the sooner they returned to dust, the quicker their soul would be released. "I don't think they would like doing this at all."

She nodded. "I'm Jewish too, but Reform, and many of us believe in embalming. Ryan wasn't Jewish and he was embalmed, so he's probably more preserved." She sighed. Daniel had made it easy for her to discuss what was really bothering her—namely, the condition of her husband's body when it came up out of the ground.

"There would be no need for you to be there," he told her in a soothing voice. "I would take care of everything."

"If you're worried about keeping things secret, how do you do this without other people finding out?"

He gave her another reassuring smile. "I'll take these papers to a judge and get his okay. Then we'll get the casket removed by a private company. I'd prefer early evening, when no one is around the cemetery. They take the casket to the place we've designated. They remove his body and do what they have to do. The casket is then sealed again and put back in the ground before daybreak."

"Oh God," she said, wringing her hands, "I don't know if I could stand having him suffer the indignity of all that without my at least being there for him."

"I understand. Whatever your wishes are in the matter, I'll help you carry them out."

She sat in silence trying to decide what to do. It was obvious that Daniel believed her story; if not, he wouldn't be willing to go to all this trouble, which was only putting him in danger. "I realize I should be grateful that you're helping me and here I am acting like an idiot."

"No, don't say that." He shook his head, frowning. "This is a sensitive subject, and I've thrown it at you with absolutely no warning. Besides, you've been having a rough time of it."

Rebecca was deeply touched by his kindness. "Can I see the papers?"

"Sure. Do you have an overhead light you can turn on?"

"There's a flashlight in the glove compartment. That might be better."

"Right." He opened a folder and handed it to her.

Rebecca read the forms quickly, satisfying herself that they said exactly what he'd told her.

"I can't be there," she said finally, biting down hard on her lower lip and willing herself not to cry. It was important for her to concentrate solely on finding Ryan's killer.

CHAPTER
TWENTY-SIX

Almost two weeks later, feeling chilled to the bone, Rebecca waited in front of El Torito on Fisherman's Wharf in Marina del Rey. Daniel had sent her a message that he'd be there by four o'clock and that after he parked, he'd walk along the waterfront. If everything looked okay and they were sure they hadn't been followed, they would meet.

But today he was late—almost an hour late. She wished she could stop worrying. Instead, all she could think of were the terrible things that might have happened to him.

She had visions of the police arresting Daniel and his investigator on some trumped-up charges. If Daniel was in jail, he wouldn't be allowed to call her. How would she know what had happened? Or even worse, what if the people who were trying to stop the investigation found out about the exhumation and killed Daniel and his investigator, Zack—how would she ever live with herself then? She tried to force these terrible thoughts from her mind, but it wasn't easy.

It was getting windy, and even in the harbor she saw white-caps on the water. She had worn a scarf and had wrapped it tightly around her head. Pacing back and forth to keep warm, she hoped that the autopsy gave them proof that Ryan had in fact been murdered. Her nerves were shattered, and she wasn't sure how much more she could take. She prayed for this nightmare to be over and her husband's killers in jail.

When Rebecca looked up she saw Daniel walking swiftly in her direction, his head lowered as a buffer against the wind. Taking a few steps back, she shielded herself behind a piling so that she could observe if there was anyone suspicious lurking about.

He strode past her, acknowledging her presence with a nod. She waited to see if he was alone. After five minutes, seeing no one, she determined it was safe and made her way down the waterfront.

"Over here," he whispered as she came to the far end.

By now, Rebecca was shivering so badly her teeth were chattering.

"Let's go inside and get something warm to drink," he suggested, rubbing his hands together.

She agreed eagerly.

In the restaurant, seated at a table where they couldn't readily be seen, he apologized for being late. An emergency had come up at the office, and he had no way to reach her. They talked about the weather and other generalities until their coffee came.

Finally, she couldn't stand the suspense any longer. "Please, tell me what you found."

"I'm sorry," he said, with a hangdog expression. "I forgot how you must be feeling." His hazel eyes were filled with kindness. "Well, from the full toxicological screen, we were able to identify two substances in Ryan's body: ethyl alcohol and amitriptyline."

"Ethyl alcohol?"

"That's usually present when someone was drinking hard liquor."

"And the other substance?"

"They tell me it's the generic name of a drug sold under the brand name Elavil." He eyed her carefully. "Does that ring a bell?"

"No. Should it?"

"It's an antidepressant," he explained, watching for her reaction.

"You mean they use it for treating depression?"

"Right." His hands were around his cup. "Did Ryan ever take any medication for depression?"

"No, he didn't."

"I see." He sipped his coffee.

"What kind of effects does this drug have?" she asked.

"As I understand it, in the beginning it can make a person both queasy and dizzy. Drinking alcohol with it would intensify its effects."

Her eyes lit up. "That's it, then!" she cried excitedly. "Someone must have given him that drug."

"Rebecca, the drug didn't kill him—at most it disabled him. We have to prove that someone gave it to him with the knowledge that it would make him fall into the water, become incapacitated, and drown."

"What do you mean?" She observed his face closely.

"If they just gave him the drug, that's not enough," he said. "We have to prove cause and effect. We have to show it contributed to his death. Or set in motion a chain of events that led to his death. What if it made him queasy and he went out on the swim step to vomit?" His brow was furrowed. "We'd have to prove that they knew that those pills would make him nauseated. And then we'd have to prove that they also knew he'd go out on the swim step and fall into the water. Or if the pills merely made him dizzy, we'd have to prove that they knew he'd fall in the water."

"I see what you're saying, but why don't we worry about cause and effect later? Let's just concentrate on finding out who gave Ryan that drug to begin with," she said, annoyance in her voice.

"Agreed," he nodded with a large sigh. "But first I want you to do something for me."

"What's that?" She stirred some cream into her coffee and lifted her cup to her lips.

"I want you to call each one of Ryan's doctors and have a talk with them." He started counting off points with his fingers. "Find out when they saw him last, if he asked for any referrals, and if he ever discussed taking something for his depression."

She felt her anger surging. "I already told you," she said, her voice rising. "My husband wasn't taking any medication at the time of his death."

Daniel reached out and covered her hand with his. "Please, Rebecca. I know how you feel. But this is important. We must be absolutely sure that Ryan did not obtain this medication himself."

She pulled her hand away and narrowed her eyes. "It would make a lot more sense to check the medicine cabinets of everyone out there who had a reason to see him dead. Like Paul Worthington or Maxwell Holmes. Or Brandon Taylor, Catherine Dennison, and John Evans."

His voice stayed low. "Don't make this any harder on yourself than it has to be, okay?"

"That's easy for you to say," she snapped.

He remained cool. "You're obviously in a great deal of pain, and I don't blame you for being impatient. But it's important for you to remember that I'm approaching this as a prosecutor, and what I really need you to do at the moment is to think like a lawyer and help me, not fight me."

Rebecca wanted to believe this man was trying to help her, but there had been so many disappointments. Was he just another in a long line of people who were convinced Ryan had committed suicide? Did he feel this antidepressant drug meant Ryan had sought help and was on medication?

For a long moment, his hazel eyes never left hers. "I see your mind working," he told her. "And I can guess the kinds of questions you're asking yourself."

"Now you're a mind reader?" Her voice was heavy with sarcasm.

Instead of taking offense, he smiled affably. "Yes. You're trying to decide if I'm like all the rest of the people you've run into since your husband died, or if I truly share your conviction that your husband was murdered."

The earnestness on his face made her feel ashamed. "You're right," she admitted. "I want to believe in you . . ."

"Good. Because I believe *you,* Rebecca. I'm on your side."

Those words meant a lot to her. She sighed. "I'll do what you ask."

"Okay," Daniel said smoothly, then glanced at his watch.

"Do you have to be somewhere?" she asked, sure she had already taken up too much of his time.

"No. I just have a lot more work to do when I get home. The reason I checked my watch is that I'm hungry. It's almost six o'clock." He grinned at her again. "Would you like to join me for a bite to eat so a hardworking deputy D.A. doesn't have to dine alone?"

Her eyebrow arched. "Yes, but on one condition."

"What's that?" he asked.

"You let me buy you dinner." Her voice was firm.

Daniel's smile this time seemed almost shy. "How about if we compromise and go dutch?"

"Deal," she agreed.

Almost a week had passed since Rebecca had learned the results of the toxicological screen done on Ryan's body. In that time she'd called Ryan's doctors and learned that none of them had prescribed an antidepressant drug for him. Nor had any of them referred her husband to another doctor. Tomorrow she would telephone Daniel with the news.

Rebecca poured herself a glass of milk to go with the peanut-butter-and-jelly sandwich she was eating for dinner while doing her monthly bills on the computer. When the phone rang, she reached for it and spilled her milk.

"Damn," she swore, trying to wipe the liquid off the keys before her computer was ruined and, at the same time, answering the phone.

It was her mother calling long distance. Not wanting to worry her folks, Rebecca had told them she was already back at work, but that it was still best to reach her at home.

"Everything's okay, Mom. Yes. I'm eating. I'm sleeping too.

Listen, let me get back to you in a little bit. I just spilled something." Realizing how late it was, they agreed to talk in the next few days.

Between cleaning up the mess and then telephoning Lucy to go over a case, almost an hour passed before Rebecca sat down to finish her work. When she tried to call up what she'd been doing, she realized she must have hit some wrong keys as she'd wiped up the spill.

She had been working in a subdirectory, but now she went into her main directory and started looking down the list of files. Many of the names conjured up memories of things she had shared with Ryan—like the itinerary for their last vacation, and their famous letter to the IRS. The next file caught her attention: "Jenson." What kind of file was that? She couldn't remember anything she'd ever labeled that way. The only person she'd ever known with that name was a law professor, one that she and Ryan had shared although they'd attended law school several years apart.

Glancing at the numbers after the file she saw how long the document was. She was surprised. How could she have made a file that big and not remember it?

A strange feeling came over her as she brought the file up. Seeing the first words, Rebecca felt goose bumps rise up and down her arms. It was as if Ryan were speaking to her from the grave. It started:

> *Dear Rebecca. I hope if and when you find this file, everything has worked out, but if it hasn't, make sure you are alone before you read on.*

Tears started running down her cheeks as she realized Ryan had purposefully stored this file in her computer. No. He had *hidden* it in her computer. So, she'd been right after all. Ryan had realized his life was in danger. Starting to tremble, she hugged herself. She had to be strong. Terrified to see what it said, but knowing she had no choice, she slowly began scrolling down the page.

Tony kept glancing up every time the door opened as he waited anxiously for Catherine to show up at Morton's, the Hollywood deal-making hangout. She was at least fifteen minutes late, which had him worried, since she was usually so punctual. Finally, she came through the door. Her eyes located him already seated, and she gave a brief nod.

She looked stunning in one of her many Armani power suits, as he called them, and more than a few heads turned in her direction. He watched as she stopped to say hello to a few celebrities and Hollywood agents, making her way to their table.

Tony didn't really like places like this. It wasn't the kind of romantic restaurant he favored. Morton's was mostly a business-type place where the object was to be seen and counted as one of the power elite.

He started to stand up to pull her chair out, but the look in her eyes stopped him cold. She hated for him to do things like that. Tony wished she'd give him a kiss; even a peck on the cheek would be better than the businesslike greeting she issued.

The waiter arrived. "I'll have a scotch on the rocks," Catherine told him brusquely.

After he ordered and the waiter left, Tony tried to take her hand, but she brushed his away, glancing around quickly. "Please, Tony, not in public."

Her attitude was infuriating him. She was supposed to love him. Why was she so afraid to have anyone else know?

"We've talked about these public displays before," she whispered to him. "I don't need to be upset at dinner. It's already been a perfectly grueling day."

"What's going on?" he asked, suppressing his anger.

"Brandon's trying to take advantage of the shift in the polls, so he's running around to meetings and speaking engagements and leaving me to hold the firm together."

The waiter showed up, and she took a hearty swallow of her drink before continuing. "I don't mind the legal work, it's the running of the office that has me crazed. If you can believe it," she said, in an exasperated voice, "most of the lawyers working for us are actually complaining about their caseloads. Jesus, considering that we've lost two partners in three months, you'd think they'd be more than willing to pitch in." She arched her eyebrows to make her point.

"And they're not?"

"No." She brushed her hair back. "In my day, if a partner asked you to jump, the standard response from an associate was always 'How high?' "

"And now?"

She rolled her eyes. "I hear things like 'My kid's boy scout troop is having a weekend sleep-over.' Or 'My daughter is playing baseball.' Jesus. Who cares?"

"It's a changing world," he said. "People are reassessing their priorities. Not every young lawyer wants to make partner anymore if it means an eighty-hour workweek and no family life." He watched her face, hoping she'd get the underlying message.

"Then let them find another profession," she shot back. "Or let them go and hang up a shingle somewhere in the boondocks."

Before he could respond, an older man, balding and with a black goatee, came over to say hello. Catherine immediately became charming. Tony sat waiting for her to introduce him. Finally, he held out his hand.

"I'm Anthony Necosia."

The other man introduced himself. Tony recognized the name. He headed a large movie studio.

Catherine's eyes narrowed in anger, but she hastily covered it up with a wide smile. "Mr. Necosia and I are trying to settle a case." She stepped on his toe under the table and went on talking with the man about a business deal.

Sitting there stewing, Tony couldn't make up his mind whether or not to call her bluff. If he interrupted to say they were really on a date, Catherine would look foolish and so would he. Besides, she'd never forgive him for mortifying her in front of such an important person.

He'd recently complained to Catherine about the lack of depth in their relationship. Since then, to his surprise, she'd actually made more of an effort to talk about her feelings. It had given him hope. But only briefly—and there were limits to how much he could endure. This was the last time he intended to be humiliated. If Catherine wasn't willing to introduce him properly, to treat him like an equal, he was going to end their relationship. When they got home tonight, he'd make that absolutely clear to her.

As Rebecca read Ryan's letter to her, flashes of the past meshed with the present. So many things began to make sense.

> *I discovered that a case at the law firm was really nothing more than a cover-up for a phony settlement that had been run through the firm's trust account. With the use of my computer, I traced the source of the funds to an offshore account. I also traced the settlement paid out through the trust account to an entity that I'm sure Maxwell Holmes is connected with, although I can't prove it yet.*
>
> *Baffled, I went to Brandon with the information. To my dismay, Brandon told me to forget about it. But I couldn't let it go. It bothered me too much that Brandon would be involved in something dirty.*
>
> *We continued to argue over it until Brandon finally broke down and admitted to me what had happened. John had incurred enormous gambling debts, and when he couldn't pay, the bookie threatened his life. John came to Brandon, who immediately tried to settle the debt with the bookmaker. The man agreed to accept the payment but insisted John still had to be taught a lesson. If not, others would think they could stall without suffering any consequences. Terrified that these men meant to maim his nephew, Brandon went to Maxwell Holmes for help. He'd heard that the man had certain connections.*

So far, everything Rebecca was reading confirmed John's story. She scrolled to the next page.

Holmes agreed to help John in exchange for a favor from Brandon. Thinking it was a onetime thing, Brandon ran some funds for Holmes through the law firm's trust account and made it look like a settlement on a fictitious case.

Reading this, Rebecca was shocked. No wonder Brandon hadn't wanted to tell her.

Not long after, Holmes asked for another favor. Brandon balked, and Holmes threatened him, telling Brandon that if he didn't continue to help him, Brandon would not live to tell about it. Holmes also informed Brandon that the money he'd run through the trust account was dirty and that he'd in effect laundered it for some very unsavory people. Not only that, Brandon had unwittingly become part of a much larger criminal conspiracy.

Rebecca sat back utterly stunned. It was clear someone had killed Ryan because he'd discovered the phony deal and they were afraid he'd discover the rest. Who had it been—Brandon or Holmes or both of them?

Daniel Black was working in the spare bedroom of his small home in West Los Angeles. With all the phone calls, court appearances, and witness interviews that were required on his cases, he'd found it almost impossible to complete the necessary paperwork during office hours. Unfortunately, that meant that ever since he'd become a deputy D.A., he'd been bringing his case files home.

He rubbed his neck, feeling the knots of tension that were a direct result of the stress he was under. There was no money to hire more prosecutors in L.A. County, so not only was his own caseload heavier than it had ever been, trying to investigate the Morland case without anyone finding out about it was causing him nothing but problems.

Zack had telephoned earlier to say that he'd run into another wall of suspicion and had to stop one line of their inquiry. Daniel had no choice but to go along, but it angered him to be thwarted in that way.

Lost in thought when the phone started ringing, it took him a few seconds to refocus.

"Mom? Is that you? I can barely understand a word you're saying."

Heart pounding with fear, Daniel tried to calm his hysterical mother so he could find out what had happened. When he learned that his father had just had a massive heart attack and was not expected to live, he was devastated.

"Please God," he prayed silently, "let him stay alive until I get there."

Promising to get home as fast as he could, Daniel hung up and then called to book a seat on the next flight to New York.

As Rebecca continued to read Ryan's letter, she felt sick to her stomach. How upset Ryan must have been to find out that Brandon had become involved in something unlawful.

> *The threats from Holmes continued. I begged Brandon to go to the authorities. Although he'd done something wrong, there were mitigating circumstances—he'd been trying to save John from harm. The worst thing Brandon could do was to keep compounding his mistake. But Brandon insisted that if this were to come out it would ruin his political chances. He demanded I stay out of it.*

Her throat was parched, and Rebecca got up to get some water. Finally, she understood why her husband had been behaving so strangely those last few weeks. Ryan must have been devastated. His idol was caught in a criminal situation from which he refused to extricate himself. No wonder Ryan wouldn't tell her. He'd probably wished he himself had never found out.

Before Ryan's death, she would have had a hard time believing Brandon could do anything wrong. Unfortunately, she'd now learned differently. His ambition had turned him into a dishonorable, even despicable person.

Putting her glass in the sink, she went back to her computer.

> *Unable to convince Brandon to do the right thing, I decided to resign from the firm and a copy of my resignation letter is attached to the end of this document.*

She quickly hit the keys to bring it up, more than curious to see what it said. There before her eyes was something that sounded strangely familiar.

> *Dear Brandon:*
> *I've been thinking about this for a long time. There is nothing anyone can say or do to make me change my mind. Although I love this firm, and the day I became a partner was one of the happiest of my life, I feel I have no choice but to resign.*

Rebecca realized that the first two lines comprised the contents of what the police said was Ryan's suicide note. John must have found the handwritten copy of this letter and cut off the bottom and top parts.

Sitting back, she digested this information. Both Solowski and Rebecca had felt the note was unfinished somehow—it now seemed they had been right.

Going back into the main part of the document, she hurried to read what had happened next.

> *I decided to put my resignation letter in a drawer while I tried one last thing. I felt that if I told Holmes he'd better back off and leave Brandon alone, or I would personally go to the authorities and divulge*

the entire scheme, the man might listen. So I went to
see him, and Holmes went ballistic.

That night, Brandon telephoned me and told me
to stop playing God. He begged me to apologize to
Holmes, and I realized that Holmes had informed
Brandon of our altercation. Brandon indicated that
Holmes had political cronies in the highest echelons
of law enforcement and that threatening a man like
him was absolutely crazy.

Rebecca, I don't want to apologize. I feel strongly
that what's going on has to stop. But I've begun to
fear for my life and that's why I'm hiding this file in
your computer. Before I can go to the authorities, I've
got to find the evidence to nail Holmes.

Rebecca pressed her fingers to her temples. Maxwell
Holmes had obviously killed Ryan. As for Brandon, he had either
known, or guessed the man was involved and chosen to stay
quiet. Panic rising in her throat, she read what else Ryan had to
say.

Be extremely careful, Rebecca. I don't want you
to die too. If I live long enough to find the evidence, I
feel my best shot would be to go to the FBI. Hopefully,
Maxwell Holmes only has connections on a state level
and not a federal level. If I'm gone, do not look for
the evidence yourself. Turn this over to the FBI along
with all of the attached data I've been able to gather
so far.

There are two other things I want you to know.
First, I've discovered that John is probably stealing
money from the firm. There's a bankbook I've hidden
in my briefcase that will prove this. Second, Brandon
asked me to check into Paul Worthington's back-
ground. I've found something I wish I hadn't. It
should not be used in a political campaign, and I'm
afraid if Brandon knows about it, he'll use it. I've left

*the evidence in my gym locker for the moment. I'm
planning to destroy it, but in case I don't have time,
please do it for me.*

*I love you, Rebecca, with all my heart. I'm so
sorry for getting you involved. Please be careful.
These people are dangerous.*

Rebecca put her head against the computer screen and
cried, huge gulping sounds heaving forth from her chest.

When she had cried herself dry, she kissed the screen, right
over the words where he told her he loved her. "I love you too,"
she whispered.

She pushed down the sick feeling in her stomach—she had
to get a grip on herself. A lot of things had to be done, and
quickly. Stunned by the secrets she'd just learned, Rebecca tried
to figure out her options.

Realizing how incendiary all this was, she quickly copied the
file onto two separate disks. Then she addressed an envelope to
her parents with a note to hold on to it until she asked for it back.

Next, she grabbed her date book out of her purse and,
flipping through the pages, searched for Daniel Black's home
phone number and address. She was trembling and had to keep
reminding herself to keep calm.

Daniel's phone rang several times before his machine
picked up. She glanced at her watch, it was almost ten. Could
he be sleeping and have his phone turned off? Or maybe he was
out on a date. She decided to leave a message.

"Daniel, it's Rebecca Morland. I've discovered a secret document, which my husband must have hidden in my computer
before he died. It's got all kinds of facts and details as to what
was going on those last few weeks before his death. I think I
know who murdered him and why. It's getting late, but I'm
going to bring this file to your house tonight. That way you'll
have it for the morning. Call me as soon as you can."

Maxwell Holmes had been dozing in front of the television set
when he was awakened by the ringing of his phone. "Yes," he
answered, instantly recognizing the voice on the other end.

"Rebecca Morland just left a message on the phone of that deputy D.A. she went to see—Daniel Black, I believe his name was. I think you better listen to it."

As he heard Rebecca's voice speaking, Holmes felt a throbbing in his temples. "We've got to stop her and fast. It seems all our efforts to scare her off have failed. That Black guy has been nosing around, and we can't afford for this information to get into his hands. If it does, we'll have to take him out too. Get some people over to Rebecca Morland's house now and then call me."

"What if she's already left?"

"Damn!" Holmes started pacing back and forth. "Do we know where this D.A. lives?"

"I think I can get the address right away."

"Then do it. Send one person there to wait for Rebecca Morland and another to her house—and pronto. And one more thing."

"What's that?"

"Someone will have to go into Black's place and wipe that message off the machine."

"I've already got a guy working on trying to erase it through the phone wires."

"Good thinking," Holmes said. He was relieved to hear he didn't have to figure out every last detail himself. "Have the other contingency plan ready just in case."

"Will do. And what do you want us to do with the Morland broad when we find her?"

"Find out if she told anyone else. Then eliminate both the evidence and the problem," Holmes said without the slightest hint of equivocation in his voice.

From his tourist-class seat, Daniel looked down as the airplane gained altitude. It was a clear night, and the lights of Los Angeles sparkled over a vast area. He remembered the first time he'd flown from New York to California, for a job interview after graduating from law school twelve years ago. He'd been staring out the window when the person in the seat next to him had pointed down. "See those blue dots? Those are all swimming pools." Amazed, Daniel had counted hundreds, maybe thousands of them. "What do they do with all those pools?" he'd asked. The man replied, "They swim all year round."

Daniel's parents had been very unhappy when he'd decided to take the job with the Los Angeles district attorney's office. They firmly believed that family was everything, and they couldn't understand why their son would choose to live three thousand miles away from them. But Daniel had been slowly suffocating at home. There were three other siblings to watch over his parents, and he had wanted to strike out on his own.

Nonetheless, he still went home several times a year to visit his family. He dearly loved them. The thought of never talking to his father again filled him with incredible pain, and he silently prayed he'd get there in time.

Closing his eyes, Daniel thought about his cases. There hadn't been enough time to arrange for other people to take over. When he got to New York, he'd have to make some phone calls from the hospital. He might wake a few people up, but they'd be able to cover for him.

Rebecca Morland's face flashed into his mind. There wasn't another deputy D.A. Daniel felt he could or should saddle with such a large responsibility. Maybe the best thing to do was to give her Zack's phone number. That way, Zack could contact Daniel if something urgent came up, and together they could decide what to do.

He felt bad for having to run out on Rebecca this way without calling her, but her husband's death had been unresolved for almost three months. Certainly, another few days wasn't going to change anything.

CHAPTER
TWENTY-SEVEN

As Rebecca drove through the Sepulveda Pass on the San Diego Freeway, she was in a state of nervous anticipation. She hoped that when Daniel Black read Ryan's letter, he'd feel there were enough details in it for him to open a full-scale investigation into her husband's death—enough so that the D.A., as well as others in law enforcement, couldn't afford to stop him. The way she saw it, the letter definitely showed that Holmes and/or Brandon had a clear-cut motive to kill her husband.

As for Worthington, she'd have to go to Ryan's gym locker to get the information Ryan had on him and then she'd see how he fit into the scheme. She debated whether to retrieve the material regarding Worthington before going to Daniel's or afterwards. Because she was anxious to get the disk with the letter into his hands as soon as possible, and because he lived close to the freeway, she decided to go to Daniel's house first.

She exited on the Olympic off-ramp and a few minutes later turned onto a tree-lined street in West Los Angeles. The homes were small California bungalows built at least forty or fifty years earlier.

Finding the right house, she looked for the black Acura Daniel had driven. It was nowhere in sight, and there was no other car in the driveway or directly in front of the house, although there was a gray van across the street. Rebecca doubted that Daniel parked in his garage. Most of the garages in this area were detached, big enough for only one car, and seldom used because they weren't that convenient.

Just in case she was wrong, she got out and rang the bell. No answer. There was a mail chute in the door that went directly into the house. Should she just drop the disk in? Deciding that she'd wait awhile for him to come home, she went back to her car.

Sitting there, Rebecca kept thinking about all that Ryan had written. She was anxious to get this disk into the hands of someone who would know what to do with it.

Maybe she'd go to the health club where Ryan's letter said he'd left the documents on Worthington. She should have cleaned that locker out before now and cancelled the membership, but she hadn't been up to it.

The gym was only about eight minutes away. If she went there, then she could come back later, and if Daniel still wasn't home, she could leave the disk in his mail chute.

The man in the gray van who was watching Rebecca was in contact with his boss. "She's just sitting there."

"You're sure she didn't put the disk in the mail chute?" Maxwell Holmes asked.

"Positive," the man said. "I've got her every move clear as can be. Do you want us to grab her?"

"Yeah," Holmes said. "But be careful. From the way you describe the area, any noise and we could have a bunch of nosy neighbors sticking their heads out the door."

"Hold on a minute," said the man in the van. "She's just started the motor and is pulling away from the curb."

"Damn," Holmes cursed. "Did you at least get that stupid tape message erased?"

"No. We ran into some difficulties."

"Okay, I want one of you to go into the house and erase that tape manually and one of you to keep monitoring things. I've got Victor in place about a block away. He's ready to follow her. He knows that this time he has to do more than try to run her off the road."

"Will do," said the man sitting in the van.

As Rebecca drove down Olympic Boulevard toward Century City and Beverly Hills, she picked up the portable phone lying on the seat next to her and punched in some numbers.

"Rebecca," said Brandon, sounding surprised to hear from her. "It's good to hear your voice."

"You may not think so when I tell you why I called," she promised, thinking there would have been more pleasure in doing this in person, but the telephone would have to suffice right now. "Ryan left me a letter I just found."

"Oh?"

"I always figured you for being brilliant," she said, then paused. "But using your law firm's trust account to launder dirty money wasn't a very smart idea."

There was a sharp intake of breath on the other end of the line. "Rebecca, where are you? We need to talk about this."

There was a red light and she stopped. "It's too late to talk, Brandon. I gave you the chance to tell me what happened, remember? But you were too excited by the crowd of people who were waiting to cheer you as their hero."

"I know what you must be thinking," he said smoothly, "but I'd like a chance to explain. Please. I'll meet you anywhere you like."

She had to hand it to him. Faced with the ruin of his entire career as well as his political ambitions, he was reacting like an old pro. The light turned green and she stepped on the accelerator. "It's not convenient for me to meet with you," she told him, hoping that Brandon was suffering, knowing his dreams were about to come to a bitter and humiliating end.

"Rebecca, please—"

"Damn you! First you answer *my* questions!" she said loudly, knowing even without seeing his face how startled he'd be to hear her talk like that. She wanted him to feel her anger, her hatred.

"Did you conspire with Maxwell Holmes to kill my husband, or did you merely sit silently by, figuring Holmes would get rid of the problem for both of you?"

"It wasn't like that, Rebecca. You must believe me," he said in a pleading voice. "I begged Ryan not to get involved. I told him that Holmes was a very dangerous man. He wouldn't listen. What more could I do?"

"You could have gone to the authorities as Ryan asked you to," she told him, her voice cold and hard.

He sighed. "I couldn't do that. Don't you understand? If Ryan had not interfered, none of this would have happened. Your husband decided to play God with my life, but when he tackled Holmes, he took on more than he could handle."

Her fury was growing. He was now blaming her husband for his own death.

Brandon exhaled loudly. "I've suspected from the beginning that Holmes might have had something to do with Ryan's death. But what good would it have done to tell you? Your knowing about it could have gotten you killed too. I couldn't bear that." His tone dropped, and his voice came out like a croak. "You must realize, Rebecca, that I love you like a daughter."

"Spare me, Brandon," she said. "I've never been so disappointed by anyone—no, disgusted would be more like it—than I have by you."

She paused to catch her breath. "You know, Ryan and I used to talk about you as if you were some kind of god. We both admired and respected you so much." She gave a bitter laugh. "What fools we were."

"Both Ryan's and your feelings for me were always reciprocated," Brandon said, then added, beseechingly, "Don't do anything foolish, Rebecca."

"I'm not the one to talk to about doing something foolish. You only have yourself to thank for what happens."

She chewed on the inside of her cheek before going on.

"Which one of the partners called and informed the police that Ryan stole money from the firm after you had promised not to tell them?"

He cleared his throat. "I'm afraid it was me."

"Why did you do it?"

"I wanted them to close the investigation." He paused. "In a way I was protecting you too. You see, I thought the longer it stayed open, the more danger there was you'd find out—and I was right."

"That's a masterful job of rationalizing," she scoffed. "My next question is this: John told me he wasn't aware of the facts regarding the deal you made with Holmes. In spite of his being a liar, I believed him because he knew he was dying. Was he telling me the truth?"

"Yes," Brandon responded.

"And what about Catherine? Was she in on this with you?"

"No, Catherine had no knowledge of what I was doing either."

"Then why did she accuse Ryan of stealing the money?"

"To be honest, I haven't looked into it yet, but I assume it's because John fixed the paper trail to implicate Ryan instead of himself."

Rebecca was passing Century City, and the tall buildings loomed like shadows in the night, lights still on in many of the windows. "You suspected John of stealing the money too, didn't you?"

"Yes," he acknowledged. "But after Catherine said it was definitely Ryan, I changed my mind."

"And you never bothered to check it out yourself, did you?"

"No," he answered. "I realize now I should have." He hesitated. "Listen to me, Rebecca, to even attempt to implicate Holmes in Ryan's death would be like signing a death warrant. Am I so terrible because I wish to live—to still accomplish something in the world? What good would my death, or your death, do for Ryan now?"

"If I don't see that the man who killed my husband pays for his crime, I could never live with myself," she replied quietly.

"Justice is an abstract concept," he countered. "In the real world, doing the right thing can often get you killed." He cleared his throat. "Rebecca, I've been brutally honest with you. Now, will you meet with me? You owe me a chance to explain everything to you."

"I owe you nothing," she said scornfully, pushing the END button, and terminating their call. For a brief time, she reveled in the satisfaction of having beat him at his own game. Then the reality hit her—it was a bittersweet victory at best—Ryan was still dead, and she was convinced that Brandon Taylor, but for his own ambition, could have prevented it.

A short while later, Rebecca pulled into the parking lot of a rather plain-looking brick building that housed a gym and tennis courts used by a slew of young executives working and living in the surrounding areas.

It was after ten-thirty, and there were only a few lights on in the building. She'd been positive someone would still be there, but now she wasn't so sure. Quickly, she glanced around, noticing that there were several cars parked in the lot. Pulling into a parking spot, she decided to check the doors.

She jumped out of her car and ran to the building. Finding the entrance locked, she knocked on the glass. Maybe a cleaning crew was still inside and would hear her.

When another car came into the lot, she wondered briefly if it was a member who was planning on entering. If so, maybe he or she would let her in too. A tall man got out of the car. It was dark and she couldn't see his features.

Just then she heard a noise and turned around. A young woman was coming out of the building. Forgetting the tall man, Rebecca explained to this woman how she had to get something that she needed for the morning out of her locker but had forgotten her key.

Slightly annoyed, the woman unlocked the door for her and then walked to her car.

Inside, Rebecca raced to the changing room. Ignoring the sign that said MEN ONLY, she found Ryan's locker. They had once discussed that the simplest way to remember combinations was to use the same one on all their locks. She prayed he'd done that here and that the numbers matched the ones on his brief-case.

Hurriedly, she turned the knob and the door creaked open. For several seconds she was overwhelmed by the smell of Ryan's cologne, which permeated the small space. Tears welled up behind her eyes, but her adrenaline rush caused her to hurry.

Digging in the gym bag, she found a long envelope. She opened it and read the papers inside. So this was what Worthing-ton was so afraid of. However, she didn't see anything in the documents that connected Worthington to Holmes. Taking the envelope with her, she left.

Heading for her car, Rebecca realized that it was getting late and she needed to get back to Daniel's. Before she could open the car door, someone suddenly grabbed her from behind and shoved something cold and hard against her neck. "Don't say a word," he rasped.

Rebecca screamed.

He grabbed her head in a viselike hold, her screams muffled inside his palm. "Scream again and you're dead, lady."

Her entire body had started to tremble, and she found she could barely stand.

"You understand me?"

In spite of her mounting terror, she nodded.

"Good. Now, slowly, start walking toward my car."

Move, she ordered her body, which seemed frozen to the spot.

"Faster," he hissed, kicking her behind the knees so hard, she stumbled and almost fell.

When they got there, he opened the door with one hand, while with the other, he held the gun against her neck.

Although she was trembling from head to foot, her mind was racing. Should she make a run for it now, before he shoved her in the car? With all the strength she could muster, Rebecca wrenched herself from his grasp and yelled, "Help! Someone help me, please!"

"You stupid bitch," he spat, slugging her across the jaw.

Rebecca reeled backwards from the punch, her head feeling as if it were going to snap off. She fell hard against the car and immediately saw stars before her eyes. Don't pass out, she willed herself.

The man quickly grabbed her again, and with the gun pushed against her temple, shoved her into the car.

"Another stunt like that, and click," he taunted.

Her jaw was throbbing and she tasted a trickle of blood coming out of her mouth. In a flash, she realized she'd seen him before. He was the man who had visited Maxwell Holmes's house the night she'd been there.

Forcing her to slide over, he got into the seat next to her. His body was pushing against hers as she faced the window on the passenger side. He jabbed her in the back. "I hate stupid broads."

The gun pushed deeply into her flesh. She had no doubt that if she yelled again, he'd kill her. In terrible pain, Rebecca wondered if this was what they had done to Ryan before they'd shoved him into the water. Nausea crawled up into her mouth and she swallowed it down.

"Listen and listen good," he grunted. "I ain't gonna repeat myself. Scream again, you're dead. Got it?"

Her breath was coming fast now, catching and rattling in her throat. Unable to speak, she nodded.

"We're going someplace to talk to some people. I ain't gonna hurt you unless you do something stupid. Got that?"

"Yes." She choked out the words, "Who are you working for —Holmes or Worthington?"

"Shut up," he warned, pushing the gun into her so hard she cried out in pain.

In spite of all his warnings, she had to ask the question. "You killed my husband, didn't you?" It came out as a sob.

"Your husband took a swim," he snarled. He forced the gun even deeper into her flesh.

Her whole body was damp, and she felt as if she was going to be sick. At some level, she also sensed the man was close to losing his patience with her. That filled her with abject fear.

"You gonna cooperate, or not?"

Panic overcame Rebecca as she suddenly realized that if he wanted to, he could murder her right here and no one would ever know. Maybe if she played along, she'd have a chance. "Yes." Her voice quivered, and a few tears rolled down her face as she spoke.

"That's more like it." He relaxed his grip. "We've got you covered. So don't try anything."

"I won't." She wondered what the "we" meant. Was there another car close by? Were there more people involved?

He pushed her over farther. "Now gimme the disk."

Shocked by his words, she stiffened. How did they know about the disk? Then it dawned on her—they'd had a wiretap on her phone. She'd been stupid. She should have realized she wasn't playing with amateurs. For all she knew, they could have disposed of Daniel Black already.

Rebecca felt utterly alone. No one knew where she was or what she'd found except for the people who wanted to silence her, just as they'd silenced her husband. Reluctantly, she opened her shoulder bag and handed the disk to him—glad now she'd stopped to mail the other one to her parents.

"I'll take that too," he said, pointing to the envelope she had removed from Ryan's locker.

Rebecca watched as he put both items in his coat pocket. While one of his hands gripped the gun, he started the car with the other. He maneuvered out of the parking lot and onto the street. She tried to formulate some strategy. As soon as they got to more lights, more people, she'd have to do something. She couldn't just give in this way. If he was planning to take her to a dark and deserted place to end her life, she certainly wasn't going to make it easy for him.

She rubbed her jaw, which was now throbbing. She wondered if it was broken, then decided it wasn't or she wouldn't be able to talk. Everything hurt, from her arm where he'd grabbed her, to her neck, which felt bruised by the gun he shoved into it. Even the back of her knees hurt where he'd kicked her.

He headed down the street, driving with one hand on the

wheel and the other holding the gun pointed directly at Rebecca, but low enough so that none of the other drivers could see it. Surreptitiously, she wound the strap of her purse around her hand.

Forcing her mind to concentrate, she tried hard to calm herself by taking deep breaths. The sweat continued to trickle down her back. Frequently, he turned to give her a menacing look, especially when he stopped for a light. It sent chills up her spine. Where was he taking her?

After a few minutes, he made a turn. When, a short time later, he got into the left-hand lane, she knew he was planning to get on the San Diego Freeway. She had to make her move soon or it might be too late.

The cars entering the freeway at this on-ramp were regulated by a meter. Only one car at a time was permitted to go on the green light and enter the flow of freeway traffic. That meant he'd have to stop for a few seconds. When he turned, she waited for him to come to a stop. He gave her another evil glance. As soon as the light turned green, he accelerated, and she grabbed for the door.

There was a screeching of brakes when the door flew open. As she flung herself out of the car, the sound of gunfire reverberated in her ears and she realized he'd shot at her. The next thing she knew her body hit the side of the road and she felt a stabbing pain in her right shoulder. She ignored it as she forced herself to roll down the embankment. Hopefully, he wouldn't be able to stop or pull over onto the shoulder too quickly without getting into an accident. She figured she had maybe a minute at the most.

She prayed that the sound of gunshots would bring the police—but she knew she couldn't count on it—not in L.A. Besides, she wouldn't feel safe with them anyway.

A burning sensation ran up the arm that had taken the brunt of the fall. Luckily, her large purse had also been under her, and it had cushioned some of the impact. She checked and found she was bleeding, but she didn't appear to have been shot. Sobbing, pulling at the earth, she propelled herself through the bushes. She had to get out of there before he came back.

CHAPTER
TWENTY-EIGHT

S cratched and bleeding, Rebecca hid behind dumpsters and bushes as she made her way unsteadily down a dark and deserted alley. At any second she expected to hear the squeal of tires as the tall, thin man caught her in the glare of his headlights. She felt like a hunted animal.

Her breath was still coming in short rasps. The pain in her shoulder was intense, and her jaw was badly swollen, although she thought the bleeding had stopped. Should she knock on one of the apartment house doors and ask someone to call the police? It was tempting. But she remembered the thin man's threats and what Ryan had said in his letter. She was more than convinced that Holmes had the ear of certain people in law enforcement. If she went to the authorities, Holmes was liable to find her. The way Detective Walters had treated her now made sense to her. Holmes obviously controlled him too.

She'd left her portable phone on the seat of her car. For a moment she considered going back for the car. Then she realized that was one of the places they'd be watching. No. She'd have to forget that idea.

Finally, she came to an alley that seemed to back up to some small businesses. There was a restaurant. Carefully, she checked around before going inside. After making sure the thin man wasn't in there either, she asked for the pay phone.

The man behind the counter pointed to an area near the restrooms. "You okay?" There was a funny expression on his face.

"Yeah."

She dialed Daniel Black's number and punched in the number of her calling card. Again, his answering machine picked up. She didn't want to leave a message in case they'd bugged his phone too. Nothing seemed impossible for people like this.

Rebecca could barely control her shaking. Should she call Lucy? What if they had also bugged her phone? Daniel had once mentioned he had an investigator by the name of Zack. But without a last name she had no hope of finding him. Her best bet was to find somewhere to rest, wash up, and feel safe. But she needed money and she was afraid to use a credit card. It could be traced too easily. And she didn't have an ATM card because she considered them too risky. Therefore, even if they were watching her home, she needed to get some cash she had hidden there.

Hopefully, they'd look for her in this area for an hour or two before deciding to check her house. If she could get there, grab her cash, and get out, she'd be able to spend the night in a hotel, and in the morning, if he was still okay, Daniel would know what to do.

Rebecca had the cab driver drop her off a few blocks from her house. Then she offered to pay him double if he'd wait for her to return. He seemed skeptical, so she told him she was running from an abusive husband. If he could just keep his lights off, she'd be back in twenty minutes. Finally, he agreed.

Terrified that the thin man might be staking out her house, waiting for her to surface, she decided to approach from the back. Climbing up the steep embankment, she heard rustling and scurrying noises and remembered the brush around here—

part of the Santa Monica Mountains—was filled with squirrels, rats, and other small animals. It made her shiver with revulsion, but she forced herself to keep going.

Every step, every movement was painful. Her shoulder felt dislocated. She had bruises and cuts all over her arms and legs. And her jaw was still throbbing. Gasping for air, she pulled herself up and over the lower patio wall and made her way to the other side of the terrace.

She tiptoed to the back door and listened. She heard nothing. Inserting her key, she entered, quickly turning off the alarm. It was probably safer not to put on any lights. That way, if someone were watching from outside, he wouldn't know she was here.

Lighting a match, Rebecca found a flashlight. Keeping the beam very low, she made her way down the hallway and into the master bedroom. All the while she kept looking over her shoulder. She was never going to feel safe here again. Never.

Even with a flashlight, it was hard to see where she was going. Which drawer had she hidden the money in? In a frenzy she pulled things out of several drawers and left them lying on the floor.

She had just gotten some clean jeans, another sweatshirt, and the cash, when she was jolted upright. A car door had slammed. She held her breath. A few seconds later, the doorbell rang. Then someone rattled the knob.

Terrified, Rebecca picked up a heavy bookend. If someone got into the house, she'd have to find the courage to hit him over the head.

One more time, the doorbell rang. She could feel perspiration along the back of her neck and shoulders. Then she detected the sound of metal clacking and realized whoever was at her door had put something into the mail chute. A few seconds later, she heard retreating footsteps, followed by a car door slamming and an engine starting. Headlights formed shadows on the walls as the car turned around in her driveway and drove away.

Her heart pounding, she made her way to the living room. Dropping to her knees and feeling around on the carpet under the chute, she found a folded piece of paper. She opened it and held the flashlight up.

"Must talk with you. Call this number. Juan." A telephone number followed.

Who was Juan? Was this some kind of a trap?

More than twenty minutes had passed by the time Rebecca returned to where the cab was supposed to be. Her heart sank because it wasn't there. Then she heard a honk. Her pulse racing, she turned around and discovered that the driver had parked farther down the street. Sighing with relief, she raced to the vehicle. As she slumped down into the backseat, Rebecca realized she was close to collapse.

"Where to now, lady?"

She hesitated, knowing he was watching her in his rearview mirror. What a sight she was. Even though she looked horrible, she decided to have him take her to the Century Plaza Hotel.

He glanced at her in the mirror. "Sure you want to go in there looking like that? I mean, you can tell the old man beat you up."

She nodded. "Yes. But leave me off at the corner. I'm already checked in. I'll enter through the back."

"Whatever you say," he replied, his tone of voice making it clear that he thought she was crazy.

After giving him double the fare plus a big tip, she got out of the cab and waited until he'd driven away before she walked up to Little Santa Monica Boulevard. A few blocks to the west there was a small motel. She'd stay there. Under an assumed name, of course.

An hour had passed since Rebecca had checked into the motel. She'd washed her bruises and scratches as best as she could. Her shoulder felt dislocated, and her jaw was swollen, which gave her face a rather misshapen look, but there was nothing she could do about either of those injuries now.

She fingered the piece of paper in her hand and wondered again who Juan was and what he wanted. She figured a phone call couldn't really hurt her if she made it too brief to be traced.

"Bueno," someone answered.

Suddenly, the image of the dark-haired young Hispanic watching her in the passageway of the *Majorca* came into her mind. Was that who this was?

"My Spanish isn't very good," she told them, then launched into what she called Pig-Latin Spanish.

The person on the other end of the phone told her to hold. Before long, another soft-spoken person was on the line. In brief bursts and spurts of Spanish and English, they somehow communicated. She had been right. Juan was the cook's helper on the Worthingtons' yacht. He was the one who had been following her that day in the ship's passageway. He said he had some important information regarding her husband's death. He wanted one thousand dollars for it and said that he had to meet with her right away.

Rebecca immediately wondered if this was a shakedown. "I'll call you tomorrow," she promised.

"No. It has to be tonight," he insisted.

Her head was splitting, and every bone in her body ached. She was also afraid of her call being traced, so she told him she'd phone him right back. During their second conversation, Rebecca said, "Tell me why this information is worth so much."

He proceeded to explain that he had seen someone on the boat that night who might have killed her husband.

Now her heart was racing. If what he said was true, this could be the key she needed. "All I have on me is five hundred dollars."

She heard his heavy breathing. Then he held his hand over the phone and spoke quickly in Spanish to someone else. "Seven fifty," he said, when he came back on the line.

"I can't. The banks are closed and I don't have an ATM card. If I have to meet you tonight, five hundred is all I have."

Again there was a whispered conversation. If it was the thin man and his cohorts, would they be haggling with her over two hundred fifty dollars? She doubted it.

"Okay," he said. "My cousin will explain where to go."

• • •

Maxwell Holmes was pacing his living room, so angry he was afraid he was going to explode. "What do you mean, you lost her?" he shouted.

The thin man, Victor Irwin, stood shamefaced. "It's like I said, boss. She disappeared into thin air."

"You idiots. I've got five men. Two in a truck, two in cars, and one at the command center, and all of you let one woman slip through your fingers." The veins in his neck were standing out. "How in the hell is that possible?"

"We don't know. One second she was hurt and, I was sure, subdued—the next, she had jumped out of the car and rolled down an embankment. By the time I got off the freeway and circled around, she'd disappeared. The guys are still searching the area for her, but who knows where she went."

"Do you have her house staked out?"

"I doubt she'd go there, boss; it's so obvious. But just in case, Kevin's on his way there now. We've also got her car under surveillance."

"Don't think for her, she's obviously smarter than you. Just send someone to every logical place she'd go. How about that little Mexican friend of hers from the legal clinic?"

"We've got someone watching her place too."

Holmes couldn't believe it! Everything could be compromised because of a stupid broad who refused to be intimidated. Well, she'd be sorry she hadn't listened. When his guys did get her, and he had no doubt that they would eventually, she wouldn't even have time to say good-bye.

The thin man reached into his pocket. "I got the disk."

"Give it to me," said Holmes, grabbing it out of the other man's hand.

"Oh, I also got something else. I figured it might be important." He handed Holmes the envelope Rebecca had removed from her husband's locker.

Holmes quickly scanned the documents that were in the envelope. At first he didn't understand, but then he put it together. "Well, I'll be damned," he said, smiling from ear to ear.

• • •

Rebecca left the motel and headed toward Century City, hugging the dark shadows of trees and buildings and trying to stay away from the streetlights. Terrified that at any second she would be stopped by someone with a gun, she kept glancing over her shoulder. Had the thin man picked up her trail?

Unable to walk very fast because she was in so much pain, it seemed to her to take her hours to reach the Century City Shopping Center. The stores were closed, but the movie theaters were still open, as were some of the restaurants. Mostly, however, the center was dark and deserted looking. Although it made her nervous, she decided to take a shortcut.

As she moved along she kept glancing from left to right. At the end of the mall walkway she turned sharply to the left. Almost immediately she became aware that a strange-looking woman was staring at her. Rebecca gazed back. The woman turned away. Rebecca felt goose bumps all over her body. Could there be two people following her, trading off to make it seem less suspicious, and this woman was one of them? She scurried around to the side of a building and hid behind a planter, her chest heaving as she waited to see if the woman was pursuing her.

You're being silly, she told herself. The woman was probably staring at her because Rebecca's face was swollen and badly bruised. Trying to quell her anxiety, she took the escalator to the underground garage.

Every few seconds, Rebecca turned around, half expecting to see the tall, thin man in close pursuit. Her heart was beating rapidly as she finally stepped off the moving stairway and scurried across the garage. At the far end of the building, after peering around one more time, she hiked up the ramp.

Outside, she ran across the street, continuing on until she came to the ABC Entertainment Center. There she disappeared into the bowels of yet another underground parking structure. This center housed the Shubert Theater, which was between runs of shows. There were also two high-rise office buildings, a few restaurants, and a movie house in the complex. After working hours when the Shubert was closed, this center seldom had much business.

The garage extended all the way across to the huge Century City landmark Twin Towers, making it one of the biggest subterranean structures in Southern California. Tonight, the gray concrete bunker seemed deserted—eerily so. Rebecca shivered with apprehension and pain as she traversed the vast expanse of space.

Hearing the sound of a siren in the distance, she wondered where it was going. If someone attacked her down here, would it be morning before her body was found? In the stillness, she heard footsteps but couldn't see anyone. Her heart pounding, she ducked behind one of the cars and held her breath.

The faint footsteps were coming closer. Perspiration ran down her back. Oh God, she prayed, if it's that horrible man or his accomplices, please help me.

Two young men dressed in Levi's and leather jackets appeared between the cars, and Rebecca realized that they must have approached her in a crouched position. Did they work for the thin man? Although she knew it was dark and deserted and no one would hear her, she screamed.

CHAPTER
TWENTY-NINE

Diana and Paul Worthington were hosting a gathering for well-to-do Republicans at their home, and she was thrilled that it had turned out to be a beautiful evening. The party was beginning to wind down, but there were still many people out on the dance floor. As she surveyed the scene, twenty tables set out on the terraces and the lawn facing Newport Bay, she was pleased with the turnout. Closing her eyes, Diana envisioned doing this kind of thing at the White House someday, and a shiver of anticipation ran up her spine.

"Excuse me, ma'am," said her butler. "But there's someone on the phone who insists he must speak to you."

She felt a surge of annoyance. Her staff knew better than to disturb her when she was entertaining. "Tell whoever it is I'll have to call them back," she said, dismissively.

"I tried," he told her. "But he insisted, said it was urgent. He also said something . . ." He hesitated, "I wasn't sure, but I think he said to tell you it was about your mink coat." There was a puzzled expression on his face.

Suddenly, Diana understood who it was. Holmes knew better than to insist on speaking to her this way—they had an agreement regarding phone calls. She'd also recently informed him that Paul suspected she was having an affair and that they would have to be more careful.

A sense of panic welled up as she pondered what could be so important. Glancing quickly around to see if Paul was within earshot, she breathed a sigh of relief when she spotted him at the far side of the terrace, talking to several guests.

"All right, I'll take it," she said quickly. With a smile, she excused herself from her guests and headed for the house.

Her hands were shaking as she picked up the extension. "Hello."

"Ah, Diana," Holmes said, sounding unbelievably happy. "How are you?"

"I'm entertaining two hundred people and wouldn't have answered except they said this was extremely urgent." She didn't bother to disguise her chagrin.

"I'm sorry," he chuckled. "But this was so good I just couldn't wait to share it with you."

"Then tell me," she said impatiently. "I've got to get back."

"I've just come into possession of the most extraordinary document."

"Really, Maxwell, why would I be interested in some document when I've got a party going on at my home?"

"Oh, this document will fascinate you. I think I've just discovered why your husband never wants to fuck you, my darling."

Her heart began pounding wildly. "What is it?" she asked, warily, terrified to find out.

"Well, it seems to be a birth certificate."

"What's so important about that? I already have Paul's birth certificate as well as mine in our safe. You need them to get a passport, or did you forget?" Her tone was chiding.

"That must be the birth certificate that was given to your husband's adoptive parents. This one is the original; you know, before it was sealed."

How could Holmes have gotten something like that? she

wondered. "What does it say that's so astonishing?" Her voice betrayed her nervousness.

"Are you sitting down?" he asked, the glee in his voice unmistakable.

"No."

"I think you should."

"Very well. I'm sitting." She swallowed several times before adding, "Now, will you please tell me what this is about?"

"It says here," he paused as if for dramatic effect, "that your husband's natural mother was a Negro."

Diana blanched. Paul's mother had been black? How could that be? "There must be some mistake," she protested. "The birth certificate we have doesn't say he's black. I don't think they're allowed to hide something like that when an adoption goes through."

"Maybe his adoptive parents didn't care," he responded. "And maybe they doctored the certificate or paid someone off. In any case, now we know why your husband didn't want any little kiddies running around. What if his natural mother's genes had dominated? Quite a scandal in *your* circle, wouldn't you think?"

The room swirled around Diana, and for a moment she thought she might be sick. Could it be true? Was this why her husband had insisted there would be no children? Was this why he had so seldom touched her? Had Paul been afraid?

"Are you there?" Holmes asked.

"Yes," she replied softly.

"You're so quiet I thought maybe you'd fainted."

It frightened her to hear how jovial he sounded. "What are you planning to do with this information, Maxwell?" she finally managed to say, holding her breath for his answer.

"Oh, I don't know. I think that's something we'll have to discuss the next time you come over here in your mink coat." This time he laughed out loud. "Why don't you go back to your party. We'll talk about this later."

Through the window, Diana saw that the party servers were now offering her guests nightcaps. Everything seemed to be the same as before—only it wasn't. And clearly it never would be again.

If it weren't for the fact that Rebecca Morland was still out there somewhere, hiding from his men, Maxwell Holmes would have been having the time of his life.

As he paced his solarium, he silently cursed the woman. This room was his refuge from the world. In here he felt like an old-time plantation owner with hundreds of servants to command at will. They would find her—they had to. At least she no longer had the disk.

In the meantime, he had another call to make. Lifting the receiver, he dialed.

After several rings, Brandon Taylor answered. "Hello."

"It's me," Holmes said. "Sounds like I woke you?"

"No," Brandon replied, in a dull voice. "I was just sitting here thinking."

"Well, cheer up then. I've got some good news for you."

"What's that?"

"I think I've found the magic bullet to get rid of your nasty rival, Paul Worthington."

There was a deep intake of breath on the other end of the line. "What do you mean?"

Holmes proceeded to tell Brandon what he had discovered about Worthington. "Once he hears I've got this in my possession, I predict he'll drop out of the race. Maybe we'll let him claim ill health or something."

"Where did you get that document?" Brandon asked.

"Oh, let's just say it fell into my hands through an angel of mercy."

There was silence. Holmes spoke again. "I thought you'd be dancing for joy when you heard this. What's wrong?"

"Nothing. I guess I don't feel too good. I think I must be coming down with the flu or something."

"That's too bad. Well, I just wanted you to know that you don't have any more worries." He snickered. "You will now be assured of winning the primary and hopefully the election."

Holmes was pleased. Brandon was in his pocket for life. He

couldn't think of anything more delightful than having his very own senator in Washington. Now, if he could just find that Morland bitch, everything would be grand.

As Brandon Taylor hung up the phone, he was filled with mixed emotions. The news Holmes had just given him about Worthington should have made him ecstatic—instead, he felt ill. He was positive that the price for having this information on Worthington was going to be too high. Maxwell Holmes never did anything for free, and Brandon had already sold his soul for his chance to become the next U.S. senator from California. What else did he have left to give the man?

There was also a terrible certainty in his heart that Ryan had discovered the same information. Now he knew why his protégé had been reluctant to divulge any details of his investigation into Worthington's past. It made him even sadder to realize that Ryan probably hadn't shared it with him because he felt it shouldn't be used and hadn't trusted Brandon to agree. Well, Ryan had been wrong. Brandon chose to believe that if Ryan had given him the option, he would have said no. Unfortunately, saying no to Holmes wouldn't do any good.

His mind replayed the earlier conversation he'd had with Rebecca, and he again wondered if he had done the right thing. If he'd told Holmes about the letter Ryan Morland had left for his wife, it would have been like signing a warrant for Rebecca's death. Somehow, he had to find her and convince her not to use the material in her possession. It wasn't worth dying for.

Suddenly, everything he'd ever wanted seemed meaningless and left a bitter taste in his mouth.

After Rebecca screamed, she stood frozen to the spot, unable to run.

The two young men meanwhile had stopped in their tracks. "Hey, lady," said one of the men, putting out his hands. "We don't wanna hurt you. Juan sent us to bring you to him."

Shaking badly, her breath coming in short gasps, Rebecca tried to ascertain if they had guns. "Why did he send you?"

"He just wanted us to make sure you came alone. That's all."

"Are you armed?" she asked.

"No. Honest."

The sound of a car's squealing tires assaulted her ears. Was it an employee who had been working late? Should she run and ask for help? Or did these two have other accomplices? Listening, she could tell the car was circling as it climbed the ramps from the lower levels of the structure.

The men heard the car too and turned to look. She held her breath. The seconds seemed like hours before she caught sight of the driver. It was a man. No one she recognized. When she saw him head toward the exit of the building, seemingly oblivious to them, she decided to go with the young men.

"Follow us, okay?" the one who had been speaking instructed her.

She nodded her head and walked behind them across the empty garage. When they reached the yellow numbered section, one of the men pointed.

"He's up there."

It didn't appear they were going into the stairwell with her. She glanced over. The door was slightly ajar. Quickly, she looked around again. She hadn't yet seen any of the security guards who were supposed to patrol this garage.

If these men only wanted the money, wouldn't they have taken it by now? Or were they waiting to grab it when she went into the stairwell, where no one would hear her screams if they killed her? For a moment, she again contemplated running, but she couldn't move quickly enough, and there were two of them.

"Please God," she prayed silently. "Let Juan be who he says he is." Rebecca opened the door, almost jumping out of her skin when it slammed shut behind her. The noise was deafening. Slowly, every nerve in her body on alert, she started up the dimly lit stairs.

"Up here," someone whispered in a thick Spanish accent.

The voice jolted her. Her heart pounded—her stomach tightened. Another few seconds and she'd know whether she'd been a fool to come here alone.

A blinding light caught her by surprise. "What's . . ."

"Here, Mrs. Morland. You alone?" His English was not very good.

It took a few seconds for her to realize the beam from a flashlight was raking her face. She couldn't see anything as her terror mounted.

"Two more steps."

Her heart in her mouth, she climbed one step . . . then, hesitating briefly, the second one. A dim shape. As she got closer, she recognized the man she had seen on the boat. She couldn't tell if he had a weapon.

Again he whispered, "You alone?"

"Yes. But you're not. I met your two friends."

"My cousins," he said. "One works in building. Parks cars."

Now she understood why they had picked this place.

"Sit," he said nervously, making a waving motion with his hand.

"In a second. Someone attacked me earlier. I want to check first." Glancing around quickly, she climbed a few steps above him and opened the door, peering out at another level of the empty garage. She needed to reassure herself they were alone.

"I very careful," he explained. He was crouched on one of the stairs and looked as nervous as she felt.

Squatting down on the step above him, she placed her back against the wall, situating her body so that she could see both above and below her. "I don't even know your full name."

"Juan Martez."

Catching her breath, she said, "What did you want to see me about?"

"You have money?"

"Yes." She reached into her purse and pulled out the five hundred dollars.

"*Gracias.*" He stuffed the money into his pocket without counting it. "My aunt reads paper. Says you think husband was murdered."

"Yes. Do you know something about it?"

"Maybe. Man on boat night of party—not on lists."

She bolted straight up. "There was a man on the boat whose

name wasn't on any of the lists?" Her heart was hammering in her chest.

"*Sí.*" In Spanish mixed with English, he told his story.

"I help cook on *Majorca.* Before party starts, Mrs. Worthington, she comes to boat with much clothes and things. A man help her. Captain says only crew and people with names on list okay on boat because many important people coming. He says if strangers come, tell security men." He paused to take a breath.

"Go on," she urged.

"I wash potatoes and watch, but man no go. Later, security men check boat, say everything okay. I think man hiding. I tell cook."

There was a loud noise, and Rebecca jumped. "What was that?"

"I dunno." Juan scurried up the stairs and stuck his head out the door.

"Do you see anything?" she whispered loudly, coming to stand behind him. Her pulse racing.

He shook his head. "No. My cousins there. I think must be okay."

Convincing herself it was nothing, she sat back down. "Go on."

Continuing, Juan explained that the cook said the man must have left. "I not think about it more until later."

"Did you see this man again that night?"

He nodded. "*Sí.* I see him in hall. The same hall where you go that day you come to boat."

She realized he was referring to the passageway leading out to the cockpit. "Can you remember what this man looked like?"

"*Sí.*" He began to describe a man who was tall and thin. Her pulse racing, Rebecca immediately recognized that it was the same man who had abducted her earlier this evening. If he had been on the boat, then he must have been the one who had killed Ryan. But who had sent him? Holmes or Worthington?

"Why didn't you come forward sooner?" she asked, trying to watch his face. "I mean, why didn't you tell this to the detectives who were investigating the case?"

Even in the dim light, she saw his face redden. *"Lo siento."* He apologized. "No have good papers. Worthingtons very careful. I use false documents. Afraid they find out. I talk to cops— they check me out—I have to leave country. *Mi madre*—she sick in Mexico. If no money for medicine, maybe she die."

"Why are you coming forward now?"

"Mi madre—she die two days ago." He gazed at his feet. "I go home. Is why I need money."

"I'm sorry about your mother," Rebecca said. She paused for a moment. "Does anyone else know about this man?"

"Just the cook."

"Is he a friend of yours?"

"Sí."

"Can you trust him not to tell anyone else?"

"Sí."

Rebecca explained that there were some crooked cops involved in her husband's death. Juan seemed to have no trouble understanding that concept. She said she would like to give his name to a certain deputy D.A. they could trust, and wanted to know how the D.A. could reach him.

Juan explained they had no phone in Mexico. As for the cook, it was very dangerous to try and contact him on the boat, because the captain and most of the crew would lie for the Worthingtons. But Juan's aunt could be relied on to get a message to Juan and the cook both. He wrote his aunt's phone number on a piece of paper that Rebecca gave him from her purse.

There was the sound of a door slamming and footsteps.

"Let's go," yelled a man.

"My cousin," said Juan, standing up.

Would they try to hurt her now? Somehow, after meeting him, Rebecca didn't think he was dangerous—in fact, he seemed to be just as scared as she was. She crammed the scrap of paper into her purse. "I'll follow you."

Her heart pounding, Rebecca descended the stairs as quickly as she could and reentered the underground garage. Every few steps she glanced back, expecting at any second to feel a hand on her injured shoulder or a gun at her head.

CHAPTER
THIRTY

After watching Juan and his cousins leave, Rebecca wearily made her way back to the motel. Every part of her body hurt, and she was exhausted. She was also very hungry.

She remembered seeing a candy machine in the motel office, so she stopped there and bought several selections before going to her room. Once inside, she quickly checked to make sure no one had been there, then she collapsed on the bed. Sleep was something she needed desperately, but at the same time it was something she feared. What if the thin man found her? What if he traced her there?

Once more she tried to reach Daniel, but when the machine answered, she hung up. Finally, totally drained and worn out from the pain as well as the stress, Rebecca fell into a deep sleep.

Early the next morning, as soon as it turned nine, Rebecca was on the phone to the district attorney's office in downtown Los Angeles.

"I'm sorry, ma'am, but Mr. Black has been called away on a family emergency. Is there someone else who can help you?"

Rebecca felt tears welling in her eyes. Without him, who else could she turn to? She thought of Solowski, then discarded it—it wasn't fair to put her in such a dangerous position.

"Ma'am?" the receptionist said again, impatiently.

Rebecca could hear the ringing of other phones in the background. "Uh, yes. Mr. Black had an investigator he worked with by the name of Zack. I'm afraid I can't remember his last name."

"Zack McKenzie?" the woman inquired.

"Yes. I think that's who it is. Can you connect me with him?"

"I'll try. Hold on."

A minute later, a deep voice came on the line. "McKenzie here."

"Uh, yes . . . I'm not sure if Daniel Black spoke to you about me, but—" She hadn't decided whether she should give him her name when he interrupted.

"Is this Rebecca Morland?"

Shocked, she said, "How did you know?"

"Daniel phoned me about you very early this morning. His father had a heart attack yesterday. Daniel had to fly home to New York." He cleared his throat. "I've been trying to reach you."

She was trembling with relief. "Why is that?"

"While he was still on the plane last night, Daniel picked up a message from you—he called me right away, but I wasn't home. Then when Daniel checked his phone again later and realized that your message had somehow been erased, he started to worry that something had happened to you."

"It did," she said, thinking that was the understatement of the century. Taking a deep breath, she asked, "Are we on a secure line?"

"Should be. Tell me where you are and I'll come get you. We can talk in person."

She hesitated briefly, then yielded, realizing she had to trust someone. "I'm in a motel on Little Santa Monica," she said. "Oh, and can you bring some first-aid supplies?"

"What happened?"

Rebecca heard the concern in his voice. Gently touching

her throbbing shoulder, she told him. "I jumped out of a moving car."

"Sounds like you need a lot more than first aid. I'm going to bring a doctor too."

"Thanks," Rebecca said, gratefully.

The doctor thought Rebecca's shoulder should be x-rayed, but she wanted to wait, so he fixed her up with a sling. As for her bruises and abrasions, he bandaged the more serious ones and gave her something for the pain if it got too bad.

When the doctor left, Rebecca told Zack McKenzie everything that had happened. Afterwards, Zack telephoned Daniel Black in New York, and Rebecca had to repeat the story a second time, with frequent interruptions to answer questions.

Then Daniel wanted to speak to Zack again. The investigator nodded his head several times, said "Yes," and then gave the receiver to Rebecca.

"We've decided to bring in the FBI," Daniel said. "Zack has a friend in the L.A. bureau. He's going to go and speak to him now. Then, if everything looks good, Rebecca, he'll come back and get you and you'll meet with them. Okay?"

"It sounds like a good plan to me," she agreed, thankful to have all the help she could get.

Zack ordered her to lock the door securely behind him and promised that he'd be in touch shortly.

While he was gone, Rebecca showered and washed her hair and then changed into the clean jeans and sweatshirt she had grabbed when she'd surreptitiously returned home.

In a conference room at FBI headquarters in the Federal Building in West Los Angeles, Rebecca glanced nervously at Zack McKenzie as they waited for his friend to join them. It was late afternoon, and the sun was beginning to set, although its bright rays were still streaming in through the windows. "Thanks for coming with me," she said.

Zack smiled at her and nodded his head.

The door opened and a slim, serious-looking young man,

with light brown hair, came into the room. "Mrs. Morland, I'm Special Agent Roy Conners."

She noticed that he spoke with a Midwestern accent, and it entered her mind that he didn't seem old enough to have such a responsible position. But then she reminded herself that looks could be deceiving, and that if both Daniel and Zack trusted him, she should too. They shook hands.

"Zack here has told me what a rough time you've had. What I'd like to do is hear the story from you, ma'am. That way I can ask some questions as we go along." His blue eyes crinkled at the corners when he smiled. "But before we do that, I understand that you recognized the man who abducted you?"

"Yes. I saw him at Maxwell Holmes's house one night not too long ago. I wrote down his car's license plate number."

"Zack gave us the number and we're running it now," Conners advised her. "I just wanted to know if you'd be able to identify him after we pick him up?"

"Oh yes," she said, with a shiver of apprehension. "That man's face is permanently etched in my mind."

That afternoon, Diana Worthington glanced up to see two handsome, clean-cut men in suits walking up the lawn from the dock. She wondered who they were and how they had gotten onto the property. Not long afterward, the houseman announced that there were Special Agents with the FBI who wanted to talk with her.

Her hands turned icy. What could the FBI possibly want to speak to her about? Perhaps she should call her attorney? He'd know what to do.

She paused, however. A nagging feeling in the pit of her stomach told her this surprise visit had something to do with Maxwell Holmes. If that was the case, she certainly didn't want her attorney alerted. He'd feel compelled to tell Paul, and she didn't want to risk that—not when they were still recovering from that terrible battle they'd had. Maybe she could handle this herself. Deciding she'd merely see what she could discern, she stepped out onto the patio to meet the men.

"Special Agents Roy Conners and Jack Burton, ma'am."

"What is this about?" she asked, her tone of voice letting them know she didn't appreciate being disturbed this way.

"We're sorry to bother you, ma'am," said Conners politely. "But we'd like to ask you some questions about your party the night Ryan Morland disappeared off the back of your yacht."

The mention of that night sent a jolt of fear through her, but she tilted her head and spoke in a dismissive manner. "That's already been thoroughly investigated by the local authorities, and to my knowledge Morland's death has been determined to be a suicide. What does the FBI have to do with it?"

"It's been brought to our attention that Mr. Morland's civil rights might have been violated that night. We're conducting our own investigation. We'd appreciate your answering a few questions, ma'am."

Still debating whether or not to call her lawyer, Diana paused while she held up her hand to shield her eyes from the sun. "Well, I'll try, although it seems entirely redundant to me," she said finally.

Conners smiled at her. "Thank you, ma'am. Now, we've just had a chat with some of your crew members, and we understand that early on the afternoon of the party, you came aboard the yacht with your clothes and other things you needed for that night. Is that correct?"

"Yes," she responded, fearful of where this conversation was going.

"And we also understand that someone was with you who was helping you." He shifted his feet. "Right?"

"There was someone helping me," she admitted, tensing up inwardly. "What's wrong with that?"

Not responding to her question, Conners asked, "Who was this person, ma'am?"

"I don't recall his name," she replied, trying to ignore her nervousness. "A friend asked me to give the man some work and I agreed he could fetch and carry for me."

Conners raised one eyebrow. "As we understand it, there was supposed to be no one aboard the yacht that night except for the people whose names appeared on either the guest list or the crew and caterer's list. Is that true?"

Her hands were clasped tightly together because she didn't want the agents to see they were shaking. "Yes."

"Was this man's name on the list?"

She decided to go on the offensive. "No. It wasn't necessary because he was only aboard for a short time."

Conners appraised her carefully as he asked his next question. "Do you recall just when this man left your yacht?"

Diana hesitated briefly, her pulse racing. "I don't remember the exact time. It must have been a little while after we arrived. Why?"

"We understand that he didn't actually leave the yacht. That, in fact, he was seen about the boat during the party."

Trying not to show her distress, she stated emphatically, "I could have sworn he left before the party began. Perhaps whoever told you that is mistaken."

The agent's gaze was intense. "Two of your crew saw this man arrive, but they did not see him leave."

She glanced over at the dock, where there appeared to be more activity than usual. She noticed another boat alongside the *Majorca*. That must be how these men had arrived without her seeing them.

"Mrs. Worthington," Conners said, getting her attention and repeating his statement.

"Well, I never saw him again," she finally claimed, waving her hand, which set off the jingling of her bracelets. "As far as I know he was long gone before the party started." She looked at Conners's serious face and wondered if he believed her.

"You said you were doing a friend a favor," he continued. "What friend would that be, ma'am?"

Diana inhaled sharply. There it was, the question she didn't want to answer. "Look, Special Agent Conners," she said, enunciating each word very clearly. "If this is that important, then maybe I *should* call my attorney." Her eyes challenged him.

His light blue eyes did not blink as he stared directly back at her. "If you feel you need some legal advice before answering that question, then by all means, please call your lawyer. We'll be happy to wait."

He was calling her bluff, she realized. Maybe if she gave them the name, that would be the end of it. After all, as long as she maintained that she knew nothing more, what could they do to her?

"Ma'am," Conners said, interrupting her thoughts, "would you like to tell us the name of your friend, or would you rather call your lawyer?"

"Why are you so interested in a man who carried some clothes on board for me?"

"We have reason to believe he's a murderer."

"A murderer?" She gripped the back of a patio chair. "That can't be. You must be mistaken. Who is he supposed to have murdered?"

"Ryan Morland, ma'am."

"No!" Her hand came up to her mouth. "Ryan Morland committed suicide. Everyone says so. Why, he left a note."

Special Agent Conners seemed to be assessing her for a long moment before he spoke. "Can we have the name of that friend now, Mrs. Worthington?"

Feeling as if she were going to faint, Diana managed to say, "It was Maxwell Holmes." She fought to retain her self-control. With a supreme act of will, she added, "As I said, I was under the impression that the man left shortly after he helped me. That's all I know. Is there anything else—or are we finished?"

"We're finished for the moment," said Conners. He cocked his head. "And thank you, ma'am, for your cooperation. We certainly appreciate it."

As she watched them leave, Diana was barely aware that her intense grip on the back of the chair had broken two of her perfectly manicured nails.

Maxwell Holmes was lying nude on the couch in his solarium, talking on the phone. "No problem, pal," he said, listening with one ear while he checked the positioning of his three sunlamps. Directly overhead, each one of them was aimed at a different area as they shone down on him. In the crevices of his body, fine beads of perspiration were already forming.

"Right." He took a puff on his cigar, then slowly blew the smoke out. "I said I'd get you a beauty and I did. If I make a friend a promise, I keep it."

He listened distractedly as the man on the other end described last night's date in graphic detail. Holmes could care less. He knew all about the woman he had set the man up with. Didn't he realize Holmes tried them out first himself?

There was a knock on his door. "Hold on one second," he said to his caller. "Who's there?"

"It's me," said his houseman.

"Well, come in, dammit. Where have you been? I've been waiting for my iced coffee for an hour."

"Sorry. We ran out of your favorite, and I had to go to the store."

"Well, keep better tabs. What the hell am I paying you for?"

The houseman put the tray down on a table next to Holmes, who took a sip of the frothy drink, then noticed that the man was still standing there.

"What is it?" he barked.

"There are two men here to see you." The houseman handed Holmes a card that identified his callers as being FBI Special Agents.

Had that bitch Rebecca Morland gone to them? he wondered. When his men hadn't found her, he figured she was hiding out. Well, the Feds would never believe her. Besides, she had no proof. "Buddy, I'll have to call you back," Holmes said into the phone. "Some guys are here to see me." And he hung up.

"Hand me my robe," he said, pointing to a white terry lounger on the chair. "Then show them in."

"What can I help you gentlemen with?" Holmes asked, quickly assessing the two agents when they came into the room.

Listening to them explain that they had been to see Diana Worthington about a person whom two crew members saw board the boat with her before the party, Holmes was incredulous.

"I have no idea why Mrs. Worthington would say she was doing me a favor." He shook his head vigorously. "I don't know what she's talking about."

"Does that mean that you never asked Diana Worthington to give someone a job?" Conners asked in a clear voice.

"Never," Holmes replied emphatically. He saw the skeptical look on the agent's face. Well, screw them if they didn't want to believe his side of the story. They couldn't prove a damn thing and they knew it.

"Besides," Holmes added, waving his hands in a dramatic fashion, "there was a full security detail that came on board and checked that boat from stem to stern before the party. I'd be willing to bet my last dollar that they made damn sure there wasn't a soul on board who wasn't accounted for. I mean, the mayor was there, and a bunch of other dignitaries. Not to mention all the jewelry the women were wearing. It's ludicrous to suppose that a man could hide on that yacht without being detected." He saw the look the two agents exchanged. This was an angle they hadn't covered.

"You have the name of this security outfit?" Conners asked.

"I'm sure I can get it for you." Holmes offered them a sly smile. "If you guys want my opinion, I'd check the source of this story again. Those crew members could have a vendetta against Mrs. Worthington for some reason. Maybe she didn't give them the raise they wanted. Or maybe they want to see their names in the newspaper." He shrugged in a casual way.

Conners nodded. "Mr. Holmes, what is the nature of your relationship with Diana Worthington?"

Holmes gave them another sly smile. "We're just friends."

The agents glanced at each other again. "That's all we have for now. Thanks for answering our questions."

After closing the door behind the agents, Holmes hit the wall with his fist. What the fuck was Diana thinking of when she sent those goons to his house? It sounded like she had lost her mind. For a moment he considered calling and lambasting her for being so stupid. Then he decided not to. He had the disk with the letter Ryan Morland had left behind, and he'd made sure the original was no longer on the wife's computer. So let Rebecca Morland run off at the mouth. These guys had no real proof of anything.

Earlier in the day, at the request of the FBI, Rebecca had looked at photos until she identified the thin man, whose name she had learned was Victor Irwin. A short time later they had tracked him down and brought him in to headquarters.

Now she waited nervously as they continued to question him. They had let her stay behind the one-way glass, so she could hear them pounding away at Irwin and could watch his face. It was surprising, but he hadn't once asked for a lawyer.

Whenever she allowed herself to admit that this man had in all likelihood murdered her husband, the rage that had been building inside her these past months came close to exploding.

She continued to listen intently to the interrogation, hearing the man's repeated denials of having any knowledge of what had happened to her husband. Each time Conners restated the charges they had against him arising from his assault on Rebecca —kidnapping, attempted murder, to name only two—the agent also reiterated to Irwin that he'd end up getting the death penalty for Ryan's murder unless he cooperated with them.

Finally, Irwin slumped forward in his chair. "Okay, okay. I'll tell you guys what happened."

Heart beating furiously, Rebecca stood transfixed in horror as Irwin recounted how he'd been hired by Holmes to get rid of Ryan Morland and to make it look like either a suicide or an accident. He explained that he had boarded the boat with Diana Worthington, but that instead of his leaving, she'd hidden him in a secret compartment in her closet while the boat was being searched by the security detail. Later, after the security detail left, she had let him out.

Rebecca kept taking deep breaths, almost overwhelmed with anger. She'd never considered herself capable of either murder or mayhem. Now she was shaken by the fury this man evoked in her. She envisioned torturing him until he was in total agony for what he had done to Ryan—to her.

"Look, I'm telling you the truth," Irwin said emphatically, his eyes fixed on the two agents. "When I got to the cockpit to take care of the problem, Morland was gone. I didn't kill him. I couldn't kill him, because he wasn't there."

Watching the faces of the two FBI men for their reactions, Rebecca saw that they didn't believe Irwin any more than she did. He was obviously lying.

They left the subject of Ryan's murder alone for a while and took another tack. "Do you have any idea why Diana Worthington was willing to help Maxwell Holmes?" asked Burton.

Victor Irwin shrugged his shoulders.

"They were having an affair, weren't they?" Conners said, his blue eyes focused on the hit man.

"Not sure," Irwin said. "But probably, since Mrs. Worthington was over at Mr. Holmes's house a lot."

"Did she ever say anything to you, or acknowledge in some way, that she was helping you because Holmes had asked her to?"

"Oh, yeah," Irwin nodded. "She said Holmes wanted me hidden from sight and that there was a special place in her closet where I'd be safe. She also said not to worry, she'd make sure I wasn't in there too long."

Conners and Burton exchanged glances. "I think we need to pay Mrs. Worthington another visit," said Conners.

"Right on," Burton agreed.

CHAPTER
THIRTY-ONE

A fter the FBI Special Agents had read Diana her rights, they took her to their headquarters to answer questions. She had a hard time believing that this entire thing was even happening to her. In her bewildered state of mind, she figured that if she leveled with the agents, they'd be forced to see that she had no actual knowledge of anything. When Special Agent Roy Conners explained that the man she'd hidden on the boat for Holmes was in reality a hit man, hired to kill Ryan Morland, Diana went into a tailspin.

"I can't believe that," she kept saying, shaking her head in confusion. "Maxwell said the man merely had to talk to Morland." She looked up at them to see if they understood.

"Did he tell you what about?"

"No," she admitted.

"Did you ask?" Conners prodded her, his eyes narrowed.

Appearing somewhat abashed, she said, "I'm afraid I didn't."

He regarded her with a skeptical expression. "After Morland disappeared, didn't it enter your mind that Holmes and the man you brought aboard might have had something to do with it?"

She could feel the color rising in her cheeks—she had considered the possibility that the two things were related, but Holmes kept reassuring her it wasn't the case. Tears welling in her eyes, she replied, "Holmes said Morland was despondent and killed himself."

Fear slicing through her, Diana tried to read their faces. Her heart sank when she saw nothing but doubt. "The detectives said there was a suicide note," she stuttered. "I had no reason to think otherwise." She fought a rising panic.

"You realize, don't you," said Conners, his voice turning hard, "Maxwell Holmes and Victor Irwin will be charged with capital murder? And because you helped in the conspiracy, you'll be charged right along with them?"

Her breath caught in her throat, and she clutched the edge of her chair. "That can't be!" Diana cried, shaking her head. "I only hid someone on the boat for a friend. I didn't murder anyone!"

The agent planted his feet wide apart as he stood in front of her and related the facts. "You were a willing participant in an illegal conspiracy. That means you can be held accountable for what the other members of that conspiracy did."

Turning white, Diana suddenly seemed to collapse into herself. Her body started to slump forward.

Grabbing her shoulders, Conners asked, "Would you like some water?"

"Mmm," she mumbled, nodding, unable to speak, more terrified than she'd ever been in her life. Her mind was reeling. This was a nightmare. She'd never be First Lady. She'd be sent to prison. Diana began shaking uncontrollably.

Burton returned and handed her the glass. Diana took a few sips, almost choking.

"Why did you want to help Holmes?" Conners asked, his eyes focused on her.

Her heart beating erratically, Diana struggled to catch her breath. "It didn't . . . seem like such a big favor at the time." She kept her head down, barely able to get the words out.

Conners squatted down on his haunches in front of her, trying to make her look him in the eyes. "Did your husband know about it?"

"No," she managed to say.

In a low voice, he inquired, "Ma'am, did you do this for Holmes because you were in love with him?"

"In love with him?" She saw the compassion on Conners's face and gave a harsh laugh that came out sounding hysterical. "I detested him!"

As Conners stood up, he and Burton exchanged startled looks. "But Victor Irwin said he saw you at Maxwell Holmes's house quite a number of times," Conners pointed out.

"Yes." She bowed her head, tears trickling from the corners of her eyes.

After waiting for a further response, which didn't come, Conners said, "Ma'am, we can't promise, but if you cooperate, we might be able to help."

"What would . . . I have to . . . do?" she asked.

"Turn state's evidence so we can convict Holmes and his henchman Irwin. We'll do our best to see you're treated fairly by the system."

Diana glanced up, tears now streaming down her cheeks. Was it possible she could have back her life? "If I testify against them, I'd get a reduced sentence or something?"

"Like we say, ma'am, we'd need to get the prosecuting attorney and the judge to okay it. But we'd certainly recommend leniency. That is, as long as you level with us under oath." He held out a wad of tissues to her.

Diana wiped at her eyes and tried to sort it all out in her mind. How had this happened to her? She took a deep breath and made a decision. "Contrary to what you must think, I didn't help Maxwell Holmes because I was in love with him." She paused. "I helped him because I had no choice." Playing with the charms on her bracelet, Diana kept her eyes focused on her hands, unable to meet the penetrating gaze of Special Agent Conners. "You see, Maxwell Holmes was blackmailing me."

Hours later, Rebecca was told by Roy Conners that Diana Worthington had confessed to her part in what had happened that night on the boat and would be testifying against both Holmes and Irwin.

"Blackmailing her?" Rebecca was incredulous. "What did he know that would compel her to take part in something so terrible?"

He sighed. "It seems Diana Worthington had dreams. She wanted her husband to be a senator and then someday President. His backers were all staunch conservatives who were dead set against abortion. They made it very clear to Worthington and to her that if there were any skeletons in their closets they had better come clean."

He stopped for a moment before adding, "Of course, both Worthingtons said there was nothing. But Mrs. Worthington had a secret. She'd had an abortion at one time. It was before she met her husband, but knowing how he felt on the subject, she'd never told him."

Rebecca was listening intently. "How did Maxwell Holmes find this out?"

He gave a grim laugh. "Holmes is one of those people who will go to extraordinary lengths to find out things about people he can use against them for his own benefit. We've been hearing rumblings for years that he was extorting money, but no one would ever come forward and finger him."

"Wow," said Rebecca, feeling overwhelmed by this new information.

Conners thrust his hands in his pockets as he went on. "From what Holmes told Mrs. Worthington, we learned there was a doctor who was about to lose his license because of a drinking problem until Holmes fixed things for him. In turn, the doctor had been paying Holmes for years. When Worthington's name and picture began showing up a lot in the media as a possible future candidate, the doctor recognized Diana and saw a way out of his own predicament. He turned over to Holmes the records on the abortion he'd performed on Diana, and in exchange, Holmes let him off the hook."

"My God," said Rebecca, sitting back and digesting these details. "Holmes was blackmailing Brandon Taylor. He was blackmailing Diana Worthington. He ordered my husband murdered. What a totally evil man!"

"Yes ma'am," Conners agreed, then added, "You probably came a lot closer to losing your own life than you'll ever know."

Rebecca shivered as that revelation hit home. For a short time she was pensive. "You know, when I staked out Holmes's house, I saw the way he and Diana Worthington kissed at the front door. They sure looked like lovers to me."

"That was part of the deal," Conners divulged. "Mrs. Worthington had to wear a mink coat with nothing on underneath whenever she went over to see Holmes. When she handed over the envelope with the cash payoff, she had to take off the coat and stand there nude." He paused. "Having intimate relations with him was also part of the deal." His face clouded. "She said his demands on her were getting worse."

Gazing up at Conners, Rebecca asked, "Do you believe her?"

"Yes," he said with a nod. "She's also offered to take a lie detector test, and we're planning on giving it to her."

"Did Paul Worthington know about any of this?"

"She says no, but we're planning to question him ourselves. In fact, we're far from through. We have to talk to Brandon Taylor and quite a few others." He gave her a meaningful look. "So it's imperative that you don't mention any of this to anyone."

"I won't say a word," she promised, shaking her head.

"We're going to move you to another hotel and keep you there for a little longer, Rebecca." Conners folded his arms across his chest. "We still don't know who else might be involved, and it would be premature to think you're safe."

"I understand." She chewed on the inside of her lip. "What about Solowski and Walters?"

"That's another issue that remains to be resolved. Both Sheriff Quentin and Detective Glen Walters have been placed on administrative leave pending an investigation. There seems to be a long-standing friendship between Holmes and the sheriff. We've also located Detective Solowski and taken the precaution of installing her and her two kids in the room next to yours at the hotel. We want to make sure they're safe until we've got all the players behind bars."

There was sudden noise in the outer room, and then the

door burst open and Paul Worthington came striding in. "Where do you have my wife?" he demanded in a loud voice.

"She's giving a statement at the moment," Conners told him. "It seems she hid a hit man hired by Maxwell Holmes on your boat the night Ryan Morland died."

"Well, I hope you don't think I knew anything about that. I had no idea Diana had allowed some thug to come on our yacht. Maxwell Holmes is a scumbag." He stopped to take a deep breath and shook his head. "You know, from the day I met Diana, I had the feeling she wasn't good enough for me. I guess I was right."

Hearing him put his wife down that way galled Rebecca. Ignoring the fact that it wasn't her place to question the man, especially with Conners and Burton in the room, Rebecca plunged in anyway.

"If you didn't know about what your wife did, how come you wouldn't let me question your crew?" she demanded.

He seemed startled for a moment, as if he hadn't realized she was even there. With a scowl on his face he explained, "That had nothing to do with a man being snuck on board."

"What *was* your reason, then?" she challenged, her voice rising.

Worthington's neck grew red as he peered around the room.

"Why don't you tell all of us why you wouldn't let Mrs. Morland speak to your crew?" said Conners.

"Oh, what the hell," Worthington mumbled under his breath. "I didn't want you talking to them because I was afraid you'd sue me for negligence," he told Rebecca. "When you have as much money as I do, you worry about things like that. That's also why I wanted your husband's death to be ruled a suicide. That way, I couldn't be held responsible."

"Then why were you so freaked when I told you my husband was murdered?" Rebecca asked, still unable to believe him.

Worthington's eyes narrowed noticeably. "While I knew, of course, that I was innocent, I was afraid I would be a suspect, and even a hint of that would ruin my chance for the nomination." He made a loud noise, clearing his throat. "Not that it matters anymore, since my own wife has effectively taken care of whatever hopes I had."

It was impossible not to hear his bitterness. Rebecca had the feeling that he'd blame his wife for all his misfortunes, regardless of who had caused them. At the same time, Rebecca wasn't satisfied that he was leveling with them. "You knew my husband was digging into your past, looking for skeletons in your closet, didn't you?"

"I heard something to that effect," he admitted.

Her mouth compressed. "I think my husband told you what he found."

This time his eyes grew fearful. "What do you mean?"

"Until you got to him and persuaded him to change his story, Scott Reed at Brandon Taylor's campaign headquarters said you and Ryan had an argument on the phone a few days before he died. He also told me that my husband ran out to meet you. Isn't that really the truth?"

A cloud descended over Paul Worthington's features. "I don't see why we have to discuss matters like that in here, Rebecca. If these men are through with us, we can go have a drink and talk."

"I'm afraid that's not possible," she said coldly.

"We'd like to hear your answer to Mrs. Morland's question," Roy Conners said. From the amused glint in his eye, Rebecca realized she wasn't the only one enjoying watching this arrogant man being humbled.

Worthington exhaled loudly. "Fine. We did have a disagreement," he confessed. "You see, I was quite impressed with your husband, Rebecca. After all, he saved Brandon Taylor's name twice by putting a brilliant spin on what some of my people had uncovered and fed to the media." He fingered his Rolex watch as he continued. "I figured if Ryan was that good, I'd hire him. I offered your husband a lot of money to come to work for me."

He must have noticed the surprise on her face. "I take it he didn't tell you about that, did he?"

"No, he didn't," she admitted, feeling the color rise in her cheeks. "But I realize now that there were a lot of things in those last few weeks of his life that Ryan didn't tell me because he was afraid that it might put my life in danger too."

"So I take it Mr. Morland turned you down, completely?" Conners asked.

"Yes," Worthington conceded. "Of course, that impressed me even more." He sat up straight in his chair. "I'm a man used to getting my own way. Rarely, if ever, do I find anyone who will turn down money. Anyway, Morland claimed that he honestly believed in Taylor and what he was trying to do."

Rebecca wondered if that statement was made before or after Ryan discovered what his idol was up to. Pressing for more answers, she asked another question. "Was this large sum of money you offered Ryan tied to his squelching the information he'd dug up from your past?"

The wariness returned to Worthington's eyes. "Stop toying with me, Mrs. Morland," he said, his voice hard as steel. "Did you find something I should know about? Or are you waiting until all this dies down before you come riding up to my doorstep one day with your hand held out?"

Caught off guard by the viciousness in his voice, it took Rebecca a moment to recover. "I'm not into blackmail, Mr. Worthington. Neither was my husband. In fact, in the letter Ryan wrote me before his death, he said that the secret from your past had no place in a political campaign. That's why he didn't turn it over to Brandon Taylor or anyone else. He actually ordered me to destroy it."

Worthington looked shamefaced. "I'm sorry. Your husband told me that too—I just wasn't sure you'd feel the same way." Then he stared straight into her eyes. "Did you destroy it?"

"Not yet," she admitted.

He raised one eyebrow. "May I have it, then?"

"It's not mine to give," she admitted. "I'm afraid it was forcibly taken from me by the hit man hired by Maxwell Holmes."

This news seemed to render Worthington speechless. After a few moments, he recovered enough to say, "There goes everything."

Conners inserted himself into the conversation. "Want to tell the rest of us what this is all about?"

Turning around, Worthington took full measure of Conners. "Why not?" He shrugged. "If Maxwell Holmes has it, I'm sure he'll try and blackmail me with it. Might as well tell the world myself for free." He took a deep breath. "You see, I was adopted. I never knew who my real parents were until about fifteen years ago. That's when I found out my biological mother was black."

He glanced at the faces of those in the room as if to gauge their reactions, but as far as Rebecca could see, no one appeared shocked. It struck her that he'd lived for years in fear of something no one else really cared about.

"I was afraid of what others would think. I didn't know how to deal with it, so I told no one—not even my wife," he added.

Rebecca wanted to say, why not be proud of your heritage instead of ashamed? But looking at this man's arrogant face she realized she'd be wasting her breath. There was still one more thing she had to know. "Was it you who broke into my home and destroyed my husband's computer files?"

There was a look of alarm in his eyes before he skillfully covered it up. Without answering, he rose and walked to the window and stood looking out. "Are we talking prison time?" he asked, most likely of Conners.

"I don't know," Conners responded. "That's probably a local matter."

"It had to be you," Rebecca insisted. "You already told us that you weren't sure I'd honor my husband's promise not to use what he'd found."

His jaw muscles worked. "Surely you can understand that, with your husband dead, I had no guarantee that someone else wouldn't use that information? I had to have the files wiped out to protect myself." He rushed to add, "However, I waited until no one was home. I wished you no harm."

Suddenly, Rebecca felt extremely weary. "No harm? I lose my husband, then you break into my home and savage it." She looked at Worthington's implacable face, then shook her head.

Turning to Conners, she said, "I'm very tired and I really don't want to be around this man. Do you need me here any longer, or may I go?"

Conners nodded his head and gestured to Burton. "Why don't you take Mrs. Morland to where she's staying."

CHAPTER
THIRTY-TWO

As soon as Rebecca got to her room at the Century Plaza Hotel, she spoke to Detective Solowski on the telephone. They decided to have dinner together in Solowski's suite after her kids had been bathed and put to bed. That way the two of them could talk.

An hour later, when Rebecca entered the room, the table was already set up, and she was amused by the array of food Solowski had ordered for them. Soup, steaks, baked potatoes, onion rings, and two pieces of decadent-looking chocolate cake covered the room-service table's entire surface.

Solowski's eyes were dancing. "Isn't this great?"

While she fiddled with the food on her plate, Rebecca told Solowski what had transpired.

"All those secrets," Solowski said, shaking her head. "Money sure didn't make those rich people happy, did it?"

"No, but it makes their misery more comfortable," Rebecca said with a grin.

"That's something I'll never know about, not on a cop's salary."

"Given all that's happened, are you going to stay in the sheriff's department?"

"Yeah," Solowski said, nodding. "My dad was a cop. My husband was one too. It's all I know. Besides, most cops are really honest."

The phone rang, and Solowski answered it. "We're doing pretty good. Yeah, she's here too. Wanna talk to her? Hold on a second." She held the receiver out to Rebecca. "Daniel Black, for you."

Taking the phone, Rebecca asked, "How's your father?"

"He died this morning," Daniel said dejectedly.

"Oh, I'm so sorry."

"Yeah. Me too," he replied. "At least he didn't suffer. He was unconscious from the moment he had the attack." Daniel exhaled loudly. "Anyway, I spoke to Roy Conners, and he told me what's going on. It sounded like you came close to being killed, and I feel terrible I wasn't there for you."

"It was pretty scary for a while," Rebecca admitted. "But fortunately you'd alerted Zack. If he hadn't been here to help me, I'm not sure how things might have turned out."

"Zack's a great guy," Daniel agreed. "Conners also said you were hurt."

She heard the concern in his voice. "Just badly bruised. I'll be okay."

"Make sure you get that shoulder taken care of—that's important." Daniel cleared his throat and dropped his voice to a more intimate level. "I was worried about you, especially after I heard your message and then it got erased."

Rebecca sensed he was trying to say something, but she wasn't sure what. "Well, I'm okay, now. And I can't thank you enough, Daniel, for believing me. Without your courage, this case never would have been solved."

"That's my job. And you're the one with the courage." He paused. "Anyway, it sounds like they've got everything under control. I wish I could be there. But I'll be back after the shivah."

He was referring to the Jewish mourning ritual. "Are you going to sit for the full seven days?" she asked.

"Yes."

"Don't worry about things here," Rebecca counseled. "Just take care of yourself and your family. How's your mother doing?"

"So-so. I have two brothers and a sister and lots of nieces and nephews—all the commotion helps. Mom loves that."

Rebecca nodded, picturing the kind of woman his mother must be and smiling to herself.

"Well, I hope you feel better," Daniel said. "I'll call you the moment I get back."

"Okay. Take care."

After hanging up, Rebecca turned back to the table and admitted to Solowski that she wasn't hungry. "I'm too tired. If I don't get some sleep I'll collapse. With two Special Agents out in the hall, this is my chance."

"It's super having them," Solowski said, smiling. "We've got a refrigerator in the bar. I'll just wrap the food up, and if you get hungry during the night, you know where it is."

"Great." Rebecca looked at the detective solemnly. "I want to thank you, too, for believing in me and sticking your neck out to help me find my husband's killers."

Solowski blushed. "I only wish I could have done more."

Rebecca gave Solowski a big hug, which only seemed to further embarrass the woman detective.

Agent Conners called Rebecca the next day to tell her that Holmes had been arrested.

"Did he say anything?" she asked, sighing with relief.

"At first he denied it all, but he finally came around," Conners said. "Although he still maintains he had nothing to do with your husband's actual murder, because when the hit man went to kill Ryan, he wasn't there."

"You don't believe him, do you?"

"No, but it is the same story Irwin told us, so we're going to have to keep up the pressure until one of them cracks and tells us the truth."

"What did Holmes have to say about influencing the sheriff's department?" Rebecca asked.

"He denies that too, insists he never put pressure on any law enforcement officials. I don't believe that either, of course." Conners gave a dismissive snort. "The guy's a born liar. With both Diana Worthington and the hit man ready to testify against Holmes, it's more a question of what charges will work best. But don't worry, we're gonna get him."

"I certainly hope so," Rebecca said.

"We've talked to Brandon Taylor too," Conners continued. "He basically told us the same story he told you. That he suspected Holmes was involved in your husband's death but didn't know for sure and was too afraid to find out. Anyway, he feels bad and says he wants to talk to you. I told him we had you incommunicado for now. But, of course, if you want to talk to him, that's okay."

"I have nothing to say to him," Rebecca stated forcefully. "If Brandon had spoken up sooner, my husband would still be alive."

Later, after getting off the phone with Conners, Rebecca sat by the window looking out at the Century City Twin Towers. On each floor of those buildings, people were working in their own little spheres, she thought, most of them probably oblivious to what was going on around them. Would any of them believe her if she told them what her life had been like for the last several months? Probably not. No one could know what it felt like until it happened to them.

And it still wasn't over. Yes, Ryan's killers were in custody, but if they persisted in denying the murder charge, there would be a trial and she would have to go through the whole thing in court.

It bothered her that Irwin wouldn't tell them the truth. Especially since he'd been offered a deal, although the prospect of him ever being a free man again made Rebecca angry.

She got up and paced around the room. Why couldn't she let this go? With her husband's killers behind bars, she'd expected to find a certain kind of peace. Instead, she had this uneasy feeling, as if the puzzle of Ryan's death was not yet completely solved.

• • •

Two weeks later, Rebecca still hadn't been able to shake her feeling of unease. Since she'd moved back to her house from the Century Plaza Hotel, she'd spent the time clearing up her paperwork and figuring out her financial picture as well as sorting Ryan's things and figuring out what to pack up and give away.

She'd promised the director at the legal clinic to have things wound up on the home front and return to work by the middle of the month, now only a week away. With that in mind, Rebecca had asked Lucy to drop off the files on some of the clients that she'd be dealing with on her return.

"I'm looking forward to getting back," Rebecca told Lucy, "but first I plan to drive to Palm Springs and just lie in the sun for a couple of days. Want to come—my treat?"

"Sounds great," Lucy replied, "but I can't. I've got finals soon. But if you're talking about treating, you must have heard from the insurance company."

"Yes," nodded Rebecca. "They're going to be paying off on the policy."

"That's great," Lucy said enthusiastically. "Then you'll be able to keep the house."

"Yeah, I guess." Rebecca's tone was pensive. "You know, the books I've been reading on grieving all advise someone not to make any major life decisions—like selling a house—until at least a year has passed. But there are just too many memories for me here. I've decided to sell."

"I'm sorry."

"It's also a matter of trade-offs," explained Rebecca. "If I want to work at the legal clinic, and I do, it's going to be a tight squeeze trying to support myself while having something left over to give Ryan's mother."

"What about the law firm?" Lucy asked. "There should be some money coming to you from them, right?"

"Yes, but I don't know how much yet," Rebecca responded, taking a deep breath. "Brandon and Catherine have promised a quick settlement of Ryan's partnership interest, but I'm still waiting. At least they've released a statement to the press exonerating Ryan for the theft of the funds and placing the blame on John Evans instead."

"Yeah, I read it in the paper," Lucy said. "And I also saw that both Brandon and Worthington have disclosed that they won't be running for the Senate."

"True." Rebecca sighed. "It's all starting to come together. But until the trial is over, until Holmes has been convicted of Ryan's murder, I still won't be able to rest."

"Have you been talking to Daniel Black?"

Rebecca nodded. "In fact, I'm going downtown to see him today. I need to thank him in person for all his help. I'm going to beg him to please get this thing over with so I can go on with my life." She paused, then added as an afterthought, "Whatever that may be."

CHAPTER
THIRTY-THREE

Downtown in Daniel Black's office, Rebecca and he chatted for a while about his father's death and his family.

"So how are *you* doing?" Daniel finally asked.

"Okay. Just anxious for the media coverage to stop. I feel like I'm surrounded by vultures."

"Yes. But soon the trial will get started, and once that's over they'll forget about you and go on to the next scandal. You'll be able to get on with your life."

"Will I?"

"What do you mean?"

"Daniel, something's still bothering me," she admitted. "Not all of the pieces seem to fit."

He eyed her carefully. "Such as?"

"The chemical substance amitriptyline the autopsy found in Ryan's body, for example. I've been trying to work that out, but I can't. Why would the Elavil be there? Irwin's method of operation as a hit man would seem to be more direct. He'd be more likely to use a club or a gun. Drugs are way too subtle for him. Besides, he still maintains that he didn't do it."

Daniel seemed taken aback. "Are you saying you believe him?"

"I'm not sure."

"Rebecca, we've brought charges against Holmes and Irwin for your husband's murder. We're getting ready to go to trial. The only thing we're still working on, and the Feds are handling it, is checking into Holmes's background, the organized crime connection, and the corruption in the sheriff's department."

"Then I think you may have been premature. I think Ryan's killer is still out there."

There was a look of surprise in Daniel's eyes, as if he couldn't believe what she was saying. "And who do you think that is?"

"I don't know for sure, but I've got an idea. Please humor me. Let me go through your files; let me study everything. If I find the connection I'm looking for, I think you'll see that you need to pursue this further. If I don't find it, I promise to let it go. Okay?"

"I don't know, Rebecca," he said, his fingers playing with the letter opener on his desk. "It's not that I don't respect your instincts, I do, but I've got bosses over me who would view all this as unorthodox. They're still smarting from the taint of corruption themselves in having yielded to Sheriff Quentin's pressure."

"Please, Daniel."

"Okay," he said with a sigh. "But promise you'll come to me with your suspicions if you find anything to support them. If you're right, it would be far too dangerous for you to be looking into this yourself."

After spending several hours going through Daniel's files, Rebecca had come up with a couple of things that seemed suspicious to her. She held up a copy of one of the photographs that had been taken the night of Ryan's death and debated whether or not to show it to Daniel.

It would be better to have more evidence before she approached him again. Feeling guilty, but assuring herself that they were only copies, not original evidence, she put a few of the photos in her purse. Then she made arrangements to visit Diana Worthington at the Regent Beverly Wilshire Hotel, where she'd taken up residence after being asked by her husband to leave their home in Newport Beach.

Rebecca was hoping Mrs. Worthington would be cooperative, since she had made a deal with the state.

"Come in," said Diana, when Rebecca arrived at her hotel room door.

Rebecca was shocked by Diana's appearance. Although she wore makeup and was elegantly dressed, her eyes were dull, and she looked surprisingly old.

"I've got a few photos I'd like you to look at," Rebecca said, ending the pleasantries and getting directly to the purpose of her visit.

"Of course."

After removing them from her purse, Rebecca handed one of them to Diana, who gazed at it for a minute.

"That's Catherine, standing by me on the yacht," Diana said.

"Yes." Rebecca then pointed to the hem of Catherine's dress. "Do you know what that is?"

The other woman held the photo up to the light, her eyes squinting. "No. It appears to be spots of some kind."

"Do you remember Catherine's dress looking like that at the party?"

"Certainly not at the beginning of the evening. It was a designer dress and I would have noticed. But later, things got so confusing . . ." her voice trailed off. "I'm not sure."

"So you think this picture was taken after my husband disappeared?"

"Well, the tables behind Catherine have been cleared. Her hair is also rather messy, as if she'd been standing in the mist. I'd say it was late."

"Would you happen to know how I could reach Catherine's friend, Tony?"

"All I know is that his full name is Anthony Necosia and he's an associate at a law firm in Century City." Diana paused. "Why all these questions about Catherine?"

"Oh, nothing," Rebecca said. "I was just curious as to how such a beautiful dress got ruined. I recall admiring it early on in the evening."

Diana's eyes seemed dazed, as if she too were remembering back to that night. "Yes, everything was perfectly splendid that night until—" She didn't finish her sentence.

On the thirty-second floor of a high-rise office building in Century City, Tony Necosia leaned back in his black leather chair. He had just gotten off the phone with Rebecca Morland and had agreed to see her in half an hour. He glanced at the piles of papers that covered his walnut desk: depositions, motions, interrogatories, and all the other documents that made up the minutiae of a civil litigation practice.

Tony had been a lawyer for over five years, and he didn't like it any better now than when he had first started. He admired Catherine Dennison's love of the law. Every detail of it fascinated her. It was as if she were playing a high-stakes game of poker. From the moment a case started, she could spend hours, days even, planning her moves, plotting her strategy.

He sighed. For all Catherine's faults, he really loved her. But lately he had begun to doubt that they had any kind of a future together. Her inability to introduce him as her boyfriend made the handwriting on the wall very clear. She'd never treat him as an equal; her career, her status, her reputation—they were all too important to her. She was one of those people who truly was married to her work.

At first, Tony had hoped that the reversal in the firm's fortunes—owing to the scandal over Brandon Taylor and John Evans—might show Catherine how meaningless it was to base her entire life on her career. But clearly it wasn't working out that way. If anything, she was more driven than ever, determined to restore the practice to its previous glory. Knowing her as he did, he was sure she would be successful in that too.

Tony thought about Rebecca Morland and the devastating loss she had suffered. What kind of questions did she want to ask him, he wondered. She'd said they would be a combination of personal and professional. Undoubtedly, things about Catherine would be included in those questions. It could be difficult. Should he tell her the truth?

Rebecca sensed, at first, that Tony Necosia was reluctant to tell her what he remembered about the night Ryan had died. But after a while, he seemed to relent, especially after she showed him the photograph taken of Catherine on the yacht that evening.

When he finally told his story, Rebecca tried not to interrupt him too many times with questions.

"The night of the party, Catherine came to my place. It was really late. Almost two. She told me what had happened, I mean about Ryan, and said she was too upset to go home. I was surprised."

"Why was that?" asked Rebecca, curious about the kind of relationship Tony had with Catherine.

Tony seemed disconcerted. "Catherine had refused to let me escort her to the Worthingtons' party. She has a hang-up about our age difference and was afraid of how it would look. We had a big argument, and I wasn't sure if we would ever see each other again. So when she showed up—it was unexpected."

"I see," Rebecca said, nodding. "What happened next?"

"Catherine said she wanted to shower, and when I went into the bathroom, her brand-new dress was crumpled in a heap on the floor." He glanced up at her. "I knew how expensive it was, so I picked it up, and I noticed there were some kind of stains on the bottom. Offhand, I'd say they were water stains."

Rebecca sat up straighter when she heard that, surmising how the water stains had gotten on the dress. "Go on," she urged Tony, who had stopped for a moment.

Looking embarrassed, Tony said he'd been planning on joining Catherine in the shower, but she had turned it off and reached for a towel. "That's when I noticed the large bruise on the underside of her arm," he said.

"What part of her arm?" asked Rebecca, leaning forward now.

Tony lifted his arm and pointed to the area near his elbow. "Of course, I asked her what had happened. Catherine seemed discomfited. She quickly explained she'd bumped into something on the yacht." His mouth became grim. "I asked her how she could get a bruise there unless her arm was raised. She gave me a look that said, 'Don't question me.' And then she changed the subject." Tony's voice dropped. "It's been bothering me ever since." He stopped to take a deep breath, and his face looked troubled.

"Have you seen that dress since that night?"

"No."

"Do you know where Catherine gets her dry cleaning done?" Rebecca asked.

"Yes, she frequently has me pick it up for her." He gave her the name of the establishment.

It was Rebecca's turn to be pensive. "You and Catherine spend a great deal of time at one another's homes, including nights, don't you?"

Tony shook his head sadly. "She comes to my place more often, although she seldom stays over. Most of the time, after we are . . ." — he hesitated, his face coloring — "well, afterwards, she usually says she wants to go home to work."

"The times you've stayed over at her place, did you ever look into her medicine cabinet?"

"Yeah, I guess so." ·

"Did Catherine ever take a drug called Elavil?"

"That doesn't ring a bell. What kind of a drug is it?"

"An antidepressant."

"That doesn't sound like something she'd take."

"I wouldn't ask if it wasn't really important, but do you think maybe the next time you're at her place you could check that out for me, just to make sure?"

He seemed reluctant again, but after Rebecca pressured him some more, he finally relented.

"Will you call me as soon as you know anything?" she asked. Tony nodded.

"Oh, and it would be a big help if you'd get me the name of

the drugstore she usually uses," she said, as she walked out his office door.

It was the next night when Rebecca returned to the parking lot behind a drugstore on Wilshire Boulevard. Tony had telephoned her that morning to report that Catherine didn't have a drug called Elavil in her medicine cabinet. But he gave her the name of the drugstore she frequented, and Rebecca had visited it earlier in the day.

She knew that the information a pharmacist had about a customer was confidential, and it would have to be subpoenaed. Not knowing if Daniel would feel comfortable doing that, it would be best if she knew the answer before she asked him. Having noticed that a young clerk periodically took over for the pharmacist, she was hopeful of convincing the man to help her.

Making her way to the back where the pharmacy was, she waited ten minutes for the young man to be free. Rebecca then showed him the picture of Catherine and explained the situation.

"If you could just check for that two-week period, I'd really appreciate it."

"Lady, I'm not sure I can do that."

"It's terribly important," she told him. "Please."

He looked hesitant, and she flashed him her warmest smile. "I'd really be grateful."

"Okay," he finally said, "but you can't tell my boss or I might get in trouble."

He began looking through the records. Finally, his face lit up. "I think I've found something. See this card," he said, pointing. "It shows we filled a prescription for Elavil for a Catherine Dennison."

She squinted at the card, her breath caught in her throat. The date on the entry was the day before Ryan had disappeared off the back of the *Majorca*. She felt a surge of elation. She'd been right.

"Thank you so much," she said, committing the name of the doctor to memory.

After thanking him profusely again, she left the drugstore. Under her breath, she whispered to Ryan, "I told you I wouldn't rest until I found out what had happened and why. I'm beginning to understand the what, but the why has me stumped."

Catherine was rushing to get her documents ready for a big meeting she had scheduled for the next day. She was exhausted. The scandal over what Brandon had done had been devastating. Several of their high-profile clients had left the firm. But Catherine refused to allow herself to think negatively, as she worked relentlessly to hold on.

As far as she was concerned, all of the firm's troubles had been caused by John Evans. From the day he'd joined the firm, it had started to go downhill. As for Brandon, she could tell that the fight had gone out of the man. Certainly his political ambitions were shot to hell, and he still wasn't sure if he was facing criminal charges. Either way, he'd be retiring soon. So that left just her, alone, working like a demon, trying to salvage what she could.

When her secretary buzzed her to say that Diana Worthington was on the phone, Catherine decided to take the call, even though she was swamped. Poor Diana, she thought, living in a hotel. That Paul Worthington was a real piece of work.

She picked up the receiver. "Hello, Diana. How's it going?"

"Lousy. Everything I've ever wanted is lost—utterly gone," she moaned. "I'm so humiliated."

"Don't be silly. This will all blow over soon. We're living in a changed society," Catherine pointed out. "Lots of people rehabilitate themselves. With money—anything is possible. You'll see, you'll be a celebrity. They'll probably ask you to write a book."

"I hope you're right," Diana said, then paused. "Anyway, yesterday I had an interesting visit from Rebecca Morland."

"Oh?" Catherine found herself curious. "What did she want?"

"She showed me a picture of you on the yacht the night her husband disappeared. It was really rather odd. She pointed to some spots on your dress and asked me about them."

Catherine felt a chill sweep over her. "What did you say?"

"Nothing, really. I had no idea what they were. Do you recall how they happened to be there?"

Alarmed, Catherine nonetheless kept her voice calm. "There were no spots on my dress that night that I can remember. It was probably just a defect in the film."

"Oh, I never thought of that."

"Thanks for alerting me anyway," Catherine said. "I've got to run, I've got a meeting. I'll call you tomorrow."

After she hung up the phone, Catherine sat contemplating her options as she wondered what Rebecca was up to. Actually, when she thought about it, Rebecca had caused Catherine as much misery as John had. Both of them had tried to ruin her plans. She'd suffered enough setbacks. She wasn't about to let Rebecca Morland interfere in her life again.

CHAPTER
THIRTY-FOUR

Rebecca sat across the desk from Daniel, explaining to him where her recent investigations had led her. At first, he was angry because she hadn't come to him as she'd promised. He also wasn't thrilled to learn that she'd removed photographs from the file he had let her look at. But then he cooled down and listened.

"So you're saying that Catherine obtained a prescription for Elavil and then filled it, and Elavil was the same chemical substance found in Ryan's body—and therefore Catherine is the murderer?"

"Right."

"Let's back up here for a minute. What made you suspicious of her in the first place?"

"After reading through all the reports, I saw that Catherine was the only witness who actually knew that my husband had been drinking scotch that night. She also described him as unsteady on his feet, with bloodshot eyes, and slurring his words. There are several other people, including me, who are willing to testify he looked fine."

"That doesn't mean much."

"But it does. It means she either saw Ryan become that way after she gave him the drug, which I surmise she did along with a glass of scotch. Or she planned ahead of time to say it, figuring the Elavil would be found in his body and everyone would naturally assume he took it because he was depressed."

"I see," he said, rubbing his chin.

"Don't forget what Tony Necosia saw that night. The ruined dress, the bruise under her arm."

"And you can't find the dress?"

"The dry cleaners said she never brought it in," Rebecca said. "For all we know, she dumped it in a trash can the next day."

"All of it, including Catherine's obtaining and filling the prescription for Elavil, is powerful," Daniel admitted. "Although, what that young clerk told you wouldn't be admissible. But say we got the information with a court order. Still, at best, you have a so-so circumstantial case—one that I'm afraid wouldn't be good enough. Catherine would get herself the best criminal defense lawyer money can buy, one who would poke holes in everything we put on. Not only that, if the judge allows them to bring in the evidence of the other suspects who have already been arrested for your husband's murder, she's got a good chance of establishing reasonable doubt."

"But both Holmes and Irwin say they didn't kill Ryan; that he was already gone."

"No one will believe that."

"I do," she said stubbornly.

"Rebecca, it certainly looks like you may be right, but without a stronger case, my superiors would never let me go to court—not when it would be virtually impossible to prove the connection."

"Are you saying that after all this information I've brought you about Catherine, you're not going to have her arrested?"

"I can't," he said, shaking his head. "There are a lot of inferences, but there just isn't enough evidence."

"So," she lashed out in a bitter voice, "it sounds like you're more afraid of losing in court than you are in seeing that justice is done."

Daniel turned pale, as if her statement had wounded him. "Rebecca, that's not true. I want to help you." He moved from behind the desk and took the chair next to hers. He reached for her hand. "I've come to greatly respect you." He paused, and seemed to be searching for the right words. "The truth is, I've also come to care for you. I would do anything in my power to help you." His eyes were pleading with her to believe him.

It was her turn to be startled. The thought of Daniel Black having special feelings for her was not totally new, nor was it unwelcome, but she couldn't let anything get in the way of what had to be done. "Does that mean you're not going to arrest her?"

"Not now, not based on the evidence we have. Come on, Rebecca, be reasonable. As a lawyer you should understand that there are definite limits to what I can do."

"I don't want to be reasonable," she retorted angrily, pulling her hand back from his grasp. "Not if it means Catherine Dennison is going to get away with killing my husband."

Without saying another word, Rebecca stood up. As she left Daniel's office, she heard him calling her name, but she refused to respond. She was positive Catherine had been involved in Ryan's death, and she'd be damned if she was going to wait another day, another minute, for that woman to be arrested.

Driving home from Daniel's office, Rebecca felt frustrated. There was no doubt in her mind that Holmes and Irwin had set out to kill her husband—and she wanted them punished. But she was also positive that Catherine had beaten them to it. She was sick and tired of the legal system and the roadblocks being put in her way. Catherine was the murderer, she was convinced of that. She just had to prove it.

What if she confronted Catherine with the evidence—the picture of the stained dress, the prescription for Elavil, the things Tony saw—and she was able to provoke the woman into telling her the truth? If she had a tape recorder hidden in her purse, she'd get the confession on tape. That should be proof enough.

On her way home, Rebecca stopped to get a new tape for her recorder. She'd wait a while until she was sure Catherine was home, and then she'd call her house.

When Rebecca got home, there were two messages from Daniel, but she didn't return his calls. She was angry. He was playing it too careful; too much like a prosecutor. Why couldn't he just take a chance and trust his instincts as she was doing?

It was after eight that evening when Rebecca dialed Catherine's home number.

"Hello."

"It's Rebecca Morland," she said. "I need to see you right away. We have things to talk about."

"Very well," Catherine replied. "You know where I live. I'll be waiting."

As Rebecca hung up the phone, she was puzzled. Why had Catherine acquiesced so easily? It wasn't at all like her. She thought it over for a minute, then decided that maybe Catherine was tired and figured it wouldn't do her much good to argue.

She was just walking out the door when the phone rang. Thinking it was Catherine, she picked it up. It was Daniel.

"Rebecca, why haven't you returned my calls?"

"There isn't anything to discuss at the moment, Daniel. You said there was nothing more you could do without more evidence, and I'm going to get it for you."

"What is that supposed to mean?" he asked, sounding worried.

"Just what I said. I've got to go now."

All the way to Catherine's house, Rebecca felt her rage growing until it was almost choking her. After parking her car, she made sure the tape recorder in her purse was turned on. For the first time, she noticed that Catherine's house was dark. That was odd. The woman knew Rebecca was coming.

Rebecca rang the bell, but there was no answer. She rang several more times. When she got no response, she tried to figure out what to do. In frustration, she rattled the doorknob, surprised when it turned in her hand.

For a moment she stood on the threshold, uncertain, then she pushed open the door and stepped inside. "Hello," she called. "Anybody home?"

No answer. Nothing. Gathering her courage, she moved around from room to room. Maybe something had happened to Catherine. She thought of turning on the lights but decided not to. If Catherine wasn't there, Rebecca didn't want to alert the neighbors. She might be accused of breaking and entering.

Could Catherine be sleeping? she wondered. Not likely with the door unlocked. Now that her eyes had grown accustomed to the dark, there was just enough light from outside to keep her from bumping into things.

Rebecca could feel her heart pounding in her chest, her breath coming fast now, in short gasps, as moving slowly, she located the stairway and started up the stairs.

Listening carefully, Rebecca strained to pick up any noise, any sign of life. The house was eerily silent.

At the door to Catherine's bedroom, Rebecca paused. Then, her pulse racing, she went in.

Suddenly, Rebecca was blinded by a light.

"Come in," Catherine said, her voice cold as steel. "I've been waiting for you."

Rebecca's first impulse was to run, but Catherine must have anticipated that.

"I've got a gun and it's pointed directly at your head. So don't get any funny ideas." She gave a throaty laugh. "You wanted to have a little chat, so let's chat."

Her eyes had acclimated to her surroundings, and Rebecca saw Catherine beckoning with the gun for her to step farther into the room.

"Come on, I haven't got all day," Catherine said.

Too scared not to obey, Rebecca reluctantly moved closer to Catherine and the gun.

"So," Catherine said, when Rebecca was standing directly in front of her. "What did you want to talk about? Maybe the spots on my dress?"

Rebecca was startled. What a fool she had been. She should

have known Diana Worthington would tell Catherine about her questions. Feeling she had nothing to lose now, she confronted the other woman. "You killed Ryan, didn't you?"

"Don't be silly. There are two men in custody who admit they set out to murder him. Everyone else is satisfied. It's only you, Rebecca, who can't let go." She paused, and a cruel smile twisted up the corners of her lips as she shook her head. "You know, you're really a foolish woman."

Heart thudding, Rebecca said, "What do you mean?"

"I could shoot you and get away with it," bragged Catherine.

"I've no weapon," Rebecca pointed out, slipping her purse onto her shoulder so she could hold her hands out in front of her. She noticed that her hands were shaking.

"Ah," said Catherine, her eyes glinting, "but I didn't know that. I surprised an intruder going through my things; you pointed something at me, and I shot. How was I to know it was a . . ."—she waved her hand in a dismissive gesture—"a whatever. I'll find something logical to stick in your palm after you're dead."

"They won't believe you."

"I'll take my chances." Catherine grinned.

With an air of calm she did not feel, Rebecca said, "If I'm going to die, then at least tell me the truth."

"What is it you want to know?"

"On the yacht that night, down in the cockpit, you gave Ryan Elavil, right? And you probably had him wash it down with something like scotch."

Catherine's eyes opened wide in disbelief. "How did you learn about the drug?"

"They exhumed Ryan's body. Secretly. They found the chemical remains of the drug in his system. I've even found the pharmacy where you had the prescription filled. I believe you saw a Dr. Marvin Spencer to obtain it."

Catherine looked horrified as Rebecca went through her litany of evidence. The police reports, where only Catherine said that Ryan was drinking scotch; her description of Ryan's behavior and appearance that night, so much more detailed than everyone else's; the prescription. When she got to the part about Tony, Catherine turned white.

"I don't believe he told you that!" she hissed.

"Then how did I know?" taunted Rebecca. She wasn't as frightened now as she'd been earlier. Even faced with the knowledge that Catherine could kill her at any second, her hatred for the woman filled her with an icy rage. "They're on to you, Catherine. If you kill me, you'll make their case."

She could see that her words were having the desired effect. Catherine seemed to be thinking.

"Why, Catherine? Was it because I took Ryan away from you?"

The other woman gave a derisive laugh. "No man is worth that."

"Then what was it? Were you part of the whole scheme? I mean, everyone else was upset because Ryan was threatening to go to the authorities about Holmes. Did you know about it too?"

"What if I did?"

"Brandon told me you had no idea what he'd done."

"That man must think I'm a moron. I've always known everything that went on in that firm, although I didn't find out about Brandon's stupidity and Ryan's pitiful attempt to rescue him until two nights before Ryan died."

"Is that when Brandon finally told you?"

"No," said Catherine, her mouth compressed. "I found it out for myself. I'd forgotten something, so I went back to the office. I heard shouting. The door was partially closed, but I recognized the voices. At first I thought Brandon and Ryan were both in there, but then I realized Brandon was on the speaker phone with Ryan. I couldn't believe it when I heard Ryan say he was going to the authorities, and especially when I heard what he was planning to tell them."

Every nerve ending in Rebecca's body was on alert. "And that's why you killed him?"

Catherine's eyes grew wild. "I couldn't let your husband ruin everything I'd ever wanted, everything I'd worked for my entire life." She laughed bitterly. "I knew the scandal would destroy everything. Brandon wouldn't become a senator. The prestige of the firm would go down the drain. Worse, Brandon's deeds might be imputed to me and I'd be held legally culpable too." Her voice lowered. "I had no choice but to get rid of him."

She advanced on Rebecca. "And everything would have been fine, if you hadn't yelled murder. It was you, Rebecca, who singlehandedly managed to ruin our firm. I hope you're proud of yourself."

With that, Catherine waved the gun at Rebecca. "In there," she said, motioning toward a large walk-in closet.

Rebecca's mind raced. Was that where she intended to kill her? Would the clothes muffle the gunshot? She prayed that Catherine wouldn't think to look inside her purse and that the police, when they were finally summoned, would discover the tape recorder with Catherine's confession on it. It wouldn't be fair, if Catherine got away with killing Ryan and her too.

She backed into the closet, her heart pounding. "After you gave Ryan the pills and something to drink them down with, what happened? Did he feel sick and that's when you told him to go out on the swim step?"

"I gave him three pills with a triple scotch," said Catherine, a tight smile forming on her face. "Poor dear had a really bad headache. When he felt sick, I told him he couldn't dirty the beautiful yacht. I promised to hold on to him. Once he was out there," she gave a small shrug, "I merely let go."

Hands perspiring, her throat dry, Rebecca managed to get out, "And he landed in the water?"

"Of course." Catherine laughed. "There wasn't anywhere else to go."

Rebecca tried to ignore the pounding in her temples, the pain in her stomach. "Didn't he scream?"

"Oh, yes," replied Catherine. "But the engines were making a lot of noise. I reached out my hand to him, and he stopped yelling and started swimming." She seemed lost in thought for a moment.

"Ryan actually surprised me, considering he must have been very ill from the combination of the pills and the liquor. He swam like a madman until he caught onto the swim step. That's when I made like I was giving him a rope." Her eyes had taken on a frightening intensity that terrified Rebecca.

Catherine continued now, as if she couldn't stop. Her face had turned into an ugly mask of hatred. "Instead, I leaned down and cut his hand. In surprise or pain, or maybe both, Ryan let go. By then he was losing his strength. I figured if he was bleeding, it wouldn't be long before he attracted sharks." She started to laugh —it came out sounding unnaturally high-pitched and hysterical. "That's when I left."

"How could you do such a thing to someone you had once been in love with?" cried Rebecca. Trembling from head to foot at the horror of what this woman was describing, Rebecca backed up until she was against a large chest of drawers. Clothes hung on either side of her. She could go no farther. In that instant she knew that she was going to die.

Rage filled her. She wanted to choke Catherine. Hurt her. Make her suffer. In a blind fury, Rebecca lunged for the other woman, pulling clothes and other things with her.

Surprised, Catherine was caught off guard. Before she could regroup to shoot, Rebecca had grabbed her by the neck and wrestled her to the ground. The gun flew out of Catherine's hand and skidded across the hardwood floor. Each of them tried to reach it as they rolled about. Rebecca attempted to pin Catherine's arms down, intent on making her pay for what she'd done to Ryan. But the other woman had turned into a tiger, biting, kicking, spitting at her.

Suddenly, Rebecca saw movement out of the corner of her eye. The next thing she knew, someone had picked up the gun. It was Daniel. She went limp with relief.

"Oh, thank God you're here," cried Catherine. "This crazy woman broke into my house, and now she's trying to kill me."

The gun was in front of him as he spoke. "I heard some of what you said, Catherine." His voice was filled with disgust.

"And I have the rest of it on tape," Rebecca said, scrambling to get her purse and show Daniel that she had Catherine's confession recorded. When she opened her bag, she saw happily that the recorder was still running.

"Go and call the police, Rebecca," Daniel said.

"You're making a mistake," Catherine insisted, now struggling to get to her feet.

"Don't move, Catherine," he ordered in a harsh tone, his eyes hard, "or I'll shoot."

Adrenaline and fear mingled with relief shot through Rebecca's body as she pulled herself up and hurried over to the phone. After calling for help, she couldn't judge how long she stood there, frozen, before she heard sirens in the distance.

After Catherine had been taken away, Daniel explained to Rebecca that, following their phone call, he'd been afraid she'd do something foolish. Figuring out that she'd probably attempt to confront Catherine, he'd decided to try and intercept her. From what Rebecca had told him about Catherine's working habits, he'd decided she'd still be at the office. When he went there and found it deserted, he realized his mistake and headed for Manhattan Beach. But by that time, Rebecca already had a good head start on him.

"Why did you risk challenging Catherine by yourself?" he demanded, his voice rising in anger.

She listened as Daniel's irritation with her was given expression, understanding that he'd been concerned for her safety and needed to get it off his chest. When he'd calmed down, she explained that the idea of Catherine getting away with Ryan's murder had been destroying her.

Later, Daniel insisted on following Rebecca home. As she drove, her mind tried to grasp and understand all that had happened. Why, oh why, hadn't Ryan confided in her, she wondered. Maybe together they could have gone to the FBI or done something else—and he wouldn't be dead. Then she realized that all the wishing in the world wasn't going to change anything, it wasn't going to bring Ryan back.

At her house, Daniel walked her to the door. "Would you like me to come in for a while?"

She heard the soft tone in his voice. It made her feel warm and cared for again, and she realized how much she had missed things like that. Daniel was a wonderful man. Maybe in the future, she thought, but for now, she was still too raw.

"Thanks, I really appreciate the offer." She gave him a smile. "But if I could, I'd like to take a rain check on that."

His face broke into a wide grin. "You've got a deal." He leaned over and brushed his lips against her hair. "Take care. I'll talk to you in a few days."

She nodded. Then, after taking a deep breath, she exhaled, and went inside.